PSYCHO-MOMMY

Mira Harlon

Psycho-Mommy

A Novel

Red For All Publishing, LLC

Psycho-Mommy is a work of fiction. Names, characters, places and incidents either are the product of the author's imagination or are used fictitiously. Any resemblance to actual persons, living or dead, events, or locales is entirely coincidental.

Published by Red For All Publishing, LLC

Library of Congress Cataloging-in-Publication Data

Is available from the publisher

ISBN 978-0-9894802-8-4

ISBN 978-0-9894802-9-1 (ebook)

www.redforallpublishing.com

Book design by Shirl Fitzpatrick

To my husband, for being my first reader and first fan! And for not laughing (too much) when I first told you I was writing a book! Thank you for the two extra sets of heart-wings. Without whom I would not have had the inspiration within me to write this book. There are no words, nor are there earthly ways to describe the love and joy they have brought me.

PSYCHO-MOMMY

ONE

OK! OK! Get a grip! Don't panic!

This has to be a mistake. I mean it's not possible. How could this have
even happened? I have taken every precaution! I mean this is absolutely
impossible. There is just no way!

I notice my heart is starting to thump harder and harder, and my palms
are beginning to sweat. All of a sudden I seem to have zero lung capacity,
as I am only capable of short breaths in and out. The water from the faucet
is dripping slightly, and suddenly instead of a light dripping in my head, it
sounds like a sudden downpouring of rain reverberating all around the
bathroom. I look at the stark white tiles surrounding me, and they feel like
they are closing in on me. I begin to feel trapped. Take a deep breath.
Innnnn – Ooooout! Again, Jessica! Innnnn – Ooooout! I grab on to the
sink for support. OK, this is no big deal. I can make myself relax – for
Christ Sake! I calm people down for a living. I close my eyes to block it
out.

Jesus, Mary and Joseph! It's not working! I'm not calming down. I'm
starting to hyperventilate.

You see, I am standing in our bathroom gawking at a pregnancy test. I
examined the instructions very carefully, very thoroughly. Ok, well maybe
that's not true. I looked at the pictures, and how hard could it be? I've
done everything correctly–I think–and I've waited three minutes. So the
problem is the little screen changed from clear and empty to a pink + sign.
A fucking pink + sign! In the directions, that means I'm pregnant. But, I

can't be! For starters, I'm on the pill! This is ludicrous! Ludicrous, I'm reiterating again, and instantly there is a tune in my head …

"Bop-Boom-Boom-Click….Bop…Boom-Boom-Click," I'm bobbing my head to the beat.

I can't place the song yet. It will come to me. It's a rapper. Yes. It's definitely a rapper.

"Bop-Boom-Boom-Click….Bop…Boom-Boom-Click"

What are the words? Something about… Starbucks?

"Bop-Boom-Boom-Click….Bop…Boom-Boom-Click"

Ok, I'm getting something… That's it. "Yes," I yell out! It's Ludacris, the rapper.

What the?

Stop it!

Now I hear "Ludacris", the rapper, belting out lyrics in my head. Well now it's really bothering me. What song is that again? You know it's pretty catchy.

"Bop-Boom-Boom-Click….Bop…Boom-Boom-Click"

It's with that cutie-pie Justin Bieber and Ludacris together. What's it called? Oh, it's on the tip of my tongue. It's really bothering me that I can't think of the song name. Then suddenly it hits me, "Baby!" I yell out, quite proud of myself that I remembered it. It's called "Baby," of course. I'm smiling at myself in the mirror…………….. Wait a minute?

Baby!?!

No, no, no, I tell myself. I don't want to hear baby songs because there is no baby! I can't be pregnant. For Christ Sake, what is wrong with me? Does that happen to anyone else I wonder? Music in your head? All the time … without the slightest warning? I seriously have an internal radio.

Always have. For instance, when I walk down the street and am feeling particularly confident, I can actually hear Nancy Sinatra's, *"These boots were made for walking"* or Justin Timberlake's *"Sexy Back."* And I start walking like a super model shaking my hips and pouting my lips.

Stop it! Back to the situation, Jessica, I tell myself.

OK, let me establish something here. It's not like I'm unmarried or anything. I mean let's face it, that would be a disgrace — like that girl Carrie from our sister office who named her kid Apple. I mean, trust me, with my training I know how a kid named Apple is going to turn out. Yes, Gwyneth can get away with it but not a single mother who still lives at home with her parents! But that's beside the point. You see, my fabulous husband and I are only married, not even 3 months. And this wasn't supposed to happen. I have a very important meeting in an hour, and I have to pick up our newly engraved wedding bands on the way. I don't have time for this. And the only reason I took this stupid test in the first place was because Simmi said I looked different in the face, and I'm two days late and she swears I'm pregnant.

OK, Jessica, THINK! You must have done this wrong. There has to be a logical explanation for this. You were in a hurry, and you must have screwed it up somehow. Well you know ...... come to think of it, it said in the directions, *"ensure a steady stream of urine on the test stick for 30 seconds."* Well, I did try, honestly, but you know it is surprisingly difficult to pee on a stick. As I play back my attempt in my head I recall trying to pee straight down on that stick but the pee got everywhere and hardly on the stick at all. What really happened is it hit the stick then as I maneuvered to see what was going on down there the urine kind of ricochet off and sprayed all over my hand instead. It flew everywhere but on that damn stick. Honestly, I have an entirely new appreciation for how men have to aim in the bowl. We have it easier in that department I have to say. I mean granted we can't just whip it out, but we don't have to aim. If I were faced with the option to whip it out or learn the art of aiming, I think I would definitely stick to what I have. Besides it's kind of comforting in the morning when you can just stumble out of bed and sit on the bowl to go in the morning. Think about it. Men have to hold themselves upright first thing in the morning.

Have you ever fallen back to sleep on the bowl, like I have? Ok, maybe that's TMI. I'm going off on a tangent here; let me get back on track.

So, back to the pregnancy test, after the pee on the stick fiasco, I spent the three minutes waiting for the results, washing my hands. Come to think of it, I probably waited longer than 3 minutes to read the results, when it clearly states in the instructions that results read after 10 minutes are invalid. As I review the instructions more carefully, it also says – *"hold stick directed downward."* I can't be entirely sure I even did that part correctly. I mean it's 6:30 in the morning. How does anyone do this correctly the first time anyway? No wonder they sell pregnancy tests in packs of multiples. You probably need to attempt 3 times or more before getting it correct. Shouldn't they make this a little easier?

I'm reading the directions now a third time, and it clearly states – *"the test may not work correctly if the test stick was not laid flat after urine was applied."* Well, that just explains it then. I waited longer than 10 minutes, AND I was waving it back and forth and blowing on it like it was a freshly painted manicure. How am I supposed to know you need to gingerly lay it flat? So, clearly this is inconclusive at best. Yes! That's it! So, I am not pregnant after all. I mean I knew I couldn't be, but Simmi was so adamant. I hear myself make an audible sigh of relief. My shoulders drop, and I can feel the muscles in my neck and back relax. I just close my eyes for a moment. That was a close call. We are so not ready for a baby. Nolan and I will just have to be more fastidious about our, um, relations and this won't happen again. Even so, I do hear a nagging voice deep inside saying, "Well maybe you should take another one just to be sure?" I consider going through the steps all over again, but I'm interrupted.

"Jess?" comes Nolan's voice from the bedroom. "What are you doing in there?"

Shit!

"Um, Uh … just a minute, honey."

I hurry up and throw all the evidence away and put tissues all on top of the box in a big heap so that he won't see it. I mean, why should I bother

11

him with this? In fact, Mom always said she didn't bother Dad with things she deemed unnecessary for sharing, and it worked well for her.

I take another deep breath and turn the handle. "Morning, sweetheart," I say. "I was just lost in thought, thinking of our rings." I walk over, rise on my tiptoes and kiss him softly on the lips. God, he has great lips! And as I do I can smell a slight hint of his cologne from last night. He smiles at me and I become lost in his eyes as he pulls me closer with a knowing smile. As my body presses up against his, I can feel the muscles in his chest. As I slowly move my hands down his arms, I can feel his strong biceps flex as he grips my waist. I giggle and tell him, "We don't have time for that. I am already running late."

"Jess, there is always time for that" he jokes back.

If he only knew what I just went through a few minutes ago, he wouldn't be saying that. I push him gently away and say, "Good things come to those who wait," with my sexiest little grin.

"You're killing me," he sighs as he passes me to the bathroom and shuts the door.

Ok, now that my little morning nightmare is over, I am feeling much lighter on my feet. I'm just going to put this all behind me. I mean as it is I have a very busy morning. I have to get our rings and then get to my meeting. I'm desperate without them. A newly married woman just feels naked without her wedding band.

You see we were married in this amazing ceremony in the West Indies on this precious little island called, Nevis. It's divine. You should really go there if you can in your lifetime. It's so unknown. And apparently celebrities and high-profile New Yorkers go there during high season but nobody knows about it. It's all like a hush-hush secret get-away spot. It's really true. Our maître d' at the plantation we stayed at told us Kelly Ripa and her family were there and Michael Douglas and Katherine Zeta-Jones and their children and even Britney Spears, you know, back in the pre-shaved head, more Britney hearts Justin days (no offense to the new Mrs. Timberlake but I heard they really let loose there). Of course, they could just tell stories to us   tourists about who was there and how would we know the difference? Anyway, we were married on the beach and we started our honeymoon immediately after with a two-week stay right there on the island in the honeymoon suite.

As I close my eyes to think about it, I am reminded of the enchanting scene of me standing there holding Nolan's hands, my strapless white flowing dress gently drifting in the wind, with beautiful, soft white coral sand under our feet and a family of dolphins going by like musical notes floating up and down the scale. I can recall instantly the smell of the Caribbean Sea. In the faint distance was the vision of the sister island of St. Kitts, which is much larger than quaint little Nevis. And turning your head would give you a glimpse of the in-land which echoes a time of long-long ago with rustic ruins of the sugar plantations that reigned supreme for such a stretch of time supporting a huge sugar industry. It was a clear day, and the water was bluer than ever.

The sun beamed down on us brightly and strongly as if the entire sky-

.... no the entire world

… no better yet, the entire universe was in absolute approval of our union.

Just our family and a couple of intimate friends came along. After they left the following day, we just stayed in our honeymoon suite for days. And we just......... well we, well you know.

Anyway, we finally decided we would go for a guided hike in the rain forest on the 4th day. And during the hike, our tour guide, Garon, taught us all about the island and what it was like back in the days of the sugar plantations. He educated us on the nature and wildlife, although I have to admit I blocked out everything he had to say about the bats! Instead, I focused more on the monkeys. He told us how the screeches and chatter we could hear up above in the trees were the green vervet monkeys native to only Nevis, Barbados and St Kitts. They were first brought to the island by English settlers. He called the chatter, *monkey love talk*. He told us the monkeys were quite romantic to one another in those trees. I remember Nolan and I looking up into the vast sky of branches and greenery hoping

13

to get a glimpse and giggling at this. Garon went on and on about the *monkey love talk* and sure enough we heard them all along the hike. Garon would say that the *monkey love talk* naturally guides him along the way, and he never does the same tour twice. He just follows the monkeys, and they take him on new adventures each time. "Oh those monkeys; they love that monkey love talk," Garon would say in his island dialect, with a gleam in his eye. We would see these adorable creatures about town. They would just be sitting up on a rock or running across the street with their dark mischievous faces and their bright, stark, white bellies —walking two together— holding the others tail or even sometimes in a little family with babies.

One morning, as we were enjoying one of the famous Nevis breakfasts on a private patio by the beach, one of those little buggers ran up and stole my mango. I watched as the tiny thief ran back to another smaller monkey and gave the mango over. There was a twinkle in their eyes. I swear it was like they were a newly married husband and wife, so in love, just like me and Nolan. I could tell what was going on – that little monkey husband was fending for his darling monkey wife, who was hungry. He ran back with the mango and grunted and screeched at her. I remember thinking; this is so whimsical, the *monkey love talk,* up close! Right there in front of me. And she, the monkey wife, accepted his triumphant score with all her heart, looking at him as her hunky monkey hero, giving him some *monkey love talk* back. Ah, those monkeys ......

Suddenly, I'm musically plunged back to reality as I hear in my head "Monkey" by the Counting Crows. I shake my head as if to free myself from the music. I've got to get myself dressed. And go get those rings.

Nolan and I loved those monkeys so much and Garon's description of their romantic ways that we decided to add another engraved saying to our rings which already has our wedding date of 7-1-2012 engraved and now will also say "monkey love talk!" And I just love it because only Nolan and I know the meaning. Nobody else in the whole wide world will know what it means but us.

Well, except Garon.

…. And I guess every other couple he takes on a tour.

…. And Britney

…. And probably the native Nevisians. Oh well, who cares. The meaning is special to us. This is about our union in Nevis. Our love. Our marriage. Our *monkey love talk*!

OK, now I'm dressed in my super marvelous purple pencil skirt and white blouse and purple heels. I pulled my hair back into a sophisticated twist. And I have to say my entire look is awesome today! Why is it you just look better after a honeymoon? I bet Dr. Ruth would say it's all that sex!

I have had my banana and yogurt with Nature's Promise whole grain oats sprinkled on top, and I am finally ready to leave. I kiss Nolan good-bye while he is putting his case papers in his carrier bag.

As I'm half way out the door, I yell out, "Remember, good things come to those who wait."

Nolan grins back at me longingly.

TWO

$\mathcal{A}$s I approach the jeweler I am getting giddy. The cab pulls up but is stuck in some traffic, and I feel like I can't get out of the cab fast enough. I tell the cab to just let me out at the corner of 8th and Walnut.

I am so excited once I get out that I find myself running down the street up to the door. Well, probably more like a light jog in these purple heels, but in my mind I'm running just like Kara Goucher in the final leg of the marathon. In my head I am hearing, dum-da-da-dum, da-da-dum-da-da-dum from the Rocky movie theme song! I get there and open the door with an enthusiastic whoosh, slightly winded from my run!

"Good Morning!" I say with great excitement.

"Yes, top of the morning to you Mrs. Reed. We've been expecting you. How was your honeymoon?" says the man in the blue-striped tie.

I giggle to myself. It is still so humorous to hear someone call me Mrs. Reed. I mean I am Mrs. Reed! ME! Well, of course to be technical it's Dr. Reed. I do have a PhD. in psychology from the University of Pennsylvania, thank you very much! And for a half a second I wonder if I should correct him.

"Mrs. Reed? Are you OK?" comes the blue-striped-tie-man's voice.

Yes, right, better not correct him. "Um, yes, Hi ….. Of course I'm just on Nevis time. Very relaxed there, you know. Not so rush-rush. I took off my watch and never put it on again," I say with a smile as I walk close to the counter.

Of course, now I always have to check my phone for the time, but I love telling people how I took off my watch on my honeymoon and never put it on again. It just sounds so romantic. I mean it is true, you know; time does not matter when you are in love. Like the other day, I woke up and thought to myself, being married is so blissful. I mean, each new day, I just

16

look at my new husband and somewhere deep in my being I know that together, as husband and wife, we will follow whatever path, good or bad, comes our way, and at the end of it all there will always be our love. And nothing else is truly more powerful than that.

"Ahh!" I sigh out loud looking out into the distance.

"Mrs. Reed?" the blue-striped-tie-man's voice is a bit louder this time.

Gosh, I know I should remember his name but I can't. Nolan did most of all the ring buying, and I only met this man once before.

"Um, ah, yes, I'm sorry. I'm here to pick up our rings. They are supposed to be ready? I'm in a bit of a hurry. I have a meeting at 9 this morning."

"Yes, I have them right here. Let me just polish them for you."

I am waiting for the polished rings with our super special secret engraving when I start to look around the shop a little. All these beautiful diamonds in every shape and size, you can't help but be dazzled. And the lights in the store must be some magic digitalized LED lighting because the diamonds look like little glistening stars. It's all about the lighting. It's just like what actresses say about achieving the right look with proper lighting. At least that's what I've read in my trusty US weekly magazine. I should get new lighting in my office. Maybe it would make my eyes glisten like these diamonds do. Nolan does so love my green eyes. He tells me all the time that he first fell in love with my eyes.

"Ding-Ding" goes the door-chime. I swivel around to look at this adorable little couple who just came in hand-in-hand, smiles beaming. You can spot them a mile away… newly engaged, for sure. I can't hear what they are saying, but they are talking to another sales assistant, probably to pick out wedding bands. I can just tell with my training. Their body language is so "new-engaged-couple". It's true you know, mind-body-behavior. It's all connected. That's Psych 101.

"Mrs. Reed, here we are, here are your newly engraved rings," blue-striped-tie-man says as he approaches me from the back offices. I can't contain myself. I have the biggest grin on my face, and I hop a little closer to the counter and put my hands out willing him to approach faster. Suddenly he can't put them in my hands fast enough. I have to see them. And as soon as he gets close enough to hand them over, I grab at them, squeeze them in my hands and pull them close to my heart, gripping them tightly. Ah, finally I have them back. I instantly feel more complete with them in my possession. I love these rings. They symbolize so much... all our love, commitment to one another, our union and even what the future will bring. It's true what they say, the circle or ring has no end. It signifies a journey that is forever. I glance inside to look at the new engraving.

What?

Wait a minute?

My smile fades and my eyes widen and I can feel my heart start to thump, thump a little faster.

"What the hell is this?" I gasp

"Mrs. Reed is there a problem?"

"Yes, there is a problem. This is all wrong. I can't believe you've gone and messed this up!" I say outraged. The ring is engraved with *monkey dove talk* not *monkey love talk*.

"It is supposed to say *Monkey Love Talk*!" I can hear my voice elevating to something akin to a high pitch hissy fit sound. And the newly engaged couple turns to survey me.

"Oh, my word, I am terribly sorry Mrs. Reed, but you know it was such an unusual saying and the sales assistant who took the information over the phone said she asked you to spell it two times for her and everything. Are you sure you didn't mean dove?" He looks at me inquisitively.

How can he even ask me this? There were no doves in Nevis! There were monkeys! Little sweet monkeys who had sweet monkey love talk!

"No, I most certainly did not say dove. I said love – L-O-V-E!" I spell it out quite dramatically. "You have to fix it." I demand.

18

"Mrs. Reed, the only problem is that the particular font you decided on and this ring type required what we refer to as a deep etching and there is no great way to fix it."

"What do you mean there is no great way to fix it?" I say in shock. I mean these are one of the most sacred symbols of our marriage. I can feel tingling behind my nose and eyes, and I blink back the sting of fresh tears I can feel welling up.

"Well, if we grind it off, it lessens the total weight, and with the diamonds on this ring, it's probably not a good idea. Sometimes we can solder it, but I have to check with the jeweler." He is motioning with his hands, and I am staring at him completely agog! How can he speak about this so matter-of-factly? There is not an ounce of understanding in his expression.

"I don't want you to do any of those things!" I snap back. "These are the rings I had our family priest bless before we left for Nevis. And these are the rings we wore on our wedding day. I don't want you grinding them or whatever you just said!" I say incredulously.

"Well those are the main options. I'm terribly sorry," he says, "I usually advise people to just do a simple 'I love you' or 'Forever mine' in the rings … makes it easy for the jeweler and less risk for this kind of mistake."

I can't believe this! He is acting like this mistake is my fault. This guy has serious blame shifting issues. He probably has an underlying personality disorder. I mean it's a classic case. Yes, yes that's it. I mean it's very close to *labeling theory* where one tries to induce irrational guilt at an unconscious level. You know, it's often a propaganda technique, to use repetitive blaming behavior in order to apply a negative status to the opposite individual and protect oneself. Well, he messed with the wrong psychologist today. I suddenly imagine reaching across the counter and grabbing that blue-striped tie with my fist, to pull him close and yell at him through a clenched jaw so that he can actually see the blood vessels in my eyes almost burst in frustration, but no instead I will be calm and professional.

"First of all," I say, "remind me of your name again?"

He smiles and says, "Yes, Mrs. Reed, its Jimmy."

"OK, Jimmy." I begin in professional work tones as I brush down my outfit as if to physically remove my anger. "First of all let me tell you it's best to know your customer, and I would appreciate it if you addressed me more accurately as Dr. Reed. Now this is a big mistake on your part. My husband has spent a lot of money here, and we are good standing customers. I am outraged by this mistake and would like to remind you that it is my prerogative what to have engraved on my rings, and it's your job to get it right. I have a very important meeting that I need to attend immediately. I ask that you stop giving me excuses and kindly tell your jeweler this was the mistake of the store, and I want every single option carefully explored so that this can be fixed with minimal change to these rings. Do I make myself clear? Also you might want to look up *blame shifting* in your spare time!"

He looks at me utterly agape and says, "um ....yes of course, Mrs., Um. I mean, Dr. Reed."

"I'll expect a call today on my mobile with the options for me to consider!" I retort as I turn on my heel and make my way to the street. As I walk away I hear in my head a big, loud, screaming rendition of "Rockstar" by Nickelback.

Well that was satisfying. It just goes to show you. Professional Jess rocks! I just stand tall, switch to my Psychologist training and bang! I mean I hate to have to get all serious on someone, but that blame-shifter-blue-striped-tie-what's-his-face had it coming! How upsetting. I mean us little people get no respect. I'm sure when Prince William and Kate got married nobody messed up their engraving. And I'm sure they didn't go with a simple "I love you" or "Forever mine". I mean, I bet they totally had some amazing royal saying that has been passed down from royal to royal engraved in their rings! No-one would dare accuse them of misspelling love for dove. The nerve of that blame-shifter!

As I reach the corner to hail a cab, I pull out my phone and text Nolan:

Me: How do you feel about Monkey Dove talk?

Nolan: Ohhhh. I can't wait. Sounds kinky.

Me: OMG I'm not sexting you. They messed up the engraving

Nolan: haha that's funny

Me: It is not! I'm furious

Nolan: calm down, honey, I love you … that's all the matters, right?

Me: I guess so

Simmi: Well, are you knocked-up?

Me: No, I'll call you later Simmi

Simmi is my best friend in the whole wide world. We met at the University of Pennsylvania while we were studying as psychology majors. She specializes in children, something I don't think I could ever do. Simmi's family is straight off the boat from India. Simmi has so many funny stories about her family. Like the time her Father first arrived here and became obsessed with exploring his new found love of fast food places. He went into a McDonalds and felt enticed to order a hamburger and of course loved it. The problem was that in Hindu religion it is like this huge serious sin if you eat anything from a cow. He thought because it was a HAMburger with the actual word "ham" before the "burger", it meant it was from a pig, and a pig is not holy like a cow. So he ate hamburgers every day for like 2 months until someone told him it was actually from a cow. He was devastated! And then of course he assumed since he already disgraced himself by eating a cow that it wouldn't make much difference if he continued. The rationalization of which is a perfect case of rationalization defense mechanism. He instead adopted the strategy during his morning worship to ask for simple forgiveness from Brahma, Vishnu and Shiva, the three main deities in Hindu religion. He still eats hamburgers now. Simmi and I laugh so hard about it every time we see him eat a hamburger. Simmi's family is the greatest. I love them like I love my own family. For the longest time I didn't even know this but Simmi's real name is Samudra. It wasn't until I went to her home for the first time freshman year and her parents kept talking about someone named Samudra. I was so confused, until Simmi leaned over and said, "that's my real name, but if you ever call me it, I'll kill you."

I think her real name is beautiful and exotic and so amazing; it sounds just like she is a princess. …Princess Samudra. I don't get it. What's so wrong with Samudra?

I do love Simmi, and normally I would enjoy greatly texting banter back and forth, but I have to get going and will just call her later. I put my phone away as a cab finally pulls up. That's strange. I'm feeling dizzy and a little nausea. No wait it's not nausea … what is that …. I think I'm hungry? Starving, actually! But that's strange. I always make it till at least 10:30 before having a snack. I mean I had my usual banana and yogurt with the whole grain oats on top. Hmmm. Well hold on, of course, I would be hungry. I mean I just experienced such a draining experience with that blame-shifter. I probably used up all my normal morning energy on that fiasco.

Wow, I am really hungry.

Could I possibly stop for some food?

I look at the phone for the time once more. Arrgh! I am a few minutes late as it is, and now I really have to pee. There's no time. This morning is not going very smoothly. This is going to be dangerously close. "Please hurry!" I tell the cabbie.

THREE

Oh boy, here we go! There she is, Captain Crunch, staring at me with that *how-dare-you-make-me-wait for-you-don't-you-know-how-important-I-am* glare in her eyes. I rush in all frazzled only 3 minutes late and that's only because I had to rush to pee. Can this morning get any more insane? I'm starving. And for some reason I have to pee like every 30 minutes, and I haven't even had my second cup of green organic tea. And Simmi is blowing my phone up with texts about how I better call her if I'm pregnant. Which of course, as we have established already, I'm not! The test was invalid, inconclusive and just plain wrong. Ok, let me just take a deep breath and relax. I'm here, and I just have to give myself a moment of credit. I mean I just experienced a total blame-shifter who was overly committed to ruining my entire morning, and I have to give myself a pat on the back. I am quite pleased with how I handled ol' blame-shifter!

Woo-hoo, Jess, I think to myself.

Woops, suddenly I feel a prickling feeling on my neck; you know when the hair on your neck stands on end during a horror movie or when you drive past an accident. Suddenly I notice, uh-oh, Captain Crunch is still looking at me as if I'm an ant she wants to step on in order to put me out of my misery.

"Gloria," I say with a bright and respectful tone, "I am so incredibly sorry about being late. I hope I didn't keep you too long. I know how busy you are." I say sort of bowing slightly to show her she's in charge.

See you just need to know how to deal with these types of people.

I add, "You are looking so gorgeous today in that red suit of yours. Where did you get it?"

Her facial muscles relax, and I can tell that she has warmed up a bit because her pen tapping on the desk has calmed to the point of just three taps a second instead of the more aggressive 15 taps.

"Oh this, it's brand new……. My husband surprised me with it after I told him I just had to have it. We saw it in Saks a few weeks back." She shrieks sauntering her hips back and forth to show how smart and on top of the world she feels in it. And of course, that's what she thinks of herself all day long, all the time.

You see Captain Crunch, aka Gloria Vanderbine, is my department chair. If you meet her once she instantly becomes the most memorable case of narcissistic personality disorder you have ever seen. I mean the mock cases we studied back in college came nothing close to this, but she lives in total denial. She has this total need for constant attention and admiration. She is so pre-occupied with being on top that she is totally unaware that the entire department can't stand working for her. Which is probably our fault because we each spend about 80% of the time doing our real jobs and about 20% of the time satisfying her ego. All of us, of course, except Richard.

Anyway, she is totally obsessive about her self-interests, and if you work under her, you better be interested in them too or you will find yourself at the unemployment line. I mean one of the best Captain Crunch narcissistic-in-high-gear stories is her obsession with being possibly related to the famous fashion icon, Gloria Vanderbilt! Get this; Captain Crunch changed her middle name to Laura last year. Why? Because her last name is so close to Vanderbilt and Gloria Vanderbilt's middle name is Laura. Captain Crunch tells us routinely how she identifies with Gloria Vanderbilt so much and swears that they are long lost relatives. She has this entire made-up back story where she thinks her great-great-great grandfather came over from Europe and when he got off the boat in NY he gave his name as Vanderbilt. But C.C. concocts this story where the clerk scribing for the passenger arrival records obviously wrote the name incorrectly as he heard it instead of its actual spelling. And in her case the clerk wrote Vanderbine and her great-great-great grandfather was forced to keep it all along. But his more fortunate brother must have gotten off the boat and in line with a more careful and more intelligent clerk instead. Therefore, alas the Vanderbilt and Vanderbine names would be forever unlinked. And Vanderbilt would eventually give rise to the famous Gloria Vanderbilt. Of course, she hasn't been able to corroborate any of this, but she tells it as if it's the gospel truth. So anyway, Captain Crunch wanted to acknowledge her family connection (albeit bat-shit crazy fake) by changing her name to be more similar. So she changed her middle name from Gloria Rose to Gloria Laura. The best is when she starts to rattle off her list of character traits that are virtually identical to the famous Gloria. It's even more comical when she is on her second glass of wine, like at last year's holiday party.

"I mean the similarities are uncanny," Captain Crunch will begin with her back straight and nose in the air, holding her fingers up as she ticks them off for you so you can follow along:

1. Our names are so practically identical (Then she goes over her formulated theory of incompetent passenger clerk)
2. We are both only children
3. We are both from New York
4. She is the daughter of a railroad heir and I am a daughter of a taxi company heir. (Her father ran a taxi company. I hardly think that allows for the term 'heir')
5. We both went through a rough custody battle as children
6. We both have impeccable fashion sense.
7. We both are philanthropists

Then right when you are about to blurt out an excuse to get yourself out of this god-awful conversation before you burst out laughing in her face, she will start to tell you how she has taken up art and painting in Vanderbilt's honor, and she expects everyone in the department to buy tickets to her upcoming art charity event to support her efforts. And then you've no way out. You have been Captain Crunched! My next Captain Crunch charity event is this coming Friday. I may fake a sprained ankle.

Simmi and I always talk about her in code as Captain Crunch or even more covertly as C.C. The nickname came to me after a terrible nightmare. In my nightmare, she was on the bow of this big ship coming into port in NY. She had a captain's hat on and she was dictating all the Vanderbilt's to get in one exit line while all the other lesser sir-named families were to remain 10 minutes behind the Vanderbilt line. The non-Vanderbilt's would be told to walk the plank if they jeopardized her name-sake in any way. When I awoke I couldn't get that image of her out of my head. It reminded me of an evil version of Captain Crunch from the cereal box. I laughed out loud thinking how suiting a nickname that could be, given her narcissistic disorder not to mention how she crunches you down to size with everything she does. And so it stuck. She will forever be C.C. to several of us lesser-sir-named psychologists in the department.

Fifteen minutes later my meeting is coming to an end with Captain Crunch. She wants me to get involved with a new study in the department for Alzheimer's disease. I nod quietly throughout the meeting and allow her to jabber at me. I notice at some point there is silence, and she is looking at me as if waiting for a response. I think I've zoned off. Shit! Did she ask a question?

So, I quickly summon my psychologist training and go with a suitable response to any narcissist by saying, "Gosh, Gloria, its lovely that you are spearheading new research for Alzheimers, and I would be delighted to be a part of it. This will give me a greater opportunity to continue to learn from someone as expert as you!" Basically to break it down I am telling her she is amazing, she is better than me, please teach me because you are of superior intelligence. Please, please, please!

After exiting her meeting, I feel faint, tired and hungrier than ever. Gosh C.C. can actually physically make you feel sick and tired. I have just 10 minutes until my first client comes in. I need to grab something to eat.

So, I, Dr. Jessica Reed, see patients from 9-1PM each day. I evaluate their current and past situation, then I chart up a psychological profile and I put a plan into action of moving each patient from their C spot to their B spot and then hopefully to their A spot, which is their ultimate desired psychological reference point. Of course, Nolan each day asks me, "Did you find your clients "G-spot" today?" So inappropriate! You know that Freud stuff is so dead-on. I'm convinced that men think about sex at least once every ten minutes of every hour. I mean, how do they get anything done?

Anyway, today I have Mrs. Carter coming in. She has reached her G-spot ...... uh, um .... I mean B-spot, so we are really making great progress.

26

And she is a handful, so I am very proud of the milestones we have reached. I mean, she came in hating her mother and now she can totally stand her for 30 minutes at a pop. That's progress. And I just adore helping people move along to their desired path. It helps them immensely in so many areas of their lives. For the first time in years Mrs. Carter has been able to have coffee with her mom without storming out of the coffee shop. I even have past clients who have reached their A-spot, and they still send me Christmas cards and credit me for changing their life. You know, people ask me what I do and I tell them, *I change lives*! You just can't beat that. Nobody has a better job than me.

Well, except maybe Julia Roberts …

…And probably Angelina Jolie. I mean Angie gets to smooch Brad Pitt all the time and get her hair done and act in these great films, and help third-world countries and adopt all kinds of children and did I mention the smooching Brad Pitt part?!

But all the same, I wouldn't change my job in a million years.

Well, I better grab a granola bar to calm down this hunger and read over Mrs. Carter's chart to catch up on our last visit. I quickly scarf down the granola bar and read over the chart. I am feeling confident about the ground we need to cover today. At our last visit, I delivered my standard *empowering talk* and discussed how this is her life to take charge of, and she must acknowledge that and take the power back from her mother. We did an exercise where we put a picture of her mother in the chair and she spoke to her mother in the power state and not the child state. It was a very powerful moment. I am just about to re-read my notes when Ella the receptionist buzzes in to tell me Mrs. Carter is waiting.

"Dr. Reed," screeches Mrs. Carter. "I hope you ate your Wheaties today!"

"Oh no" I say in surprise, "Mrs. Carter did we have a setback?"

"A setback? Would you agree that calling your mother a *'backstabbing bitch'* in the middle of the train station a set-back?" She uses her fingers to make quote signs for emphasis.

OK, quick think. Obviously something upsetting happened, and Mrs. Carter's ability for sublimation failed. I need to first get her calm.

"OK, Ok Mrs. Carter," I calmly walk over to her and take her hand to guide her to the couch. "Let's just have a seat and see if we can get to the bottom of this."

She sits.

I sit.

I smile at her and nod knowingly, "Just start at the beginning and tell me what led to the setback?"

Mrs. Carter goes on to explain how she had been dating an investment banker and that she had met him at one of her Mother's fancy parties. Her mother is well-to-do and a widow who became instantly rich after her husband's passing. Now, apparently, this investment banker man she is dating is 12 years older than her. And apparently her mother found out about their relationship and promptly informed the investment banker that if he did not stop dating her daughter she would have him blackballed from the social network they are involved in. Boy, her mother is very controlling. I picture her as a little Endora from Bewitched, you know the mother who never pronounced Darrin's name correctly and always messed their lives up. I always do that; picture my clients and their life stories as either cartoons or TV sitcom characters. And I always picture them as mini versions. And before you dismiss my technique, I would like to defend it by saying how brilliant it is, because it helps me to visualize my client's life situation and in the end provide better advice. I mean, everyone knows that most people learn and remember better with visual cues.

"Mrs. Carter, what do you think your mother's motivation was for doing that?"

"Because she is a crazy controlling bitch who doesn't want her own daughter to be happy!"

"OK!" I say, "However could she perhaps know anything about this man that might be worrying her? Did you ask her the reasons why?"

"No, I just yelled at her and started to cry! I'm 40 years old. He could have been the one. I love him!"

I am taken a little by surprise by this remark. Mrs. Carter has never told me about this man and has never used the word ... love! I smile at her and put my hand out to reach her arm. "Mrs. Carter, I am so sorry, I didn't realize you were in love. You've never mentioned him. What is his name and how long have you been seeing him?"

"His name is Frank, and we've been dating for 4 weeks." Silently I giggle to myself. 4 weeks – love!?

"Mrs. Carter love is typically something that takes time to establish. But in new relationships we often feel an infatuation or an emotional connection that arises from the limbic system in the brain.

"It's not infatuation. At my age love comes quick. It has to."

"OK, yes I see," I say with understanding.

Mrs. Carter tells me a lot more about Frank, and my assessment is that he is a decent man and cares for her. However, I advised Mrs. Carter to not try to convince Frank to move to England as she suggested, but rather discuss with him her feelings and then more importantly discuss it with her mother. I set her up for her assignment. She is to listen to a CD I have for these types of situations. It contains certain classical music from the Romantic Era of course, some Beethoven, Offenbach, and a little Strauss. The steps are easy. Find a quiet spot, get comfortable and then put on the CD. Her focus during this time is to try to achieve a calm state. I instruct her to make sure she is undisturbed the entire time. No phone!

This is necessary to let the music penetrate her thoughts.....

Allow it to calm her.....

Feel the music....

Imagine the composers' intentions of the music....

Then, at the moment she feels that she has reached a point of inspirational calm she is to write a letter to her mother from her heart asking her to reconsider her opinion of their relationship. It's important for her to not react out of aggression or impulse because that will escalate her mother's already negative stance. This is my signature therapy. You see I did some post-graduate research work on the effects of combining music with social psychology therapy. I had some really interesting findings. Music can help in so many ways. So, I personally have about a dozen CDs that I have made, and I pair them with assignments for my patients. My dream is to one day start my own music psychology practice and produce my CDs. You know so when Britney shaved her head, for example, they would bring her in and say you need to listen to these Jessica Reed CDs. Or when some strung-out star is in need of rehab for the 8th time, they will say you need this Jessica Reed CD. You get the picture. This could possibly be why I have a heightened internal radio. Songs randomly come to me all the time without warning. And sometimes after a song has come to me I realize it's of use for these therapy CDs. It's a very creative and stimulating process. It's like I am a musical genius! Except, well, I don't actually make the music, nor do I play an instrument, and really all I do is just hear it in my head all the time. Anyway, you get the idea.

By the time she leaves, she is relaxed and hopeful, and I feel we reached a good spot before she parted. I still have a giggle inside about her 4 weeks in love. You see in psychology, we know that love at first sight isn't really love. It's more chemical and scientific if you will. You see, when mating, all mammals are similar. A mammal has limbic response or a limbic resonance. I don't mean to sound totally unromantic, but it's true. What people refer to as "Love at first sight" is really experiencing "limbic resonance at first sight" through experiences with the senses of sight, smell, touch, and sound. Think about it ...... dogs do it best. They sniff around, their ears perk up they lick and all. That's all love at first sight really is. As this continues for a long period of time with a committed couple, similar neural patterns become activated in the limbic system causing increases in neurotransmitter activity and neuronal connections, leading to the long lasting feelings of what most people think love is and feels like .... Happiness, Devotion .... Love.

I can remember when I had limbic resonance at first sight. My friends and I were in our final year of graduate study. We had decided to go to the River Rink at Penn's landing after a particular grueling week of studying. River Rink is an outdoor ice rink in Philadelphia. I close my eyes and recall and suddenly I can remember it all like it was yesterday....

You see on that day, I really didn't want to go because I never ice-skated before, and I don't quite like the cold. But everyone said it would be fun. And how hard could ice skating really be? I remember arriving, and it was really a beautiful night. We went into the heated facility and waited in a long line to rent skates. I was surprised at the crowds. I mean did people really like ice skating that much? I rented my skates, and I recall giving myself some really positive self-talk.

"You can do this Jessica."

"You probably are a natural ice-skater and could have possibly missed your calling for the Olympics. You will probably unlock some hidden talent you never knew about."

"If these little kids running around here can do it then so can you. It's probably a lot like walking."

"No problem!"

I laced up the skates and went out on the ice. It was cold and the sky was clear and there were little twinkling stars above in the clear night sky. And just beside the rink there was the sound of the gentle moving waterfront, and as you turned to look from side to side you could see panoramic views of the entire city. Imagine beautiful buildings all lit up and the Benjamin Franklin Bridge in the distance. I remember thinking; *I quite like ice skating already.*

UNTIL

I took the first step on that Ice.

AHHHHHHHHHHHHHHHHHHhhhhhhhh!

31

OK, hold it together, I remember chanting. Hold on to the side. Breathe. My legs were suddenly Jell-O. My ankles felt like they would give out at any moment, and these little stinking kids were zipping by me as if they were professionals. I was waiting for them to do a triple lux right there in front of me. Show offs! How can you ice skate that well at six years old?!? At six, I could barely walk and chew gum at the same time. I steadied myself as much as I could and held on to the side for dear life. I remember just trying to get once around and off that rink. I remember closing my eyes and envisioning a nice hot cup of hot chocolate to motivate myself, when all of a sudden I heard, "tag your it" behind me and a kid zipped by and another one crashed into me and my legs went out in front of me and I fell backwards and smacked my head on the ice. In that moment I realized what it was like to "see stars". I couldn't quite focus. I saw little speckled lights and the noise level became very loud and then very quiet and then .... it happened. I heard a faint voice say, "hey there little doll-face, are you ok?"

At first I thought I was hallucinating or maybe my head injury was so severe the voice was an angel on the other side about to guide me to the light. Slowly, I opened my eyes, blinked a few times and there he was ..... Nolan. This giant godlike guy wearing jeans and a blue sweater and a wool hat over his head, but the kind that just hugs the head and you could see his brown hair sticking out everywhere. I looked at his eyes, which were a pale brown with a slight hint of green. And I closed my eyes again thinking I was dreaming. He, by that time, had knelt down next to me and said, "Are you going to lie there all night?" with a humorous tease.

"I think I hit my head." I remember whispering.

"Yes, you sure did. I saw it from the other side of the rink. Let's get you up doll-face!" He put both arms under me from behind and scooped me up like I was a toddler. "Bend your knees a little and push each foot out one at a time; just a little to the side gently and I'll help you around."

He skated to the front of me so he was facing me. Held my hands and skated backwards to help me all the way around and off the rink. I remember, blushing, feeling tingles all over and staring at him. I thought he was a god!

32

We eventually made it inside, and he bought me a hot chocolate and asked me if I needed to go to the doctors. He teased me a lot, and from all my training in psychology I could tell he was having a limbic reaction too. He told me all about how he was an ice hockey player, and as a little boy his dream was to be on the Philadelphia Flyers. I eventually left to go home with my friends, but he wouldn't let me leave until I gave him my phone number. He called me that night. When the phone rang, I remember thinking it would be a friend wanting to hear about the hunky guy I met, and instead it was him.

"Hey doll-face, when can I take you out on a real date?" he asked smoothly.

It was love. I mean, it was a limbic resonance that led to love. Whatever! It was love! Then like clock-work I hear a song coming in my head.

"da-da-da-da-dadadada! Boom! Boom! da-da-da-da-dadadada!"

Oh, God! It's "Ice-Ice-Baby!"

Seriously, is that the best ice related song my subconscious can come up with? Sometimes my *musical genius* is so flakey.

Coming back to the moment, now, I suddenly feel even worse for Mrs. Carter. I am going to help her fix that old bitchy Endora!

FOUR

"Two more s'mores martini's, please, John!" I yell out.

Simmi and I are at our favorite place to go after work. We love the s'mores martinis. This martini has to be one of the most incredible inventions since the telephone. It's a heavenly mix of vodka and chocolate liqueur, with scrumptious graham crackers around the glass rim with tiny little marshmallows floating on top. It's heaven. It is so soothing. I call it a grown-up-hot-chocolate!

"So, tell me again how you messed the test up?" Simmi sarcastically cracks.

"Look, Simmi, will you just drop it. I'm not pregnant ok! I'm drinking you see."

"Jess, I'm telling you. You look different to me!"

"That's what love does," I retort. "I'm still on a honeymoon high."

"It's not love; it's a bun in the oven. Look, I know these things. It's an ancient Indian wisdom my family has. I can always tell when someone is prego." Simmi is confidently sashaying her head back and forth at me.

It's quite endearing when Simmi brings up her Indian background because she is usually torn between rejecting it for her adopted American ways versus accepting it when it suites her. Her way of accepting it is through shopping around to choose the Indian frocks and jewelry she likes, calling it her cultural duty. You see, Simmi likes the dancing part, the traditional party and garb part and sometimes the spiritual part. I think it's adorable when she brings it up like this, and it makes me love her even more as my best friend.

"OK," I roll my eyes at her, "If it will make you happy I will take the other test. I have the other pregnancy test in my purse. We can go in the bathroom at the event and take another test, and I will prove your Indian Voodoo is a bunch of crap. Will that shh—, shut-you up?" I grimace and realize I am slightly slurring.

"Yes, thank you!" Simmi smiles victoriously as she hoists her s'mores martini in the air.

We are about to pay our check to head over to Captain Crunch's god-awful charity event. The martinis are a necessary pre-requisite in order to pretend we are interested. It's going to be horrible. And at least Simmi is meeting Vishal. Vishal is Simmi's long-time boyfriend. He totally fits in with her family which is great. She used to date a "100% white boy", as Simmi puts it. I mean the whitest white boy you could find. And she never told her parents about him because they would have flipped. In her parents' minds she must marry another Indian.

And preferably a doctor or a lawyer with a lot of letters after his name.

And preferably from the same part of India.

And preferably from a family who upholds the Hindu religion. But I always wonder if they would allow a son-in-law who ate hamburgers?

You see this is a classic case of parent-offspring conflict on mate choice. This is of course very common. Parents have a daughter and think to themselves she will grow up to be something they have envisioned, perhaps a doctor, a lawyer, an Olympic swimmer, or the first woman president. Perhaps the next Meryl Streep!

Well, ok, maybe not …. That Meryl Streep part is something I want for my future daughter.

Now the kicker is that some cultures have more parental influence than others. In Simmi's case her parents are quite adept at the guilt building from early childhood. Hence, no more white boy! But less you think Simmi is a big wimp, she did go through a Romeo and Juliet phase. She was going to stand-up and profess her love for white-boy. She had a big speech planned and was going to accuse them of being narrow-minded and racist against non-Indian's. We even practiced it, and I pretended I was her father. She was so stoked up to deliver the speech, but then she met Vishal at a party and he could dance like a rock-star and white-boy danced like, well, a white-boy. And that was the end to her Madonna, Papa don't preach speech she had been working on.

Suddenly, I hear "*Papa Don't Preach*" loudly in my head. I close my eyes after a sip of s'mores martini and get a little lost in my Madonna moment. Then I see Simmi looking at me strangely and realize I was doing a little chair dancing to that one.

OK, so, turning the internal radio off now. As for me, I am man-less this evening, because my Nolan coaches the *mites* hockey team on Friday nights. And usually the only thing that makes this type of event bearable is when you can make it a date-night.

We finish up, pay and leave John a fat tip.

We arrive, slightly tipsy, to the art charity event. Everywhere we look we see sophisticated, smart looking people, who all smell like money. You know the smell. It's not any kind of perfume or cologne you have ever smelled in Macy's before. It's something that was probably purchased at a shop on the Champs-Elysees in Paris. Or imported from Rome and blessed by the pope during a recent visitation with his holiness himself. They are all standing around drinking champagne and gathered in huddles in front of the most ridiculous looking abstract art you have ever seen. A four year old could make these stupid paintings.

"How can anyone actually pay good money for these things?" I say incredulously to Simmi.

"Because they are rich dumb-asses, who think they need to have fancy art hanging in their offices and homes and someone tells them this is fancy art, so they buy it. Now come on to the bathroom so I can prove I'm right!" I love Simmi after a couple martinis. She gets so sassy.

"Simmi, we can't; here comes C.C."

"Gloria, you are looking lovely tonight!" I fake smile at her.

"Yes, you do Gloria! You are absolutely stunning in that blue dress. It shows off your eyes!"

Oh, good one. Simmi is so good at working C.C. I have to remember that eyes bit myself for next time I need to flatter ol' Captain Crunch-o.

I become entranced with her hair which she has in this huge bouffant, and I'm wondering how she can get it to stay like that when suddenly I hear my stomach growl. They both look at me. "Oh, sorry I skipped dinner to get here on time. I'll just get some snacks here."

"NO YOU Did—" Simmi is trying to say as I cough over her and take her arm.

"We were just about to head over to see your work, Gloria. We will let you get back to your mingling." I yell over Simmi, who is looking at me utterly astonished.

"Yes, please do," Gloria eyes us suspiciously. "It's a silent auction, so if you like something, bid away. It's all for charity you know." Her voice trails behind us as I head towards her paintings, pushing Simmi in front of me.

"What are you doing?" Her face is grimacing at me. "We ate salads and pasta and garlic bread?"

"Shut-up Simmi, ok, I didn't want her to know where we were. She knows we get the s'mores martinis there. Suck-up Richard told her." I say with a strained yet cool undertone.

"But why is your stomach growling?"

It is strange. I am suddenly hungry again. I grab something off one of the passing Hors d'oeuvre trays. It's a cracker with something on it. I eat it.

We stand in front of three paintings with signs that read Gloria Vanderbine – distant cousin to Gloria Vanderbilt. Oh no she didn't!?!

Another platter passes by, and I grab two more quick snacks. A mini crab-cake and an asparagus wrapped in prosciutto.

Then I eye a crudités platter. "I'll be right back, Simmi."

I run over and fill a little plate with veggies, cheese and crackers.

When I come back over to C.C.'s paintings, Vishal is standing there now holding hands with Simmi.

"Hello, Vishal! How is residency?"

"Not too bad." He leans over and kisses my cheek.

"You're totally right. She looks different," I hear him whisper to Simmi.

"Oh my God, Simmi, you told him?"

"Jess, calm down. Vishal isn't going to say anything. He works non-stop anyway. Who is he going to tell?"

"Vishal, I'm not pregnant and if you say anything to anyone I will…" I pause trying to think of what I can hold over his head. "I will tell everyone about summer of 2009!"

Vishal looks at me agape. Yes, those are harsh words, but I've made my point.

Vishal is this super intelligent, yet funny guy: Indian, of course. He is so sweet to Simmi and totally loves her. They are really close, and Simmi and I think he will propose soon. He is almost at the end of his residency. He just finished medical school, and we were all so happy when his residency ended up being here in Philadelphia at the University of Pennsylvania because that meant he didn't have to move. As soon as residency is over, we think he'll pop the question. Simmi was at his apartment one night recently. He was running late so she was waiting for him when she noticed a book she hadn't recognized before on his nightstand. She was totally snooping, but it was a great find. It was a "How to buy a diamond" book. She opened it up, and it was obviously well read through with ear marks on several pages and with all the important parts highlighted with yellow. I mean is that incredible or what? That's the kind of moment where you want to do cartwheels in the room and immediately call your best friend. You have to give him credit. How many guys go to that trouble? I mean he is quite thorough. She took a picture of it with her phone and texted it to me. I was hysterical. That is so Vishal! He is always studying or working, but he can be really fun too and as I said he can dance like Usher. Anyway, in 2009, we all had a summer beach house together, and Vishal got really drunk and anyway I have some real dirt on him.

God, here comes another tray. This one is some kind of puff pastry.

"Yum," I say, grabbing one and taking a bite. As I start to chew I immediately realize it's a mushroom something or other.

"It's mushroom and duck liver pate. Enjoy!" The server is saying.

Oh my god, I hate mushrooms. I try to spit it into my napkin. But all at once I can feel my stomach lurching and Oh My god, I'm going to be sick. I think I see a trash can nearby. I run over grab it and throw-up in it hoping nobody has seen me.

"What are you doing," screams some woman in a black tight dress with her voluminous breasts popping out.

She's waving and pointing at me and then motioning towards a sign. I turn to look at the sign. It reads Marilyn Moore modern art collection – hand painted modern vases.

OH MY GOD! I just threw-up in her art.

"I'm sorry! I'll buy it!" People are starting to look. I can see suck-up Richard in the distance ogling me. "I'll just be right back!" I run to the bathroom covering my mouth with one hand and my throw-up bucket art in the other. I feel sick again, and I feel faint.

Simmi comes bursting in.

"Jess, are you ok? Maybe we should get you to a hospital. Vishal can get you in quick."

"No, I'm fine. I just need to ….to …. To ..." I rush into the stall. I'm vomiting again and am suddenly reminded of how much food I've eaten in the last 90 minutes.

"Get me home, Simmi!" My eyes are all watery and I feel light-headed. And my heart is racing.

"Jess, let's take that test!"

"NOW? I can hardly stand Simmi, let alone pee on a stick!"

"I'll hold you up, you just do the pee part." Simmi is trying to convince me.

"Are you crazy? It was those mushroom things. You know I hate mushrooms!"

"OK, OK. We will drive you……." Simmi begins, but she is cut-off by the door smashing open.

"She's in here," comes a shrill voice. "Young lady, what are you doing with my art in the bathroom?"

Simmi snaps, "Look lady, she's pregnant …"

"Simmi!" I screech!

"…and she threw-up in your bucket; it was an accident. Leave her alone. We will pay for it!" I can hear her ushering the woman out.

Twenty-five minutes later Vishal and Simmi bring me to our condo, after I had to pay $300 for a stupid hand-painted vase that looks like a trashcan. And we had to explain to Captain Crunch that I must have the flu. She also seemed pretty upset that I bid on a trashcan instead of her paintings, but thank goodness she didn't see what had happened. I never have been so humiliated before in my life. And I never knew I could have such a terrible reaction to mushrooms. Simmi gets me into bed with a cold wet towel for my forehead. She insists on waiting, but I tell her Nolan will be home very soon and not to worry. She makes me promise to take the test in the morning. And just to appease her, I tell her that I will. After Simmi leaves and I lie down, I notice that the phone light is on indicating there is a new message.

I pick it up and push the button.

"Hello Mrs. Reed .… Um I apologize … I mean Dr. Reed. This is Jimmy from Robbins. Our jeweler has evaluated your rings, and we have some options for you. Unfortunately, each option does require minor changes to the ring. Can you call me at your earliest convenience and we can go over it? Thanks!"

I hang it up. I start to feel a tingling behind my nose and eyes. My heart starts thumping, and my hands feel hot. And then, all of a sudden, I'm sobbing. What is wrong with me? I can't calm down. Jesus, I am a mess!

I lie there for what feels like forever. Still sobbing into the pillow, I slowly recount the week wondering why I can't calm down. I still feel nauseous from those awful mushrooms. At least I think it was the mushrooms or maybe it was the s'mores martinis? But I've never gotten sick from those. Simmi and I treat ourselves to them almost weekly. But, I should be feeling better by now. Come to think of it I have had some odd symptoms this week. Maybe I do have the flu. I go over it in my head .….

Jess, think, what are your symptoms?

Nausea and vomiting …

I have felt a little dizzy here and there.…

And, oh my, how hungry I've been.…

And it's the weirdest thing; I've been peeing all the time!

And I've been really thirsty. I've started to bring a glass of water to bed, and I wake up in the middle of the night to drink it. Then while I'm up I have to pee again.

And I have even been a little moodier than normal, and now I can't stop crying ……………

"Oh My God!"

I sit straight up in bed.

I run to my purse.

Rip out the other test.

This time I read it carefully. OK, I can use a cup instead it says. Yes I'll do that. I pee into a plastic throw-away cup. I take the test stick. Put it in the cup just like they say. I lay it flat after, just like they say. I wait for exactly 3 minutes. I time it on my phone. Then I walk slowly over. I close my eyes and say, "God, it's in your hands."

I open them and ....

A huge smile instantly comes across my face.

Before I can do anything else, I feel tears falling on my cheeks.

It's positive. It is, and I feel this amazing joy. I'm not upset. I'm not at all terrified. I feel fearless and totally content.

I twirl around, and I cup my arms together pretending to cuddle a make-believe baby.

I can't believe it. Nolan and I are going to have a baby. I really am pregnant! Simmi was right. And I had no idea I would be this happy.

I mean it's a total shock. This is so unplanned. And earlier in the week I was in complete denial, but now it all makes sense.

Then all of a sudden I realize, Holy Shit! I need to tell Nolan!

FIVE

This is huge!

I can't just tell him with words. I can't just show him the test. This is our first child. Yes, it's a surprise! He will be shocked. But it has to be memorable. It has to be special. I look at the clock.

8:05.

I have another 55 minutes until the shops close.

Thinking quickly, I throw my jacket on and flats. I run out the door. I'm practically floating. My head is racing. Will it be a boy? A sweet little boy with Nolan's eyes! Or a girl? A darling girl with my hair. The next Meryl Streep, perhaps?

I approach first the greeting card store on 7th. I race in and run to the card section for babies. I can't decide and so I buy three cards. One is from wife to husband and is all loving and romantic. One is from child to new Father with a picture of a little baby hand in a big father's hand. Oh my Gosh that made me tear up again. And one is a "Surprise you're going to be a daddy," card. That last one is a bit of a joke card because it shows the newly knowledgeable father passed out due to the news. Which suddenly I think, uh-oh, could he pass out?

OK, I have cards. Check.

Next I float over to the liquor store and buy champagne.

OK, I have champagne. Check.

Next, I know exactly where to go. A few months back I bought a baby shower gift from this adorable baby boutique up on 12th. I am practically skipping up the street. There it is. "Little Loretta's Lambs" it's called. I open the doors.

My breath is taken away. I look around and see everywhere adorable baby clothes and infant toys and picture frames and so many things I never noticed when I was in here before. The walls are painted with pastel greens and yellows and purples, and there are little lambs floating along the wall. It's incredible. ....Babies and their stuff.

It's just incredible. I have a moment of concern. BABIES! I know nothing about babies!

Suddenly the woman behind the register is approaching me with a box of tissues. I don't quite realize it, but I am crying.

"What's wrong dear?" She twitches a sympathetic face.

"Oh, dear, my .... I'm sorry. It's just ...... I just found out I'm expecting!"

"Oh is that all ...... honey come on over here with Miss Loretta. Have a seat."

She is the nicest woman in the world. She gets me a glass of water. Then she hands me a new expectant mother gift bag with all kinds of information and a complimentary baby keep-sake book. And I tell her all about throwing-up in the trashcan. She laughs and says I might think about carrying around that trashcan for a few more weeks because I could be in for some rough days. She advises me to watch my diet. Eat every 2-3 hours and drink plenty of fluids. Gosh I was so excited that I hadn't even thought about my proper prenatal care. I need to read about this. I need to get books out of the library. I need to do some literature searches. I need to make a doctor's appointment. I need to start pregnant-lady yoga. Wow! I have a lot of work ahead of me.

Loretta also eyes the champagne and says, "You know dear in my day they didn't know much but now they know for sure you shouldn't drink while you're pregnant."

44

"Um, uh...... yes, I know, of course," I stammer. "I just picked it up for my husband as a new father gift. You know a surprise!"

Shit! Of course I can't drink. What am I thinking? I need to adjust my entire outlook. Then it hits me. No more s'mores martinis! Oh My God. How will I survive?

The next 30 minutes are a blur as Loretta gives me a crash course on babies.

"Bye, Loretta. Thanks for everything. I'll be back next week." I joyfully wave to her as I exit the store.

Loretta has all these great programs on safety for expectant mothers, and she can show you how to look up if a toy is on recall. And she even has a day in the spring when the fire department comes and helps you learn how to properly install a child seat. Loretta told me 8 out of 10 parents do it wrong. Well not me. I'm going to learn every right thing to do. So, I signed Nolan and I up already for this safety program next Saturday. I left with two huge bags. One was full with all the information and free stuff she gave me. And the other had these adorable hand knitted little booties. The pair of them can fit in the palm of my hand. I also purchased three adorable newborn onesies.

The first says: "*Daddy's little peanut*" and it has the cutest cartoon peanut with a face on it.

The second one says, "*add me and we are three,*" and there are three peas in a pod. Two big ones for the parents and a little one for the baby.

And the final one says: "*ipood.*" I couldn't resist that one. Nolan loves his iphone so that will be a hit.

I rush home and set the condo all up with candles, and I wrap up the gifts I bought and I write loving words of encouragement of what a great father he will be in each of the three cards I purchased. I think I'll give him the romantic one first and the joke one last. The champagne is chilled on the table, and I've organized a quick playlist of songs that have the word Baby

45

in it. One song is even the Justin Beiber and Ludacris one I heard in my head. See how it comes in handy later?

While I am waiting for Nolan to arrive, I am searching on the internet. I have come across some website I am really learning a ton from. One even has a calendar function. I put all my info in, and it tracks my growth and how big the baby is and how much it is growing. According to the calendar, my baby is just a small blastocyst, and right about now it is embedding into my uterine wall. This is so cool. I look at my belly and say, "I love you little blastocyst!" I continue reading ahead and have learned that I am way behind. I start making a list:

1. Must buy prenatal vitamins
2. Must make urgent appointment at OBGYN
3. Must start walking 30 minutes a day
4. Must eat diet full of folic acid
5. And diet full of iron
6. And diet full of fruit
7. And diet full of green leafy vegetables
8. And diet with the correct protein portion
9. And must immediately start doing kegels for proper birthing

And, Oh My God, there is an entire list of foods I can't eat such as sushi, peanuts, cold cuts and tuna fish. Honestly, how are you supposed to know this material well enough to deliver a healthy baby? I bet Reese Witherspoon didn't have to worry about this. Her nifty Rodeo-Drive-Nutritionist probably just delivered her the exact pregnancy portions with every nutritional item necessary. And when she finished with her prego-perfect meal, I bet a personal trainer probably came over for personal preg-o-lates, some new-fangled exercise that makes you bounce right back into shape. And you know those celebrity trainers keep it a huge secret and the rest of us losers are researching how to make a banana, kale and cucumber smoothie while stretching our labor muscles at the same time. What are labor muscles, anyway? I need to research all weekend and chart it out and make lists and ………. just then I hear footsteps and then a key in the door. I leap up. I'm a ball of nerves. I am so excited but I am not sure how Nolan will react.

The door opens, and Nolan rushes in.

"Jess, doll-face, what's wrong? Simmi texted me you were sick, and you didn't answer my calls or texts?"

"Oh, I ran out for a bit, and I must have left my phone here," I say trying to calm him.

"What are you doing running out? You should be in bed!" He hasn't noticed anything, the candles or the cards or the champagne. He is totally engrossed in me. He scoops me up in his arms and walks me to the bedroom. I am giggling.

"Nolan, honey, put me down. I have something to tell you."

"Tell me once you are lying down, doll-face." He is so loving and caring. God, I'm so lucky.

He lays me down and sits next to me holding my hands and says, "I'll make you Mom's famous chicken soup."

"Nolan, I'm not sick!"

"But Simmi said you barfed in some expensive art vase?" he looks confused.

"I did, but it's not what you think. If we can just go out to the dining room, I have some things that will help." I start to get up, but he stops me.

"What things? You stay here. I'll get them." He stands up from the bed to go out into the dining room.

I come out behind him, and he appears to be taken aback as he looks around the room and for the first time takes in the champagne and cards and gifts. He turns and sees me and says, "What on earth is all this, Jess?"

"Just open that little box with the yellow bow," I gesture towards the box with the booties in it.

He walks over, and I can feel my heart beating. I can't help the massive smile that is plastered across my face. He picks it up and looks back at me unsure of himself. I'm smiling so much my cheeks hurt.

"Go on open it!" I provide an encouraging nod.

He opens it and looks inside. He pulls out the adorable hand knitted booties and places them in his hand. In his large hands, the booties look so petite as if they belong to a tiny doll. His face is blank for a moment. But then his features soften a bit, and he stands upright a little more. Blinks a few times, and I can see a hint of a grin starting.

"You want me to start a doll collection?" he questions me with a smirk.

I just beam back at him and my eyes well up a little.

He walks slowly towards me. Our eyes locked.

"Does this mean what I think it means?"

Unable to speak I just nod at him, smiling, crying.

With that he runs over and lifts me in the air. He twirls me around and then brings me to his chest to hug me. My feet still are dangling in the air.

"I love you doll-face!"

"I love you too, and I love our blastocyst," I reply.

"Blastocyst? What's that? I thought you were pregnant?" Are these for some weird science project that you are doing?"

I laugh out loud, "We ARE pregnant," I emphasize derisively, "but right now the baby is just a collection of cells called a blastocyst." I look at him for signs of acknowledgment.

"Oh cool, a blastocyst!" Nolan says in a deep manly tone. Then he puts me down. And pretends to ice-skate across our floor and makes a make-believe slap-shot and throws his arms in the air. "SCORE," he yells. "Me and my boy will be on the ice all the time. I'll coach his team, and we'll get matching jerseys," he's rambling while doing fancy imaginary stick-handling moves with the sofa cushion.

"Babe, you know it could also be a girl," I quip.

"Oh right, a girl! OK, in that case I don't want her anywhere near those hockey guys!"

We fall to the sofa laughing.

Nolan and I stay up together half the night. I tell him all about the symptoms I was having and how Simmi insisted that her Indian voodoo was telling her I was pregnant. I tell him the whole story about Captain Crunch and show him the vase I vomited in. I did manage to clean it out earlier. Then we settle in to bed and talk all about what the baby will be like. Part me. Part him. And I name all his best qualities that I hope the baby has, and then he names all the things he loves about me that he hopes the baby will have. He tells me he hopes the baby is more like me and less like him. But I hope the opposite. Nolan is one of the most genuine, thoughtful men I have ever encountered, and he is always so relaxed. I, on the other hand, am always so high-strung and over-worried and so I hope the baby does not get the worry gene from me. I would love for the baby to be cool and calm like Nolan!

We talk and talk for hours. And we decide that we aren't going to tell our parents just yet. We want to get one doctor's visit under our belts, and also we want to just have this be our special secret for a while. We come up with the code name Blasty, short for blastocyst and if we need to talk about it around someone we will use the term blasty. Although I suppose I need to tell Simmi so her head doesn't explode.

We have the most amazing night. We even find time for ….. Well, you-know and then the next morning I wake up still enveloped in Nolan's arms. My head is resting on the pillow. Nolan is still asleep. I place my hands on my lower abdomen. This is incredible. I have all weekend to research. There is no time to waste. I gently slip out of Nolan's arms. I quickly get dressed and leave a note on the table.

Dear Daddy-To-Be,

Going to library for research on blasty. Meet me at Pod for lunch at 12.

Love,

Mommy-to-be

Then I send a quick text to Simmi.

Me: Meet me at Franklin if you want the results to your Indian Voodoo!

I arrive at Franklin library at the University of Pennsylvania. I love it here. There is a familiar smell of old books and journals. And it's so serene. I always imagine the collective brain power of those who have entered and exited this building over the years. I mean someone like Raymond Davis, who was honored with a Nobel Prize for pioneering contributions to astrophysics, probably came up with his ideas right here in this library. Or even before Ray-Ray, Laura Alber, president and CEO of Williams Sonoma, probably was first inspired here at Franklin. I bet it was here at this very brown wooden table that her passion to expand the quality of the lives of those of us at home came alive, later giving birth to Pottery Barn Kids and Pbteen. Note to self – request Pottery Barn Kids catalog. And yes, I'm sure there are the Norman Tweed Whitakers of the world who sat in here too. I mean what kind of chess master gets involved with planning the most notorious kidnapping of the 20th century? Using your intelligence to plan a kidnapping of poor 20 month old Charles Augustus Lindbergh, Jr just proves that the profession of Psychiatry and Psychology is deeply needed. But that's beside the point. Looking around, I see people studying, writing, tapping away on their computers and slowly browsing the aisles of books. It puts me in an instantly tranquil state. Some people go to a yoga class to relax, but all I need to do is come here. I'm not quite sure what I am looking for, but I think I will know it when I find it. I definitely want to read up on proper nutrition. Suddenly, I also wonder if there is any psychology fetal research that I should be aware of. I'll ask Simmi; she will know. Just to get started, I head over to the catalog computer. I'll just put in some search words and see what kind of resources are here. I stare at the screen. The cursor is blinking at me as if to say, "come on now, type something!" I type in "Pregnancy". Immediately a vast list of references pops up, and I smile at the screen. But hold on, as I glance down the list I'm not so sure I like this.

*Low birth counts: statistics and **pregnancy***

*Cancer in **pregnancy**: treatment options*

*Fetal-alcohol syndrome in **pregnancy***

*Folic Acid deficiency in **pregnancy**: Cleft palate risk*

***Pregnancy** by age-group: live birth to fetal death ratio*

*High Risk **pregnancy***

*Intrauterine surgery in **pregnancy***

*Hemorrhoid development and surgery during **pregnancy***

Holy blasty! Every reference is more terrifying than the one that preceded it, especially that hemorrhoid one. As I think of these unknowns, my head feels a little heavy, and I feel like I might ....

Next thing I know, out of pure reflex, I'm up and sprinting to the bathroom.

Oh, right, I forgot about this nausea and vomiting thing. I reach the stall and barely make it. I'm basically heaving in the bathroom with nothing actually coming up. Ok, Jess you are not doing so well with this whole 2nd-day-of-knowing-you're-pregnant thing. Now that I think practically, I was so excited to get to the library, I didn't eat. And Ms. Loretta said I'm supposed to eat every few hours. I'm washing my hands and unexpectedly the door busts open.

"There you are. I was right, wasn't I?" Simmi rushes in. Her hair is totally disheveled. Half of it is in a ponytail and the other half is just hanging off her head in wiry clumps. She is wearing her slippers and sweatpants and a tee-shirt that reads Bieber Fever.

"Wow, Simmi you shouldn't have glammed up for me," I eye her from head to toe. And then I can't believe the sight of her and start sniggering.

"I wouldn't be laughing there Dr. Reed. If you are what I think you are, you are the one who will be looking quite funny over the course of the next nine months!" Simmi gestures to my body with a big circular movement and a pointed finger, indicating a larger girth around my mid-section.

We both start giggling.

"Well, I know I didn't rush out of bed for nothing. And I know you, Jess. You are starting your baby prep research, aren't you? That's why you are here. I bet you'll have posters, ghant charts and PowerPoint presentations by Sunday night."

Simmi continues to tease me, but I am distracted by the thought of my belly growing and I am unable to stop smiling because from deep inside I think I can actually feel my heart swelling. I am smiling from ear to ear.

"OK, Jess you're tormenting me over here. Say something?"

I look down at my feet and pull a fake frown to string her along a bit, "Well, Simmi I brought you here to ask you if I could borrow your blue dress?"

"Shut-up! You did not. Spill the beans!"

"OK .... well, does your Indian Voodoo predict a girl or a boy?"

"I knew it. I knew it!" She wraps her arms around me.

"Oh God, Simmi, you didn't even brush your teeth?" I frown at her again, this time a genuine frown.

"Well, forgive me for running out the door to celebrate with my best friend. Now tell me everything. Did you tell Nolan? Did you tell your parents? OH MY GOD! You're pregnant! I just knew it. How are you feeling? Oh and I better be the godmother! Are your boobs bigger? I hear your boobs get bigger," she continues.

"OK, yes, I will tell you everything," I say. "But first we need to eat! I was told eating often is supposed to help the nausea and vomiting."

So we go to a nearby breakfast and coffee shop and grab some egg-white vegetable omelets, and Simmi gets a latte and I get some orange juice for vitamin C. From the internet last night I learned when you are pregnant caffeine is also off limits. And of course no alcohol and I mean no alcohol and did I mention no alcohol. Naturally, now I am totally vexed about those s'mores martinis from the other night. That's top on my list of questions for the doctor. And, of course, it didn't help that one of the first references filtered on the library catalog was *Fetal-Alcohol Syndrome*. What if I already gave that to the baby? I tell Simmi all about the catalog search results and all the scary things I saw. And she tells me that her Grandmother provided her mother with whisky during pregnancy to calm nausea and vomiting, so not to worry because she turned out great!

"But Simmi, you didn't see the list of articles that darted up!" I say alarmed.

"Oh Jess, you always did select such poor search words for research activities!" Simmi provides a compassionate look.

I look at her a bit deflated.

"Well, I am not taking any chances. I have already downloaded the pregnancy diet app. I can put in everything I eat before I eat it, and it tells me if it's ok and what nutritional value it delivers to the baby."

Simmi rolls her eyes at me and begins.

"Here, I, Simmi the great library search term wizard, will write down what you should be searching for, and you go back to the library and then let me know later what comes up. I have to get myself together before I see some parent of a patient on the street."

Simmi is this amazing child psychologist. She helps so many parents and children, but she always gets uncomfortable when she runs into a family on the street. And for some reason she always runs into a family when she is looking her worst! But the kids love running into Simmi on the street. You see Simmi has such a great nature about her, and she develops this powerful connection with these children. It's like they are friends for life. It's a gift really. Simmi is scribbling down search terms for me to try. She hands me the list and gives me a peck on the cheek.

"I'm out! No more scary stuff, you hear me. And lay-off that silly app! Our parents ate whatever they wanted. You are becoming paranoid. Nolan and you are healthy, and you will have a healthy baby!"

As she walks towards the door, I read her list:

Jess's revised search terms

Great Sex during Pregnancy

Happy Pregnancy

How to relax in Pregnancy

Healthy Pregnancy

Exercise in Pregnancy – also see great sex during pregnancy

Achieve Blissful mother-to-be-state – also see great sex during pregnancy

I can't help giggling, and I look up at Simmi who looks back to get my reaction. She lifts her perfectly manicured eyebrows up and down, indicating she is pleased with her naughty suggestions. Oh Simmi!

I head back to the library, and 4 hours later I have about 8 books and have photocopied an entire bag full of journal articles. I have some great resources on exercise, nutrition, calming exercises, stages of pregnancy, and I even found a book for Nolan on being an expectant father. But there is too much to read and catch up on.

I text Nolan.

> Me: N – change in plans. Blasty knowledge severely lacking. Super-mom status in jeopardy. Meet me at Franklin to help carry home heaps of info. We can order food at home and catch up.
>
> Nolan: Seriously?
>
> Me: Have you met me?
>
> Nolan: Yes doll-face, I'll be right there.

SIX

Stay Calm. Don't freak out all at once! Follow your notes. Speak calmly. I'm practicing a little calm self-talk. I use this with my patients all the time.

"Doll-face," Nolan looks at me amusingly "it's only our first appointment. There is no need to stress about this!"

We are sitting in the waiting room at the OB/GYN office. There is hardly a place to sit. Every chair is filled with a body–bodies of all types–women who don't look pregnant at all and others who look very pregnant. Young, old and in between. It's actually a great mix for a social research project. I should think about that.

I'm distracted from my thoughts by a woman who opens the door and comes in with a circular donut shaped cushion. She looks about to pop, and according to her facial expressions, she looks miserable.

"They better take me today. I can't take this anymore. And this is all your fault!" she is saying through gritting teeth to a man behind her. The man is walking a few feet behind her. From my training, I quickly analyze their body language. And my professional scientific impression of the two of them is he is afraid of her but needs to help her. And she, well she wants him to fall off a cliff, most likely as the result of pushing him off herself.

"Just calm down, sweetie," he is saying as he signs the sign-in sheet at the front. He looks petrified.

She plops down the donut cushion and sits on it. They are arguing, but I can't quite make out all that they are saying. Then suddenly her voice rises and she says, "I didn't even want to have a baby and now I'm 65 pounds over-weight. I'm not sleeping, my back is killing me and I have to sit on this stupid, fucking pillow so that I don't pass out from Hemorrhoid pain!"

Oh My God! Hemorrhoids, just like my search at the library showed. Oh, this is not good. I am starting to sweat. Now, I am staring at them out of even greater interest. What is that thing she is sitting on? Do I need one of those? I look at Nolan alarmed, and he just starts giggling.

"I'm glad I'm not that guy!" he leans over and whispers.

I wish they would just call me back already. We've been here for thirty minutes at least, and all these other pregnant women are freaking me out. On a positive note, I feel well informed from all my research, but I have at least 20 questions for today (well to be exact 27). When Nolan met me at the library the other day, we took home heaps of articles and books. I sorted through them all and read so much in the last few days I am practically an expert. Nolan keeps telling me to just relax and let it progress naturally. Of course, that's easy for him to say. He doesn't have a person growing inside of him. He has been really sweet and loving though. And he offered to take all the nutrition books and articles under his expert management. You see, Nolan is a sports nutritionist. He works for the Children's Hospital of Philadelphia at the Sports Medicine and Performance Center. He writes up different calorie diets for athletes. And he has some really interesting cases. There are underweight athletes, overweight athletes, and athletes with iron deficiencies. Then he has the poor athletes who experience gastrointestinal distress with exercise and even severe muscle cramping due to a lack of proper nutrition. He loves his work and is really good at it. His dream however is to one day work for the Philadelphia Flyers. So he also in his spare time writes a sports nutrition blog that frequently caters to the hockey athlete in particular. He is hoping to get discovered by the Flyers.

He stayed up half the night one evening and read all the nutritional information, so now each morning he prepares me some kind of delicious smoothie. This morning was yogurt, blueberry, kiwi, celery and spinach. It sounds gross, but he is a smoothie God. It was delicious! I told him if he was going to manage the nutrition piece of "the blasty project" he has to ensure 110% consumption of every essential vitamin, mineral and nutrient. And so far he has hit the mark! He's even charting it all out for me, which I love. When I put the smoothie ingredients in my pregnancy diet app it pings me back with 5 stars and "way to go, super healthy mama!" It's pretty impressive how Nolan just whips these smoothie's together.

"Mrs. Reed, we are ready for you now," booms the nurse's voice.

Here we go!

"Hi," I say. "This is my husband Nolan, and my name is Jessica."

The nurse's name badge reads "Marge."

Marge seems less then enthused by my introduction.

"OK, Mrs. Reed step over here to the scale. I am going to get your weight, blood pressure, and then I need you to give me a urine sample in this cup."

"Well, Marge I have a few questions for you." I say brightly.

"Hold them for the end, please. I need to get three more ladies back to their rooms!" she quickly shuts me down. Geez! She's not very friendly is she? This is not at all how I pictured an OB/GYN nurse to be. I was expecting someone like, well like Mary Poppins.

After I do everything she requires, she ushers us down to room 5 and hands me a gown.

"Put this on, opening in the front."

"In the front?" I say doubtingly.

"Yes, dear, in the front! Don't be shy, we've seen it all before."

I'm not sure how I feel about that statement. I mean she could have said something more encouraging like, "don't worry sweetie, everyone is a little nervous their first time. I'll fix you a tea to help you relax and bring it back to you!"

OK, a few moments later, I have the opening in the front and a flimsy paper sheet over top of me. I'm holding together the opening so I'm completely covered up. This seems all wrong. I just want to ask some questions first. I can feel myself getting hot all over and anxious.

There is a knock on the door. "Mrs. Reed may I come in?"

"Yes," I say apprehensively.

"Mrs. Reed, Hello, I am Dr. Lange." She shakes my hand and then turns to Nolan. "And you must be Mr. Reed?"

"Yes, I am and proud of it!" he smirks.

The doctor turns back to me, she smiles and sits next to me.

"I'm sure you have a lot of questions Mrs. Reed. All first time expectant mothers' do, but let's go through some basic medical history first and do an initial exam and then we can talk in my office and I can answer all the questions you have."

"I don't think you want to promise that kind of time, Doctor. She's an expert questioner!" Nolan is saying under his breath.

"That sounds great," I say enthusiastically, ignoring Nolan altogether.

This is going much better. I feel myself relax a little. She asks me all about my medical history and then has me lay down on the table. Of course, this is the uncomfortable part where I am basically butt naked and subjected to a cavity search.

"Everything feels normal, Mrs. Reed. Let's do a quick breast exam, shall we."

She moves up towards my head and reaches up to palpate my breasts.

"Oh, good for you, you have what I call designer nipples." She says brightly.

Did she just say I have designer nipples?

"Excuse me?" I question

"Designer nipples! I would kill for these nipples. They are perky and perfect for latch-on?"

Suddenly I feel very uncomfortable. "Latch-on?" I question again.

"Yes, for breastfeeding of course!" she nods with a reassuring look. "You are going to breastfeed aren't you?"

"Oh, um ….. Yes, of course!"

Oh my God, I never even thought about the breastfeeding part. I haven't allowed myself to actually think about the baby. I am so preoccupied with the "blasty phase." I have to go back to the library now and research breastfeeding! Shit!

"OK, why don't you get dressed, and you can both meet me next door in my office." She leaves us alone.

Nolan looks totally stunned or is he nervous, or perhaps thrilled? I'm not sure which when he finally says, "That may have been one of the closest lesbian-like encounters I think I will ever witness!"

"What?" I say incredulously.

"Come on, you know what I mean, another women touching your boobs and saying you have designer nipples."

"Honestly Nolan?"

"Look, I'm just saying I will be happy to come to all your appointments if this is what goes on. Plus you look pretty hot in that open to the front gown. Maybe we can steal an extra one for home to play doctor!" He's looking at me yearningly.

It's official. I do not understand men. We are in one of the most sterile and clinical environments possible. Everything in this room is white and made of steel and there are medical supplies everywhere, and somehow he is thinking about sex?

We walk into her office and sit down.

Dr. Lange begins, "Here is a new parents' welcome packet. It reviews all that you need to know at this stage. I warn all my patients to stay off the internet and to not overstress about potential pregnancy problems."

Too late!

"Also," she continues, "I have a list of prenatal vitamins that I recommend. Please make sure to start taking these immediately if you haven't already. An extra calcium and magnesium supplement is also recommended."

"Again, please try not to read too much off the internet. There is no sense in worrying about things that aren't happening to you. OK?"

I nod. Nolan smirks.

"So what questions do you have?"

"Well," I say "just a few"

I hand her the questions that I have prepared in triplicate; a copy for her, a copy for me and one for Nolan. It reads:

I had exactly 2 s'mores martinis which contain 4 ounces of vodka, 1 ounce of chocolate liqueur in each drink before I knew I was pregnant. Have I subjected my baby to fetal-alcohol syndrome?

I was diligently taking my birth control pills, so can you please explain to me how I became pregnant?

I understand at approximately 22 days after conception the neural tube forms. What kind of test do we order to make sure the neural tubes are well formed?

What other foods should I avoid besides peanuts, sushi, cold cuts, tuna fish, soft cheeses, smoked fish, Caesar dressing, homemade ice cream and pate? (I ate a half of a puff pastry that contained mushrooms and pate but vomited immediately after. What are my risks for listeria?)

60

How much weight do you recommend I gain week to week? I would prefer down to the ounce via a chart if possible.

Can I get a handicap parking sticker to avoid the risk of involvement in a pedestrian parking lot accident? I figure if I am closer to the entrance I have less risk of being struck.

How do I avoid Hemorrhoids?

Do you recommend any preg-o-lates instructors?

At what point can we rule-out heart problems in the fetus or other vital organs?

I understand at 5 weeks that ears are developing. Should I start playing Mozart and reading Shakespeare out loud at that point? Do you have any study data on this type of activity and the best media to invest in?

This question is for a friend of mine: If she wanted her baby to be the next Meryl Streep should she read the baby books on acting methods?

I'm a social psychologist and practice at the University of Pennsylvania and I understand from my research that there is new data indicating that behaviorally and psychologically a 32 week fetus is equivalent to the newborn. So what specific actions should I take at 32 weeks to ensure I use this time wisely? That's an 8 week jump start.

Turn page …

Dr. Lange looks up from the paper. She doesn't turn over the page to look at the second side. She looks a little bewildered.

"Um, Mrs. Reed, might I suggest we set you up with our social worker, Mia? Mia will be able to help you with a lot of this. What you are experiencing is very common for our first time moms. My job is to focus on your health, and I really stress that you stay away from reading too much extraneous information." She looks at Nolan to emphasize this statement and then looks back at me. "And please try to enjoy your pregnancy. That really is the best gift you can give your baby! Your first pregnancy is the one where you can focus solely on yourself. I can tell you there is no concern about your drinks and the pate, although I do advise that you refrain from alcohol during pregnancy. You should be just fine. You are a very healthy, young woman, and as long as you continue with a healthy diet and regular low-impact exercise, and get plenty of rest, you will be doing all that is necessary to develop a healthy baby. We don't order any special tests unless they are warranted, and unfortunately, I can't get you a handicap parking sticker unless you develop back or leg problems. Now as for being on the pill, you have stopped taking it I assume?"

"Yes, as soon as the test was positive," I reply.

"Great. Were you by chance on any antibiotics recently?" she inquires

"Yes, as a matter of fact I was about a month ago."

"And do you remember which antibiotic it was?" She questions.

"Um, I'm not sure. Something like metro-something."

"Ah, was it metronidazole?"

"Yes, yes," I answer enthusiastically as if I won the lottery. "That was it!"

"Well. There you have it. Patients on certain antibiotics are warned to use back-up contraceptives because the antibiotic can cause estrogen containing pills to become less effective. And metronidazole is one such antibiotic, so if you didn't use back-up contraception that could likely be the reason you became pregnant. I generally recommend to my patients using a condom or spermicide as a back-up method when on certain antibiotics. Your pharmacist should have advised you as well.

"What? My pharmacist never told me that!" Stupid pharmacist! All she said was something about eating more yogurt to avoid a yeast infection. I mean in terms of priority messaging to a patient shouldn't the part about – *look you can get pregnant on this stuff* – come before the yeast infection part? What the hell? I'm going to go back and give that pharmacist a piece of my mind. I mean I could probably sue her. I can feel my eyebrows furrowing.

"Mrs. Reed, are you ok?"

"Oh, yes, sorry, I was just recalling that the pharmacist didn't mention anything about getting pregnant. Can't that be considered like malpractice or something?"

Dr. Lange smiles, "Actually nowadays the warning labels are so obvious that it's expected that the patient read all the materials before taking the medication, and you usually sign a paper that says you understand how to take the medication and indicate that you have no further questions."

Oh, so that's what they have you sign. I always thought you were just signing to say you've picked up your medication, like when you sign for a FedEx package. Those tricky pharmacists!

"Well. Mrs. Reed, beyond that, why don't you read over the packet, and we can pick up on your next visit, ok?" She is standing up from the desk.

"But, but …." I begin.

"Thank you for your time doctor. We will read over the information you gave us." Nolan is saying and grabbing my hand. "Come on honey, let's read the packets and maybe call Mia to set up an appointment."

I'm stunned. I don't want to talk to Mia; I want to talk to my doctor! Here I am, trying to be an active participant in my pregnancy, and she is pawning me off to Mia. I feel like I am receiving a pat on the back and a push out the door. Nolan is leading me out towards the waiting area, and I am still in a daze at what transpired. My questions were not taken seriously. She didn't even look at the other side of my question list. Just as I gather my wherewithal, I turn to challenge the doctor with the rest of my questions, but she has already disappeared.

"Doll-face let's go grab some lunch and look over the new parent packet together." Nolan squeezes my hand gently.

"I can't. I'm supposed to go in to review the options for our wedding bands."

"Don't worry about that. Let me handle that. I don't want you getting upset over those rings again!"

Nolan reaches out to hug me. Suddenly wrapped in his arms, I feel immediate relief. Everything will be ok. And to be honest I don't think I am in the best state of mind to deal with Mr. blame-shifter-what's-his-face! What a relief that Nolan will handle it instead.

"Honey, it would be so wonderful if you would handle the rings. I really have so much on my mind right now!" I blurt out.

"Of course you do. Don't give it another thought. I will take care of it!"

I am still feeling slightly disappointed in my first pregnancy appointment when all of a sudden, I hear—

"Mrs. Reed, wait! You'll want this information," Marge is yelling.

Oh my gosh, I don't believe it. The doctor must have hand written all the answers to my questions. Of course! It's just like with my patients; documentation is so important. I should have known she would be professional about answering every last question. I hold my hand out, and she hands me a piece of paper. I look at it. But, it's not the question paper at all. It's blank.

"It's blank." I crack

"Turn it over dear," Marge counters.

I turn it over and stare at it. It's not the answers to my questions, but suddenly it's the only information I actually care about. It's my due date. I'm staring at it unable to speak.

"What is it?" Nolan looks concerned. I hand it to him.

Karen Lange, MD

Women's Care Center

Patient Name: Reed, Jessica

Approximate Due Date: June 16th

64

Unexpectedly, I do a little skip and hug Nolan. Nolan is grinning down at me.

"Nolan, we're having a summer baby! How exciting!" I squeal.

Ok, so now I feel excited and happy, and I guess my first visit wasn't so bad. So, we go for a quick lunch and have a fabulous time reading over all the pamphlets, and we are particularly giddy about the pamphlet entitled, "Pregnancy Do's and Don'ts".

"I will call the pregnancy police on you if you sleep on your belly!" Nolan is kidding me.

"And I will call the father-to-be-police on you if you don't run out in the middle of the night for pickles and ice cream on demand. It says right here, in the "do" category that the husband should support the mother's cravings."

"Oh yeah, well I better not see you getting Botox!"

"Botox?" I scream, "It doesn't say that!"

"Yes it does, right here. Pause your Botox treatments." Nolan is pointing to the pamphlet.

We are both giggling.

"Actually, tomorrow I have a Botox session scheduled, and we usually have wine and cigarettes right before the treatment." I'm saying gaily, when a women passes by overhearing me and stops dead in her tracks. I'm suddenly embarrassed that she might scold me for such terrible behavior, when she says, "Oh Honey, who do you go to for your Botox? You look fabulous! And cigarettes and cocktails? You have to tell me!"

I stare at Nolan, and Nolan stares back at me.

"Um, it's not my doctor. I just have … a … friend that goes there. I actually don't get Botox done."

She looks at me disappointed and then takes out a business card from her purse. "Get that name and email me ok! I'm serious. I need that name!"

She saunters off. I look at the card.

"Well I guess Polly Huxley of Huxley Publishing and Communications won't call the pregnancy police on me!" I say in disbelief.

We both practically fall off our chairs in hysterics.

We part ways. I head home to enjoy my last "sick day" before heading back to the office tomorrow, and Nolan goes to see about the rings.

As I am heading home I can't stop thinking about what an amazing father Nolan is going to be. He is so attentive to me. If people walked a little too close to me in the restaurant, he would quickly maneuver himself so that he would be between me and them. Kind of how I would imagine a soldier would jump in front of his best friend on the enemy line to take a bullet. He is quite heroic. Come to think of it Nolan would make a very handsome soldier! I imagine him in a soldier uniform marching ahead of me, looking for enemies. He really is being so protective and supportive. I simply am the luckiest girl in the world. And even though this pregnancy thing was completely unplanned, I just feel as if it was meant to be. But there is this tiny little niggle about the pregnancy, which is how do we tell everyone? In the pamphlet it says the highest risk of miscarriage occurs during the first trimester. Apparently it's quite a high risk! I never knew that. I feel like a walking time-bomb. How will you know if you are going to miscarry? The pamphlet recommends waiting until you reach 12 weeks to share your news. Once you have reached that milestone, you are in the second trimester and there is a much lower risk of miscarriage. I am only about 8 weeks, so I don't exactly feel like shouting from the rooftop that we are expecting. At lunch, we decided for now that we will make a special trip to tell our parents, but we will wait to tell everyone else at 12 weeks (except Simmi, of course, because she already knows).

SEVEN

(O)h Shit! Here he comes, suck-up Richard. I've been totally avoiding him. I took a few sick days after the whole pregnancy news and played it off like I had the flu. But I know suck-up Richard saw me throw-up in the trashcan and everything.

"Oh Jess-er, Jess-er?"

I hate when he calls me that!

"Jess-er, there you are. We have all been so worried! What's the haps, girl, on your barf and carry?"

"Oh, hi Richard. I'm feeling much better now. Thanks for asking."

"Jess-er, you know rumor has it you could have a bun in the oven!"

Shit, what's he talking about? How could he possibly know? What if he overheard Simmi and I talking that night in the bathroom? That would be just like him to totally spy on us. He could be bluffing! He has been known to do that sort of thing. Yes, that's it. He is bluffing. Unless, he cornered Simmi, and she broke down and told him the whole story about her Indian voo-doo and everything? No, no way would Simmi crack like that. Ok, he's bluffing.

"Richard, don't be ridiculous. I'm newly married. Now-a-days, we ladies really plan these things out. Plus I hope you are not starting any rumors because I'm sure HR would not look kindly on that!" I say casually.

"Oh Jess-er, I'm just kidding you, girl. Don't get all law-and-order on my ass!" he screeches and giggles.

"One more thing Richard, can you please stop calling me Jess-er?"

"Aww! Why? Jess-er is such a cute nickname. I love it."

Richard is notorious for making up obnoxious nick-names for people. You see, right around the time I was to be married to Nolan another Jessica

67

was hired into the department. It was a big issue in the beginning because other staff would accidently mix us up on emails and correspondence. This, of course, was a huge concern because of the need to keep patient confidentiality. And in staff meetings there was a lot of confusion regarding which Jessica was who. So Richard came up with calling me Jess-er (the "er" is to denote "R" — for Reed — my soon to be new last name). I objected, but it stuck anyway. Well, the other Jessica only worked here for 6 months and then transferred to Johns Hopkins in Maryland, but Richard still insists on calling me Jess-er. And did I mention I HATE it?

"Well, Richard, unless it's ok with you that I start calling you Ricky, please stop calling me Jess-er!"

"Oh, my-my, don't you pull the Ricky card on me! OK, you win, no more Jess-er!"

"I have to run Richard. I have a patient coming in!"

Richard cocks his hand at me and yelps, "Tootles" then saunters off, and for a moment I am transfixed, imagining him walking to Ricky Martins, "Shake your bon-bon!"

I race around and tell Simmi what happened, and she tells me that Richard definitely was asking if I was pregnant. However, Simmi denied any such claims and distracted him by talking about her new manicurist. You see, what you need to know about suck-up Richard is that the instant he knows anything it goes straight to Captain Crunch. He is such a little suck-up to her! We think his lips probably have made a permanent tattoo on her butt. I knew Simmi wouldn't have cracked with him. Just one of these days I would love to get some dirt on Richard that we could use to embarrass him. He could stand for a dose of his own medicine. But the problem is Richard is such an open book that I can't imagine there is any dirt to get on him. He is openly gay, and with me he mainly channels his bitchy-gay attitude, not the he-is-so-fun-be-my-best-friend gay. He tells us all his weekend stories and leaves no details out. I mean no details out. He posts all kinds of outlandish pictures on-line so it is near impossible to catch any dirt on that boy!

"So Simmi do you have time for lunch today? I have to catch you up on the latest." I gesture to my stomach.

"Sure Jess, I have to get through 3 patients, but a late lunch at 1:30 would work!"

Suddenly my phone vibrates. I take it from my pocket and check it.

> Vishal: J- it's me Vishal. THIS IS A SECRET. Don't tell Simmi. Can you meet me next Friday at the Philadelphia Art Museum at the gazebo in the back?

I'm standing in Simmi's office and am frozen with fear. Oh My God, how do I get out of here without her wondering what's going on.

"Who's texting you," she looks at me suspiciously.

"um, oh, nobody."

"Nobody?" she grins

"Oh, it's just Nolan. He is getting our rings from the jeweler. He is so wonderful. He insisted on doing it himself and not worrying me anymore about it!"

"Oh that's nice," Simmi becomes instantly uninterested.

Whew! That was close.

"See you for lunch," I blow a kiss and leave her office. Quickly I jab into the phone.

> Me: WTF, next Friday is Halloween?

> Vishal: Yes I realize that, just can you meet me at 5. I need your help!!

> Me: Tell me why?

> Vishal: No! Meet me or I'll ask someone else.

> Me: OK, OK fine! Can I bring Nolan?

69

Vishal: Yes! BUT DON'T TELL SIMMI

OMG! This is it. It has to be the proposal. Simmi loves Halloween. It is by far her favorite holiday. But it does seem a little soon. He hasn't completed his residency. But he does have that highlighted ring book. And he is a thoughtful guy; he most definitely would plan something thoughtful like a Halloween proposal. OMG! I'm dying. Today is only Tuesday. How am I going to keep this a secret from Simmi? This is going to be torture! But if it really is the proposal I must sacrifice the best friend bond for the more powerful moment of a great proposal experience. It's my absolute duty as maid of honor. I mean, of course, I'll be maid of honor. Oh my God! Maid of honor! I'm smiling ear to ear. But then suddenly I see a flash of myself nine months pregnant. Oh no. What if they get married before my due date? They can't get married until after I have this baby! I can't be a big pregnant looking elephant at my best friend's wedding. I just can't.

Quickly, I jab into my phone again.

> Me: Vishal are you sure it has to be next Friday? I don't know if this is going to be your proposal, but Halloween is kind of cliché' don't you think? Just saying, maybe you should wait until Valentine's Day?

> Vishal: Jessica – I am not discussing when or what my proposal plans might be. Honestly can you just be there and stop all the questions.

> Me: OK, you are right. I'm sorry. No more questions.

> Me: Actually, sorry, one more question. Are you going to tell her you are taking her somewhere nice? She will want to be dressed nice.

> Vishal: I'm sorry I asked you.

> Me: OK, right, sorry. Too many questions. You can count on me. See you then at 5.

OK, OK, I have 15 minutes to focus. I have two patients this morning. The first is Clara Teevan. Clara is a dear old lady. She is retired and has severe anxiety ever since her husband who she married when she was 15 died eight months ago. After I meet with Clara, I have a brand new patient. Looking ahead to tomorrow I feel a tickle of excitement because Mrs. Carter is coming in. I am very excited to see Mrs. Carter again. I hope that my exercise and instruction allowed her to make some progress with her Mother. But I am even more excited to tell Simmi at lunch about all the great summer birthdays we get to plan.

Summer birthdays are just so exciting. I have a winter birthday, and I vividly remember on my 7th birthday my mom had worked all week to get ready for my birthday party at our house. I was so excited. It was a smurf theme party, and we had smurf cupcakes and decorations. It was going to be smurftastic! And then a snowstorm dumped 12 inches of snow, and nobody showed up. I spent the night crying in my room until my Mom brought up about 6 smurf cupcakes, and we ate them until we felt sick to our stomachs! But, a summer birthday, I mean the possibilities are endless! There is no way a snow storm will come ruin my baby's party in June. If it's a girl we can have a tea-party in our backyard. Granted we don't have a backyard yet, but we will one day. If it's a boy we could have a superhero party, and the boys will swing heroically from the play set in our backyard and pretend to blast each other into Asgard or something. Granted we don't have a play set yet either, but we will one day. I'm so excited!

OK, focus, Jess, focus!

Quickly, I review the charts for the day and set-up my new patient file. First time patients are very intriguing to me. It's like unraveling a great mystery, and every single patient is different. On the first visit some want to talk and talk, and others are so nervous that they have trouble finding the words until they get more comfortable. I always start by introducing myself and my methods and then ask a ton of questions to get started. The questions depend on the situation of course. But, I love to try to get to the bottom of the issues so I can move them along their C-B-A spots. I am just printing out the new patient forms when my assistant chimes.

"Dr. Reed, Mrs. Teeven is here."

Clara insists I call her Clara. I never call a patient by their first name until they ask me too. But, Clara hates if I call her Mrs. Teeven.

"Clara, come on in. How have you been?"

"Oh, hello dear. You know ….. Same old stuff for this … same old gal," her soft crackly voice replies.

"Can I get you some tea Clara?"

"Yes, dear, I love my tea!"

I have tea available especially for Clara. It helps her relax. She actually has gotten me back into tea drinking. I used to drink tons of tea when I was a teenager with my Mom, but then in those harried evenings of graduate study I switched to a high octane version of coffee. But since sipping tea with Clara I have slowly started to switch back to tea. I really do love tea. I don't know what it is about tea, but it does have such a comforting effect, like a big hug!

I bring Clara her tea. She picks up a spoon and stirs it slowly, just staring at the spoon.

"So, tell me Clara, have you continued to go to the support group I recommended?"

"Yes, dear I have, but I have to tell you I feel worse sometimes after leaving," She replies.

"Well, that is natural in the beginning. When you are surrounded by people who are experiencing the same emotions as you it can be very emotional. But I promise you if you stick with it eventually you will find great comfort in it. It's definitely part of the healing process."

Clara and Maurice were married 62 years. 62 years! That's amazing. I often wonder what it will be like to grow old with Nolan, but it's hard to imagine what things will be like 10 years from now let alone 62 years from now. Maurice was a pilot in WWII, and after the war he became a commercial pilot for PanAm until he retired. Clara describes him as a wonderful man with a love for the outdoors. He was an avid fisherman and raised their three boys to fish and keep a garden of their own fruits and vegetables. Since he passed she said the garden has become overgrown. It pains her greatly to look out of the window at the garden. But she wishes she could gain enough strength to go out there and take care of it. But every day she tries, and she just can't do it. Of course, now that the weather is changing there is not much point.

You see, Clara is experiencing a typical grief process. The death of a spouse is one of the most traumatic experiences in someone's life. And when a couple has been together as long as Clara and Maurice, the impact can be even more severe. One aspect I focus on routinely with this sort of patient is quickly identifying and strengthening a social support system. Sadly, however, many of those who are up in age don't have a strong social group. And in Clara's case she has no daughters. You see, daughters are more likely to support the mother who has become a widow. For a moment I am side-tracked by the thought that perhaps my first daughter is growing inside of me right now. I touch my stomach briefly. Anyway, when I administered a *Grief Reactions* test with Clara, she performed so badly that I even referred her to a psychiatrist for depression treatment. She did allow herself to grieve, and she is improving a great deal but the anxiety is now one of her worst complaints. She can't sleep through the night most nights, and she wakes up alone in the house and is scared. She has what I would assess as a panic attack, feeling shortness of breath and chest pain. So, I am working with her to use some coping strategies and also consider some life changes, such as moving in with one of her sons or considering a retirement community. The focus right now has to be increasing her social support. I've seen this too many times. There are numerous studies of elderly spouses who die within the first twelve months following a spouse's death. It's no coincidence. There are a lot of factors that play into that, and one is lack of a social support system. Or it could just be dying of a broken heart. I really do believe that.

"So, Clara, how has your sleeping been going?"

"Oh, not so good dear. I just wake up nervous and scared, and then I think of Maurice and I miss him so much. I just wish the Lord would take me. You know sometimes when I first wake up I feel like he is there next to me, but then I remember he's gone."

73

"Well, Clara I can understand how upsetting this is for you. But you have so much life to live and so much to give to your family." I say confidently.

"Have you tried the coping strategies with any success?"

"I have dear, but reading is tough on my eyes. I have tried your tea suggestion and I have started to just put on some old movies. The kind Maurice and I would watch together. Our favorite was, *"There's No Business Like Show Business."* Do you know that one, dear?"

I nod. I can remember my grandmother watching that.

Clara begins again, "But then I am still up half the night watching the movie. Then I eventually fall back to sleep but can't get up the next morning. Then I feel exhausted all day and then the same thing will happen the next night."

"Clara, I really think you should reconsider living with one of your sons. Maybe it could just be temporary. You don't have to sell your house. Maybe think of it as a temporary, long-term visit."

"I know dear, but that wife of Scottie's is just too much to bear. You know she had that boob job, and I go over there and those boobs are unbelievable. I thought I raised my son better than the kind of man to marry a big booby dim-wit."

"Yes, well a lot of women today struggle with their appearance."

"Yes, well, she struggled all the way to double D's." Clara is gesturing to her chest with these big outstretched arms.

I can't help but giggle a little.

"Oh, Clara, what if you willed yourself to look past that and focus on the baby?"

Her youngest son and boob-job girl just had a baby.

"Well, you know, dear, I do love that baby."

"I think it would do you a world of good to be surrounded by family. This would certainly help you cope, and I think the most important thing is hopefully it will help your anxiety subside."

We end with Clara agreeing to talk to her son. I am quite pleased with the progress today. It is so refreshing meeting with Clara. We sit and have tea, and I feel like I am talking with my grandmother. I also provide her with my signature relax CD that contains melodies and soothing songs that I put together for my patients who have trouble sleeping. She is excited to use it but said she would have to buy a CD player and asked if I had it in a cassette form. I don't even think you can buy cassettes anymore, can you?

Next is my new patient. I am not sure what to expect. Normally I have some background information, but this patient was scheduled very last minute. It seems this person is a friend of Captain Crunches. So God only knows what this patient could be like. I will soon find out. I start busying myself with finalizing my new patient documents, when a pang of hunger overwhelms me. Suddenly, I find myself leaping up to run towards the kitchen. But I have no food in the kitchen. I am supposed to be going out with Simmi for lunch but that's not for another 2 hours. I make my way to the staff kitchen, and I open the refrigerator. It's filled with all kinds of food containers and trendy lunch bags labeled with names and "DO NOT EAT," messages. I never realized so many people packed their lunches. I have to eat something right this minute. I am contemplating searching through the bags. I start to move things around to see if there is perhaps something nobody would miss. When all of a sudden my peripheral vision catches someone standing directly next to me, and I jump sky high in the air.

"Oh my goodness, Richard, how long have you been standing there?"

"Jumpy are we Jess-er?"

"Uh, I just have a new client and I, uh, skipped breakfast and am famished." Quick think. I need to give a reason why I was snooping in the fridge.

"And, um, I left a lunch in here recently that I didn't use, and now I can't find it," I say feeling quite smug that I came up with a quick explanation.

"Oh, those office thieves! You know at least once a month I am missing something from my bag. It's un-fucking-believable Jess-er," Richard rolls his eyes and places his hand on his hip with a thrust.

I am just about to get snippy with him about calling me Jess-er, when he interrupts me.

"You know I keep an extra stash of granola bars, protein bars and dried fruit and nuts in my office. You can help yourself?"

I can help myself? I stare at him? Is this kiss-ass Richard I'm looking at or am I hallucinating?

"Earth to Jess-er?"

"Oh, um sorry. Yes, Richard I would really appreciate that. That is so nice of you."

"No probs. You know you never know when you are going to get a text from some young honey badger you just met to meet you clubbing right after work, so a granola bar and a protein bar and I'm out shaking my bon-bon in minutes."

Did he just say shaking his bon-bon? Oh God! And what the hell is a honey badger?

"Well, thanks so much, I'll just pop into your office, shall I? I'm expecting my next appointment any minute."

"Yup, just look in the bottom right drawer."

I dash out of the kitchen and rush down the hall. Captain Crunch is coming out of her office.

"Jessica, aren't you supposed to be meeting with Gail right now?"

"Oh, um, yes, Gloria. I don't believe she's arrived yet. Looking forward to meeting her. I just have to pick something up, and I am working my way back to my office."

Geez, you can't do anything around here without everyone questioning you.

"Ok, well, Gloria is a dear friend. Please give her 100%."

"Yes of course," I smile brightly.

100%? The nerve! I give all my patients 100%. I mean I give even more than that … 110%. And even if I didn't why should her friend get any better care than any other person off the street?

Ok, I've reached Richard's office. God this place is a mess. How does he find anything? There are papers strewn everywhere and books flipped open and post-it notes with little reminders stuck everywhere. In the corner there are about 15 different size shipping boxes piled high. It's giving me a headache just standing in here. I am half tempted to tidy it up a bit. But I really have to get back. Quickly, I open the bottom drawer, but there is no food in the drawer, just more papers. Damn, what did he say? Left drawer? Right drawer? I can't find it. I feel like I'm getting dizzy I am so hungry. I can't control it; I have to find this food! Suddenly I glance over at the boxes. Maybe it's in one of those. Without thinking I rip one open. And then immediately I wish I hadn't. I am staring into the box. And staring back at me is a ….no is that what I think it is? Oh My God! It is! It's an enormous pink vibrator in a plastic container and in glittery letters the top reads, PINKY THE PUMPER! I think I'm going to be sick. I quickly close it up and put it back on top of the pile. I stare agog at the pile. There are boxes piled higher than my head. Are they all boxes of PINKY pumpers? Or worse, are there other sex toys that I've never even heard of in those boxes? My head is spinning. What the hell is Richard doing with boxes and boxes of sex toys in his office?

"Did you find it, Jess-er?" Richard unexpectedly appears.

Oh My God it's Richard.

"Um, uh, um, no, no I didn't find it. I didn't touch it."

"Geesh, you're such a neat freak. This place is giving you anxiety, isn't it?"

"Um, yes, neat-freak, yes, anxiety," I repeat like a robot.

Richard looks at me suspiciously. He looks at his boxes and looks back at me again.

"Ok, Jess-er." He opens a drawer and hands me a couple of granola and protein bars.

I take them from him, but I feel sick to my stomach now. I don't think I can eat them. Then suddenly I find myself thinking about where he keeps his food and is it ever comingled with the sex toys?

"Ok, Thanks Richard. I have to run for my appointment." I rush out of the hall and barely make it to the restroom to vomit. I can't be sure if that was from being pregnant or the thought of the granola bars fraternizing with the sex toys.

I need to get myself together. I'm staring at myself in the bathroom mirror. I look pale and my eyes are watery. I have to tell Simmi about those boxes.

"Jess, are you in here?" Comes my assistant's voice.

"Um, yes just a minute," I manage to respond.

"Your next appointment is in your office!"

Just great! How do pregnant women function like this? Thankfully, the restrooms are stocked with various toiletries, and there are individual mouthwashes. I quick splash some water on my face and rinse my mouth with the mouthwash and throw the granola bars in the trashcan. Then I wash my hands 3 times as I think about what I found. And then finally rush out to my office, feeling light-headed.

As I enter my office taking deep breaths and trying to focus, I can see that my new patient is sitting already in my office. I can only see that her legs are crossed, and she is wearing a pair of Manolo Blahnik heels and a deep blue dress with a flowing yellow and blue scarf. She has a curly head of blonde hair that looks like it has been professionally styled. I'm not surprised that she is one of Captain Crunch's friends as she looks like money.

"So sorry to keep you waiting," I begin.

And then as she turns to look at me I gape at her, take a step back and take a surprised breath in. Quickly I realize my reaction and try to pretend I tripped over something. Staring back at me is a face that looks so distorted by plastic surgery that she doesn't look human. She looks more like a star trek character. Her lips are blown up to at least three times that of any normal lips and her cheek bones are jutting so far out with the skin pulled so tightly I wince a little for fear she is in pain. Her eyes look more like an Asian woman's eyes, and her nose is by far the worst of it all. It is so small for her face. It resembles a nose that belongs on an 8 year old, not a full grown woman.

"It's ok if I have startled you. I do tend to surprise people." She says looking away from me.

"Oh, um, not at all, let me introduce myself, my name is Dr. Reed."

"It's so nice to meet you Dr. Reed! My friend Gloria highly recommended you. This is my first trip ever seeing a psychologist, so I asked her for the best."

I smile awkwardly at the thought of C.C. actually recommending me as the "best".

Despite her awkward features, her eyes are kind and warm.

"Well I have some standard questions for all my first time patients, but let's start by discussing why you made the appointment in the first place?" I say in my most professional and accepting tone.

"Well, Dr. Reed, I am a bit obsessed with plastic surgery as you can probably tell by my face. I know I shouldn't get it done but I can't help it. As soon as I finish a procedure, I am back out there setting up another appointment. I have had 32 procedures in all. And it's just controlling my life. I want to stop it." Tears start to flow from her eyes, and I suddenly feel sorry for her.

I walk over to her with a tissue box. I place my hand on her shoulder and kneel down in front of her.

I begin, "Gail, you are a beautiful person. I can see that already. I would be willing to bet that you are seeking the plastic surgery in order to try to repair something that has hurt you early on in your life."

She looks at me. Our eyes lock. She is silent for a long time and then says, "How did you figure that out so quickly?"

"Well, I didn't figure anything out yet. I just have learned over the years about obsessive behavior triggers, and I think I can really help you."

For the next hour I listen intently, as through tear-filled eyes, Gail recounts how constant teasing from schoolmates over her appearance led her to a long-lived obsession and disapproval of her body and face. At the catholic school she went to, her classmates called her *monster face*.

"Gail, I am so sorry! Children can be so cruel without realizing it!"

"That's not the worst of it," she said in a whisper.

"What else happened?" I probed.

"Well, they would chase me." I can see that she is having trouble getting the words out. She is struggling through her tears to explain, but she can only take breaths.

"Ok, they would chase you and then what? Would they catch you?" I inquire.

She looks up at me with her warm eyes, distorted by plastic surgery and filled with tears. And she just nods.

"Gail, tell me what would happen when they caught you."

"They would .... They would ....pretend to ......"

"Pretend to what?" I openly draw myself closer to her as if to will the words out of her mouth.

"They would pretend to crucify me!" She puts her head in her hands and sobs.

I'm silent. I can't even formulate my next question. It takes me a minute to regroup.

Finally, I ask her in utter outrage why other classmates would pretend to do something as horrific as crucify her. She explains that they had just learned about the crucifixion of Jesus Christ. I can't recall if my mouth was wide open in shock at this or if I even cried a little too. She told me how her first procedure was on her nose at 16 after she begged her parents for the procedure. She was so depressed that they would have done anything for her. After that she had one procedure after another. She recounted how she wished she stopped with the nose job as she actually grew into her features in her twenties and was quite attractive. At that time she met a wealthy businessman whom she married. With access to wealth, she just had no limits. Her husband since divorced her, and she continues to go through her alimony money to support her addiction to surgery. At the end of the meeting I told her that I need to evaluate her further, but I believe it's possible that she may have Body Dysmorphic Disorder (BDD). It is becoming more prevalent with our new society obsession with appearance and plastic surgery. You see the classic presentation is an extreme form of body image dissatisfaction driving patients to take bizarre actions or become severely depressed.

As I part ways with Gail, I am so affected by her story. I really feel for her and desperately want to help her, but this is my first case of BDD. I need to do some research. On the positive side, I have forgotten all about Richard and his sex toy boxes. Well, at least I had forgotten about them until just now. Oh, great! Now I can't stop thinking about the sex toys again. Argh! It's time to meet Simmi finally, and I could really use a break from this office. One weird thing after another is happening to me today. I have so much to tell Simmi!

EIGHT

Simmi is staring at me totally gobsmacked. She can't believe what I have just told her about Richard. We are sitting in an outdoor café near our office. It's oddly sunny and warm today, which is totally unseasonal for the Fall in Philadelphia. So we are soaking up the rays. We have our sunglasses on as the waiter approaches us.

"I need a few minutes, please, but I'll take a water," I say.

The waiter nods and takes Simmi's drink order and dutifully disappears back inside the café.

"I thought you were going to get the chicken salad." Simmi curls her nose and stares at me.

"Well, I want to," I say as I get out my phone and start jabbing into it.

"What are you doing, Jess?" Simmi peers over at my phone.

"I have to enter my food into the pregnancy diet app. It's awesome. I put in the food I want to eat and it tells me if it's ok." I turn the phone so she can see.

"Wait a minute. You are telling me that you carry around the equivalent to your mother in your pocket so it can tell you what to eat and what not to eat?" Simmi says skeptically.

"Simmi, you don't understand. There are tons of foods that I shouldn't be eating. I am telling you I could kill my baby if I don't follow these instructions. You don't understand the risks. It's a lot of pressure," I riposte.

"OK, so what do people in third world countries do who don't have the means of your fancy app?" Simmi counters.

"I don't know Simmi. There they probably have great tribal wisdom because they have been living the nomadic life for centuries. They probably eat the healthiest foods every day handpicked from the land. They probably grow organic tomatoes and carrots," I say self-assuredly.

"Besides do you want to talk about my lunch or do you want to get back to Richard?" I leer at her.

"Oh, right, yes, yes more Richard, please." Simmi says with pure enjoyment.

I have filled Simmi in on all the crazy antics from today. She is completely flabbergasted by the sex toys. And she has already begun a plot to nab Richard. She will go in early one day before patients and go to Richard for advice on a new wax esthetician and "accidently" knock over all the boxes. We giggle as we imagine sex toys falling out everywhere.

"I wonder if he has the *missile orgasmer 200?*" Simmi says thoughtfully while looking up towards the ceiling clearly in deep interest.

"WHAT?" I say disbelievingly.

"My cousin from England told me about it. Supposedly it's the best vibrator since the rabbit and all my cousins have them," Simmi retorts so nonchalantly that I laugh out loud. It's as if she is talking about vacuum cleaners she is so matter-a-fact.

"I don't know what to say Simmi; your weird cousins are quite tawdry."

"They are not weird or tawdry, Jess, just because they are up on the latest personal pleasure devices. So do you think Richard uses them for personal use or do you think he is some kind of sex toy distributor on the side?" Simmi curls up her face in curiosity.

"Um, seriously Simmi, both options gross me out," I say indignantly.

"Wait a minute! Oh my God I can't believe it. How did I not know this about you?" Simmi is staring at me smiling.

83

"What?" I say defensively.

"Of course," Simmi looks astonished at me. "You think my cousins are all weird, and you are looking down on Richard because you don't own any sex toys yourself, do you?"

"What do I need sex toys for? I have a human sex toy known to you as my husband, Nolan!" I realize I have said that a little louder then I meant to and two business men in suits walking along the street practically break their necks to look back at me. At which point Simmi is practically doubled over in laughter.

My face feels hot and piercing with embarrassment.

"Oh, Jess we have a lot to explore! Don't worry. I know just where to take you!"

"You are not taking me anywhere. I don't want to get involved in your kinky Kama sutra practices."

Simmi looks offended. For a minute she is silent and then shakes her head and laughs again. Even though Simmi is relishing in this conversation at my expense, I still love her.

"Let me get this straight… you… Princess Samudra, own a sex toy?" I glare in disbelief.

"No, no of course not," she pauses for effect and then blurts out, "I have not one but many sex toys!"

To which I nearly spit my water out, and I even feel some almost shoot out my nose.

"Simmi!" I squeal.

"My favorite is the rabbit!" She gives a look of thankfulness for its existence.

"Oh my God, Simmi!" I lean in close to her and say, "Let me just ask one question." I look around to make sure nobody is too close to hear this. When the coast seems clear I say, "Where exactly do you put it?"

This time Simmi spits out her drink for real. Her eyes are wide with amusement and amazement. "You can't be serious Jess? What do you mean where do you put it? If you don't even know that, you need more help than I thought!"

I look back at her consumed with hysterics and disbelief at her misunderstanding of my question. I laugh so hard I can feel my face getting hot, and I can barely get the words out to even respond to her outlandish accusation.

Finally I manage to say, "You jack-ass, I know where you put it mechanically. I mean where do you hide it in your apartment. What if your parents found it?"

"Oh!" Simmi laughs harder still. "I thought you meant ……… I mean I thought you didn't even know where to … you know, stick it."

We are hysterical with laughter. After a good five minutes or so we finally regain composure and Simmi tells me how she keeps it between the mattress and box spring of her bed. And that she even keeps some items at Vishal's place. Wow, I have known Simmi for years and years, but this is the first time in a long time that I have learned something new about her.

We finally get off the topic of Richard and then the best part of our lunch is when I tell her my due date. She gasps and immediately starts talking about summer parties before I even get a chance. She keeps saying things like ….

"My goddaughter will be so brilliant. She will shun frilly dresses and start reading by the age of two!"

And …

"My godson will be a handsome and charming prince, ready to rescue anyone from a burning building."

We laugh and laugh, and she has completely lifted my spirits. But alas lunch time is up and we have to high-tail it back to the office. And I am so

85

completely proud of myself. I didn't once even come close to leaking Vishal's Halloween plans.

The rest of my day is filled with paper work, eating snacks and peeing every 20 minutes. I am not even exaggerating. When you are pregnant, it is as if there is a 100 pound elephant sitting on your bladder. You feel like you constantly have to go, and the peeing is only perpetuated by the constant need to drink water. I am about to pack up for the day when there is a knock on the door. I don't look up and just say–"Come in!"–as I continue to pack up my gorgeous coach bag that Nolan gave me last Christmas!

"Uh, Jessica?" A meek voice begins.

I look up in total surprise to find Richard standing there, looking as if he has seen a ghost. And did he just call me Jessica? He hasn't called me Jessica for at least a year.

"What's wrong Richard?" I look at him concerned.

"Can I talk to you for a minute?"

Oh no! He must know I opened one of his boxes. What if he is going to confess to me that he is this sex-toy-king-pin, and he's going to involve me in his filthy ring of sex toy underground marketing? Or what if he is a distributor like Simmi said, and he is going to invite me to be in his pyramid scheme. Or worse, what if he tries to sell me something, right here in my pristine office where I see patients. Oh my, I feel myself starting to sweat, and my hands feel all clammy.

Richard is approaching and staring at me, looking like a lost puppy dog. I've never seen him like this before.

"Jessica, I have a huge favor to ask of you." He sits on the chair with his back straight and his legs crossed and both hands folded nicely in his lap.

I hold on to the arms of the chair to brace myself for what he is about to say.

86

"What is it Richard?" I finally peep out almost immediately, dreading that I've opened up the door to discuss anything. Dammit, I should have said I'm in a great rush, and it will have to wait.

He looks down at his hands, and I close my eyes bracing for the worst.

"My mom has the Big C," he begins.

Oh dear lord, what the hell is the Big C? Is that some oversized vibrator that Simmi would salivate over? It probably has some dual action function and a million buttons on it for speed and intensity alteration. It probably has to be charged every night because of the sheer size of the thing requiring some high voltage power that it needs to operate on. I can just see Simmi instructing Vishal to not use the toaster at the same time as she uses her Big C for fear of a power outage. I can't take this. I feel dizzy. I sit back in my chair in a heap and open my mouth, about to tell him I want no parts of his sex toy empire, when I notice he's crying. He's crying?

"Richard, what is it?" I now look at him more concerned.

"It's a rare type. It's called Glioblastoma Multiforme, and it is the highest grade glioma, meaning its grade 4. That's the worst grade tumor, and this kind she has is the most malignant form of something known as an astrocytoma."

My mouth gapes open, and I sit up in attention. Of course, now I realize when he said Big C, he meant cancer. What a moron I am!

"Oh, Richard, I'm so sorry. I had no idea. You never talk about your mom," I say as I bring him the tissues.

"I know," he says taking a tissue from the box. "It's hard, and I like to keep that part of my life separate, you know? If I didn't, well I don't think I could really get through the days."

"So anyway, My Dad died when I was young and so it's just me and Mom. Her sister lives far away and, the brunt of all this is on my shoulders. She doesn't have the best insurance and so I've been even trying to make some money on the side to pay for all the medical bills." He pauses and blows his nose on the tissue. He leans over to pull another one from the box.

"Anyway her doctor squeezed her in for some appointments tomorrow. Some further testing, and I need to take her. I have been able to reschedule all my patients for next week, except one. Can you see her tomorrow for me, please?"

"Oh gosh, Richard, I would love to, but you know I don't have expertise with eating disorders."

Richard is an expert in eating disorders. He used to have one himself, prior to coming out of the closet. He describes it as a self-loathing torture he put himself through, but once he accepted himself for who he was, he was instantly over it. He just came to terms and has been "flaming gay" as he puts it ever since and never looked back. He is quite good at it too. I mean being a psychologist…he's good at it, but he's also good at being gay, I guess. I mean how would I know what being good at gay means? Anyway, you get the idea, everyone sends their eating disorder patients to Richard.

"It's a cinch, her name is Ambi, and she is doing extremely well. The reason I thought of you is she just broke up with a boyfriend and her mother is concerned about a relapse, so I think you would be perfect to see her for a consult. Not to mention I trust you. I know you'll be discreet."

He trusts me? This is a new development.

"Ok, sure, that I can do. Don't worry about a thing. I'll take great notes and leave them on your desk after I meet with her."

"Thank you, Jess!"

"Don't mention it Richard. I really hope things go well with your mom!" I lay a hand on his shoulder.

"Me too!" he stands and gestures to his lips with his index finger. "Can you keep this on the down-low? You are the only person that I've told in the office. I haven't even mentioned it to Gloria yet."

"Yes, of course!" I nod enthusiastically.

I have never in my life seen Richard like this. And he didn't once call me Jess-er. I feel so horrible for him. It goes to show you that you can think you really know someone. You can be an Ivy League trained psychologist and everything, but some people can still be a huge mystery. Richard probably puts on this super extraverted exterior on each day because truly if he let people in on his sad life he would have to actually deal with all of this on a higher level. God this makes so much sense. And ... the sex toys? Is that what he meant about making money on the side? Oh my God! This is so depressing. I think I judged him all wrong. The entire walk home to the condo I am consumed with thoughts of Richard. What it must be like to see your mom suffering like that? What it must be like to feel helpless? He probably wants to just take it all away but he can't. Then it occurs to me all of a sudden. Is she in pain? What if she is in horrific pain? Poor Richard!! On the way home I vow to never talk meanly about him again. And I will offer to take on more of his patients if he needs me to. And maybe I'll make him a care package. Yes, that's it. I'll make him a care package.

As I enter the condo I can hear the TV on. Nolan must be home early. I walk in, and he turns to me. The site of him conjures up all the feelings from my entire day. It feels so overwhelming, and I feel vulnerable now that I am home with him. I think of the morning sickness, the new patient, the sex toys, and Richard's mother. I hardly can understand what is happening to me, but all of a sudden I'm crying. Nolan rushes to me.

"Dollface, what is it?"

Through tear-filled eyes I try to find the words to begin explaining what happened today, but all I muster out is ....

"Glioblastoma Multiforme. It's horrible! I have to call my mom!"

"The baby? Our blasty? What is it? Is it bad? Will it survive? I don't care what we need to do. We will get the best doctors and the best everything," Nolan is continuing.

"Huh? No, not blasty! Nolan, you are incredible. I love you! The baby is fine! Glioblastoma Multiforme is a brain tumor."

"You have a brain tumor?" he looks limp.

"No, not me!" I respond.

"Your mom has a brain tumor?"

"No, I just want to call my mom. OK, let me start over. First, hug me, and then I'll explain."

We sit. He hugs me for a long time. His strong embrace and the familiar smell of him calm me. I take several deep breaths and then begin telling him about the day.

For the next hour I tell Nolan all about my day and the new revelation of Richard's home-life. And he makes me promise to not enter the door saying medical terms. After he calmed down, Nolan seemed very interested in the sex toys. Am I the only one who doesn't seem to be interested in them? Nolan told me to sneak one home. I mean the nerve of him. Does he expect me to go in all ninja style and sneak in with my black gloves to swipe a Pink Pumper? Never in a million! We do agree that this is the weekend we will visit our parents and tell them about the baby. After hearing Richard's story I really want to see my mom.

NINE

Mmmmm! The freshest smell of strawberries and apples wakes me up. I rub my eyes and look at the clock by the bedside table. It is still early. I am about to get up as Nolan comes into our bedroom. He has a morning glow to him. He is not wearing a shirt just pajama bottoms, and he is carrying a serving tray. On it is the source of the strawberry and apple aroma.

"Good morning, doll," He says as he approaches me.

I smile at him. As much as I appreciate him bringing me a morning smoothie, he looks so good that I wish he was still in bed with me.

"What's all this?" I gesture at the tray.

"Well Mrs. Reed, this morning we have strawberry, mango and banana with some rolled oats, and a hint of mint in your pregnancy smoothie. This is what I like to call the 'Nolan original, super-rockin' smoothie', a pregnant girl's dream source of vitamins, iron, potassium, antioxidants, and some whole grains. This will keep your energy up all morning. Plus, I also made the love of my life this whole grain toast with an apple cinnamon spread I made in the food processor." He is grinning ear to ear.

I am utterly dazed, "You are a complete god! I am the luckiest girl in the world."

"Where do you want it?" he inquires.

I gesture to the desk in the far corner.

"Can I kiss the cook?" I say, knowing my eyes are twinkling with the need for him near me.

"Well, the establishment usually frowns upon it, but if you insist; I have to keep the customers happy!" he replies with a grin.

I chuckle at him as he puts the tray down and hops on top of the bed at the bottom of the covers. And he rips them off me with one swoosh. I gasp at the coldness I feel from the morning brisk air. I am only wearing a tank top with matching boy shorts from Victoria Secrets, and without the blanket, it is freezing. But he quickly starts kissing my legs, then the inside of my thighs, then lifts my tank top and kisses my stomach until he reaches my breasts. He gently sucks on my nipples, and I am no longer cold, but hot all over. I am overcome with the desire of wanting to feel him inside me. The heat from his body is incredible, skin-on-skin. The feeling is dreamlike. I grab his pants and push them down with my hands and then with my feet. All along I'm thinking I don't need a damn pink pumper. Nothing in the world could top this. I wrap my legs completely around him and grab his back feeling his muscles working as he thrusts.

I am so in love!

I dazedly float through the next part of the morning. Drinking my smoothie, eating my toast, showering, and then as I slowly allow my thoughts to drift from my morning with Nolan, I realize it's Friday. It's Halloween! It's Simmi's big night! Oh my Gosh!

"Nolan!"

He appears in his work clothes looking so absolutely sexy and manly.

"Ready for round two?"

I pretty much ignore his advance, "Nolan its Halloween. We have to meet Vishal at the art museum tonight."

"OK, no problem. I'll just meet you there after work. I'll stop at home to change into my coaching gear."

"No, you can't. It's Simmi's big night. We have to be dressed fancy." I say

"Well, if we both come from work, we should be fine. I'll just bring my hockey gear in the truck and can change at the rink," He answers.

"Ok, but don't spill any coffee on your tie!" I point to him. He has completely ruined a few good ties that way.

"Ok, doll. I gotta run." Nolan kisses me on the lips and then turns to leave.

"What ever happened with the rings?" I inquire as he's leaving.

"It's all sorted out, Doll. Don't you worry. I love you!" he calls before he shuts the door.

What does, "all sorted out" mean? Now I'm dying to know what he did. My thoughts are yanked back to that frustrating day. Monkey Dove talk. Ugh! The thought of that blame-shifter guy angers me. Just then my phone beep-beeps alerting me to a text message ......

> Nolan: Stop obsessing about the rings. It's a surprise. You will love them. Trust me!

He knows me so well.

> Me: OK Smoothie King

He is right. I don't have time to obsess over the rings right now. I need to find something to wear for tonight. I search through my closet. I finally settle on my Stella McCartney dress. I found it one day in a consignment shop. It's beautiful. It's a black cotton blended, sleeveless shift dress with an all-over tonal design, bust darts, and a hidden rear zipper. It's so flattering. I swear it makes me look taller. I bought it for one of Captain Crunch's charity events. I shimmy into it. But hang on a minute.

It's not zipping up?

Is the zipper stuck?

Wait a minute. It's not the zipper. It's ME! I feel a jolt of shock zing through me.

My belly is too big! But I'm not supposed to be showing yet. My pregnancy tracker and calendar says I shouldn't even gain more than 5 pounds in the beginning. I rush to the bathroom and jump on the scale.

126 it blinks back at me. Holy Shit! I gained 11 pounds. How is that possible? I take the deepest breath in and stand tall and straight and pull on the zipper as hard as I can. After 3 minutes of tug-a-war I get it up. I look at myself in the mirror. I have a total pouch jutting out. I can't have that. I grab a black blazer from the closet to pair with it. I can wear the blazer at work and it should hide the pouch. Well I don't look as fabulous as I usually do in this, but it will have to do. This night is about Simmi anyway. I am so eager for tonight to arrive for Simmi. She has been waiting for this forever. Not to mention, it's been so hard keeping a secret from her. I am practically jumping out of my skin. I so badly want to call Simmi, but I don't dare for fear she will know something is up by my voice.

Resisting the urge to call Simmi, I try to think of something else to occupy myself. I know…. I will distract myself by calling Mom.

I get out my phone as I am walking to work and dial Mom.

"Good Morning, dear!" She answers.

"Hi, Mom! I miss you!" I bellow. "How are you and Dad?"

"Oh sweetie, we are just fine. Your father has left already for the shop."

My Dad owns a taxidermy shop. It was really gross as a kid because he would bring these dead mounted animals and fish home and set them right on the dining room table and I always thought it was really creepy. It was also embarrassing to have friends over because they would either be totally startled or overly interested, both of which detracted from my personal playtime. But I have to say Dad is quite good at it. And he really loves doing it. It's his expression of art. The name of his shop is actually "Don's Taxidermy Art Studio". He also serves as the Vice President of the Pennsylvania Taxidermy Association so we are all quite proud of him. Nolan calls him "VP" for fun! It is a pretty noble profession when you think about it. So many people consider their pets members of the family and become distraught after the loss of a pet. My dad can be there to aide in their grief. He can preserve their beloved pet for them to have forever! Case in point, my Aunt Laurel had a beloved cat that Dad conserved because she couldn't live with the thought of burying her. Till this day at thanksgiving we see little Casper on the mantle. I've actually had a few

94

bereaved pet owners that I have had to counsel at the office. It's a very interesting area of psychology. There are a few people that even specialize in it now.

"Well, Mom, I was just calling because Nolan and I wanted to visit on Saturday. Is that ok?"

"Honey, you know you never need an invitation. Just come over anytime!" She says.

"OK," I say and then hesitantly I approach another topic, "Mom, how are you feeling?"

"Well just fine, why do you ask, dear?" she says suspiciously.

"No reason. I just want to make sure you and Dad are taking good care of yourselves."

"Oh, don't worry about us dear. We are doing just fine. We take our nightly walks, and we have your father on his low cholesterol diet. And we've even been following Dr. Oz's low carb, high protein, high omega fatty acid diet too."

My mom and dad are sticklers for anything Dr. Oz says. They set their DVR to *Dr. Oz*, and they consider everything he says the gospel truth. She told me recently about the time she went into the pharmacy asking for fennel seeds to help with Dad's gas problem. The pharmacist looked at her like she had 3 heads and told her she should try a health food store. When she finally made her way to the organic food store and asked about it the clerk said, "of course aisle 3." She said he even added, "Did Dr. Oz send you?" Boy does he have a following.

"Ok, mom, well just make sure you pay attention to any unusual pains," I hear myself saying.

"Oh, dear aren't you sweet. You must really miss us. We'll see you on Saturday dear. Drive safe. Love you!"

My phone goes beep-beep in my ear. Another text.

"Love you too mom." I hit end call and look at the text. It's Simmi.

Simmi: Come quick. I've totally nabbed him.

Me: Nabbed who?

Simmi: Richard! Captain Crunch saw the whole thing from the hall. He's in so much trouble.

Me: No, Simmi. OMG!

Simmi: I know. It's so great. We finally got him.

I struggle in a furiously chaotic moment to try to put my phone away and then start running towards work. I have 3 more blocks to go. I finally reach the corner of our building. I stop for a second to catch my breath. I open the door and look up to run again, but it's too late. I see Richard being escorted down stairs by someone from security. He has a box in his hands.

I run up to him.

"Richard, are you ok? What is going on?"

"Why don't you ask your friend Simmi?"

"Oh Richard, I'm so sorry. We didn't think anything would ….."

Quickly his head jerks up to meet my gaze. "You were in on this?"

"Uh… uh… no of course not!"

"I trusted you Jessica! You know what I'm going through!"

The security guard steps between us and says, "We have to move it along here."

Richard stares at me coldly as he exits the building.

I'm left standing there. I feel nauseous and dizzy. I can't move. Then I take a deep breath and look out at Richard on the street exchanging some parting words with the security guard. I run to the door in a final effort.

"Richard," I scream swinging open the door. "I will fix this. I'll do something! I promise!"

He just turns towards me, looks me up and down and shakes his head in disgust. Then he turns and walks away. I'm left there frozen. The guilt is like a dark ominous cloud above my head with the threat of an impending storm to come. This is my entire fault. I have to find a way to fix this. I rush to the elevator and head up to my office. I throw my stuff down on my desk and rush out towards Simmi's office. I can see several groups of colleagues in hushed huddles all for sure talking about Richard. He will be the new office gossip. I reach Simmi's office. She is on the phone but gestures for me to come in.

"I just don't understand why you want to go there tonight. It sounds boring," she is saying. She rolls her eyes at me.

She must be talking to Vishal about tonight. I can't help thinking of the dichotomy of this day … perhaps being the happiest one for Simmi. A day she will remember forever and tell her grandchildren about. While, for different reasons entirely, Richard will remember this day forever too, but with disdain and regret and probably hatred toward me. Ashamed to even mention this day to his loved ones, he probably will come up with an alternate story to make it more comfortable to discuss when asked what happened to his job. And I feel a compulsory need to take a hard look at my place in all of this, how I am entwined in each outcome. If it weren't for me sharing what I found in Richard's office with Simmi and encouraging her to nab him, Richard would still have a job right now. And tonight whatever Vishal's plans are, I have a feeling I will play a big part in one of the happiest days of her life, the proposal that will start her journey as a married woman. In this single day, I will have ruined a life and helped create one.

… Just like that.

"OK, well I've gotta run. Jess is standing here," I can hear Simmi saying.

Simmi practically slams down the phone, "Holy Shit," Simmi begins, "where have you been? You missed the whole thing!"

I collapse devastated into Simmi's chair.

"What's wrong are you feeling sick?"

"You could say that!" I angrily reply.

"Is it the morning sickness?"

"NO SIMMI, it's not the morning sickness. Have you any idea what we've done? Richard was fired!"

"What? No he wasn't. We were just having a little fun."

"He was, Simmi, I saw him. He was escorted out by security. We got him fired!"

"No, that can't be true. For what?"

"I don't know. I wasn't here, remember? What the hell happened?" I look at her accusingly.

"Jesus, Jess. Calm down, nothing happened." Simmi looks affronted.

"Nothing, Simmi? Are you serious? A man was fired! Have some empathy!"

"I did exactly what we talked about. I went in early. He was getting ready for his patients. The boxes were stacked in the corner. I asked him if I could come in for a minute to ask his advice. I told him I was unhappy with my current waxer, and he said he knew a great esthetician that he could recommend that does all his man-scaping. As I was leaving I pulled a fake mishap and fell into the boxes. Oh my God, Jess, it was hysterical. A bunch of boxes fell to the floor. I immediately started apologizing and said I didn't even see them there. He jumped out of his chair when he saw them topple over. Several things exploded onto the floor. That Pink pumper thing you told me about, which by the way I could immediately see why you were so freaked out about it. That thing was huge. And a few other things... stuff I've never even heard of before. Things of all sizes, shapes and colors, and I think I even saw a package of anal beads and something called a banana massager, which now I am dying to know what that is by the way? And the best part was something must have gotten switched on by the impact and started vibrating on the floor making this racket. There were several people gathering outside looking on in total astonishment. You had to have seen it. It was so unbelievable!"

Simmi is laughing.

"Simmi, how can you be laughing? Richard was fired!"

"Well, first of all, I'm sure it's a mix-up, so don't worry and also even if he did get fired it's his own fault for having that stuff in his office. And why are you all of a sudden so pro-Richard. He's been nothing but rude and condescending to you!"

I recall my promise to Richard that I wouldn't share his story about his mother, and I don't want to break my promise to him now.

"Look Simmi, Richard confided in me about something, and I just know he is going through something terrible right now. He needs his job!"

"What did he confide in you about?" Simmi is practically salivating over this news.

"I told you I can't tell you. That's the meaning of confide."

"Come on. You're my best friend. You tell me everything!" Simmi looks irritated.

"Not this Simmi, it's too sensitive, and I gave my word." I abruptly get up and start walking to the door.

"Where are you going, Jess? Are you mad at me now?"

"Look, Simmi, I have to try to fix this. I'm going to see Gloria."

"You can't be serious?" Simmi is following me out of her office.

"As a heart attack!" I say with my head held high, striding down the hall.

"Well then I'm coming too!" Simmi matches my stride.

"Suit yourself!"

This is the closest thing to an argument we have had in years. The last time there was this much tension between us was the time I wore Simmi's Cleopatra looking outfit which I thought was a costume. I wore it to surprise Nolan one night for some role playing. We accidently ripped it, which I didn't think was a big deal because I would just buy her another costume. But then I learned that it wasn't a costume. It was a wedding dress for her cousin's wedding, and it was specially made in India and shipped over to her. It took four months to hand bead. And the wedding was a week away. I am reminded of this because even though Simmi was furious, she quickly forgave me. Even though I am upset with her, I look over at her walking side-by-side with me and feel more confident with her there.

"What is your big plan, Jess?" Simmi probes as we walk towards C.C.'s office.

"I am not really sure yet. I'll wing it!"

We enter C.C.'s office. Her assistant Julie is front and center. She looks up from her computer through her glitzy reading glasses. They are black and pointy at the sides with little red and silver gems bedazzled on the corners. She wears them low on her nose, and when she looks up at you from her reading material, it always seems as though you have greatly disturbed her. Every time she does that I have this overwhelming feeling that she must hate her job. I mean she is an assistant to the department head. Her job is to assist!

"Good Morning, Julie! We are sorry to bother you, but we need to speak to Cap... I mean Gloria. Is she available?" I say completely deadpan.

"I see, well Jessica, she is already behind this morning, so it will have to wait." She looks back down at what she is reading as if to indicate the discussion is over.

"Actually Julie, It can't wait. It's very urgent!" I ignore her remonstrating look and walk straight to the door.

Julie stands from her perched location and throws her arms up. "You can't see her now. What are you doing? STOP!"

I can see Simmi from the corner of my peripheral vision smiling. She is obviously proud of my buoyancy.

I knock on the door with one hand while turning the handle at the same time.

"Gloria, I am sorry to interrupt but I need to urgently speak to you!"

Captain Crunch looks up at me with disdain. There is a short older man opposite her desk, and he slowly turns to me quite shocked that their session has been interrupted.

"Jessica, what on earth? I am in the middle of a session here."

"Yes, but as I've said it is urgent." I muster.

"If you'll excuse me a moment Lester, this will not take more than a few seconds," She smiles at him reassuringly and then walks towards me giving me a horrific look. "This better be important!" she whispers as she passes by me and then closes the door behind us.

We are now standing outside of her office. Julie has her arms crossed and is surveying me with repugnance. Captain Crunch looks even more upset than Julie. Simmi is still smiling.

"Jessica what on earth is this about?"

"Well, Gloria, I think there has been a terrible mistake. It seems Richard was let go this morning."

"That is none of your business Jessica!"

"Well, as it happens, it is. And I feel I need to address it with you. You see, I was in on it!"

She stares at me disbelievingly and opens her mouth. She closes it again, gives me a once over and then begins again, "Nice try Jessica. And very sweet of you, but I know you weren't in on it."

101

"I was so, please, just hear me out."

"Yeah and I was in on it too," I hear Simmi add.

"Now, that I can believe," Captain Crunch acknowledges Simmi with an irreverent look.

Simmi gasps as if she has been slapped across the face.

Before Simmi can get a word out I confess the entire story. Talking quickly and directly I explain how I was hungry and Richard offered me a granola bar and while I was searching for it I knocked over one of his boxes and that Simmi and I were just trying to play a little prank on him to get him back for all the jokes and remarks he dishes out.

Gloria looks totally unaffected.

"Well, Jessica and Simmi, I am glad that you see fit to turn our professional environment into your personal comedy hour; however, we are running a clinical practice here, and as you are well aware, there are patients walking these halls at all moments of the day. And it's quite unfortunate that Richard's first appointment of the day was approaching his office just as the aforementioned items were carelessly strewn throughout his office. This said patient is a long time sufferer of bulimia, a disorder she developed after suffering as a rape victim." She pauses to let this sink in. She begins again, her voice raised, "She was greatly disturbed by this scene. Do you have any idea what this means? She was greatly distressed. She could sue us! She could ruin our reputation. We could be shut down! I liked Richard as much as the next person, but there are repercussions beyond my control here. I am going to have to report this to my department chair later today. Now if you will excuse me, I have another important patient waiting in my office who has been equally disturbed by your antics this morning. And I highly suggest you ladies think long and hard before pulling a prank like this again or you will be following in Richard's footsteps!"

"But…. But …." I manage, but it's too late. Captain Crunch has left and is securely behind her door again. In the meantime Julie walks over to the door and places herself in between me and the door. Her arms are crossed in front of her chest, and then she lifts one arm and points to the opposite door for us to leave.

Simmi and I exit into the hallway. I am not completely sure what just happened. I know I had good intentions. But in the course of about 5 minutes, I was insulted, reprimanded, my career was threatened, and I can't help but feel we were also treated like children. I feel such colossal regret and guilt. There must be a way I can fix this.

TEN

Think, Jess, think! A new plan ... you need a new plan! Ugh! I can't think under this pressure. I have a patient in ten minutes. OK, I am going to have to put the plan off until later.

I need to quickly cheer myself up for the sake of my patients. I know what will cheer me up. Today is Friday, and that means I've made it to my 9th week of pregnancy. I will look up my online pregnancy calendar and read what happens in the 9th week. Within seconds I have it pulled up.

Congratulations on reaching week 9! Your little bun in your oven is about an inch in length – the size of a grape and weighs just shy of an ounce. Your baby is a fetus now. Believe it or not, even though your baby is so small, most of the body parts are in place already. Your precious baby's heart will be completing a miraculous feat by dividing into four chambers. And there is no more embryonic tail.

Hold on! Rewind! My baby had a tail?

Now even though the external sex organs are now in place, you won't be able to detect the sex of the baby for a while longer. Have you thought about if you will want to know the sex of the baby prior to the birth? It is probably a good idea to discuss this with your husband now as you may have differing opinions. The placenta is now beginning to take over most of the work. Although you can't feel it yet, your baby is moving around all the time. Soon rapid weight gain will begin and soon you will feel little kicks and punches.

Oh Lord! This is making me feel worse. Finding out the sex – should we do that? I don't know. Placenta? Weight-gain and heart dividing? Oh My!

Well, the feeling-the-baby-move part is kind of amazing. I imagine what it will be like and place my hands on my belly. I can't wait. OK, this is cheering me up a little. I have a smile beginning on my face. I close my eyes and think of the baby. Ok, this is better. This is what matters most right now. I must stay calm and collected for the health of the baby. It's working. I'm feeling happy and calm thinking about the baby. Let me read a little more....

How has your mood been? Even though you may not yet be in maternity clothes, the symptoms of pregnancy are usually their worst right about now. You may experience severe morning sickness. Beware, your hCG levels are peaking and will range from 255,000– 285,000 mIU/mL this week. That means you could be in for your worst morning sickness yet.

Well, of course. Isn't that just grand! My thoughts are doing gravity-defying acrobats in my head about what I need to accomplish this week, as if I'm trying to schedule in the morning sickness. Let's just see what other joyful symptoms I may need to fit into my schedule....

Mood swings are inevitable. Cut yourself a break. It is normal for the hormones to throw you into fits of anger and then quickly into sobbing sadness. If your family, friends and co-workers are not aware you are pregnant at this stage, they may become worried about you.

Hmm... There's a thought. I could go to Richard and Captain Crunch and explain that I'm pregnant and all this is because I was hormonal, and maybe that will fix everything?

Who am I kidding?

I'm never going to be able to fix this!

I am a loser pregnant lady losing grip on reality. I'm ruining everything. I ... I can't take this ...

I am so angry I could scream! And why doesn't this online pregnancy tracker calendar just speak the truth. It should say, "You are going to be sick as a dog this week, then after that you are going to blow up like a moose and everyone is going to hate you because you are going to be bitchy, crazy, and annoyingly depressed." Then with the thought of that, I let out an ugly grunting noise followed by uncontrollable tears. I am officially a basket case.

There is a knock at my door.

I take a deep breath, but it's no use. I am still sobbing.

"I need 10 minutes, please," I manage to get out in a shaky voice.

"OK, your 9 o'clock is here. I'll tell her you are delayed," My assistant says.

"Thank you!" I grumble.

I really am a hormonal mess. I try frantically to think of what might calm me down before seeing my 9 o'clock, which is Mrs. Carter, so it's important I get it together. I go through the list. Call Nolan? No. Call Simmi? No. Call Mom? No. Call Dad? No! Sit here and cry for 5 more minutes than do some jumping jacks? No. Then it hits me. I frantically go on to our intranet and search for contacts. I type in Richard's name and ... there it is ..... His cell phone pops up. I write the number down and stare at it. Should I call him? Will he even talk to me? Will he hang up on me? Well, I have to try!

I dial the number from my office desk.

It goes right to VM.

Shit! He probably can see it's the University calling.

I think about leaving an apologetic message, but instead I just end the call.

I get out my personal cell phone. He won't recognize it.

I dial. And sure enough he picks up.

"Richard, here!" he sounds upbeat!

At the sound of his voice I realize I am still crying. I can't talk to him like this. I hang up.

Oh my God–I just hung-up on Richard. This is not going well.

Ok, I gather my composure. Then dial again.

"Richard here!"

"Um, uh, hello? Richard?" I say my voice still a little raspy.

He laughs, "Don't be shy, let me guess, you were at the party last night?"

He doesn't know it's me. I contemplate this for a minute. I realize that if I tell him it's me he is likely to hang up on me. I won't have a chance to help. I have to go along with this. Maybe we can agree to meet somewhere.

"Um, yes I was!"

"Perfect. No worries darling. I get about 5 calls a day like this. Ladies like yourself that are interested in purchasing more items or having a party of their own, but once they call they get a little nervous."

"Uh, right that's what happened to me." I say in a huskier voice trying to conceal my own voice for fear he will recognize me.

"So which is it?"

"Which is it? I repeat.

"Yeah, more items or a party?"

I am not sure what we are talking about here. "Um, a party," I say not knowing what that means.

"Perfect. I am booking up fast, but I recently just had a, um, well, a big change to my schedule, so I could fit you in soon. When were you thinking?"

I am halted at his mention of a change of schedule. I immediately can imagine him sitting in my office asking me for help, and then I think of his poor mother. I feel tears stinging at the back of my eyes. I can't believe I've done this to him.

"Um, yes soon would be good."

"OK how many people are we talking?"

"Um, uh, I guess about 5."

"5! Oh honey I don't come out for 5. Can you get closer to 20? That's my minimum."

"Okay, um 20, okay."

I am so confused. What is he talking about? Why do I need 20 people?

"Oh, honey, look–I know if this is your first one it can be a little odd. But trust me there are a lot of freaks out there–if you know what I mean!! Everyone secretly wants to be invited to a sex toy party.

A what? Oh my …? He wants me to have a sex toy party??? I can feel my heart quickening.

He continues, "It can be a lot of fun! You'll want to arrange for drinks and snacks and some fun stuff, like at one of my last parties there was even a penis shaped ice luge to do shots from. The girls went wild for it. What a site, let me tell you I have some great pictures from that little event. Is this your cell number?"

Stunned, I can't quite respond and then squeak out "uh, yeah—"

"Ok, great. I'll shoot you a picture of the penis luge."

There is silence.

"Are you still there?"

"Um, uh, yes. I have to go though. Can I call you back?"

Sure, what's your name?"

"It's Jes,… I mean Joy."

"Ok, Joy. Call me back, and we'll book your "*Joy bringing joy to others*" party. OK?" He cackles into the phone.

"Uh, em-hmm, bye!"

Beep-beep my phone goes. I am still so stunned from that conversation. I look at my phone thinking it could be Nolan, and instead I see a giant picture of an ice sculpture. This is not just any ice sculpture. It is shaped like a giant penis. A giant, frozen penis sculpture designed to deliver shots of alcohol. It's enormous! I practically loose grip of the phone, I am so perturbed. That's it. PAUSE! Can we take a step back? Who on earth comes up with the manufacturing of a giant ice penis luge anyway? Is it just me or does that seem insane? I mean ... wow! Just WOW!

I close my eyes to re-group. I try to put the image out of my mind. But, as I close my eyes I can still see the image. It's getting brighter and brighter. I think I'm going to pass out. I finally open my eyes again. I can't resist, I look down at the image on the phone again. For some reason I can't bring myself to look away. It's just like looking at a car accident. I can't help myself. I clasp my hand over my mouth in shock. With the ice penis staring back at me I feel waves upon waves of revolting sickness. But, I can't help acknowledge some interference between the waves. I think it's a feeling of intrigue. Yes, that's it. I am also quite intrigued. How do you implement the use of this thing? What are the mechanics? After several seconds of staring, I notice there is a text attached to the picture which reads:

> Richard: It's called the "Iceman" ... isn't it gorgeous! You can get one on amazon.com

Utter and complete bewilderment rushes over me!

I am stunned. The strange thing is I no longer feel sad or guilt at this moment. I am in pure shock! I feel as though that image is permanently burned into my mind. When I blink I can still see it.

Mrs. Carter is waiting. And I guess a shocked psychologist is better than a crying one.

I call out to my assistant's desk.

"You can send Mrs. Carter in now," I say with slight apprehension.

In she comes.

"Mrs. Carter, I'm so sorry to keep you waiting. It's been a big ... well just a huge ... I mean it's been one of those days."

I can't get that picture out of my head.

"So, Mrs. Carter, why don't you begin today with where we left off? Tell me how your assignment from last time went, please. The luge .... Ah, I mean the letter to your mother about Frank?"

Mrs. Carter opens her mouth to begin, and I am just relieved to stay quiet for a bit.

"Yes, so Dr. Reed, I've be so excited to meet with you and tell you my progress." She beams with a smile. And, instantly, I feel a little spark inside.

"Every night after work I would come home, go through the mail, have some dinner, get into my pajamas and then get the CD out. I would listen to it near my fireplace. The first time, I just couldn't relax, and it took me about 35 minutes listening to the music to even just close my eyes and feel my shoulders give a bit. In fact, that first night I remember pausing the CD to go make a cup of chamomile tea in hopes that the tea would aide me in my effort. Then the second night I did the same routine, but I made the tea first and that night it only took about 20 minutes for me to feel relaxed, and the music did just kind-of infuse me with relaxation. Then by the third night as soon as I put the music on, I just closed my eyes and could feel the weight of the world roll off my shoulders. It was just pure calm. The music just faded to the background, and there were no rushing thoughts anymore, no images of what I needed to get done. I just sat there alone– sitting silent. And it made me wonder, why I haven't been doing something like this each night for years. No wonder I am so stressed. I never give myself time to relax! But you, you gave me this CD and told me to write the letter, and I just can't say enough about it. You are a genius. You really are!"

I beam at her but don't interrupt her story.

"So," she continues, "I waited until about the fifth night or so when I was totally relaxed and felt a particularly strong blissful moment. I had finished my chamomile tea, feeling a strong sense of tranquility, and it was then–at that moment–that I went and sat at my desk with the music still playing and began to write to my mother. I wasn't sure what I wanted to say in the letter or how long it would be, but I knew I wanted to write it from my heart. I remember this overwhelming, potent instinct deep within

110

compelling me to begin with my childhood. And so I began to write. I didn't have to think about it because it felt so natural. As if these were the words I needed to say to my mother all my life. It poured out of me. Before my Dad had died and before my mother remarried, she was like a different person. And I wrote about how much I missed her – not the 'her now', but the 'her then'! I lamented and told her I knew there was still some shred of that person deep within her. I brought attention to her obsession with wealth and control ever since she re-married and how it's worsened since becoming a widow. I mean, it was such a cathartic process. Towards the end of the letter, I explained my feelings for Frank and requested she accept it, but that if she didn't it would be her mistake. And even if she threatened Frank with blackballing him from her social circle, I didn't care because it would confirm to me, both, her true feelings towards me as her daughter and Frank's true feelings about me as a significant other."

She pauses and looks up at me. There are tears in her eyes. I've never seen Ms. Carter cry before.

She begins again, "I wish I had done something like this years ago. You've changed my life." She stands up, walks over to me and puts her arms out. I meet her by standing and reach out to give her back a hug, saying only, "I am so happy for you! It was there inside you all this time! I just helped you find it."

I am so proud of Ms. Carter. I've forgotten all about Richard and am just beaming back at her. I am quickly reminded of why I love my job. It's truly the best job in the world.

"Ms. Carter, I am so incredibly proud of you. You followed my assignment in the way it was intended, and your outcome was just—"

"Perfect!" she bursts out.

I smile at her, "It really sounds like you have reached a wonderful new level in our sessions." I marvel at her in wonderment.

"So, please tell me, what was the response?"

111

"Oh, well my mother called me, and when I didn't answer she left this message."

Ms. Carter pulls out her phone. She pulls up her voicemail messages and begins to play it on speaker phone for me.

"Eve, I have been in receipt of your whimsical letter! You are quite the drama queen aren't you? You know you were always that way as a child, so I am not surprised. I'm glad you brought your father up because it is clear to me now more than ever that you are a complete replica of that man. When he was alive, he completely squelched all of my potential. I am not obsessed with money and power. I am simply a successful woman. When (or if) you become one, then maybe you will understand. And as far as Frank goes, you do not have my blessing. He is too old for you, and your promenading about will be a complete embarrassment to me. I warn you, don't continue this relationship. Now, I will see you for our normal coffee next week!"

Wow, that Endura is something else. I mean I am completely gobsmacked. Not an ounce of warmth or understanding in that voicemail at all. I mean her only daughter poured her heart out in that letter. Ok, let's think. How can I break this down for Ms. Carter?

I think for a moment and then straighten up in my chair for effect. "Ms. Carter, I am quite surprised by your mother's response. She clearly has some real issues going on. Nonetheless, I think you did a marvelous job," I say.

"Thank you, Dr. Reed. I am very proud of the letter, and as I said I think it really was more for me than for her. I learned so much about my own feelings through the process. And if she does try to step in then it will show me Frank's true feelings too. I think he is a better man than that."

"Have you told him about this?"

"He knows about her threats, but not about the response to the letter."

"OK, here is what I recommend you do. Confide in Frank the situation and your mother's reaction. Explain that it is very possible that she may retaliate on him. Then, I want you to–from this moment– end all contact

112

with your mother. It may seem harsh but that's the next step to convey your seriousness of your relationship with Frank. DO NOT go to your regular coffee. Do not speak to her by phone. If she tries to call you, do not answer it. Instead keep all communication to email to avoid an opportunity for her to berate you. You can simply tell her in the email that you reached out via your letter and felt her response was insulting and underscored that she is not willing to work on improving the relationship between you two. And until she is open to that, you do not want to be a part of her life."

"Wow, ok, are you sure about this?" Ms. Carter looks sheepish.

"Yes, think about it logically. Your mother is in a current ego state. If she only cares about herself then she will not come to your level ever, no matter how hard you try. There is nothing in this scenario for you, except heartache. On the other hand she will hear your message of silence loud and clear. It will make a statement. If she is willing to talk to you on your level than that's the only path forward. You need to wait for her to come to you."

"Thank you, so much, Dr. Reed. Everything you say makes so much sense. Please, can I call you if I run into any problems before our next appointment? This will all be new ground for me."

"Yes, of course," I hand Ms. Reed my card and circle my cell number. "Call this number if you have an emergency." I point to the number and then look at her again and say, "I am so very proud of you Ms. Carter!"

"Please call me Eve," she responds.

"Ok, Eve, I am very proud of you!"

She nods and grins.

As we end the appointment, I remind her to continue to listen to the CD. It should help her in many ways over the next several weeks as she gets through this rough time with her mother. She explains that she has already copied it for her car and now listens to it at least two times a day if not more. I am very pleased.

I finish with Eve and walk her to the door. Feeling accomplished, as I lead her out I see an unfamiliar young woman in the seat outside my door. I don't think anything of it until my assistant says, "Are you ready for Ambrosia?"

I look at her in confusion, "Ambrosia?" I question.

"Yes, Richard's patient you agreed to see yesterday. She had a conflict so we moved her to today."

"Oh yes, of course!" I turn to Ambrosia.

"Pardon my confusion. My schedule has gotten a bit switched around here. But please come into my office."

She is a skinny little thing, but then again I guess that makes sense if she has been suffering with an eating disorder. But she doesn't look sickly. Not at all! She appears quite healthy and has beautiful flowing blonde wavy hair. She is petite, and I can see her nails are perfectly manicured. As we walk in she takes her time over to the chair and then hesitantly sits down on the edge of the chair. Like you do when you are in a dirty subway station and you are afraid of germs.

"Ambrosia, what is your last name?"
"Harrigan," she states in a soft tone.

"OK, Miss Harrigan, I am delighted to meet you. My name is Dr. Reed."

I write down Ambrosia Harrigan on a new file folder, and I print out a new patient form.

"What a beautiful name you have!" I smile at her trying to connect and put her at ease.

"Thank you!" She says just above a whisper.

"Miss Harrigan, I understand you have been seeing Dr. Richard Amado for a long time so it may be a little awkward at first talking with me. But how about just to get started, you tell me what you felt was positive in your interactions with Dr. Amado?"

114

With that she seems to perk up a bit and speaks more comfortably. She begins by saying, "He is the best. When I was going through my hardest time, he still treated me like a person, while everyone else treated me like a china doll. Nobody would be themselves around me. They were afraid to break me. Dr. Amado would still joke with me. He made me find my self-worth again. He is such a wonderful psychologist. I have to admit I am sad he is not here today, but I really look forward to seeing him next time!" She beams at me.

Oh Lord! What is C.C. going to do with all of Richard's patients? He is the only one here with expertise in eating disorders.

"OK, well I am so glad to hear that. Now, Dr. Amado shared with me that you are going through some relationship troubles, which happens to be one area I am expert in. Tell me what's going on and maybe we can make some progress today."

"Well, my boyfriend of a little over a year told me he needed space. But I know it's directly related to me not wanting to go through with having sex with him. I do love him and all, but I am so young still and after everything I've gone through I'm just not ready yet. To tell you the truth the thought of getting undressed in front of him makes me want to ... to just do it again?"

"I'm taking notes …. Do what again?" I say deadpan.

There is silence. I look up at her and she looks completely alarmed.

"You know, purging!" She stares at me.

Holy Shit! I didn't see that coming. "Oh, I'm so sorry. Now I understand. My apologies!" I am not used to this type of patient.

"OK, well I can understand your feelings on this. A first sexual experience can be very scary, and you need to know you are ready. If you feel at all like reverting back to purging then you are not ready."

"Well, duh, but I don't want to break up with him either."

I am a bit taken aback. This is the first time a patient has ever said "well, duh …" to me. Of course, she gets along with Richard! It totally makes sense.

"Yes, I can see that," I try to recover. "Truly the best thing here is for you to voice your true feelings to your boyfriend. And more importantly you have to evaluate what you find most important in your life. Your health should rank higher than everything else."

"So, what I would like to see you do is write a list of reasons why you don't want to have sex and why you are not ready. Make it concrete so that you can see it on paper. Then approach him with it and explain that you simply need more time. If he loves you, he will wait."

She looks frustrated.

"Are you ok?"

"Richard doesn't have me go home and write."

"I, uh, I see. Well each of us has a different style. But it might help you. Give it a try."

"Or maybe I can just run it all by Richard the next time I meet with him."

Gosh, this is going horribly. Why did C.C. fire Richard? Clearly, this poor girl needs him.

"Well, that sounds fine but please don't do anything you will regret. Can we talk a little more about what your next steps might be? I have some other ideas for you."

She begins standing. "Actually I think I will just discuss this with Richard. Honestly, I shouldn't have come today. I had a feeling this wouldn't feel right."

"I'm sorry. I know a new psychologist can be difficult. No worries at all, and call me if you run into any emergencies in the meantime." I say as I hand her my business card. I want her to have some connection because as soon as she finds out Richard isn't here anymore she will probably lose it.

As she exits, I think about Richard and realize I have to handle this. I get out his number and dial again from my office phone. It goes to VM again. I hang up. I wait 5 minutes, and then I dial again.

"Richard here," he answers.

"Richard its Jessica Reed from …."

"Seriously, you think I forgot who you are already?"

"Um, no, of course not, I just… I just … anyway I just am calling because I wanted to check on you. How are you doing?"

"How am I doing? Well, let's see I got fired because two catty bitches threw my side business products all over the place. I'm sure it's probably up on YouTube by now. I probably will get my license revoked. So basically my career is screwed and oh yeah, my mom's dying. Yeah, I guess you could say I'm just peachy. I have nothing to say to you Jessica. Don't call me again." And he hangs up.

So it seems he will call me Jessica when he is sad or angry and Jess-er when he's happy. Strange because I like when people call me Jessica and loathe when he calls me Jess-er. Complete opposites! I wonder if I could try some reverse psychology there to counter-act it. Well, anyway, that's not the point here is it?

ELEVEN

I am in desperate need of a break. I head over to Simmi's office. I can see her through her office window working on paperwork so it's a good time.

"Knock-knock," I say through the cracked door.

"Are you still angry with me?" She questions with a frown.

"How can I be mad at you for long? You're my best friend!"

"That's right and don't forget it!" She sneers up from her pile of paper work.

"Ok, but you have to help me fix this thing with Richard," I say sternly.

"Yes, of course. I'll do anything." she states affirmatively.

"OK, well first I have to catch you up. I tried calling him. He won't talk to me."

"Well, that's no good," Simmi surmises.

"Yes, but I have another in," I say raising an eyebrow for intrigue purposes. "But, I need your help!"

"What do you know about Iceman?" I say mockingly expecting her to look perplexed at which point I will show her the Iceman picture Richard texted me.

"Oh, tons," Simmi responds.

I am completely shocked! It was meant as a rhetorical. "Simmi, you never cease to amaze me!"

"Well, you know, I had a little brother. He loved the Iceman."

My eyes practically pop out of their sockets, "Your brother! Simmi that's so bizarre even for your family."

"No, it's not. It's a boy thing!"

"Yes, I know it's a boy thing. I'm not that naive! I've seen one before." I shake my head derisively.

"So what's the big deal?" She snaps.

"Well, we need one. So does your brother have one?" I say a bit disgusted.

"Have one? He has a whole collection and accessories!"

"Yuck! Simmi!"

"What?" she queries in surprise as if it's normal to have accessories to Iceman!!

"It comes with accessories?" I scathe at her, "What kind of accessories?"

"Oh you know the standard stuff, like a ramp for the iceman to slide down."

I feel complete vile. "Why would you want to slide it down a ramp?"

"You know, that's the power of the iceman, shooting out the ice liquid! The iceman shoots out the liquid and then you slide on it."

"Oh My God Simmi, seriously? What is wrong with you and your brother? Your parents let him have that?"

"What is wrong with me?! What is wrong with you?"

"Look, just forget about it! You just get the Iceman, and let's move on to the next topic."

"Fine, weirdo!"

"I'm not the weirdo I assure you!"

"Whatever! Next!"

"OK, so he wants me to have a sex toy party!" I announce.

"You? He wants YOU to have a sex toy party?"

"Well, not technically me. After he wouldn't take my calls, I called him from my cell phone because I knew he wouldn't recognize the number. I was flustered when he answered. I imitate for her his "Richard here" greeting. I couldn't get any words out, and I didn't exactly own up to who I was at first and so he assumed I was some shy lonely woman from a previous party of his, and I just went along with it. So, I figure let's fake a party. Have him show up, and then we can corner him."

"Why fake the sex party? I mean, if we are going to all that trouble, then we should just have it."

"Simmi, I am not having a sex toy party at my house! For Christ sake, I'm pregnant!"

"Well, what does that have to do with anything? Pregnant ladies need lovin' too!" Simmi starts shaking her hips around in her seat.

"Oh, Simmi, I'm not having it. End of story!"

"Fine, I'll do it. I got you into this mess; I'll have the sex toy party. Leave it to me, just tell him my address."

"Really... really? You would do that for me?"

"Of course, what are friends for?" Simmi says smirking. I can't help but feel that she would want to have the party regardless, but I am still very grateful.

"So why did you start this discussion with Iceman?"

120

"Oh, because Richard recommends we have the Iceman at the party. I guess he incorporates it into the demonstration or something."

"Hmmm, that's creepy!"

"Yes, that's exactly what I thought."

"Ok, well, I will have *Joy*, my alias, text him to confirm the party, and he wants at least 20 people there."

Simmi quickly responds, "No Problem! And Joy – couldn't you come up with a cooler name?"

"I like Joy!" I furrow my brows at her.

Simmi gives me an Olympic-gymnast-McKayla-Maroney-styled not impressed face.

"Ok, what day do you want to do it?"

"Let's do three weeks from now on a Friday."

"OK!"

I take out my phone and jab into my phone:

> Me: Hi Richard, I checked my Calendar I can do the Friday 3 weeks from today.

"OK, I'll let you know what he says."

"See you tonight."

"Tonight?"

Shit! I clear my throat stalling for time, "I mean… Later… you know what I mean." Simmi eyes me suspiciously, and I am worried that I may have just tipped her off to Vishal's surprise.

"Hey, I've been meaning to ask you. Why are you wearing your McCartney dress?"

"Oh, um, you know, I have pregnant brain. I thought we had another Captain Crunch gala tonight. I need to get myself to bed!" I hastily make my exit. I hope she bought that!

The rest of the day is filled with paperwork and starting training for the Alzheimer study C.C. wants me to participate in. These poor Alzheimer patients! It's such a horrible disease to begin with, but then these studies, although important to the science, subject these patients to such a lengthy battery of neuropsychological testing. The testing is so rigorous at times that the patients can break down into tears. It's quite depressing because there is yet to be any good treatments for these poor patients. After I finish with the training, I finally leave work tired and exhausted. Ever since I've been pregnant, I am not sure what is worse, the morning sickness or the pure exhaustion. I have to perk up. I only have about 30 minutes to make my way to the art museum. Just as I am leaving, my phone goes beep-beep. I check it.

> Nolan: Running few minutes late. See you in a bit! Love you and HAPPY HALL-o-WEEN!

Another text comes in—

> Richard: Hi Joy! 3 weeks from today – you are on the books. Shoot me your address.

Oh My God! My fake sex-toy party confirmation just came through. I text Simmi to let her know. She simply texts back a smile emoticon. She is enjoying this way too much!

I run over to the juice bar nearby and order a vitamin B rich protein smoothie, hoping it will energize me. I drink it up. And I already feel a little zing. It was good, but I have to say, not as delicious as the ones Nolan makes. God, he is such a wonderful man. I can't wait to see him. I begin to pack up my stuff and try to maneuver between the tight spaces within the juice bar. The tables and chairs are packed in, causing an awkward exiting process as there is a long cue of people waiting to place their orders which semi-blocks the exit. I try to put my coat on, and of course I have to suck in air to maneuver my arms behind me in this McCartney dress that was form fitting 11 pounds ago. I am in a bit of a hurry with the intense urge to be near Nolan after this insane day. As I hurry, I accidently bump into someone.

"Sorry," I smile.

"Watch it lady," this woman grimaces. She looks oddly familiar.

Without even flinching, I just exit. I don't care about the rude lady; I just want to see Nolan and be a part of Simmi's big night.

I start walking to continue making my way to the art museum, when I hear, "Hey, you, wait …wait just a minute!"

I look back, and it's the rude woman who I bumped into. Oh no, she's practically running towards me.

I ignore her and start walking faster. But, I can hear her voice a little louder and what's that? Is she running now? Her foot steps are quickening! I steal another look trying to make it seem like I'm looking at something else. Oh My God! She is running and waving her hands. I start running, but I'm not making much progress. I'm in heels and my too tight McCartney dress and holding my huge purse with all my paperwork in it. Oh My God. What if this is it. This woman is going to catch up to me and start a fight because I bumped into her. We will have a scuffle, and she will knock me unconscious. I'll miss Simmi's night and everything and end up waking up in the hospital next to some starlet suffering from "exhaustion!"

Just then I feel someone grab my arm. It's her. I turn and scream out, "I don't want to fight you. Leave me alone."

She stares at me and then bursts out in laughter. "Fight you? Good Lord, my dear. You don't remember me do you?"

I stare at her. She really does look a little familiar. Oh no, is she some patient from my volunteer clinic days or something? I can't quite place where I know her from. This is definitely pregnancy brain syndrome. I decide the safest thing is to just shake my head no.

"I'm Polly Huxley of Huxley Publishing and Communications. I met you in that coffee shop. You were with that handsome man. You were supposed to email me your friends' Botox doctor? Remember?"

"Oh, yes," It all comes rushing back to me. Nolan and I were joking after our first OBGYN appointment while reading the pamphlets, and I had said I was going for Botox and before my Botox treatment we drink wine and smoke.

"Um, I am terribly sorry Polly. I was only kidding about that. I'm sorry you are in such an apparent desperate need of Botox."

She looks at me totally affronted.

"Um, I don't mean from your looks that is. In fact, you have a very nice forehead. No lines at all. I just mean you chased me all the way down the street for a Botox doctor, which seems a little outlandish!"

"No sweetie, you have it all wrong. The communications side of my business is supporting a large business for a client of ours, a Botox franchise. It's a huge area of growth, but it's also very competitive. Women now-a-days are so overburdened by their lives, between professional careers, having children, managing their home-lives, relationships, not to mention trying to look younger and younger, that the Botox market has to be fresh and think out-of-the-box. The women of today want to pair primping with relaxation and socialization all wrapped up in a neat little afternoon or lunch break. You get it, don't you? I mean you look like a professional. We need to cram in all their desires and pair it with the Botox treatments. And it doesn't really end there. Fillers and other treatments can be offered too. When you said you had a doctor already making it a social experience, I wanted the name so I could study it. We need to launch something exciting for our client."

"Oh, now I see. I'm so sorry. I didn't mean to insult you. It's just… you see I'm in a terrible hurry. I need to make it to the art museum in … I look at my phone for the time. Oh My Gosh, I only have 15 minutes. I really have to go." I turn and start to walk away.

Polly takes a few steps to the side and waves her hand and then yells out, "Here, let's share a cab. I'll drop you there, and let's chat a bit."

I take her up on it because I don't want to be late. We hop into the cab, and she tells the driver to take us first to the art museum and then make a second stop at Rittenhouse square.

"So, I don't even know your name?"
"It's Jessica," I reply.

"So, Jessica, any other ideas about Botox? I mean you say you were just kidding but you had me intrigued. And I'm not entirely sure yet if you are just holding out on me?"

I laugh. "Seriously, I'm not holding out at all. I don't know anything about Botox."

This conversation is hopeless. I wish I could just get out of this cab. She's droning on about fresh ideas and how I exactly fit their target profile, and I am nodding but really trying to block her out. I can't help her with her Botox empire any more than she can help me with Richard.

I am still nodding at her when I hear "Well then, what is it then, come on let it out," she demands at once, her voice is raised with anticipation.

"Pardon me," I survey her with confusion.

"Tell me your idea!"

"What Idea?"

"Oh you are a tough one aren't you? Look, I've been around the block. If you nod at me when I ask if you have other great out-of-the box ideas and then play dumb that only means one thing." She opens her purse and for a second I lurch back in fear of what she is reaching for.

She garnishes a check-book. "I'll pay you our top consulting fee for one great idea."

We are pulling up to the art museum. I just want to get out of the car. I close my eyes and try to think of anything to say just to shut her up so I can get out of the car. In a last ditch effort I hear myself just blurt out ...

"Pair it with a sex-toy party."

She sits there stunned. Her mouth drops open. That did it. Perfect. I open the door and get out. I shut the door and start walking briskly away. I look around trying to get my bearings. Where did Vishal say to meet again? OK, think! This Polly has me all flustered. I look around ... Oh, that's right, by the gazebo. I believe that's in the back, but the cab dropped me at the front by the Rocky steps. The sight of the steps, ever since I was young, compels me to want to run to the top and jump with my fists held high. But I can't this time. I'm running late. I turn to make my way around to the back of the art museum. My thoughts are consumed with excitement for Simmi. I just can't wait to see how Vishal will propose. Will he get down on one knee? Is there some sacred Indian way of proposing that I don't even know about? I realize capriciously that Simmi and I never covered that topic before: Indian proposals. OK, I have to make a mental note of that.

"Jessica, Jessica?"

I hear my name being hollered but not sure where it's coming from. It's a woman's voice. I'm looking around but don't see anyone I recognize. I keep walking but then the voice gets louder. I turn again and... it's Polly.

"Boy, you walk fast." She says as she catches up to me.

Unbelievable!! This woman won't quit.

"Look Polly, I'm late for something really important. I can't help you anyway."

"Your idea is genius. Sex-toy party! Of course, it's what women of the 21st century need!"

I laugh in disbelief. "You can't be serious."

"Weren't you? Listen don't answer that. Let's just meet in my office next week when you have time."

"I have a busy week, next week," I say dodging her request.

"Ok, week after that?"

126

"Look, Polly, I don't mean to be rude, but I'm a psychologist. I don't see how a psychologist could possibly help you with your communications plan."

"A psychologist... of course, even better!" I have to give her credit. She is persistent. Wait a minute. That's it. I think this Polly has a classic case of overconfidence effect. For some reason, she is over confident that my idea will be a success. It's like when a school superintendent claims that all their students are above the average but testing scores claim otherwise. Or a group of drivers that claim they are above average drivers or even claim to be perfect drivers, but in reality that is impossible. You get the idea.

"I guess to be direct I should just tell you I am not, in any way, interested in discussing this further with you." From my psychology training I know that when you are in a situation with someone like this you need to cut it off quickly.

She looks at me knowingly and simply says, "You are a card, Jessica!"

"If you'll excuse me," I turn on my heel.

"Well don't forget this," she says.

I look down, and she is holding a check. "A deal is a deal."

"If I take this, will you leave me alone?"

"Yes, I will, but I hope if you change your mind you'll call me ok?"

She hands the check to me and then leaves.

I shove the check in my pocket and hastily walk to the back of the art museum. As I approach, I can see that Nolan's truck is already parked in the back. As I make it a little further up the hill, I can see Nolan standing talking to Vishal. Even though Vishal is very tall, Nolan still towers over him. The sight of him makes me smile. I yell, out to them ... "Vishal, Nolan ... I'm here!"

They both turn to survey me. As they do, I can see that Vishal is in his scrubs from the hospital, and Nolan has on one of his hockey jerseys.

127

"Nolan, didn't you remember….. I told you to dress nice?" I glance over at Vishal.

Nolan lifts up his jersey revealing a shirt and tie.

"Ok, well, what's with the jersey?"

He leans in and kisses me. "You are so cute, when you are confused."

"What's going on?" I demand.

Nolan looks at Vishal. "Dude, you break the news to her, I'm not telling her."

I look from Vishal to Nolan and then back to Vishal.

Then I hear myself blurting out, "Vishal, I can't believe you are not proposing. I mean will you just get on with it. Simmi wants to marry you. She found your diamond book with the highlighting and she knows you are thinking about it. I mean stop torturing her and do it already!"

Both men look at me agape.

Nolan leans over and whispers. "He is proposing."

"Oh, um, sorry about that Vishal! And can you please not tell Simmi I told you she found your highlighted diamond book?" I request. "Which was so smart and thoughtful of you to go to such trouble... to research it and all?" I add for good measure.

I can't quite tell if Vishal is annoyed or angry or just nervous.

"So what news did you have to break to me?"

Vishal points to his car.

I stare at it.

"Ok, yes I see you washed your car! That's nice."

"It's not the car. it's what's in the trunk."

128

He walks over to it. Nolan smirks at me and gestures for me to follow. So I do. We make it over to Vishal's beat-up blue Toyota. He opens the trunk, and I look in. The trunk is practically overflowing with pumpkins. I am really confused now. I look at the pumpkins, and then I look at Nolan, and then I look at Vishal. Vishal and Nolan exchange bemused glances, and then Vishal hands me a pumpkin.

"The reason I asked you here is to help me. I needed help with the way I am going to propose."

With that I can barely contain myself. I clasp my hands together and do a little jump in the air and start with fits of giggles.

Nolan grabs my arm and gestures at Vishal. Vishal hunches over waiting for me to calm down.

"Ok, sorry, please continue!"

Vishal begins again, "You see this was the first place I took Simmi out for a date. After we toured the art museum, we came out back here and looked out over boathouse row. It was nighttime with stars twinkling above, and the river was lit up, and Simmi said it was the most romantic setting she had ever seen up close. We sat in the gazebo that night and talked for hours. I knew that night I wanted to marry Simmi. So, I am going to propose tonight here at the gazebo. The same place as our first date, but I want to make it really special for Simmi!"

"Oh, Vishal, it is special. She will love it! You are so thoughtful." I gush!

"Well, where you come in is with the pumpkins."

I look down at the pumpkin still confused.

"I need you to carve the pumpkins. I need each pumpkin to be a letter to spell out "WILL YOU MARRY ME?""

"But, but ...what?"

Nolan interrupts, "Vish-dude, we got this; you get out of here to handle everything else. Just text me, when you're close, dude. Good luck!" Nolan fist pumps Vishal in a manly caveman way, and Vishal leaves.

TWELVE

I'm still standing there with the pumpkin. I take a few staggering

steps. I feel a little numb. I'm all dressed up. I thought we were going to have a glorious night out with champagne and I don't know ... Maybe ... dancing.

"I love you!" Nolan says with amusement.

"I thought we were going to a fancy private soiree in the Philadelphia Museum of Art. I wore my best dress, which by the way I can hardly fit into anymore because of blasty! And, by the way, blasty is now officially a fetus. And I am going to start to realize the full symptoms of my pregnancy this week. My hCG levels are skyrocketing." Nolan looks at me slightly alarmed. "Oh, you don't know the half of it. Let's just say I'm not in the mood to carve pumpkins!" The tears just come as I think about this day and Richard. Frankly, I'm used to the tears now. They are just always nearby, like a bad haircut. There is nothing you can do about it so you might as well embrace it. My mental state is just one small ingredient in the hormonal soup I am swimming in each day now.

"Don't cry doll-face. I'll do all the carving. You just sit there and talk to me!"

"No, I can't do that. Simmi is my best friend. I have to do this."

"OK then, grab a pumpkin and here….." He throws me one of his hockey jerseys. "Now you know why I am wearing my Hextall jersey."

Nolan and I proceed to pull every last pumpkin out. I am now sporting an oversized Rick Tochett hockey jersey that comes down to my knees over top of my beautiful McCartney dress. Nolan fills me in on the rest of Vishal's plan as we begin to carve each letter into the pumpkin. I take *W-I-L-L Y-O-U* and he takes *M-A-R-R-Y M-E-?*

We sit there and by the time we get started it's already dark. There we are in the starry night on a blanket that Nolan had in his trunk, and we carve each letter one by one. After about the second one, I realize I am quite enjoying myself. I am actually very excited because after the proposal Vishal did plan another incredible surprise. So the way it is supposed to go down is Vishal left us to do the hard work ... bastard! Meanwhile, Vishal went to shower and get dressed. He left his car here so that he could pick Simmi up via a cab to the art museum. Tonight the art museum is having a wine and cheese function for members only to highlight the new costume exhibit. And of course Vishal is a member. So that warrants the fancy dress that Vishal demanded Simmi wear tonight. And now I know why Simmi was in her office saying his plans sounded boring for a Halloween night. She thinks all they are doing is a wine and cheese event. Anyway, they will go to the wine and cheese as if it's just a date. Then afterwards he will convince her to go to the back to look out at boathouse row, and while they are exiting the museum he will text Nolan, which will be our cue to light the candles in the pumpkins. Quite romantic, I have to say! Then this is the mind-blowing part. He worked it out with the museum to set up 4 cozy tables for dinner, which he is having catered. He invited his family and her family who are going to all be seated for when they return to the museum. They will actually be there during the wine and cheese bit, but Simmi won't know because they will be wearing face masks. Costumes were encouraged for the event. Anyway, after the proposal Vishal is going to pretend he forgot something, and when they go in, she will see all her loved ones. I just think it is a marvelous expression of love to do this for Simmi. Vishal knows how important her family is to her. She is so going to cry! And Nolan and I are invited too of course. Isn't it amazing? I'm telling you ... that Vishal, I approve of him!

We are almost half way finished with our carving when I begin the story of Richard. I explain every detail of the firing and how he looked at me in disdain and how I tried to call him and how now he thinks I'm some sex-toy seeker named Joy. Nolan is mixed with empathy for how I am feeling and amusement by the story. But I know he knows I am so vulnerable inside because he puts down the carving tools and leans over to me. He gets so close to me that I think he is going to kiss me but instead he lifts his hand to my cheek and says, "Jessica, if Richard knew you, the real you, he would know that you would never hurt anyone intentionally. He would know what I know. That you are one of the most beautiful women in the world inside and out with the most loving, caring and understanding of hearts. I know you will find a way to reach him. And I love you for that.

131

Don't you dare feel guilty anymore about this! He should never have brought that paraphernalia to his work place. He has nobody to blame but himself."

His words are so powerful! I know it comes from a place of true sincerity, and he would never steer me wrong. He is right. I need to let this all go. Whenever I doubt myself, Nolan seems to have this wonderful unwavering faith in me. He always believes in me, and he gives me courage. Just then he kisses me, so passionately and urgently. We fall to the blanket. I am lost in his embrace, and for a moment I forget where we are until something in Nolan's pocket vibrates. Nolan is not fazed in the least. It vibrates again.

"Nolan, your phone!"

"Oh shit!" Nolan checks the phone.

"What does it say?"

Nolan looks at the text speechless for a moment and then blurts out, "10 min warning."

We abruptly jump up. Nolan has some long stringy pumpkin pulp on his cheek with some seeds, and I start laughing.

"Let me get that for you!"

He smiles and in turn picks some off my forehead.

I still have the 'O' and 'U' to do, and Nolan has to finish the '?'.

We immediately start carving again. We are silent and then at times burst out giggling. We are both a complete mess. The 1980's era vintage Philadelphia Flyers hockey jerseys are covered with pumpkin guts, and I can't be sure but I even think I have some in my hair. I picture the future depreciation of these vintage jerseys on EBAY and smirk at the thought that this night just cost us about 5,000 dollars in 2029. I am still on the 'U' and Nolan is only half way done with the question mark when Vishal texts again.

132

Nolan reads the text aloud, "Walking up. I'm shitting myself!"

Nolan and I are cracking up and practically crying at the same time. My heart is thudding, and we are both sweating.

Nolan texts back "STALL - STALL!! WE NEED 5 MORE MINUTES and DON'T SHIT YOUR PANTS, DUDE!"

We finally finish the carving, but we hear footsteps.

"SHIT, SHIT, Nolan hurry!"

We are desperately trying to set them up in the correct order. We put them in position, and I maneuver myself around to the front and can see that it spells, "WILL MARRY YOU ME?"

"Crap, Nolan, it's all mixed up." The footsteps are getting closer. It's dark so we can't see how far away they are.

We fix it again, and I go around to check again and now it says, "WILL YOU MARRY ? ME"

"Oh my God Nolan, we are going to ruin the entire thing. I'll fix the letters, and you get the matches!!"

"Matches?" Nolan looks befuddled.

"You don't have matches?! What the hell? Did you think your shiny white teeth were going to illuminate the pumpkins?" The footsteps sound as if they are right behind us. We stand and turn slowly. I almost want to raise my hands in the air in a *'we-give-up-you-got-us'* sort of way.

"What the fuck is going on back here?" a deep voice says.

"Um, Um, I'm sorry sir ......" Then I stop mid track and realize it's not a man at all. As my eyes adjust in the darkness, I can see it's just Simmi's brother.

"Prad, Oh My God, what are you doing back here? You gave me a near heart attack! You are supposed to be gathering inside. You can't be here!"

Prad and Nolan engage in a man greeting that involves a half hug and a sort of chest bump.

"Chill, Jess! I wanted to see what is going on."

"Did Simmi see you? You could have ruined the entire moment, Pra-douche!"

"Shut-it, Jess. They are at the end of the hill."

Prad is Simmi's baby brother. I've known him forever and sometimes feel like he is my baby brother too. His real name is Pradosh, but Simmi started calling him Pra-douche as punishment for whenever he did something completely stupid. Yes, it's completely un-lady like, but for some reason it doesn't faze me in the least with Prad. I kind of picked it up as well, but we are the only two he lets get away with it. Nolan laughs every time he hears me say it! Prad is 6 years younger than us. He is a total cutie, and he loves his big sister. Always the consummate college guy, he is constantly in search of the next big party. He is in a fraternity and everything. He goes to this private pharmacy school in Philadelphia called the University of the Sciences in Philadelphia. He refers to it as USP for short. USP is a private university and is located in University City, but you would never know it. When a Philadelphian thinks of University City, one conjures thoughts of University of Pennsylvania and Drexel University, the dominant universities in the area. USP is so small that I am quite sure there are high schools bigger than this university. Simmi always teases Prad that she went to an Ivy League school, and he didn't (even though he was accepted to two other Ivy League schools but chose USP instead). Usually this recurrent argument ends in Prad's usual confident counter statement about the average graduate from USP grossing abundantly more money than the average graduate from the University of Penn, which is likely true! Prad wants to be a clinical pharmacist and is in the doctor of pharmacy program, which is pretty cool. And the female to male ratio at that school is way in favor of the guys so he is on the crazy hook-up train week in and week out.

"Let's go Jess. They are coming up." Nolan snaps!
"Oh right!"

"Prad can you fix the letters?"

Prad fixes the letters while Nolan goes to the truck to look for matches. After he dashes to the truck I realize I think we still have a wedding match book in the glove compartment. I'm filled with frustration because I can't just yell out because Simmi could hear me, so I begin to run over behind Nolan when all of a sudden I see Simmi and Vishal in the distance. I am mid-run and need to quickly get out of their sight. I forget I have heels on, and as I heave myself to the side, I completely slip in the pile of pumpkin pulp laying on the trash bag we cut especially to be tidy. I am completely covered in goopy pumpkin guts. Nolan must see them too because he immediately gets down on the ground in a marine-like front crawl. He begins to crawl towards me, arm over arm, low on the ground like he's in combat. I am struck by the site of him. He looks incredibly sexy like that. His perfectly sculpted butt is slightly raised in the air, and I find it quite stimulating! Simmi and Vishal are getting closer, and I realize I can't exactly move or I could ruin everything. Nolan makes it over, and he looks at me.

"What happened to you?" he whispers.

"Don't worry about it, just light the damn pumpkins. And remind me to have you do that front crawl at home," I whisper. He smirks at me.

Vishal must realize we haven't lit them yet because I can make out two slight shadows in the night that look like they are moving more to the right, and I can't quite hear their voices as much. Nolan starts lighting the pumpkins and then both Prad and I help. We finally get the last one lit when I hear the voices again, and I can hear Simmi gasp.

The three of us front crawl out of there behind some bushes. Who knew how hard it was to actually do a front crawl. Trust me, front-crawling in heels and a Stella McCartney dress covered in pumpkin pulp should be an Olympic event. I am dripping in pumpkin guts, and some leaves are now stuck on top of the pumpkin pulp. I must be a sight. Nolan looks pretty much the same just less severe. And Prad still looks like, well, he looks like a cool frat boy. Figures!

We hear vague words here and there... "Love ... rest of life ... beautiful ... laugh ... forever... Grow old."

I can make out what sounds like sniffs and sighs, and I know immediately that Simmi must be crying. Then I see one shadow get smaller, and I realize that must be Vishal kneeling down on one knee. God, this is exciting! I hear another loud gasp and a booming, "Of course I'll marry you!"

Then the two shadows romantically fuse into one shadow. The three of us in the bushes are completely silent just looking on, watching the moment. I glance over at our pumpkins and from the distance it's one of the most amazing sights. There, under the gazebo, are 15 glorious pumpkins. Each one revealing a letter to spell out the words Simmi has been waiting so long to hear. In the darkness with the bright candles, it is completely mesmerizing … *Will You Marry Me?*" I can feel little tears coming. I sniffle a bit. I wonder if there is a Guinness book world record for the most crying in one day. I could be a serious contender. I'm convinced if something like that exists a pregnant woman must hold the title. I sniffle again, and Nolan puts his arm around me. And I reach out and put my hand on Prad's shoulder.

Prad responds by muttering. "Get your nasty pumpkin hands off me!"

We all start laughing. I guess a little too loud because, I hear Simmi say, "What's that noise in the bushes?" Crap we are caught.

"Prad if she sees you, she will know your family is here. You stay here, OK!" He complies.

Nolan and I emerge from the bushes, so that we can keep the rest of the secret in tack.

Simmi exclaims, "What the …"

As we get closer I can make out that Simmi has her Alice + Olivia Black striped trench coat, which looks quite exquisite on her curvy frame, belted at the waist with her gorgeous purple chiffon dress on and matching Michael Kors purple and yellow pumps, which I am dying to borrow. She looks stunning. I can tell she spent extra time on her hair. She looks absolutely radiant.

"Jess is that you?"

"Yup and Nolan! Congratulations!! I reach out my arms and go to run at her for a big hug when Nolan yells, "NOOOOOOooo, don't do it." His voice is so thunderous! The sound of his howl is reminiscent of all the times I've heard him bellow after 6 year old hockey players. I stop dead in my tracks.

"Jess, don't hug her! You will pumpkin mush her all up."

"Oh right!" I say woefully.

"Jess, look at you, you look like … like a freak forest monster!" There I am standing in a pumpkin covered hockey jersey with leaves glued on by the guts of the pumpkins we carved. Not my best look.

"Thanks, it's all Vishal's fault. He made us do all his dirty work! But I'm so glad he included us in your moment. I am so happy for you both!"

Nolan is shaking Vishal's hand, "It was close there in the end dude! Congrats man. It was awesome!"

"Show me!" I gleam at Simmi. She knows exactly what I am referring to and thrusts her hand to my eye level. And I am completely flabbergasted by the ring. It's one of the most picturesque, ornate rings I think I've ever seen. It has a total vintage look with a center round cut diamond. Around the center diamond are small rose cut diamonds, and then those are surrounded by square cut colored stones.

I can overhear Vishal saying to Nolan, "I hand-picked the center diamond. You know I was a stickler on the four C's: Color, Cut, Clarity and Carat. I went for a 1.5 carat center diamond and I wanted VVS-1 or VVS-2 for Clarity and E or F for Color. The jeweler kept bringing diamond after diamond out for me to look at, and I wouldn't settle until I saw this one. It fit perfectly with my specs." He sounds like he is talking about a car engine. "I just knew man. I knew it was the one and the sapphires …" He continues on.

"Oh sapphires, of course, your birthstone!" I say. "Simmi, it is so you! It is just perfect. I am so happy for you! So, how does it feel to be engaged?" We both squeal!

"Oh Jess, I can't believe it. I was totally shocked. I mean he's not even close to being done with his residency. I am so happy! And on Halloween night, my favorite holiday! And those pumpkins? Look at you! You are a mess." She laughs and smiles.

We both laugh for a longtime, and I can tell she is in a total state of bliss. I remember the same feeling when Nolan proposed to me.

Finally Vishal begins. "You know what Sim, I forgot my museum membership card in on the counter. I just remembered. Let's go in to get it."

"Ok, you go in, and I'll stay here with Jess and Nolan."

Vishal looks totally whitewashed.

"Um actually," I quickly begin. "I would love to go in and use the bathroom. You know, get some of this guck off of me."

Vishal looks at me with relief.

"Ok," Simmi says.

So we all stroll down together to the entrance. As we approach the entrance and walk into the great stair hall of the museum, Nolan and I purposefully recede to the background. Vishal ushers Simmi in and off to the right are the tables and some violinists. Oh my, he even organized violinists. They begin playing Tony Bennett's, "The Way You Look Tonight!" I feel total elation for Simmi. I watch, awe-struck, as she realizes what is happening. I can tell she is utterly flabbergasted. She looks around, and as it becomes more and more clear to her who is in her midst, she places a hand over her mouth and gently shakes her head back and forth in disbelief. One by one a family member approaches to hug her. She keeps blubbering, "Oh my God! Vishal, how did you?" Vishal beams at her, clearly content at her visceral reaction.

There are hugs and kisses, and I can see the female family members lining up to see the ring. The men are high fiving Vishal and shaking his hand. Nolan puts his arm around me and looks at me as if to say, "let's go join in on the moment!" But I am startled by the sight of him under the museum lights. He looks atrocious, which means I must look worse.

"Oh Nolan, you are a mess."

"So what?" he shrugs his shoulders.

"We can't join them. I have to get washed up. Let's just go home. I'm exhausted, and we had our own moment with them. I want her to enjoy her family."

"Are you sure she won't be upset?"

"I'll text her. She will understand."

"OK, well you know I have to get to the rink!"

Nolan has directed his assistant coaches to start the mites practice so he can be a little late tonight.

"Why don't you come over later? I'll make you my famous hot chocolate."

Nolan knows my favorite thing at the rink is the hot chocolate. I am not much of a skater.

"I don't know," I say. "It's been a terrible day. I have to go home and rest and try to figure a way to get this thing with Richard solved." I say resolute.

"Yes, but I know I can make it a better night. No wife of mine is going to bed sad."

I smile at him and agree to meet him after I have showered, enjoyed a cup of tea and have put on the comfiest pair of sweats I can find. He drops me off and goes straight to the rink. He has a pretty cool gig. Even as head coach he can show up in a jersey covered in pumpkin guts, and nobody would think anything of it. In fact, he will probably be showered with praise and attention for it. After I complete my pre-requisite activities— shower, tea and sweats— I make my way over to the rink. I am bundled up in a hat, scarf, gloves and a puffy winter coat. I am not one that relishes in the cold feel of the rink, like hockey players do. I like to be warm (call me crazy)! I surreptitiously sneak in the "hockey player only" entrance and survey Nolan and the kids. They are just wrapping up, and I watch him with admiration as he leads the final huddle of the evening. As the players disperse, I watch them intently. Some go to get a drink of water through their helmets from a parent on the sidelines. Some naughty ones disobey the instructions and try to get a few extra minutes of skate time, but then there are a few that linger around Nolan, looking up at him like he is someone they venerate, a hero almost. I can see him talking with them, joking with them, hooking them and pulling them a bit with his hockey stick. Then one even reaches up to give him a big bear hug. I am struck by his sheer innate ability to inspire these kids. He is going to be a wonderful father. As I look on, I feel a great sense of gratitude for how my life is turning out.

Nolan finally makes it off the ice. He is doing what I refer to as the penguin walk; you know the way hockey players walk with all their gear on. As he passes the parents who are packing up their children's gear, many issue him thanks and praise and then finally he spots me. He gives me a little wave, and I feel a little like the grand princess at the ball. All these people, big and small, are admiring him, but I'm the one he can't wait to see.

"There's my doll-face," he greets me with a kiss. He has to bend over more than usual to reach my lips, as he still has his skates on and is massively taller than me in my Ugg Boots (purple, of course). He pulls me into his office and gestures for me to sit in his chair. He kneels down in front of me, and I'm not sure what to expect next. But then he pulls out the skates he bought me a long time ago. He keeps him at his office, as I don't really use them much!

"Oh no, I'm not putting those on."

He starts to try to slip off one of my Ugg Boots.

"Nolan, I'm pregnant! Are you crazy! I can't go out on the ice."

"Jess, do you think I'm going to let anything happen to you out there. Come on. Do some loops with me, and then I'll get you that hot chocolate."

I can't resist his smile or good looks. I want to please him.

"Baby's first skate?" I say hesitantly.

Nolan smirks at this, obviously pleased with the thought of his girl and his baby on the ice with him. We head out on the ice together. We loop once around, and I start to relax a little. Nolan is holding on to me and talking about his night. It's just us out there on the ice. We are alone because the open skate doesn't start for another hour, and the Zamboni driver is smoking outside. We skate around again, but he has shifted positions. Now he is in front of me. He is skating backwards, which I have always found incredibly sexy. He gently pulls me along like I am a five year old child. He is smiling at me and just looking into my eyes. Finally he stops, abruptly. He kneels down on one knee. I am quite alarmed because I'm not sure what he is doing.

"This is our spot isn't it?" he says.

Immediately I register the spot we are standing on. We have skated to the far side of the rink, where the red goal line meets the boards. (How do I even know this terminology?) It's the spot I fell on and hit my head all those years ago when he came over and took care of me. The night we met — the night that started it all. I smile and nod yes, recalling the night he proposed to me at this spot. He pulls out something from his pocket and begins, "Jess, will you have a baby with me?"

I laugh and say, "well I think we are a little past that." He opens his hands and is holding our rings. OUR RINGS? I had totally forgotten about the rings with all the happenings at work. I quickly grab one out of his hands and look at it. There in clear print it reads, *Monkey Love Talk*. They fixed it and from what I can tell they look as good as new. I don't see an inkling of change in them.

"How did you, what did you….." I stammer.

"I told you I would fix it." He takes it back from me and slides it on my finger. I gasp and get down on my knees and hug him. I tell him how happy I am to finally have our rings back and how wonderful he is that he took care of them for me. At which point he informs me that he has something else for me. He instructs me to close my eyes. I do! Next, I feel the faintest of touch from his hands around my hair. I'm enjoying this moment of anticipation. He gently brushes my hair off my shoulders, and then I can feel his hands again brushing by the sides of my neck and under the nape of my neck. For a moment I think he is trying to seduce me on the ice, but then I notice the feel of a slight heaviness lying over my chest just below my collar bone.

"Open," he says.

I open my eyes and look down and there draping around my neck is the daintiest little ornamental pendant. As I look closer at it, I can make out it is either silver or white gold by it's color. I pick it up and bring it closer to my eye, and that's when I realize what it is! It is an artistically sculpted image of a mother and a child. I stare at it in complete wonderment!

"Nolan, it's ..... I mean it's so ....." I can feel warmth in my chest and a bouncy feeling of delight. It's the most thoughtful thing I think he has ever done for me. Through my tears (of course I cry several times a day now) he explains how the jeweler had to remove the previous etching on our bands. And so Nolan had the idea that instead of wasting what was once part of our rings, could they take the little bit from his ring and the little bit from my ring, fuse it together to make a mother child pendant. I mean who thinks of something like that? How does such an immensely thoughtful idea enter into someone's mind? It has to be the psyche. Yes, that's it! It just goes to show you how the psyche changes when you are looking forward to what by any measure can be described as a miraculous event— creating a child. The psyche, well I guess I should explain, is your total mind, both conscious and unconscious. So in this example, the psyche becomes inspired by love, and the anticipation of a child you've made together can create an unexplainable connection, the truest of loves. And from that an idea like this is born!

That night we share a deliciously warm hot chocolate and then settle in at home. Nolan accomplished an amazing feat; he made me so blissfully happy despite all my worry and concern for Richard.

THIRTEEN

I wake up to the delightful smell of citrus and what I think is an aroma of baking bread. Before I even open my eyes, I reach for my pendant and smile. I have a little internal dialogue with the baby. *Oh baby, your mommy and daddy love you so much already. We can't wait to meet you!* It's Saturday morning, and we have a busy day. We are scheduled to be a part of the BABY, SAFE AND SOUND program I signed us up for at *Little Loretta's Lambs*! And after that we are heading straight to share our exciting news with our parents. I can't wait. I am actually very excited. I thought I would be nervous, but I'm not at all. I pull myself out of bed but immediately sit back down. I feel a little queasy. I take deep breaths and remember what Ms. Loretta told me about eating in the morning. I make my way to the kitchen to eat whatever it is that smells so wonderful.

"Morning, Doll! Sleep well?"

"Nolan, I need food now!" I look at him like a tigress must look at its prey. He knows it is serious because he doesn't even protest my crankiness, and he just silently hands me a fruit smoothie. I gulp it down as he is saying, "It's a mix of pomelo and ugli fruit with a mandarin. Do you like it?"

"mm-hmmm! What about food?"

"Coming up," he replies.

He hands over a plate. On it is a breakfast burrito covered in salsa, and I think I smell jalapeno peppers. The sight and smell of it suddenly makes me feel very, very...

...I'm dashing to the bathroom.

I barely make it. My eyes are watery and my vision slightly blurred, but I can make out that the citrus concoction is half in the toilet and half on the

144

floor with speckled bits of orange on the wall. I attempt to clean it up, but another hurl of vomit comes up.

"Jess, leave it. I'll get it!"

"I'm... I'm sorry honey!"

I literally crawl back to our bedroom. The room is slightly spinning, and I feel very shaky and clammy. I feel like I am on death's door.

A few minutes pass, and Nolan comes into the room. He looks as though he has on a hazmat suit. He is adorning green kitchen gloves, a spatula in one hand and a bucket in the other. He is wearing his fishing waders along with my Christmas apron which has a picture of Mrs. Claus on the front. And well, let's just say it's not quite flattering on his figure.

"Here doll. Here is a bucket if you can't make it up to the bathroom next time. I'll call and cancel our safety class and visit to the parents."

"NO, no we can't!"

"You're sick! We can't go!"

"I'm not sick... remember? This is the 9th week. My hCG levels. I'm bound to have some morning sickness. That's all this is."

"Well, all the same, maybe we should just do all this running around in your 11th or 12th week when the hog levels have receded."

"hCG LEVELS," I say indignantly.

"Sorry, right. hcg. Whatever!! I'm canceling!"

"NO, Nolan, I will be fine. I just need to eat something. But not a god-damn burrito! What the hell were you thinking making that? I bet if I log that in on my pregnancy diet app it would beep like crazy and blink at me: Warning, warning inflicting unnecessary risk on your child!"

He looks uneasy "Ok, then what?" he demands.

"French toast! I want French Toast. The thick kind."

"Um, I don't have that kind of bread in, Jess."

I give him a look as if to say that if the bread is in Uganda then he better charter a plane and boat to get it.

"Right, then, I'll just be a few minutes," He finally replies.

I'm still sweating a little, and my heart is thudding quickly. I still taste the citrus flavor which is making me feel like I could vomit all over again. I'm alone in the room, and I hear the door shut. I close my eyes. I realize that what I really need is what I provide for my patients. I need a music CD. I need a calming soothing pregnancy CD. I contemplate this for a moment. Gosh, that's it! It's brilliant! I lay there and conjure up all the right songs or tunes that should be on the CD. Some shouldn't even be songs, but maybe sounds. Like the sound an ultrasound makes or the sound of a healthy baby's heart palpitating away. Yes, that's it. I am going to make myself a therapy CD. Not that I need therapy. I mean I'm a psychologist for goodness sake. That would be like an accountant going to HR block for tax preparation. I am just going to do this as more of a wellness program for myself.

I get to my feet feeling a little wobbly, and I rinse my mouth out trying to rid the taste from my mouth. I slowly enter the kitchen, making sure to stay very far away from the burrito that is still taunting me from the counter. I get a granola bar and slowly start nibbling on it, then go to my computer. I am fastidiously pulling songs and sounds for my CD and am making great progress. I'm on my second granola bar when Nolan walks in. He is surprised to see me sitting by the computer.

"What are you doing? Why aren't you in bed?"
"I'm not dying of the plague, Nolan. It's just morning sickness! Keep that burrito away from me, and I should be fine."

He looks at me peculiarly, and I wonder what he is thinking. I'm the one that has to be an incubator here. I am the one dealing with raging hormones and morning sickness and exhaustion each day. He's not getting up twice a night to pee. He didn't just puke up citrus and what did he call it ….. ugli fruit. What the fuck is ugli fruit anyway? Is that some kind of underhanded joke now that I have gained weight? And so what if I made

146

him rush out for French toast. I feel like reminding him that I am growing a human being over here! It's his job to provide the supportive encouragement I need. And if that means running out for French toast, then he better just do it! I mean this is NOT the 1950's when the man's job ended after a successful depositing of sperm! And if that's what he thinks, he has another thing coming! I can feel my face crunched up, and the back of my neck and shoulders tighten. I am typing a little harder on the keyboard. My back straightens as if ready for defensive action.

I hear Nolan giggle. And I almost get whiplash turning my head to investigate the source of this laughter. Oh, he better not be laughing at me.

"Geez, honey, calm down. I will have your French toast in just a few." He softens his tone and says, "Doll, how can I make these exactly the way you want them? How about some powdered sugar and strawberries on top?"

"I don't know, hold on a minute." I grab my phone and jab into the pregnancy diet app:

> French toast
>
> Strawberries
>
> Powdered sugar

It bleeps out messages back to me.

"No can do on the powdered sugar – could increase my risk of gestational diabetes." I glance at him thinking he should know this. I mean, when I brought all that nutritional research home, he said he would handle it.

He is smirking at me, "Doll you are not going to get gestational diabetes from a little powdered sugar. You eat a very sugar-free diet. A little bit for balance here and there is fine."

"Nolan, the app says I shouldn't eat it!"

"Ok, well your husband who is somewhat of a nutritional expert is saying it's ok if you want it just this once." He walks over to me, and I am hot with anger. "Are you going to trust me or some unadjusted, one size fits all, app?"

He begins again, "I am your partner in this. I am on your side. Don't take it out on me. I love you!"

His words do soften me a bit, but I can't help this rage inside. As I, Dr. Reed, assess what is going on with me, I realize, it's not directed towards him. I just feel angry. God I need this relaxation CD. I look at him and smile, letting him off the hook … this time!

We finish the French toast sans powdered sugar and head up to *Little Loretta's Lambs*. We are quickly escorted to seats and handed tons of information. What happens over the course of the next 2 hours is pure shock and awe. I mean did you know that the average non-baby-proofed home is an utter death trap for a baby? I mean, after the presentation from today I feel like running home and ditching half of our furniture and then locking up virtually everything we own. Better yet, we should just exist on white padded walls and floors until our baby is at least 6 years old. My nerves are on edge. If I only had completed that CD. I could really use it for a calming effect right about now. I mean did you know all the things that could kill your baby. Take strangulation for instance–any loose wires or electrical cords or cords to the window blinds could cause strangulation for your baby. Not only do they explain this to us, but then they read a real life account of this from a newspaper clipping. They pass it around the room for added effect. It was completely morbid. And if that wasn't enough, let's review the hazards of cleaning supplies. You have to lock all of those up. Each cabinet has to be securely locked with some kind of industrial size lock because apparently babies get into everything. They actually shared an account from the poison control center about a baby drinking bleach resulting in a surgical replacement of her little esophagus. Oh My God! And don't get me started on banisters and railings. Did you know you have to have a gap greater than 25 inches, including the rails of the crib you buy? And the dangers of a simple crib – I had no idea! You know those cutesy little bumpers that go along the bars so that your adorable little baby doesn't bump its head? Well apparently that's not the real danger. Your baby can get pushed up against those bumpers and basically be suffocated or suffer from entrapment or strangulation. Again with the strangulation! And the whole crib sleeping thing is a massive disaster with the risk of SIDS. And did you know you shouldn't use blankets with infants? I mean I didn't know any of this. I am a wreck. How are we going to remember all this?

Then you have the other list of things:

> Turn down the water heater below 120 degrees to avoid severe burns

> Put gates up near every stair set and entrance to a room with dangerous things. And basically from what I have just learned every room in our condo is dangerous.

> Secure all heavy objects on counters so that a baby cannot pull things down on themselves. They passed around another newspaper clipping about a baby that pulled an entire big screen television down on himself and was killed.

> And your toilet's! That's not even safe. The baby can actually drown in there.

By the time we were done both Nolan and I were completely stunned. But the good news is they showed us all the items we needed to buy to protect our baby, and conveniently they supply them to new parents. You can't even purchase these items in the stores so it's a really good thing I found this seminar. And lucky for us they had items we needed left in stock and would deliver them right to us. Sure it was a little more expensive, but what does that matter when you are talking about your baby? By the end of it all I'm unsure of what really happened, but I do know we somehow purchased close to $3,000 worth of certified safe baby equipment! I can't wait to receive the crib with perfect rail settings, which also exhibits a low to the ground design to decrease fall-outs. Or the perfect feeding table with wheels that's impossible to tip over and even car-seats designed specifically for newborns. I'm pretty sure we were suckered into that last one, but I don't care. If they sold a bubble my baby could live in for the first 5 years, you better believe I would have bought it!

As we are leaving I see Ms. Loretta by the register. I run over to say hello.

"Oh Jessica, dear, I was wondering where you have been?" she reaches out for a hug. I introduce Nolan and remind him that this is where I purchased the booties when I revealed that we were pregnant. We have a very nice exchange, but I tell her the safety class was a little overwhelming. She assures me that they do a nice job but notes that she wished she knew I was in the class because she would have warned me to not buy anything as they are out for your money. Too late for that warning!

I feel the urge to go straight home and baby proof, but our parents are expecting us. As we make our way to Nolan's car, I hold his hand and apologize for my antics this morning. I'm not sure what came over me. I can't control my feelings. I've never experienced anything like it. I now have a completely different perspective for hormonal imbalances associated with pregnancy and childbirth. During my graduate work we evaluated patients' suffering from Puerperal Affective Disorder, something I always found hard to wrap my head around. The lay population refers to it as baby blues or postpartum depression, but a subset of these patients actually become delusional and can commit suicide or equally as tragic kill their babies. You've seen it on the news. It's terrible. Suddenly I stop in my tracks. Could I be at risk for this? I mean I am already so hormonal?

"What is it doll, a pain?"

My face must look so affected. "No, I just am getting worried about my mood."

"Oh doll, you are fine. Really, I've seen worse!"

"You have?"

"Yeah, come on ... Rosanne! And she never even had a kid!" We both laugh out loud at this.

150

FOURTEEN

$\mathcal{A}$re you kidding me? I cannot believe Mom still has that ridiculous sign up. The election is over but she refuses to take her Mitt Romney sign off her lawn in defiance! Both she and Dad said they were going to move to Canada if Obama was elected again!

As we pull into the driveway of the house I grew up in, I glance at the red front door. Every few years my dad spends a weekend repainting the door red. If it eventually needs replacing, he just buys the same exact door and continues his painting routine. And to the right are the garage doors that Dad broke three times and the garden that mom painstakingly upkeeps. As I gaze upon the house, I feel excitement and that warm familiar feeling I get being close to home, which is always mixed with some sadness because we don't find the time to travel here very often. Which doesn't seem right, because it's only 35 minutes outside of the city! I look up at my bedroom window, which immediately conjures up memories of sneaking out with my wild and crazy high school friends. None of whom I really keep in touch with anymore, mainly because when you are a full-time working professional, where is the time? This town for the most part is home to people who don't always go to college. They are completely content pursuing an apprenticeship with the steamfitters or carpentry union or being lifelong insurance sales people, realtors or waitresses. They continue in the footsteps of their parents often and also in many cases are content with not wanting anything else in life than the same life they had growing up. Which for the sake of clarifying, I'm not judging. I just always knew I wanted to go to college, but only a handful of my friends went. And of course those who went would usually set their horizons on the state college – Penn State of course. Penn State was the last place on Earth I would have ever wanted to go. I just wasn't after a big party school, and I also knew I wanted to attach myself to something great, something that helped people. I wanted to aim higher, achieve more, and get out of my comfort zone. After much deliberation, I chose the route of psychologist over becoming a psychiatrist, and U of Penn's program was my first choice.

151

As I gaze up at my window, which still has the same purple and white curtains, I can remember Blanche throwing rocks at my window, and we would sneak out and just roam the neighborhood and talk about what boys we liked and play fun games. As we got older though, Blanche's fun and games became, well, a little advanced for me. In 8th grade Blanche stole her dad's scotch, of all things, and proceeded to drink it straight from the bottle. She came to my house and immediately started puking. My mom let her stay at our house overnight and warned her that if she ever saw her like that again she would have to tell her mother. Problem is my mom knew that she wouldn't get anywhere with Blanche's mother. This was a woman who named her child after the sultry character on the Golden Girls, a show that premiered when she was pregnant with Blanche. She was obsessed with this show. She could have chosen Rose or Dorothy or even Sophia, but instead she chose Blanche the promiscuous and morally questionable character played by Rue McClanahan, so I think in a way Blanche's mother chose her daughter's path in life before she could figure it out on her own. Blanche had a younger brother with Down's syndrome whom she took care of a lot, and it took a toll on her as a child. Everyone felt bad for her, and I think she got away with more because it was assumed she was just acting out. When she did get out, Blanche was the life of every party. She had no interest in academics, and her goals in life were to sleep with all the cute guys and drink every weekend. But she was an excellent sister to her brother and loved him dearly. I remained friends with her throughout high school, but I wouldn't try alcohol or drugs, so we started to lose touch over time. In a way I lived vicariously through her. I quite enjoyed her company and zany stories. I would listen intently to her sexual escapades in disbelief as I could simply not understand how she could just sleep with any guy at such a young age. I was so not engrossed in this personally. I wanted to get into a good college and find a man that I wanted to marry before I would sleep with him. I wanted to wait until marriage in fact. I have to say I didn't quite make it to marriage, but I didn't have sex until I was in my twenties, and it was with Nolan. Blanche would always try to encourage me to have random sex with some guy, and I never really understood why.

As I started to learn about psychology, I started to learn more about Blanche. It took me no time at all to realize she was undiagnosed, but clearly a full-fledged sufferer of bipolar mania with a dangerous comorbid substance abuse problem, and in her case the substance abuse was likely a self-inflicted effort to extend the mania episodes. She became so dependent on substances that she eventually could not engage in a social situation unless she had consumed some alcohol or drug first. I often wonder if her mother had named her Rose, would she have turned out any differently. Last I spoke to her she was working as a realtor, taking care of her brother and of course still drinking often. I tried gently to bring up the possibility that she could be drinking due to an underlying imbalance and that she should get evaluated. I even offered to go with her. She always laughed it off and claimed the drinking just took the edge off after a trying day with her brother. I do hope one day my words will penetrate her subconscious, and perhaps she will get help. I care about her and hate the stories I hear. There is the time she threw-up on a police officer's shoes. The time she flashed a bouncer to get into a club without having to stand in line. Then there was the time she peed on a Ferris wheel because she was stuck at the top. She thought she was safe because nobody would see her peeing up in her Ferris wheel cart, but she didn't think about how the pee would trickle out of her cart and land on people below. She pretended it was starting to rain when she got off but was banned for life from coming back to that carnival. Then there was the time she had random sex with a guy in a band and let him tape it, which was circulated to random people. Don't get me wrong they all sound like funny anecdotes that most would enjoy laughing about, but it also becomes very sad too. What I have taken away from Blanche is that as a psychologist, you simply cannot help people, no matter how well you are trained, unless they want to be helped.

I wonder if I'll have time to phone Blanche while I'm here. I'm lost in thought about Blanche when Nolan comes around and opens my door for me. He continues to be completely chivalrous and protective of me and our unborn child. As we approach the house we go over our plan again. We decided that we wouldn't just blurt out that we are pregnant; instead I will just wear my pendant and see if they notice. This should be fun. I ring the doorbell and then open the door.

"Mom, Dad, we are here!"

"Oh honey, your home!" Mom comes running from her kitchen, which is still decorated with the apple wallpaper she picked out when I was in grade school. The house smells of garlic and onions, my Mom's standard base to any meal.

"Your father should be here any minute. He's at the shop still."

We hug, and I am just smiling ear to ear both content to be home with my Mom but also thinking in my head of her possible reaction to becoming a grandmother. She takes our coats and my pendant is on full display, but she doesn't notice it yet.

But then she turns and raises her eyebrows at me, "So my darling, we have a lot to talk about don't we!"

Wow, she is so clever. I can't believe she has figured this out already!

She is grinning and begins again, "You will be so busy won't you? I can't wait! I'm just so excited."

"Oh, mom, us too. It was such a surprise! We wanted to tell you sooner, but we just thought it would be better to tell you in person!"

"Simmi must be over the moon!" Mom goes to the stove and lifts the kettle for water looking at us both. We both nod yes for some tea.

"Oh, yes, well, she is!" I respond.

"It's such a special moment in a young ladies life!" Mom beams.

"Yes it is," I respond.

Mom looks to the ceiling as if remembering back, "The planning, the anxiety, the excitement ..... Oh it's just so fabulous. So how did he do it?"

"Excuse me?" I look at her slightly disturbed by the question. I am new to this pregnant thing, but I do think it's unusual for your mother to ask you how the baby was conceived. That's kind of private!

"You know, how did he do it? Was it traditional or some trendy new-fangled approach? I love to hear those types of details."

I look at Nolan. Nolan looks back at me and shrugs his shoulders. "Um, traditional I guess."

154

"Oh, I love to hear it was traditional. Did you wear something special?"

I scrunch my nose up at her and cock my head to the side. Then, suddenly I realize we might not be talking about the same thing. "Mom what are you talking about?" I question.

"Simmi, of course—the engagement! She called here, by the way, looking for you. Said you haven't been responding to her texts, and she wanted to make sure you weren't dead." My mom looks bemused. "That Simmi, she is a crack-up."

Nolan and I both take a big breath in relief, while simultaneously gazing at each other in amusement. "Oh, I didn't realize she told you."

"Oh yeah, she called and told us the entire story. I put the phone on speaker so your father could hear too and—"

She trails off and then looks confused at both of us.

"Wait a minute!" She approaches us both slowly, taking tiny steps in her orthotically correct loafers. "If you weren't talking about Simmi, then what were you talking about?" She surveys us both suspiciously.

I stand and smile and point to my pendant. Mom stares at it for a minute. She looks a little unstable. Nolan quickly stands and catches her as she almost tips over.

"Mom, are you ok?"

She ignores my question. "Are you saying what I think you are saying?"

Nolan answers first, "Yes, we are going into the jewelry making business." I laugh and slap him on the arm.

"Yes, mom, we are going to have a baby. You are going to be a grandmother!"

She squeals in delight and engulfs me in a hug. Her hug is familiar and warm, and it feels like it lasts forever. Then she backs away and picks up the copy of family circle sitting on the table to fan herself as she slowly sits down.

"Oh darling, what a surprise!" Her eyes are shifting quickly, and she takes a lot of deep breaths.

"I am so happy for you. Oh, what a surprise!" She takes another audible breath in.

"You will make such an amazing mother. Oh, what an amazing surprise." She says for a third time, fanning herself more quickly.

She turns to Nolan and surveys him from head to toe and begins once more, "And Nolan, I know that you will be just a marvelous father. Just don't take any grandchild of mine on that ice with those hockey sticks, ok?"

Nolan laughs and looks alarmed at the same time.

"Well, we gotta tell the VP," He responds tactfully, steering clear of the ice hockey remark.

"Oh, Jessica, your father! He is going to burst into tears. You know your Dad. Just the thought of him being a grandfather... Oh, this is just such a joyous day! Wait until I tell Father DeVane tomorrow at mass." I can tell my mother's thoughts are racing from one category to the next. Father De Vane christened me and also blessed our rings before we went to Nevis. My mother worships him and even encouraged (made) us to have a small church officiating mass too with Fr. De Vane when we returned home.

"Oh honey, what am I thinking? There is so much for you to tell me! Tell me all about everything, leave nothing out! When is your due date? How have you been feeling? How are your feet? My feet blew up like balloons when I was pregnant. And are you resting properly?" she continues, in a machine-gun approach of questioning. We hear the sound of a car door close outside.

"That must be the VP now. I'll go see if he needs help with anything." Nolan always buddies up with my Dad on visits to escape the girlie conversations my mom and I have.

I begin to tell my mom all about how I found out and the morning sickness when she interrupts me. She hunches over the table towards me. Looks out into the hall to confirm the men are still outside and whispers, talking out of the corner of tightly pursed lips, "Pregnancy is a great time to tell your husband you can't have sex. Oh, it worked like a charm with your father!"

"Mom!" I say incredulously.

"It's just some motherly advice, honey. How has your sex drive been?" She deadpans.

"Mom!" I exclaim again. Since when is it appropriate to talk about your daughter's sex life in the kitchen like this? I could see if we were having several martinis at a holiday party, but we are stone cold sober and sitting in the apple decorated kitchen of my youth. I used to bake cupcakes in my easy bake oven right here, for goodness sake!

"Right, of course. I know honey." She is shaking her head back and forth with empathy, clearly identifying with what it must be like. "Men, they want that sex all the time! So how often does Nolan expect it?"

I shudder at this statement from my mother, and my eyes are practically hanging from my eye sockets in absolute shock!

She opens her mouth again. I quickly beat her to the punch, "Mom, if you say one more thing about sex I'm going out with Nolan and Dad."

"Oh boy, ok honey, sorry, sorry, sorry!" she shakes her head as if we should be able to have these kinds of talks. "Well go into the living room will you and grab my pregnancy album. I'll pour our tea!"

"Ok," I say glad to be done with the sex talk.

I enter the living room. As I enter the room, I can see Harold and Burt studying me with watchful eyes. Those are the names I gave the two deer-heads that adorn the wall. They are perched above the fireplace. They have been there for some 25 years. I remember initially being scared of them as a little girl, but eventually I got used to them. They just became a part of the living room, as much as the TV, the couch, my dad's special recliner

157

and the coffee table. The thing is they are oddly very lifelike. And eventually you start to feel like you're not alone in the living room, but it's in a comforting way. I guess they can provide the kind of security that a stuffed animal would to a child. My Dad really believes in all that ... Don't get him started on that topic.

"Hi, Harold and Burt," I warmly acknowledge them.

My dad is very talented, I must say. Their eyes and eyelashes are incredibly restored. I remember one time I had been out with friends, and Blanche wanted to sleep over. Of course, she had a few drinks prior, and she came in and started talking to Harold and Burt. She created this game where we pretended Harold and Burt were our husbands. She would get really into this game and have a 30 minute dialogue with the dead deer. Why I didn't question her sanity back then, I will never know. I find the pregnancy picture album and venture back to the kitchen.

Finally Dad comes in. Mom is giddy with excitement and begins with a completely phony greeting at a volume that is unnecessary as we are all standing within earshot. "Oh honey, doesn't our dear Jessica look so grown-up, so matronly? Oh she is the apple of our eye isn't she, Don?" I feel a surge of laughter that wants to erupt, but I hold it at bay. My mom is no good at surprises. She talked to me this exact way the morning of my wedding shower. I called her in the morning, and I can remember she spoke three decibels higher than she normally does. I later learned it was for the benefit of the other people in the room with her at the time. She said things like "Oh, hi my bride-to-be ...." And, "Oh not doing much of anything today, you know same old same old ...."

It was a huge giveaway because Mom usually provides great detail of her daily schedule whenever I call. Then the end of our conversation culminated in a practical full admission of the shower when she asked about what color manicure I had and quickly noted that I should be sure to wear something nice to the brunch Simmi had planned for me to join with her family who was visiting from India (which I had never told her about).

She so gave it away!!

158

My Dad, before he gets a chance to greet me, says, "OK, Emy, why are you acting like you just spent a fortune on the credit card? What is it? Just come out with it." My dad calls my mom Emy. Her full name is Emilia.

"Hi, Dad," I say smiling and rolling my eyes for his benefit at my mother's poor acting skills.

"Oh Don, don't be silly. I'm not hiding anything from you."

Then a full two minutes tick by, and we are just smiling at each other, waiting for Dad to see the pendant.

Mom looks like she is feeling wobbly yet again. She reaches for the family circle once more and begins to fan herself. I realize I can't let this go on much longer or Mom might pass out.

"Dad," I begin and reach for Nolan's hand. I glance at mom who is now leaning over the counter for support and has wide eyes. "Nolan and I, well, we have some news, we…"

"Oh for Pete's sake, Don, look at her new pendant would you!"

Dad looks at it but then says, "I need my glasses, Love!"

"Oh Jessica just tell him already. My heart can't take it."

"Dad, we are pregnant!" I hear myself blurt out!

Dad's eyes widen and start to glisten. He picks me up and spins me around the kitchen. As he steps away from me, I see the tears. Dad is such a softie. He wears his heart on his sleeve, always has. I remember him crying on my first day of kindergarten! He shakes Nolan's hand vigorously and then grabs him and hugs him too. "Well, this is … This is just … absolutely incredible! Well, this calls for a drink."

I clear my throat a bit.

"Oh right, well a drink for the non-pregnant." He grins at me.

I drink my tea as Mom, Dad and Nolan have some Irish Bailey's on the rocks.

The rest of our visit is filled with funny stories as we flip through Mom's pregnancy photo book which documents her pregnancy and my birth. I realize that I am not doing such a good job at keeping a pregnancy memorabilia book and silently vow to do this as well. We have such a wonderful time. I wish we didn't have to leave, but we still have to tell Nolan's parents.

FIFTEEN

On the way to Nolan's parents' house we talk about how real this is all becoming and what wonderful grandparents our child will have. We are so happy and content. Within about 15 minutes we pull up to Nolan's parents' brownstone. As we get out of the truck, we notice Rosanne's car is parked a few cars up, a red jeep.

"Oh Nolan, you didn't tell me Rosanne was going to be here!"

"I didn't know either. It's OK, at least we will get over telling her too all at once."

"I guess!" I say with dread!

We walk up the steps, and Nolan bursts in.

Nolan's Dad is in his usual spot parked in front of the TV with the football game on. He perks up when he sees us and gets up and shakes Nolan's hand and kisses me on the cheek.

"Barb the kids are here!"

Nolan's Mom comes in from the kitchen. "Oh, there you two are. I thought you were going to be here 30 minutes ago."

"Yeah, we got held up in traffic." Nolan says. He doesn't dare mention that we stayed a little longer at my parent's as this would illicit jealousy from his mom.

"Oh well, If you had called I would have held up dinner, but instead we had to eat. You know how your father gets. I really wished you called. I like to make sure you get a nice hot home cooked meal when you're here!"

That was an obvious knock at me.

"What can I get you to drink?" Barb inquires while taking our coats and hanging them up.

We follow her out to the kitchen and under the bright lights of the kitchen, Nolan's mom screeches at us, "Ah, sweet God above! Barry, get in here right now." She says with alarm. Barry comes running in, and Nolan and I are in a bit of a daze, not quite sure what is happening. At the sound of the commotion, Rosanne pushes past me without acknowledging Nolan or I, and then we are all staring at Barb.

"She's knocked-up!" She laughs with a Cruella de Vil laugh. I am not quite sure how to react. Nolan laughs. And Rosanne cackles. I can't laugh as I am a bit miffed that she referred to my first born child and me as knocked-up. She elbows Nolan and says, "That's my son! Good job!" Again, I feel offended by the crassness of this conversation. Barry congratulates us and is genuinely excited. But quickly he hears a roar from the television and dashes back to the TV. Then Rosanne has a delayed reaction, "Oh this is so great. I'm going to be an aunt!" She pulls her phone from her pocket and dials a number and within seconds she is blabbing into the phone … She leaves the room and I can hear her saying. "Yeah my brother is having a baby. I'm going to be an Aunt. Isn't that so cool?"

I am still speechless.

Finally I muster out the words, "How did you know?"

"Oh, I saw your pendent straight away. I just knew. Of course I've been waiting for this! So I look for signs. You're a little round in the face too! I was hoping this would happen soon!"

OK, did she just say I'm round in the face?

"Mom, Jess has been so amazing. She has been really sick and has been so good about taking great care of herself and reading all about being pregnant. And even though she is sick she makes it into the office every day to take care of her patient's. She is amazing!" Nolan is gleaming and he looks so proud.

162

I smile at him and feel a little more relaxed when I hear, "Oh, well, it's good to get the time in before the baby comes... those last few professional moments!"

Hang on, last few? What does she mean? I look at her inquisitively.

"Well, of course you are going to quit–to raise the children!"

I just stare at her.

Nolan answers for me. "Oh, come on Mom, it's not the 70's! A lot of professional women are able to balance family and career."

"The bad mothers that is." She quips.

If my eyes were daggers!

"Oh Nolan, when you were born, I knew I would never go back to work. They couldn't pay me enough to leave you with some stranger for the day. Miss all your first steps. Your first words! Unbelievable how these women just pass off mothering to some Spanish speaking nanny!"

I am outraged at her judgmental and obviously targeted words.

Finally I can't take it anymore. In the nicest voice possible I say, "You know Barb, I didn't go to school for 8 years to only work for a couple years and—"

She interrupts me, "Of course not dear, but think about the math. You quit for the sake of the children and, so what, you don't work for 18 – 20 years, you still have another 20 good years in you after that to work. And you know there are lots of great things you could do from home, like sell Avon!"

I can't believe this. She thinks I'm going to give up my career, my passion. She wants me to sell fucking Avon? I help people transform from their moments of desperation, and she says give it up and sell Avon!

I straighten my back and say, "As a psychologist and a professional in the world of mental health, I can tell you countless studies have demonstrated that women who are fulfilled in their careers have adult children who

163

benefit greatly from this and recount their childhood as a more positive experience than mother's who were frustrated as parents and did not enjoy the same escape!"

Barb smirks at me and says, "Oh darling, I never wanted to escape my children!"

Oh my gawd! It's pointless. I don't even know why I try?

I begin again. "Trust me, I think staying at home is a noble and extremely satisfying choice for many women. My mom stayed at home too, as you know. I'm just saying that it is equally noble and satisfying to contribute in the professional world. Besides, I have a great career to be a mom. Once I have my own practice I can set my own hours!"

Nolan can tell I'm frustrated, and he chimes in too. "Mom, I didn't marry someone who was going to stay at home. I want her to follow her dreams as much as she wants me to follow mine. And our kids will understand that."

"Of course they will, hon!" She pats him on his back. "They just might end up knowing a lot of Spanish too." She cackles again. I can feel my blood pressure boiling.

Rosanne re-enters the room. "So I just called all my friends. They are so excited for me. They want to take me out to dinner to celebrate."

Somehow Rosanne manages to always make everything about her.

"Oh that's nice!" I manage!

"When's the due date?"

I perk up and tell her it's in June!

"Oh great!" she says sarcastically. "I'm going to the Bahamas in June. You can't have that baby while I'm away. Tell the doctor to sew your legs together if they have to!" Rosanne and Barb laugh, and I feel nauseated.

I stand up.

"You ok, doll?"

"Um, I'm just feeling a little queasy!" I say.

"Oh, let me help you up!" Nolan says, and he immediately is at my side.

"It's Ok. I can make it!"

"I never had morning sickness!" Barb spouts out as if she was a superior pregnant woman.

I provide no response and slowly walk to the steps as I hear Nolan in hushed tones scolding his mother. It's so strange. The Reed family really is a loving family, and they were always so welcoming to me. But at some point his mother became competitive with me. If I had to pick a time point I would say it began as we approached our wedding date. She started to become oddly controlling of our wedding plans and scoffed at the idea of us getting married in Nevis. I think she actually expected us to cancel it on account of her wishes. I make it upstairs into the bathroom and let the water run until it's very cold. I splash water on my face several times. I try to think of the songs I started to gather for my pregnancy relaxation CD to calm myself. OK, it's working a little. I feel myself calming. I am taking deep long yoga like breaths. I look in the mirror, squat down, lift my arms wide to the side and over my head, taking a big breath in. Then I let it out as I bring my arms to my sides again and stand straight. I do this again a few more times. At least until the last time, where I farted accidentally and realized that was enough. OK, let me now look at this from a psychologist point of view. So Barb is definitely in the parent ego state. She is trying to exert herself as the controlling parent in this relationship rather than the more acceptable adult ego state. You see in psychology, the parent ego state is just saying, "Look I'm in charge here you little insignificant daughter-in-law. I raised my son. Now you take care of him the way I would!" There is no point in me reacting to this. I need to patiently wait for the parent ego to regress and for the adult ego to surface. Then we will all be in the same place together, and things should return to how they were pre-marriage. Yes, that's it! I just need to ignore her.

I slowly make my way back down to the kitchen, and I can hear Rosanne droning on about how she will need a greatest aunt shirt and bumper sticker and she has the nerve to tell her mother – *get it for me for Christmas*! It's said in a demand like matter, not a request. Nolan is waiting for me and stands up as I enter.

"Are you ok, doll, did you-"

I interrupt him, "No, just splashed some cold water on my face. I'm feeling better. You know it comes and goes."

Nolan looks at his mom with a probing look. Barb clears her throat. I can see that she looks in a bit of pain as if she has some gastrointestinal distress. "Um, Jessica, dear, I hope I didn't upset you. You know we all love you, and we are very excited about the baby. We just get a little over-zealous sometimes."

I smile at her. Gosh, she so didn't want to say that to me.

"Thanks, Barb! I'm so excited too!"

Nolan smiles at his Mom and at me. "Well, I'll let you girls talk baby stuff. I'm gonna catch up on the game with Pop!"

I feel like screaming, DON'T LEAVE ME IN HERE! Ok, self-talk. Jess, remember Parent ego state. Let it all just wash over you. Do not react.

"So, Jess what do you think, boy or girl?" probes Rosanne.

"I'm not really sure," I say "I just want a healthy baby. I think it would be exciting either way. I really—"

"Oh, it's a boy!" Barb interrupts. "Yup a boy. I know these things."

What does she mean, she knows these things. Who the hell does she think she is—the Dalai Lama? My body is different from hers. If anyone knows these sorts of things it's me!

"Are you going to breastfeed?" Barb continues.

"Um, I hope too!"

"There is no hoping to. You either do it or you don't! You know it hurts at first. You have to be tough. You can't wimp out on the first few tries like some of these tarts these days." I am just staring at her befuddled. "Oh, I overhear them in the shopping malls and in the super market going on and on about how they didn't produce enough milk and oh please! What do they think people did in the 1800's before formula? If you love your baby, you will breastfeed!"

I open my mouth to speak, but the words just don't come out.

"Oh, I am going to breastfeed for sure!" Rosanne says condescendingly.

First of all, who does she think is going to marry her? And if I want to breastfeed, which I do, that's my own prerogative and nobody else's business. And what broom did she fly in on. I know from experience that many of these women who suffer from Puerperal Affective Disorder have such an incredible psychological burden that it is very possible that they can't produce milk. And for her information in the 1800's so many babies died shortly after childbirth, and this could have been due to low milk production. Who does she think she is? I am hardly paying attention when I hear ...

"You have to name the baby Nolan if it's a boy and if it's a girl you should name the baby Noelle. If not the first name, Noelle should be the middle name because that is Nolan's Godmother's name."

Did she just tell me what to name the baby? Oh screw this parent-state-ego-bullshit! This just became a power struggle and she is messing with the wrong person.

"Barb, you know what? I'm not even in my second trimester. I don't really want to discuss names with you. You understand! That's a private discussion between Nolan and me. We might even keep the name a secret until we come home from the hospital."

She looks like she was punched in the stomach. Perfect—that's what I was going for. Of course, Nolan and I have not discussed names or keeping anything a secret, but now I might just have to suggest that.

167

Rosanne gets up and whispers something to her mother while opening the fridge, as if I didn't notice.

"Nolan, honey, remember we have to get going soon for that thing!" I yell out to him.

"Huh, what thing?" Nolan says distractedly.

I notice Barb's suspicious eyes. "Oh you know how men can be. I'm supposed to meet a friend for her birthday. Nolan probably just forgot."

I stand from the kitchen chair and head towards the front door to urge Nolan to leave. But he doesn't react; instead we end up sitting with his Dad for quite some time watching the game. I don't mind because his father is not telling me what to, or what to name my baby. He just sits there merrily and even told me I was glowing! Meanwhile Barb and Rosanne are hunkered down in the kitchen discussing me I'm sure. Finally, we make our exits with hugs and kisses as if nothing was brewing beneath it all. As we drive home in the car, I contemplate what to say to Nolan. I resist the urge to report to him all the comments in the kitchen. I wonder how many daughter-in-laws have these same thoughts at this very moment. I mean the Duchess of Cambridge is pregnant. Does the queen tell her what to name the baby? Does she tell her she better breastfeed? Or Reese Witherspoon, I mean did her new husband's mother tell her triumphantly that she never had morning sickness, and does she have a sister-in-law who demands "I'm the best aunt" shirts. I bet not!

"Penny for your thoughts?" Nolan says.

I look over at him. He is cute! I love him so much.

"Just thinking about the baby. Hey do you have any ideas for names?" I ask, hoping he doesn't say Noelle.

"Not really, you?"

"Not yet," I reply. "But I was thinking we should keep it a secret when we decide. You know, reveal the name when we leave the hospital."

"Great idea!" he says. I sigh in relief, he is so easy going.

"I did have one name in mind," Nolan continues with a smirk.

"Oh yeah, what" I question, quite intrigued.

"Apple," he says and waits for my reaction.

"Shut-up!" We laugh and laugh! He knows there is a girl in my department who named her child Apple, and I discussed the psychological ramifications for about a week with him.

We had a joyful return home where we joked about all the names we wouldn't name our child. I threw in Noelle for good measure. And he simple just said, "Yeah, that's my godmother's name. I wouldn't want my daughter to be named after someone. I want her to have a name unique from any family members." Then he hesitates, "Unless of course you had a special family member in mind!"

And it's times like these when I know Nolan is the most perfect match for me!

SIXTEEN

*H*oly Nipples, Batman!

I am staring at a large breasted, dark nippled, woman in front of me, in all of her glory. Her breasts are much bigger than mine and her nipples are at least twice my size! I am startled by the sight, mainly because it's me. There in the mirror looking back at me is a woman's body I don't recognize! I'm at week 11 and definitely have a pouch in my belly and have definitely started to wear my "fat" clothes. You know the ones that usually remain in the back of your closet. You wear them on weekends or around that time of the month when bloating sets in. I am desperate for maternity clothes. I did get up the courage to venture into the local maternity store, and quickly I realized that there must be a conspiracy against pregnant women. Not only are you going to get big and round and ugly, but you have to wear bigger, rounder, and even uglier clothes. As I walked into the store, I looked around and saw shirts with big floral prints emblazed on the front and slacks with no style at all in horrible washed out colors. I don't think I took more than 4 steps before I quickly turned around and ran out in an anxiety stricken fritz! I wish I could ask some friends I know that have been pregnant where to go, but we are waiting until Friday to spill the beans. Friday will be officially twelve weeks and past the danger zone of miscarriage. Even more exciting, we have another prenatal visit this week, and I will get to hear the heartbeat. I am thrilled. In fact, I cleared it with my physician to record the sounds for my CD. In fact I have every song and sound on there. I just need this for the final touch. I've already been listening to what I have so far, and it has been amazing. I just use some fancy apple plug-ins, and it's simple to record any sound.

Anyway back to the nipples. I don't exactly have the biggest boobs in the world. OK, let's be honest I have always been a B cup. But, now, all of a sudden, my boobs are huge and what is more affronting is the way they appear. My nipples seem as though they have spread to the size of a silver dollar. And they are really, really dark all of a sudden. And out of nowhere there is this weird looking freckle that has appeared right next to my nipple.

Worse than that is that I have developed what can only be described as underarm fat. What is that exactly? Is it part of your boob or part of your underarm? And the most disturbing part to me is I can now see the faintest of blue curvy lines jutting out from my nipples. I guess it's my boob veins. I'm so disturbed I rush out of the bathroom and over to the computer to look up this week in my pregnancy calendar, searching for something, anything about blue boob veins.

"Whoa, where are you going?" I hear Nolan call after me.

I'm too rushed to answer. Quickly, I pull it up on the computer.

Week 11

Congratulations! This is your last week in Trimester one. By the end of this week you should be feeling much better, and you should start to have significant relief from morning sickness...Blah... Blah... Blah...Your baby is about the size of a lemon ...Blah ...Blah ...Blah...............

I am interrupted by Nolan who has appeared behind me. I am bending over the chair frantically reading the computer screen, and he is saying something and is trying to hug me or something. At least I can feel his body pressed up against mine.

"Nolan, please!" I say disdainfully.

Baby is growing rapidly now and it is a good time to check out some maternity clothes ...blah...blah

Yeah, tell me something I don't know. I am distracted again by Nolan who is now fondling my breasts. I stand erect and swivel to face him.

"What on earth?" I say.

"What? Oh doll, you can't come running out here with no clothes and expect me to not get excited." He smiles at me while trying his best to rub up against me.

"Nolan, get off!" I push him away. He laughs with a frustrated chuckle.

171

"First of all I am not naked. I just got out of the shower and as you can see I have a towel on. I look down and realize my towel is still loosely around my waist.

He looks at me in disagreement.

"And besides I am looking up why my breasts are freakishly weird today."

"Oh, doll, these are not freakishly weird. They are magnificent." He goes to give them a squeeze, but I slap his hands away.

"They are sore too!" I say. He ignores me and tries again as if he is a 5 year old who decided to not hear what I just said.

"Nolan, can you please stop?" I say noticing his eyes are transfixed on my boobs. I cover myself up. "I'm serious." I say while tightening the towel in the back above my shoulder blades.

"Ok, ok, ok, but you've been warned. Naked hot wife evokes horny husband! I'm going to go take a shower ... a cold shower! Your smoothie is on the counter. It's a Veggie boost!"

I face the computer to finish week 11:

Blah...Blah...Blah ... Changes in hair, toenails and fingernails
....

I can't believe this. I read all the way through and nothing, not one word, about weird blue-veined, silver-dollar-nippled breasts.

I grab my phone and text Simmi.

Me: I have dark, huge nipples.

Simmi: Welcome to the club.

Me: I don't want to be in the club. It's gross!

Simmi: You callin' my tits gross?

Me: No!!!! You—big dark nipples is hot. Me— it's gross.

Simmi: Stop talking about nipples… you're creating a lesbo moment here.

Me: I'm seriously freaked out.

Simmi: Meet me early for coffee so we can talk wedding plans, nipples and sex toy party!

Me: Ugh! Don't remind me!

Simmi has been so incredibly adorable about the wedding. She has made this little website about the wedding, and she keeps updating it every time she plans something new. It's going to be a grand event. Naturally, they will have a traditional Indian wedding, and I am so excited because as her maid of honor I get to rock an authentic Indian wedding dress. Sometimes they have the belly out though, so we will have to really avoid that because contrary to my plan they are having the wedding smack at the end of my 38th week. I've told her she may need to pull me in on a float with a whale harness. I also begged her to change the date because anything could happen. I could go early. It's in the window. But, she said there is nothing she can do about the date. That there is practically an international board of Hindu deities deciding these things as it involves a mass exodus of Indian family members from both the bride and groom's side, not to mention the London relatives. So, basically, although I am very important to Simmi, I am low on the totem-pole when it comes to this day. In fact, they are trying to find places to put family members, and somehow I've agreed to host her cousin and her husband in the midst of birthing my first child.

I meet Simmi at our favorite coffee shop near work. We have at least 25 minutes to chat. Simmi gets a vanilla skim milk latte, and I get a decaf vanilla chai latte. I confirm with the barista 3 extra times that it's decaf, while Simmi rolls her eyes at me.

"You gotta chill on the decaf thing, girl!"

"Simmi, you have no idea what it's like to be pregnant. I told you already all the foods I can't eat. And caffeine is a no-no. There are studies that claim it can increase miscarriage, and if that wasn't enough the safety knowledge you must commit to memory is obscene. You have no idea. I already moved most of our cleaning supplies to the garage storage area. I wanted to see what it would be like. Nolan is ready to kill me because he has to run down there almost every day for something."

Simmi adjusts in her chair and raises her eyebrows at me.

"Simmi, do you want my baby to drink bleach?"

Simmi smirks!

"I mean it. It happens, and I'm hardly going to sleep because that safety course scared the life out of me. Do you know how many babies die from SIDS?"

I pause to punch in the ingredients of the fruit yogurt smoothie sitting in front of me into my pregnancy diet app when Simmi rips it from my hands.

"Simmi, give that back—I need it!"

"Jess, listen to me," she begins in her psychologist voice. "You do not need this. How do you think women managed before pregnancy apps? Do you think all the babies died whose mothers ate a yogurt parfait without checking the ingredients first into a computer? You are stressing yourself out, girl. That baby is going to be born with OCD!"

"Look Princess Samudra, don't you talk to me in your haughty psychologist voice. I know that voice. I'm not one of your patients."

"I'm not talking to you like one of my patients. I'm talking to you like one of my patient's mother's!"

"Excuse me?" I say a bit bewildered.

"Jess, you are becoming a psycho-mommy!"

"I beg your pardon?"

"A psycho-mommy! That's what I call it. A psycho-mommy is my little technical term—"

"Oh yeah, real technical Simmi—"

"Let me finish. A psycho-mommy, in my eyes, is an overly stressed mom, usually type A, who obsesses over every detail of their child's life. There are moms out there bringing their children up Vegan who were meat-eaters their entire life and suddenly they have a baby and boom—Vegan. They change their entire life and personality to fit to an unusually high standard. It's not their fault. Our society has pressured moms and even scrutinized them, requiring them to rise to impossible standards, creating a perfect life for their children. Now, it even affects pregnancy. You need to relax. Nolan showed me that list of questions you went into the doctor with and—"

"He did what?" I say stunned.

"Jess, that's not the point. He was just worried about you and for good reason. You should be enjoying your first pregnancy."

"I am Simmi, and how dare you call me a psycho-mommy!"

"It's just a term!"

"Oh, really, is that a medical term. Because if you gave me my phone back I would enter it into the medical dictionary app, and I bet it wouldn't come up!"

"Jess, it's a term that I coined for moms who become so stressed out about making everything perfect that they cause themselves psychological harm. I'm telling you it's becoming a big problem. I wouldn't be surprised if it's in the next DSM update. And all I'm saying is I think you're on that path. Your research, your obsessing, your—"

"Simmi, my research is me being responsible. And I do that for patients, too."

"You're not one of your patients. You don't need to research yourself."

"I'm not researching myself. You think I'm the first pregnant woman to look up in a book what to expect? I mean there is a best-selling book called, '*What to Expect When You are Expecting*' for Christ's sake, Simmi!"

"Jess, I'm just—"

"Simmi, not another word about this, OK? Let's talk wedding!"
"OK," she perks up, "Well, we have to pick out the color of your dress. It's going to be beautiful."

I'm nodding and genuinely excited, but in the back of my head, I can hear Simmi's voice ... *You're a psycho-mommy!* Am I a psycho-mommy? A PSYCHO-MOMMY?!?

We cover the wedding and a bit of the sex toy party, which somehow seems like it is becoming an early bachelorette party for Simmi, but I'm not in the mood, so I interrupt and say we really should get to work.

Once I'm back to my office, I start to prepare for work, but I can't shake Simmi's words, "*psycho-mommy, psycho-mommy, psycho-mommy!*" And I can't believe Nolan showed her the questions I asked the doctor behind my back. That's the first time he has ever done anything like that. I need to get my mind off of this. I go to the break room. There is a fresh fruit platter half eaten so I help myself to some strawberries, kiwi and pineapple. I open the cabinet and see there are some new selections of tea. I look them over and realize that I am not sure about most of them. I pull out my phone and start randomly typing them in my pregnancy app. Finally, I settle on ginger and mint. The pregnancy app agrees that's the best choice. I wait for the tea to brew and adjust my bra several times. It's very uncomfortable, and this thong is really riding up. I guess even my underwear isn't fitting me right anymore. I am desperate for some maternity clothes, and I never thought I would say this, but granny panties would be so comfy right now. Perhaps Simmi will know where to go for maternity clothes. As I wander back to my office, I stop dead in my tracks in front of Richard's office. I look in his office window agog, as I see Captain Crunch with some person I have never seen before sitting at Richard's desk. I scurry to C.C.'s office and interrupt Julie. She gives me her typical look of disdain by tipping her chin down and looking up at me above the top rim of her bedazzled glasses.

"Um, excuse me Julie, I don't mean to bother you, but who is C.C., I mean Gloria with? She's in Richard's office?"

"Jessica, that's not Richard's office anymore remember? She is interviewing a new psychologist in there."

"What?" I say in disbelief. "But, but I don't understand. I was hoping this whole thing would blow-over."

Julie just shakes her head at me to indicate that it will not just blow-over. And then stares at me, as if to say, *why are you still standing there?*

I go back to my office and drink my new tea. It's pretty good. I have to say my morning sickness is letting up. I still feel nauseous in the morning, but I drink down my Nolan smoothie and eat something, and then it usually subsides. I pull out my first patient's chart. I do a few breathing exercises and a new pregnancy yoga move that I read is supposed to help open the pelvis for birthing. That was a mistake as my thong is really irritating me now. I adjust my bra again, and then I have a brilliant idea. I can just unhook my bra and put my jacket on. Nobody will notice a thing. So I do and sigh in relief. I feel more relaxed. OK, I really need to focus. My first patient is C.C.'s friend, Gail, whom I have grown quite fond of. We met once about a week and a half ago for another follow-up session where I tried to gather more details from her past that might be helpful in our therapy process as we move forward to treat her BDD, which I think I have conclusively settled on as a diagnosis. She is truly a beautiful person inside with the warmest and kindest eyes. And I hardly notice the disfiguring facial features anymore that have resulted from all her surgeries. Instead, now, I see Gail, a loving woman who misses her husband who divorced her as a result of all this. I also see her as a philanthropist who wants to impact the world around her and also try to heal her young wounds. I have done a ton of research on BDD, so I feel informed and ready to help her, but I think it's a tricky situation.

SEVENTEEN

"*You're* 9 o'clock is here," my assistant chimes.

"Send her in, please." I answer.

In comes Gail. She is wearing a gorgeous blue and black Burberry basket weave check coat. It's to die for! She has on knee high black boots with a small understated heel. She looks so sophisticated.

"Gail, you look gorgeous today. That coat is absolutely stunning on you!"

"Oh, stop, Dr. Reed. I know I don't look gorgeous! I've never a day in my life."

"Now, wait just a minute, Gail. Let me take your coat and have a seat." I run my hand over the coat. Boy, it's a beauty.

I smile at her, "Now, I genuinely meant that compliment, honestly. You have to learn to accept compliments about yourself, and we need to get to the bottom of why you wouldn't take my compliment."

"Can you think for a minute why you rejected my comment so quickly?"

"Well," She begins as she looks down at her folded hands, "I guess I just never believe those words: *You're pretty! You look nice! You have beautiful hair or eyes.* I guess I just think it can't possibly be true."

"OK, well, why don't you believe it?"

"Because, I'm not those things," She says shaking her head in disbelief.

"If you are not those things, then what are you?"
She shifts awkwardly in her chair and doesn't respond.

"Gail, be honest with yourself and with me. What thoughts are in your head?"
"I just know, Ok? I know I'm ugly, repulsive, and even monster-like!"

178

I shudder slightly inside at her remarks, knowing these feelings have so much to do with her early childhood and those mock crucifixions. "Gail, you are none of those things. You are beautiful the way you are! You need to believe that first before you can move forward with your therapy. It may take a while, but that's the first step!"

We talk for a great while longer and I give her instructions. I tell her next time she comes in I will have a therapy CD for her. I explain how we are currently at her C spot. In order to get to her B spot, I want her to truly believe she is beautiful. I underscore that beauty can be in the form of many ways and to think hard about this. I already have some great ideas for her CD. I want to keep it upbeat. I'm thinking *"Beautiful"* by Christina Aguilera, *"Born this Way"* by Lady Gaga and even *"The Most Beautiful Girl"* by Charlie Rich. I am getting so excited I can't wait to put it together and give it to her. I give her the assignment for this week. She needs to write down ten things she loves about herself and then describe in detail why those 10 things make her beautiful. She has to re-read what she writes 3 times a day and then bring it to me for our next session. She leaves happy with the assignment, and I think we are really making some progress.

Next, I have little old Clara, one of my favorite patients. I run out to fill my portable tea maker because Clara and I sit and sip our tea while we talk. I love it! When I get back to my office with the portable tea maker I can see Clara has arrived and is sitting in the chair outside my office. Her eyes are closed, and as I approach her, I'm not sure if she is sleeping. As I get closer and observe her, I can see she is wearing oversized earphones and is holding a CD player that must be from the early 1990's.

"Clara?" I say gently.

She doesn't flinch. I look at my assistant who returns my gaze and just gives me a look of uncertainty by turning the palms of her hands up and hunching her shoulders up.

I say again, "Clara?"

No response. So I go in and plug in the tea maker and set up our tea-cups and then exit back out into the hallway. I put my hand gently on her arm and still no response. Finally, I shake her a bit and her eyes pop open in surprise. She takes down her earphones and looks at me a little bewildered.

Finally, she gives her head a little shake out of the dream world and says, "Oh, hello, Dear! I … I must have dozed off there." She smiles at me. "I was having the most life-like dream about my Maurice, God rest his soul!"

"How lovely, Clara. I'm glad to see you resting and, better yet, dreaming of Maurice!" It's very common for widows to dream of their spouses in many forms, but commonly they will look very healthy and happy in the dreams. Often they look 20 – 30 years younger. This is a good sign. The other side of the coin is they dream about the deceased as being sick or in the most recent state prior to death. I can tell by her smile that this was a good dream. He probably looked wonderful and was happy!

"Please come in. May I pour you some tea?"

"You know I love my tea, dear!"

I pour our tea and ask her what she was listening to. She beams back at me and says, "Dr. Reed, I'm listening to the CD you gave me, of course!"

I don't know why that didn't occur to me, but I am pleasantly surprised to find this out. "You were!" I smile. "Fantastic! How do you like it?"

"How do I like it? Oh, dear you have no idea. I take it everywhere with me. One of my grandsons gave me this nifty CD player, and it goes everywhere with me. I love it so much." She hushes her voice a bit and whispers, "I even take it into the bathroom!" We both giggle, and I blush a bit. "I was going to ask you to make me a copy of this one if it's not too much trouble. Scottie says he can put it in my bedroom."

"That's a fantastic idea. I would be delighted to make you a second one!" I say with pride!

Clara and I sip our tea. She has an earl grey, and I have a decaf vanilla tea. We sip and talk. She tells me how it took her a few days since our last appointment to actually find her nifty new CD player. She first went to electronic stores to buy one but was so confused by all the 'gizmos' as she called them that she would just end up leaving in frustration. Randomly, she mentioned looking for one at a family dinner, and her grandson said he had an old one he never uses that she could have. She is adorable when her face lights up saying how she got it for free–didn't have to spend a penny for it. I don't think she realizes it's probably 20 years old and is now obsolete with the invention of the iPod. Then we approach the topic of her son Scottie. And it turns out that he wants to put the CD in her bedroom, at his house. She is going to move in, temporarily, with the emphasis on temporarily, with Scottie and boob-job girl and the baby. She says I'm a genius and very talented because now when she sees boob-job girl she just closes her eyes for a moment, and she can hear the music playing from the CD in her head. She said in these moments where she used to get all upset, she now says she can see boob-job girl's lips are moving, but all she hears is the music. If she starts to bother her more she just interrupts her and states she has to complete her therapy under Dr. Reed's orders. She says this creates an awkward moment, and then they just leave her alone. In fact she tells me multiple stories about how she name drops me all the time.

For instance … *"I can't do that, Dr. Reed said!"*

"I have to go here, per Dr. Reed's orders!"

"Dr. Reed said I shouldn't be in large crowds!" I gasp at her. She looks indignant and says, "Well, I hate crowds, and they wanted to take me to the Philadelphia Mummers Parade this year, of all things!"

We giggle and sip some more tea.

"Anyway, dear, that CD and your direction have been magic," she compliments again!

"Clara, I am so very proud of you. Congratulations, you have officially moved from your C spot to your B spot." I show her my chart, indicating the goals for each of her ABC goals. She is quite pleased and informs me she didn't know she had an ABC goal chart. That she really just comes for the tea and good company! She is such a pleasure to be around.

"Clara, I see such tremendous progress. Now, tell me about your sleeping?"

"It's much better, dear. I listen to the CD in bed, and half the time I wake up 6 hours later with the earphones still on. Now, I do have my sad moments, and sometimes I still have trouble sleeping. And I often still wake up and think that Maurice is still beside me in bed. Then, of course when I realize he's not, well, that's a bit hard to contend with again."

"Well, that is to be expected!" I tell her. "It will take a lot of time," I explain further, "and that felling may never subside." But in terms of her overall health, she is doing incredible. And also staying with Scottie for a while should help.

Just then I hear a commotion outside, and then I can see my door handle turning. All at once, in busts Ms. Harrigan, Richard's patient, and my assistant. Clara and I stand. I immediately flinch at my thong riding up, but try to hide it. *This damn thong! No more thongs, Jessica. You are pregnant, and your ass is getting bigger anyway!*

My assistant barks at me, "I'm sorry Jess. She said she had to see you. I tried to stop her."

I can see Ambrosia is upset. "It's ok." I say. "I was just finishing up here with Clara." I take a hurried evaluating once over and can see her color is bland, her face especially looks withdrawn, her hair looks limp and her eyes are bloodshot. I can make out some cuts on her hands. And, of course, I only met her once before, and she was very thin, but today I would describe her as cachectic. I can tell she must have relapsed and is not well. I am quite concerned!

Clara comes up and gives me a hug and whispers, "I'll be on my way, dear, this one looks like she needs your magic more than me." She leaves giving me a knowing smile. As she passes Ambrosia on her way out, she puts her elderly hand on Ambrosia's perfectly tanned young shoulder and says, "Honey, you are going to be just fine. Dr. Reed can help you. She helped me!"

Ambrosia does not look impressed.

"Ms. Harrigan, please come have a seat." I greet her kindly.

She is in fits of rage, shaking her head. I can see her cheeks are flamed red with anger now.

"I don't want to take a seat! You said I would see Richard again for my next appointment! Well, he is not here, and they are trying to pass me off to somebody else! Where is Richard?" She demands!

"Um, Ms. Harrigan. I'm very sorry. You see, it's a little complicated."

"This is bullshit!" Suddenly she starts crying. "I need him. I… I've been trying to call him. I'm in a very bad place. I started to … I started to… you know … Again. I need him!"

"OK, ok!" I bring her some tissues. As I get up again I wince at the thong. Now, it's just plain hurting me. "Let's figure this out," I say. She collapses into the seat and crumbles into a ball, sobbing. She is writhing in the chair. I place my arm on her shoulder, and she flicks it off with a jolt. Finally, she looks up a little and begins.

"I talked to my boyfriend. He didn't care about my problems. He dumped me. I am a wreck, and I can't handle it. My family is treating me like a psychopath again, and my mom keeps threatening to admit me to a psych ward! I kept calling here trying to make an appointment, but I was getting this weird run around so I just decided to show up!"

"Well, I can talk to your mom and—"

"I DON'T WANT YOU TO TALK TO ANYBODY, I JUST WANT TO TALK TO RICHARD!" She exclaims at me, with anger and distress boiling up from her insides.

"I'm sure they told you out front that Richard's not hear any longer. There is nothing I can do about Richard, but please let me help you."

She just gets up and says, "You suck!" and leaves.

What a wonderful day this is turning out to be. I find out I am a psycho-mommy, and I suck in the same glorious day! And, if I do nothing else, I need to rip off this thong and throw it in the trash! I'm distraught. What do I do? Do I chase her? Do I tell C.C. she could possibly be on the road to a suicide risk?

Without thinking I am dialing Richard's cell phone. It goes to voicemail. "Richard, here, leave a message." BEEP!

"Richard, its Jess. I'm not calling about what happened between us. It's an emergency. Your patient Ambrosia, you know Ambi or whatever you call her, she was just here. She's distraught. Her boyfriend broke up with her. She has relapsed, and she wouldn't say exactly what or how long it's been happening, but she looked awful. I tried to calm her down and help her, but she stormed out when I told her you weren't here anymore. She needs you. I'm fearful of what she might do. Please call."

I hang up and stare at the phone, willing him to call. 5 minutes go by and no call. Ten minutes go by and still no call. I am rapidly tapping my fingers on my desk and biting my nails on the other hand. I'm staring at the phone, and I can feel beads of sweat forming on my forehead. Just as I am about to go to plan B and call C.C., the phone rings. I answer immediately.

"Richard, is it you?"

"Yeah, it's me!"

"Thank God you called. She is in bad shape."

"I know... I know... I just talked to her. She's coming over to my house."

"Your house. Isn't that like against—"

"Jess-er, are you kidding me? Against what ... all your rules?? I don't work there anymore, and besides you are the one who called me. I'm going to help her as a friend not as her doctor, OK? And you can consider yourself removed from the situation ... I wouldn't want you to have something dirty on your clean-slate, now would I?"

"Oh, Richard, please! That's not what I meant!"

"Well, I'm taking care of it."

"Well, wait, I need more than that?"

"Well, you are not getting more than that!"

"But, I mean, Richard, she was flipping out. Other people saw. I need to take some action."

"Fine, just file a memorandum to her chart, and I will have her call the office when she gets here to indicate she has found a new therapist!"

"OK, OK that works. And, um... Richard? Can I talk to you about the other thing. I'm so sorry, and I have been thinking about you so much."

"Gotta go, Jess-er!" The line goes dead.

Ahhhh! I just want to scream out loud! I grab my purse and sprint to the ladies room. *"Chariots of Fire"* is playing in my head. I shove open the door, and it slams on the opposite wall. I rush into the nearest stall, and all at once, I try in earnest to wiggle out of my pants the best I can, bumping and smacking into the sides of the stall walls. I mean, can't they have a changing section in the ladies rooms? Have you ever tried to undress in a tiny stall? And how the hell do two people undress in a bathroom stall? I think of all the movies I've watched where the overly attractive couple that just meets hurriedly finds a bathroom stall of a club to succumb to their fervent needs. Of course, in their search they are barely looking around because they are in fits of passionate kissing, but still they manage to find a stall, undo the appropriate clothing and find themselves in perfect unison making love in a stall! That's such crap. If anyone tried that they would have legs in the toilet bowl, and it would probably result in at least one person with a concussion. CRAP – all of it! Finally I get the thong off. I sigh in relief.

But hold on. What is going on?

It doesn't feel any better.

All at once I straighten up abruptly. I can feel my cheeks hot with fury! HEMMROIDS!!!!!!!!!!!!!!!!!!!!! NOOOoooooo!

I am having a full fledge conniption! I think I am hyperventilating. That fucking thong! Why did I wear that fucking thong???? I'm still standing there, naked from the waist down, frozen with anxiety. I don't know what to do. Then it occurs to me that I should look at it. Assess the damage. I quickly search for my compact mirror in my purse. I take it out and slowly open it. I say a silent prayer. *Please, God, please let this be my imagination! I'll do anything. I'll donate my paycheck this week to the poor. I'll never lie to anyone again. I'll cancel the sex party. PLEASE!* With a slow movement I lower the mirror down and then slowly position the angle so that I can see my nether region. The image that reflects back to me is beyond description. I'm not sure I even know what I am looking at. It looks like a tiny balloon is inflating out of my butt. I drop the mirror and start crying.

"Jess – is that you?" I hear a voice.

I straighten up in embarrassment. I'm silent. Holding my pants in front of me. Even though the stall is shut, I feel exposed.

"Jess, it's me, Simmi!"

I crack the door open. She looks at me. "Oh My God! What is it? Is it the baby? Are you in pain? Are you bleeding?"

"I shake my head no and motion with a sideways movement of my head, gesturing her to come near.

I whisper, "I just found out I have … I can't even say it …"

Simmi is looking at me in horror. "You have what … WHAT?"

"Hemorrhoids," I exclaim!

Simmi relaxes, "Oh Jess, you scared the life out of me. Is that all?"

"Is that all? How can you say—Is that all—at a time like this?"

"Let me take a look," Simmi says matter-of-factly.

"No – no way!"

"I've seen you naked before, plus, come on we are both professionals." I am so defeated that for some reason this makes sense to me. I let her come into the stall, and I turn around for her to take a quick look. I won't get into the mechanics of it, but if anyone ever saw what we were doing, I think there would be more than just one concern and perhaps HR involvement.

"Jess, it's tiny. It's not bad at all."

"Since when are you a hemorrhoid expert?"

She laughs, "I'm not an expert. It's just that Prad talks about it a lot. You know as a pharmacy intern that's like a really common question he gets. There are tons of over-the-counter things you can pick up, and if it gets worse there are even prescriptive options. And I always flip through Vishal's medical textbooks. I've seen pictures of severe ones – seriously this is nothing!"

This is not making me feel any better.

"Look you're a mess. Tell your assistant you are sick. You have to go home for the rest of the day. Go to the pharmacy, pick up some hemorrhoid cream. Take a long bath, and go to bed."

Simmi is right. I can't work the rest of today. Surely this constitutes a medical emergency! Luckily, I don't have any more patients. I would just be missing part of C.C.'s Alzheimer's study training, which I can make up anytime.

EIGHTEEN

I am at least six or seven blocks from our condo. I purposely trekked as far away as possible from my two regular pharmacies. I don't want anyone who recognizes me to see me purchase hemorrhoid cream. As it is, I wrap my scarf high around my face and hair to disguise myself. When I finally feel far enough away, I spot a pharmacy across the street. I cross the street and walk in hesitantly. What aisle is hemorrhoid cream in anyway? I browse around and look at the above aisle signs. This provides no clues! I start wondering up and down aisles. Finally, I see something with the word hemorrhoid on it. Of course, of course, why didn't I think of it? It's in the same aisle as the feminine sanitary pads, tampons, condoms, pregnancy tests, personal lubrication, and adult diapers; it's basically the most embarrassing aisle to ever be caught in. It's the aisle you get in and out fast as if you were a storm-trooper on a mission, but in reality your breakneck actions are from fear you will run into your boss or an in-law or an acquaintance holding a box of condoms. And, of course, I am lingering because I don't know what to buy. So, on full tilt, I just start putting one of each in my basket. A cream, an ointment, something called a medicated pad, a medicated travel pack wipes set, a cooling gel, suppositories, a hemorrhoid relief seat. Oh My God! Suddenly I have a flashback to that poor pregnant woman at the doctor's office – the one with the doughnut shaped seat – I'm buying a doughnut seat! Oh my God! I'm going to be walking ahead of Nolan (doughnut seat in hand) and snarling at him, spitting as I scream, "this is all your fault!" I am beside myself with grief, so in a final effort I also grab the rectal syringe, whatever that is for, a hemorrhoid spray and an anti-itch cream. I rush to the register, desperately wanting to conceal the evidence that I, Dr. Jessica Reed, have hemorrhoids! My focus is unparalleled– get this stuff in bags and rush home.

When I reach the front, I have to wait behind a lady who is complaining that her coupon didn't go through. Meanwhile a larger line is developing behind me and in my head that means more witnesses to observe my hemorrhoid relief purchase. I'm turning into a basket-case; I'm twitching and have developed a tic where I am biting my lips over and over again. Finally another clerk comes to the front and says, "Next in line?" He is about 19 or 20 with Justin Beiber type hair and an eyebrow piercing. I approach the counter and dump my items on the counter. He starts to airily ring them up not noticing anything about them. Thank goodness! But then when he gets to the medicated wipes he runs it across the scanner, but the barcode doesn't register. He takes out the gun and zaps it. Nothing happens! He pulls out the intercom and I shake my head in fright. "NO, please—"

But it's too late. "I need a price check on the store brand hemorrhoid relief medicated pads." He says it in a calm, un-judgmental tone as I stand there in an agonizing state of torrent embarrassment. But then I can tell that he finally realizes in his pea-sized brain what he's read and he snorts a little guffaw and eyes me with a jeering look. I am scorching with anger. I want to attack him! If I open my mouth, I think actual fire will come out.

I don't dare turn around. I can feel everyone's pejorative eyes on me, thinking, poor girl she's so young and has hemorrhoids! I feel like falling to the floor in a fetal position.

$147.62 later and I am out of the embarrassing confounds of the pharmacy and briskly walking down Chestnut street towards our condo. I am holding two heavy bags and my briefcase, and now I wish I had just sucked it up and gone to the local pharmacy. I still have several blocks to go. I pass a street sign that reads, Juniper Street. It rings in my head. Juniper!?! Why do I recognize that street? I am rarely down this end of Chestnut. Then it hits me – Juniper! That's the street that Richard lives on. I recall the details from when I looked up his cell phone number on our work directory. I pull out my phone and pull up his saved contact information. There it is—his address. He lives on Juniper. Before I can stop myself, I have turned down the street and am looking from side to side to get my bearings. Frantically, I look for numbers and signs of residential housing. At first it's just businesses, and I walk a few more blocks. Then I see in the distance the Naked Chocolate Café. Yes, that's it. He talked about that place all the time. He lives right near there. They make the most amazing hot chocolate he used to say, and apparently he claimed their desserts were 'orgasmic', as he would put it. I stop in front of the café and swivel around. I don't see his house number. I look some more and take a few steps and then suddenly there it is. Richard's house!

I maneuver closer and just stare at it for a while. Then I get the courage to walk up to the house. There are several doorbells with different names on it. I spot the 3rd one from the bottom which says "Amado". Before I know what I am doing, I am ringing the bell. Shit, now what? I stand there holding my bags full of hemorrhoid products. Then, I hear footsteps. I can feel my heart rate start to quicken. For a second I look around for a getaway, and I contemplate running away. Then the door cracks open, and I am quite surprised ... it's not Richard. It's an elderly woman. She has on a scarf, a plain white button down shirt and sweatpants. She is pale and thin. Strikingly, I notice the head warp she has on, covering her tiny head. I surmise by the way it's wrapped tightly around her head that she has no hair. I immediately know who this is. This is Richard's mother who has obviously been ravaged by the effects of chemotherapy.

"Um, hello, you must be Mrs. Amado?" I extend my hand to greet her. She takes it in hers. Her hand is cold and frail, and her handshake is delicate.

"Um, forgive me for disturbing you. I was just in the neighborhood and was looking to say hello to Richard."

Her face softens, and she smiles broadly. She has a beautiful smile, almost angelic-like. "Oh, well, if you are a friend of Richard's," she begins, "please come in. He's not here but should be back in a bit."

"Oh, no I really couldn't. I don't want to bother you."

"Nonsense, I would love the company. I'm not supposed to go out by myself so I hardly get to talk to anyone other than dear Richard. He's a love, isn't he?" she beams.

"Um, yes, yes he is." I respond. *He hates my guts, but let's not dwell on that.*

I don't at all feel comfortable going in, but I don't want to disappoint her. I follow her up to their place. It's beautifully decorated as I would expect from Richard. As I look around, I can see incredibly ornate antiques mixed with funky trendy pieces. It's decorated in a way that I could never effectively replicate myself, simply because I lack the creativity that Richard has. I spot several pictures of Richard with a beautiful woman, possibly in her late 40's. I look closely at one and realize … no it couldn't be?

"Is this you and Richard?" I ask gingerly.

"Oh yes, that was taken last year at the Philadelphia Flower show! Richard and I attend every year."

I am taken by surprise. The woman in this picture looks young, vibrant, beautiful and glowing. But as I turn to look at the woman before me she looks, older by at least a decade, weak, broken, pale and extremely fragile. I fight back tears and say, "You look beautiful!"

"Thank you dear, that is kind of you."

"So tell me how you know my Richard?"

"Oh, I'm a psychologist too."

"Oh, you are, that place has been so good to my Richard. It was so kind of them to give him a leave of absence so that he can take care of me. I mean I hate to put this all on him, but I have no one else nearby to help. And as you can imagine, we are in the thick of it now. I practically live at the medical offices. Between the chemo treatments, platelet and blood transfusions, scans and follow-ups, well … there is something almost every day. Today is a rather good day though, I'm feeling Ok. But I often worry about my Richard. Richard has had to rush me off to the ER more than once. I know he's going through a lot. I'm so glad he has such good friends. Another young lady was just here for him. She didn't look that good, and he took her on a walk. That's where he is now. He is such a Love, my Richard!"

I think silently to myself–the anguish Richard must be going through. Watching your mother waste away like this. Praying and hoping a miracle will intervene. Being the brave son who takes on the burden of care with pride but never letting his true emotions be detected. I imagine him crying to himself at night. And then on top of everything, what have I done? I got him fired. And he obviously doesn't want to burden his mother so he tells her it's a leave of absence. And now he is off saving Ambrosia. And I

191

think to myself all those days I would get angry or annoyed at him. I feel like such a horrible person. I guess I deserve this hemorrhoid.

I shake away these thoughts and look at her tenderly, "Your son, Mrs. Amado, is a wonderful human being. You must be so proud of him!"

"Oh, I am so proud of my baby Richard. But I do worry. Maybe you can get him out of the house sometime for me. He needs a break!"

"I smile and nod."

Then I think I better get out of here because I don't want to upset him. What if he walked in right now! That would be terrible!

"I really have to get on my way, Mrs. Amado. But is it ok to leave Richard a note?"
"Yes, of course dear, go ahead."

I leave Richard a simple note telling him again how sorry I am, and I plead for him to please meet me tomorrow morning at Naked Chocolate Café – my treat at 8 AM.

I leave the apartment in sorrow. Whatever problems I thought I had are nothing in comparison. If Mrs. Amado can deal with cancer then I can buck up about this stupid insignificant hemorrhoid. I head for home. Once I settle in, I take a long bath and have some of the pregnancy tea I bought recently. Then I spread out all my hemorrhoid products and begin my research. I look up tons of information and realize it's not so bad. If I manage this correctly, then there is hope that it won't get worse. I also am suspicious that my prenatal vitamin that contains a higher than normal iron amount could be a culprit in all of this. I make a note to discuss this at my next appointment. After a lot of reading, I go with the ointment to start. And then I rest on the bed.

I reflect on this day, my patients, Simmi and her psycho-mommy term, the changes in my body and finally Richard and his Mom. I contemplate the meaning of all of this. Not just on the visceral level but the real life meaning. I get up and put on my pregnancy CD, which is almost complete. As I listen to the soothing songs, first *"Baby Mine"* by Allison Krauss, then *"To Zion"* by Lauren Hill and *"Beautiful Boy"* by John Lennon, before the 4th song begins I am floating in la-la-land, thinking of how incredibly blessed I am. Simmi's words lay heavy on me. I am a psycho-mommy! I am obsessing. I am! She is right! But, it's a natural corollary, isn't it? It comes from a deep place of protectiveness... of love. I want to do everything correctly, not for me, but for this baby growing inside of me. I want this baby to thrive, to have all the things I never had, to feel incredible love and unwavering support. I want this baby to achieve every dream that comes to his or her imagination. I sigh, and realize that I just want to be the best mother I can be. And if that means becoming psycho-mommy, I guess I will live with it. I close my eyes and drift along with the music.

Several moments or hours later, I can't be sure, I groggily open an eye, then the other. It's dark out. I hear the door closing. I must have dozed off.

"Jess, you home?" I hear Nolan's soothing voice.

"In here," I say hoarse from sleep.

I can hear Nolan setting things down. He enters the room and trips over something and grunts to himself.

"What was that? Are you ok?" I think to myself, I left the doughnut seat on the floor, unable to look at it for long.

As he finds a place to sit amongst all my hemorrhoid products strewn over his side of the bed, he leans in and kisses my forehead. Then, picks up a box of cooling gel and regards it carefully.

He laughs, "Oh, doll, say it isn't so?"
I frown and confirm his suspicions.

NINETEEN

8:05 am: I have great willpower! I repeat... I have great willpower!

8:10 am: DAMN-IT

8:15 am: Oh, for the love of GOD!

8:20 am: OH, FUCK IT!

It turns out a pregnant lady waiting in a chocolate shop is not the best idea. I had all intentions of choosing a seat by the window so I didn't have to look at the scrumptiously inviting desserts. But by the time I waited for the two hot chocolates I ordered, my chosen seat was pilfered by some overweight man in a too tight suit. He must come here every day–I angrily observe him stuffing his face with some heavenly looking pastry. Instead, I'm forced to take the small table that faces the older German lady who stands in the back making the fresh pastries for all eyes to see. It's like watching a carefully choreographed waltz. She gently, but with authority, tosses the pastry dough and then wields it into these magnificent shapes. She applies the chocolate sometime on top and other time's pipes it inside using a pastry bag. I can't take it any longer. I have to have one. I get back in line. I'm going to get that huge chocolate cake with the pears and raspberries on top. I tell myself, because of the fruit topping, it can't be all bad. And I'll get one of those amazingly beautiful bowed up bags filled with chocolate for Richard's mom. Richard? Who Am I kidding? I glance at my watch. He is not coming! Finally I make my way to the register, order everything and then make my way back to my seat. I sit down and tell myself that even though Richard is not coming, I am going to enjoy myself and resist my inner psycho-mommy. I do not pull out my pregnancy app once. I take a sip of the delectable hot chocolate, and it is... well it is ... orgasmic – just like Richard described. This is not like your typical Swiss Miss packets. I can taste distinctively fresh melted chocolate and an infusion of cinnamon and nutmeg with a hint of something else I can't quite make out. I feel like I'm in a French café. I take another sip and oh my God, I'm in love with this hot chocolate! I want to marry it! Just then I take two huge bites of cake when I hear, "Uh-hum?" Someone standing before me is clearing their throat.

I look up, and in surprise I see Richard. "You came?" I jump up in jubilee and smile at him.

"Jess-er, I had no idea you were a chocoholic." He looks down and surveys my table which has a huge piece of cake, a bag of chocolates, and two hot chocolates. I feel my cheeks burn with embarrassment, as he also points to his nose to indicate I must have something on it.

I reach up to my nose and sure enough—whipped cream!

I wipe my nose and then say, "Actually, this is for your mother," I hand him the gift bag, "And this hot chocolate is for you!"

"Geez, Jess-er your guilt must be in overdrive!"

"Um, right, well, first off, please have a seat." I say matter-of-factly.

"Look Jess-er, bold move on your part going to my mother like that. The only reason I am here is because my Mom really liked you, and she read the note you left so I had no way out. She can even watch from the window to make sure I enter this place, so my best attempt was to purposely run late and hopefully miss you, but I can see you are getting your chocolate hoarder fix on, so I guess that wasn't going to work for me!"

"Look, Richard! I am genuinely sorry. And I am going to tell you something only a few people know."

He perks up, always the complete yenta, and his face softens just like the good ol' Richard I remember. Richard tosses everything aside for some good gossip.

I launch into my story and in great detail for the next twenty minutes I tell him everything about not knowing I was pregnant, throwing up that night at Gloria's event, which he witnessed, finding out I was pregnant, becoming psycho-mommy and my emotional roller-coaster ride. I tell him all my worries and concerns. It just flows from me like an avalanche. I can't stop it. To my utter surprise he listens intently, and I can see why his patients must love him so much. I eventually get to the part where Simmi and I just wanted to catch him in a bad situation, purely as a joke, to get him back for all the things he has embarrassed us over.

I finally end and am staring silently at him waiting for a reaction.

"Richard, please — say something."

"Look, Jess-er, that was a great story and all. And by the way, I totally think you will be a psycho-mommy. No offense, it's just so obvious! But look, you lost me my job. My Mom is going through chemo, I can't give you what you need and be your omnipotent redeemer. I need to focus on me and Mom. You're just going to have to deal with it. You screwed me over royally. Now I have to have 7 sex toy parties in a week, thanks to you, or I can't pay the bills to live, not to mention all the medical bills that are mounting!" He lifts his finger and slashes it about in my face, "Which, by the way, is all I was doing with those boxes in my office, trying to make extra money! I'm not some freak-a-zoid. I got into this to cover my Mom's medical bills. You make great extra cash on the side, and I am magnificent in this role. The ladies loooovvve me!" He says with exaggerated enthusiasm. "I'm a super-star seller! You should see me put on my show!" He leans over and whispers, "By the looks of your little chocolate fix going on here, you could use a toy or two!" I am flabbergasted by this, but he doesn't give me a chance to respond.

"But all that aside, I'm desperately trying to find something else, but there are hiring freezes everywhere. Look, Obama is my man, but this economy blows! I might have to just start my own practice or something."

"Let me help you! Please!"

"What are you going to do for me?"

"I dunno, but I know lots of psychologists. I'll ask around. I'll talk to Gloria again. I'll figure something out."

"Jess-er, look, leave it be. I gotta go!"

He stands up and waits for me, which I think is nice. We exit together. And I turn to say good-bye and thank him for meeting with me. But he interrupts me and says, "Now the only reason I waited for you is because we are going to put on a show. Look to my mom's window." I look up and to my surprise there is Mrs. Amado gaping out the window. I wonder how long she's been staring out of it.

Richard puts an arm around me. He is smiling broadly. "Smile God-damn it," he commands me, "And wave to Mom!"

There we are, arm and arm, smiling, waving. Through his grinning smile he manages to say, "This doesn't change a thing. I still hate your guts!" Inside I feel a pang of hurt, but I just go along with the show. I smile and wave and then Richard says, "You can go now, Jess-er, have a nice friggin' life!" and he blows a kiss for his final act.

I feel complete tottery in my steps as I walk along. I'm unsure of what to do next. I am in a bit of a daze. After a few minutes I realize I'm walking in the wrong direction. I have to get to work. I am overcome with thoughts of Richard and his mother. How can I fix all of this? There must be something. I can email all my friends and ask if anyone knows about a job. I can talk to C.C. again. Maybe I can tell her Richard has a sex addiction. You can't fire someone over a psychological affliction. Surely in our line of work that could be understood. Oh, it's no use, maybe Richard's right. I just have to accept that I ruined someone's life. He can go on having sex toy parties. I mean, he said himself he is a master at it. I can see him at it to. He is probably an expert show-man. He could sell anything. I mean he could really sell anything. Wait a minute ... he could sell anything! That's it! I hastily fumble around in my briefcase. Ugh! Where is that damn card? Finally, I find it and hail a cab.

Next thing I know I'm pulling up to a large building on Market Street. I get out and pay the cab and walk in. I take the elevator to the 31st floor and go into reception. People are hurried about, walking past me with stacks of paper, big huge poster-boards with colorful artistry strewn about. People are dressed quite spiffy. I approach the receptionist desk.

"Can I help you?" A young woman with her hair up in a twist says to me.

"Yes, hi, I'm here to see Polly Huxley!"

"I see," she gives me a once over and then asks, "Is she expecting you?"

"Um, not really, but she told me to stop by anytime."

She smiles at me in doubt and laughs audibly, "Polly meets with people by appointment only."

"OK, but if you could just let her know I'm here."

"Look, it doesn't really work that way. You'll need to call back and make an appointment."

This little tart is making me quite frustrated. "Look, I just traveled all the way here, and Polly herself said to stop by." She is shaking her head at me, and I can see I am getting nowhere. Suddenly I remember the check. I search in my coat pocket, and by a stroke of luck it's still there. I pull it out and open it. For a few moments I am speechless. Written on the check in flowing handwriting is $5,000.00. Oh my God! I've been walking around with a $5,000 check in my pocket!?

"Lady, I really need to get back to work, OK?" I look up from the check. "No, it's not ok!" I show her the check. I am here to see Polly… about this!

She takes the check and scrutinizes it. I can see she is looking at the signature, which she must recognize as Polly's. I take this moment to secure the upper-hand. "I am a highly paid consultant of Polly's as you can see, and I need to see her urgently." I hope that worked. I'm crossing my fingers behind my back.

"OK, have a seat. I'll call her assistant."

I sit down and look around. This place is pretty impressive. A lot of high energy, people bustling about, phones ringing, teams of people huddling in offices and tiny little alcoves. I notice some magazines to my right. I pick up a copy of "*Modern Advertising*" and start flipping through it. I start to read an article about Pixel Advertising, when I hear a shrill voice, "Jessica, Jessica, I can't believe it's you." Polly comes rushing over to me and grabs my coat. "Come with me!"

"Hello," I say while giving a snide look to twist-haired-receptionist-girl.

"I am so happy you decided to come in. Can I get you coffee, water, tea?"

"Water would be great!"

I follow Polly through a maze of long corridors and turns. The walls are draped with all kinds of framed advertisement campaigns. There are awards hanging with Huxley Publishing and Communications touted as the best advertising company in Philadelphia. I pass a picture on the wall of Polly with Mark Walberg, and it looks like it is signed by him. Finally we reach her office, which is a luxurious expansive corner office with amazing views of the city.

"Kay, can you grab us two waters please," Polly instructs before closing the door.

"Have a seat! We've been hard at work on your idea. We've made some progress, and I would love to tell you about it. Get your thoughts?"

"Yes, well, that's actually why I'm here. I had another idea." Polly perks up anxious to hear what I have to say.

TWENTY

Friday is finally here. I've made it to the 12th week. Today Nolan and I will get to hear our baby's heartbeat for the first time at our OBGYN appointment. Then, I get to tell the world my news and better yet I can openly display pregnancy symptoms and psycho-mommy neuroses without a care in the world. If I feel fat it's ok because I'm supposed to be fat. And tonight my plan for Richard will unfold. Nolan and I are dressed and ready to walk out the door to our appointment. Today was a triple berry, banana smoothie with a bowl of oatmeal. My Pregnancy app gave me extra stars for that. I am feeling great. Not a lick of morning sickness. I do have a list of questions, but I have decided I must change my approach. Instead of handing her my list in triplicate I will just ask them as they come up, you know conversationally. Before we head out I must read about week 12 in the pregnancy calendar.

Week 12:

Congratulations! You have officially made it to the 2nd trimester. If you haven't yet, it is now the ideal time to tell friends, family and co-workers you are expecting!

And every person you see, the mailman, the grocery store bagger, the dry cleaner's clerk. Who cares? Tell them all, I think to myself, and give a resilient shake of my head! Better yet, I can get a tee-shirt made up that says, "Next Meryl Streep in development" with an arrow pointed to my belly! That's actually a pretty good idea. I wonder where I can get that done?

"Come on doll, let's go!" Nolan's voice cheers. OK, back to reading.

Your baby is growing rapidly and has practically doubled in size since just a few weeks ago. Your uterus is expanding with your growing child. Your amazing uterus will eventually be big enough to hold a full-term baby, the placenta and amniotic fluid. At this time many parents are overjoyed to hear the baby's heartbeat for the first time.

Ahhhh! I can't wait. I am completely giddy with excitement. I grab my recording equipment for the CD and Nolan and I head out. As we arrive, I first notice someone standing out front of the office with a cigarette. I stop dead in my tracks.

"Jess, what is it?" Nolan looks at me with concern.

"Nolan, I can't go in there."

"Doll it will all be fine. I'm nervous too."

"No not that. There is a man standing out front of the office, smoking. I can't pass him. I will breathe in the toxic cancer inducing smoke from his cigarette, and it will go straight to the baby!"

Nolan looks at me quite startled. "OK, we can wait until he leaves."

I take the opportunity to launch into a dissertation on my research. "Did you know that cigarette smoke around pregnant women has been linked to low birth weight? It's true. The mixture of the tobacco and the smoke has about 4000 different contaminants, 40 of which are known to cause cancer. Nolan did you hear me? I said 40!"

His eyes are wide, and he shakes his head slowly back and forth to indicate that he didn't know that.

"And, you know how after someone smokes you can smell it on them, you know on their breath and clothes? Well that's because they are drenched in those contaminants. Nobody and I mean nobody who smokes will be allowed near my baby! They should make cigarette contaminant alarms for mothers. And I also think—"

"Doll?"

"I'm not a psycho-mommy Nolan. I did real research on this. I can show you the reports at home!"

He smiles lovingly at me and reaches out to grab my hand and says, "No doll, I just wanted to tell you that he's gone now. The guy with the cigarette! And I don't think you're a psycho-mommy. I think you are the best mommy in the world!" I soften immediately and feel less anxious.

201

We safely enter the doctor's office, but for good measure I hold my breath as we enter in case there is anything lingering in the air outside the door. I think about requesting that the office management consider placing a sign outside reading, "No smoking within 300 feet of this door, please! Pregnant women and their innocent babies are at risk!" I notice that the waiting room is completely full again. Geez! Business is booming for these doctors. We sign in and have a seat. I look around for any ladies sitting in donut seats. None! Thank God! I don't think I could deal with seeing that again! I fear that one day I will be in here with my bum attached to a donut seat. Nolan must sense worry on my face for he holds my hand tightly. I can tell he is just as excited as I am. I have nervous energy.

"OK, so you remember the plan for tonight?"

"Yes, how can I forget. You've gone over it three times already!" He looks at me bemused.

"Right! Well, just checking. Oh, Nolan, I'm so excited." I say in hushed tones.

"Me too, doll, me too!"

After about 20 minutes, Marge, the nurse, calls my name.

"Hello, Marge!"

I walk over to the scale before she asks. I know her routine now. Scale, blood pressure, urine sample, and then you are allowed to talk to her. I dutifully follow this like a Catholic school child.

After I complete the urine sample and place it in the designated spot I begin.

"Marge, I just wanted to remind you that I cleared it with the office to record the heartbeat with some sound equipment." I hold up my apple computer.

She looks at me annoyed, but then again she always has that look on her face, so it could just be an indifferent look. So I just smile brightly back at her. If we were in my office I would ask her to tell me about what happened in her childhood. Something definitely has affected her, and it has resulted in her micro-management of the screening process of her patients, hence the unspoken agreement of scale, blood pressure, urine sample and then talking. And she clearly has a significant non-interest in socialization. I would start her C spot at just making 30 second eye contact with patients. Actual physical smiling involving both eye contact and facial muscles would be the B spot for her. It would be a long road. I would predict at least 4 years of therapy.

"So, it's ok, right?"

"I suppose. Anything new?" She's scribbling on the chart.

"Well, we are really excited for today, and Nolan made me a new smoothie this morning. And I—"

I break off mid-sentence as I realize she didn't mean her question in a social way because she looks up from her chart with her nose scrunched up and one eyebrow arched fairly high, indicating that her annoyance barometer is increasing rapidly.

"Oh right, about the pregnancy. I developed a hemorrhoid, and the morning sickness seems to have subsided." I say this very quickly as if I've just provided the answer to double jeopardy. I guess to be accurate I should have had to say, "*What is hemorrhoid and no morning sickness for 800.*"

"Ok, room 3 please, undress waist down." She hands me the paper sheet cover. I look at it in disgust. I hate these things. I mean couldn't they invest in better more dignified covers for us ladies? I mean I have paper towels and toilet paper that are thicker and more luxurious than this thing. We head into the exam room and wait for Dr. Lange.

"So, dollface, next month is my poker game with the boys. It's my turn. December 14th."

"Oh right, I forgot."

Nolan and his friends, a mix of hockey players and guys from work, all get together once a month for poker. They rotate houses. There are eight of them, so it's totally fine because it's at our place only once every 8 months. So, usually Simmi and I make it a girls night out.

"I'll plan something with Simmi! Is it really going to be December already?" I smile at him and touch my belly, "Blasty's first Christmas!"

"How are we going to handle the holidays anyway?" Nolan inquires.

"We can go to my parent's for Thanksgiving dinner and your parent's for dessert. That's opposite of what we did last year, so it should be kosher with everyone. And as for Christmas, I'm not sure how I'll be feeling."

Christmas day is always so exhausting for us. We spend most of the time in the car jetting here and there.

"I think its best we have a quiet Christmas morning at home, and then we can visit the family later in the day or even Christmas Eve or the weekend after."

"But you know how Mom and Rosanne like us to stay overnight and wear those matching pajamas they always buy and play Christmas trivia. If you're feeling good maybe we can still do that?" Nolan asks.

Not on your life!

"Ok, sure, but you know we should get in the habit of staying home on Christmas. Now that we will be parents we will have to start our own Christmas morning traditions."

Nolan smiles at this. I can see his mind working at full speed thinking of all the fun fatherly things he will do. Dressing up like Santa, setting up a train table perhaps, videotaping our child's first Christmas or making some amazing café au lait with homemade whipped cream! I can feel my tongue salivating at the thought of this. I am deep in my café au lait dream world when there is a knock at the door, and Dr. Lange enters.

"Jessica, how are things?"

"Dr. Lange, hi, things are wonderful. My morning sickness is dissipating, and we are so excited to hear the heartbeat today."

"Excellent!"

204

"Yes, but unfortunately I've developed a hemorrhoid." I say somewhat embarrassed.

"Uh-huh ... any other changes?" She's entering information in the computer. I'm slightly perturbed at her "uh-huh" remark to my hemorrhoid. I mean doesn't a hemorrhoid deserve more attention than that?

"Yes, I have noticed changes in my breasts that ... that, well alarmed me."

"Ok, well let's take a look. Layback and put your legs in the stirrups and scoot forward. And just unhook your bra and we will take a quick look at your breasts.

I hear Nolan giggle, and then he continues, "Just to let you know the changes haven't alarmed me at all!"

Dr. Lange laughs. "Oh, I see!"

"Scoot down a little more, Jessica, please!" Dr. Lange washes her hands and applies gloves.

This is the worst part. Does the general public, and by that I mean men, realize that women are basically subjected to a full body cavity search with each pregnancy visit. I close my eyes and ask, "When do we hear the heartbeat?"

"After the exam. Ok, everything feels about right. She takes a quick look at my breasts. OK, you can go ahead and get dressed. I'll be right back." She leaves with her computer that's on wheels.

I quickly get dressed and start to get a little anxious. She hasn't answered any of my questions yet. Next thing I know Marge is coming in with a handheld device. Dr. Lange is following her.

Dr. Lange starts talking before the door even closes behind her. "Now, while Marge sets everything up. Let's go over some things. It's very common to develop hemorrhoids at any stage of pregnancy, but early on like this may be an indication that you are at risk for worsening

205

hemorrhoids. I encourage you to increase your water and fiber intake. The iron in the prenatal vitamins can increase constipation, resulting in worsening hemorrhoids. If you have to stop taking the prenatal vitamins, you can, for upwards of a week or two. If you do stop the prenatal, just supplement with a folic acid supplement. Or you could look for a vitamin with lower iron content. Also, changes in your breasts are noticeable around this stage and will continue. You can expect to go up 1-2 cup sizes and your breasts will feel much heavier over time. You will notice pigmentation changes in nipples, freckles and birthmarks. The darker pigmentation of the nipples allows the infant to have a visual bull's eye for nursing. Also, you may notice darker underlying blood vessels and your breasts may become noticeably lumpy. This is all normal. It's your body getting ready for motherhood."

Nolan says under his breath, "Bulls-eyes!" I don't even think he realizes he has said it out loud!

Marge interrupts. "All set!"

"Any other questions before we hear the heartbeat?"

"Actually, I was wondering if you could post a sign outside for smokers, you know, something to deter them from smoking outside the office door?"

Dr. Lange looks at me inquisitively. I tell her my fear of walking in the front door this morning because of that looming smoker.

"I see. Yes good point. We will definitely flag that with the office manager. Any other questions?"

I have tons more questions, but I set them all aside. I don't want another minute to go by without hearing the baby's heartbeat.

"Um no, please let's hear it. Let me just hit record on my audio equipment."

This is unbelievably exciting. I lie down, and they apply a cool gel to my lower abdomen. Dr. Lange is standing to my right, and Nolan is to my left. I don't hear anything yet except *wosh-wosh-wosh* and a crackling sound. I

206

mean, I want that part for the CD too, but I'm desperate to hear the heartbeat.

"Now, as you are only 12 weeks, it may take a minute to find it because the baby is small."

I'm waiting. Biting my lower lip. Waiting some more. She is moving the probe around my lower abdomen, and the gel is cold. Suddenly, I get extremely worried. What if something is wrong? I look over at Nolan. I squeeze his hand, and he squeezes mine. I feel emotional. I blink back tears. Please hurry up and find it. Just as I think I can't bear it any longer, I hear something. It's rapid and steady, like a fluttering sound with the *wosh-wosh* mixed in.

"Is that it?"

"Yes, that's your baby's heartbeat. It sounds great!"

"Does it sound ok, I mean normal?"

"Yes, Jessica, perfectly normal!"

Oh my God! It's the most wonderful sound I have ever heard. I gasp out loud and then laugh out loud. So does Nolan. We look at each other. "I love you!" I say! "I love you too!" he says. I squeeze his hand harder.

"146 beats per minute! Strong heartbeat!" Dr. Lange says.

Our baby has a strong heartbeat! I beam in pride!

The rest of the day is a complete joy except when I go into the pharmacy on the way to work to buy fiber bars and supplements. Of course, that's right next to the aisle of shame. But, after that I tell everyone I see. I send text messages to everyone. I bounce right into C.C.'s office and tell her without a worry. She, to my surprise, is happy for me. She sits me down and tells me how she always regretted not having a child. That she would love to have someone to pass the Vanderbine legacy too. Then she gets into an entire story about how her child would probably be just like Anderson Cooper, another silver fox, naturally because they would be distant cousins. After I sit listening to her drone on about Anderson Cooper and matching cousin bracelets, she tells me that we just will have to plan out my patients appropriately. Some may choose to wait until I get back which is fine, but we need a contingency plan for those who need support through the interim. The conversation was quite delightful. At the end she asks about Gail and her progress. I give her a bit of an update without sacrificing my patient's confidentiality. She shows real concern and worry for her friend, which is a new side to C.C. or at least a side I haven't seen before. I think about bringing up Richard to her, but I can't ruin the plan.

I feel like I am floating on air. Between appointments I go on amazon.com and purchase a personal Doppler machine to hear the baby's heartbeat. I didn't even know personal Doppler's existed, but Dr. Lange told me about it. I think she mainly brought it up because I was trying to get the technician to keep the heartbeat on longer and longer, and finally they had to kick us out. As a side note, I definitely subscribe to the feeling that I am the only patient they should be thinking about in the moment. We are talking about growing a baby here. I need full undivided attention. I had to wait for 20 minutes in the waiting room before I could cross the gates of sanctum to get back here and so can the next lady, for crying out loud! Anyway, I justified buying the Doppler by telling myself it's for the CD. But if I am honest with myself there is a bit of psycho-mommy there. The real reason I bought it was to be able to check it every day for myself, just to be sure everything is ok. And so what? What's wrong with listening to your baby's heartbeat? Nothing! I don't care! I'm doing it, and if that makes me a psycho-mommy, then fine! I receive several texts from Mom and Dad. They are eager to change the spare bedroom into a nursery for when we visit once the baby is born. Dad said he could decorate the room with baby animals. Of course, you realize these are not stuffed animals in the traditional sense! These are REAL stuffed animals. I can't have that. I can just picture myself nursing my infant in a rocking chair while having a near heart attack at the glimpse of glowing eyes from a baby owl in the corner that I hadn't noticed before. I'm going to have to break it to him at Thanksgiving — no taxidermy in my baby's room! Don't get me wrong. He means well! Dad even put up a sign in front of the shop that says, "expectant pop-pop inside!" So he is at least a little redeemed with that.

I am just bursting with happiness. I can't hold it in. But I have to be professional with my patient's. It's not appropriate for me to talk about myself with my patients. I settle down to get ready for my next patient, Eve Carter. When Eve enters my office she bounds towards me.

"I have the most amazing update, Dr. Reed."

"Oh, I can't wait to hear it." I say with enthusiasm.

She begins talking before she has even taken her coat off. "You won't believe it. I did exactly as you said. I shut my mother out. I didn't go to regular coffee with her. I did not accept her calls. It was a little tough to do, but I just remembered your words: *She is in an ego state, and I can't rationally engage with her now.*"

She pauses. I am on the edge of my seat.

"So, what happened? Tell me!"

She throws out her hand. On her finger is an enormous diamond. It glitters and twinkles in the light. I bet Vishal would approve of the 4 C's on this rock. I wonder if Frank read Vishal's diamond book too?

I stand in exuberance. "Eve, it's absolutely gorgeous. Congratulations!" She stands too, and I take her hand to gaze and admire it up close. "Well done, this Frank of yours!" I say. We are both beaming at each other. I can't hold it in. I hear myself saying, "Oh, Eve, I have news too. My husband and I are expecting our first child!" As soon as I say it I realize it was unprofessional. Shit! I try to shift back to her, but I can't because Eve has leaped towards me and engulfed me in a hug!

"Dr. Reed, this is splendid news. You will make an amazing Mother. Your child will have their head on so damn straight, I bet you raise the next diplomatic leader of the world."

I laugh out loud, "I had my sights on the next Meryl Streep, but what you envision sounds good too." We both giggle.

"Now, back to you. How are you feeling about all this?"

"I am so happy. I love Frank, and he loves me. I never thought I would get to this point. I thought I was a spinster for life! We don't even want to wait. We want to get married in a few weeks."

"Are you ready to jump into that without resolving things with your mother?" I inquire.

"Well, that's the best part. She heard through her circle of yentas that Frank proposed, and she was at my apartment within the week. She was humble and sorrowful and asked me to forgive her. She said the last couple of weeks without me completely opened her eyes to something she hadn't realized. She was still grieving from the loss of my step-father, and she thinks she was somehow taking it out on me! Isn't that amazing?"

I wonder what psychologist her mother is seeing? It is very true that we often take grief out on those closest to us!

"That is amazing!" I encourage.

"So we think we will fly to an island or something with Mom and a few others and just get hitched!"

"Eve, I am delighted. And I have to say you have reached all your goals with me. You are at your A spot." I show her the chart. We marvel at her progress. She has been coming to me for two years. When I first met her she couldn't make it through a coffee with her Mom, and she was miserable. Now, she has found a new path forward with her mother, she is engaged to a man she loves and she has relaxed through the power of music therapy.

"But, Dr. Reed, I don't want to be done. I mean ... I can't do all this without you!"

"Eve, don't be silly. You—and you ALONE—have done all this. I've just helped you open some new doors, but the doors were always there for you!"

"But I need you to show me what other doors there are for me."

"Well, that's just the thing. I think you are able to find the doors yourself now."

"But I don't want to go on not seeing you." She looks teary eyed.

"How about this? We can switch to a 6 month follow-up plan. We will set an appointment every 6 months. That way I can stay in touch with you and if anything ever pressing comes up, you are still on my schedule and we can always fit you in sooner if you need to talk to me."

"Yes, yes, please, I want to do that!"

We agree on this plan. These are the days in psychology when you feel rewarded. The years of training, studying, research, lack-of-sleep and testing all are washed away with a single patient success story. The feeling is one of accomplishment, of fulfillment, and humbleness, knowing that relationships are ever evolving and mysterious. There is never a magic bullet. This was two years of effort on Eve's part, but she stuck through it; she toiled and chipped away at it. And in the end it worked. I feel a bit like Mother Theresa right now. I picture myself with a white veil with blue stripes. This is the kind of feeling she must have felt helping the poor. OK, so I'm not like Mother Teresa exactly, but maybe a little. I mean I help people. I enjoy it. I love it. I feel it's my calling. Suddenly the thought enters my mind... *Mother Teresa would not approve of your sex-toy party.* I shake my head and get up to walk Eve to the door, dismissing that thought as quickly as I can. She thanks me profusely, and she asks my due date. I beam at her, and my hand naturally goes to my pendant. I tell her about the due date and my summer birthday party fantasies. We both bask in the happiness of her engagement and my motherhood for a few moments before she departs.

TWENTY-ONE

Simmi: Where the hell are you?

Me: I'm on my way!

Simmi: People are flooding in. And your Polly chick has been here for an hour at least with crews of people and equipment. What the fuck? They have taken over my entire apartment???

Me: should be there in 5

Crap! Crap! After work, I went home and finalized my CD with the heartbeat noises. I couldn't resist. I made the mistake of listening to it, and I fell asleep. On the good side, it totally relaxes me, and I have really found something here with this. On the down side, I totally screwed over Simmi with the party. I reach her building and dash upstairs. I take the stairs because the elevator is totally ancient, and it takes 10 minutes just to adjust between a few floors. As I'm hiking up the never ending stairs, I think to myself … *Well I am certainly getting my 30 minutes of brisk exercise today.* Which, of course, I've been neurotic about. I walk to and from work each day, so that counts. I do morning and nightly prenatal yoga moves. I also do my kegel exercises when I'm with a patient, without them knowing of course. But it works beautifully because I've trained myself so that each time a patient comes in to just start my kegels. At first it felt like a totally rude behavior. But then I realized they have no idea I'm doing kegels, so what's the harm. As a result, I get several sets in a day. But stair-climbing, this is a new one. I feel quite winded. I finally reach floor 9. I pause a minute to try to catch my breath. Boy, I feel out of shape … and I would consider myself fairly fit.

As I walk down the corridor, I can hear the commotion. There is music playing. It sounds like a club atmosphere. I knock on the door. No response. So then I bang on the door with all my might. Simmi opens the door, and I am taken by the delicious fumes of garlic that waft out to the hallway. Simmi is holding the door open with one hand, and with the other she yanks me in. "There you are. I'm going to kill you!" Simmi is dressed in a tight black dress cut fairly high with knee high boots. She looks hot to trot, I must say.

"I'm so sorry! I'm here now. Where is Polly?"

"She is setting up in my bedroom. She has like 10 people with her."

"Ok, I'll head in there!" I look around, and I can see cocktails being mixed from the bartender I hired and little delicate appetizers everywhere from the caterer. I used Polly's $5000.00 check to hire a professional bartender and catering service for the party. You see, Polly is scouting Richard as the face of her new marketing campaign based on my ideas. This will be a pilot run. He doesn't know yet. I was afraid if we told him he wouldn't show up with me involved.

I glance around some more and take in the whole room. A tray of decadent desserts is a centerpiece to the table, from Naked Chocolate Café, of course. I see old friends from college and some of Simmi's friends from her gym. People are waving and shouting out, "Jess, come have a drink!" I get excited all over again at the thought of sharing my news. And for once I don't feel the need to hide my stomach. There is an entire apartment full of people that I get to say, "I'm pregnant!" to.

I pause for a second and retreat to where Simmi is setting up a crudité platter.

"Simmi, where is the Iceman? Is it up on the roof terrace?"

"Nope! Polly has stuff set-up there. I haven't seen it yet but she mentioned something about erecting a heated tent up there, so I just put it in the front of the living room where Richard will do his little show. I figured he would want it nearby."

I'm confused by this. Isn't she afraid of it melting everywhere? Isn't she afraid of people spilling alcohol?"

I glance over, and I don't see it. Am I missing it? I glance from one side of her living room to the next. I don't see it anywhere.

"Simmi, where is it?"

"Right there!" She points to the living room with one hand as she sets out penis shaped pasta salad with the other.

"Are you playing a joke on me or something?"

"Jess, I don't have time for this. The party starts in 30 minutes." She is taking out a penis shaped cake from the fridge. Gosh she has gone all out for this.

"Just show me."

"Honestly Jess, it's right fucking there! She grabs me and points directly above the TV."

I squint and look closer. Suddenly I see it. I walk closer. I stare at it in disbelief. It's a miniature collectable of a silvery white super-hero standing on an icicle shaped platform. As I look closer I can make out the word "*Marvel*" etched onto the miniature version. I can see another one just like it connected to an ice ramp. This is her Iceman? This is the ramp? This is what she thought I meant? Oh My God! My face lights up with humor. My eyes are glued to the miniature figures. My mouth has dropped open in a wide joker-like smile. I feel my body beginning to lurch into hysterics. It hits me all at once like a great planned out Saturday Night Live skit. That weird story she told me about how her brother had one, this is what she was talking about? I laugh uproariously.

I recall her snooty words...

"It's a guy thing," as if she was all-knowing in that department.

"It's the power ... the power of the iceman, shooting out the ice liquid! The iceman shoots out the liquid and then you slide on it."

I can't control the laughter. People are starting to stare at me, but it's all just too funny and I laugh harder still. All along I had the image of the giant penis ice luge being in her brother's room. I had an image of him somehow putting it on a ramp.

Simmi comes over to me. "What is wrong with you? Have you lost it? You're acting drunk, and Polly is waiting."

"Simmi, this is your Iceman?" I point at it in mock expressions!

She looks at me in annoyance. "Yeah, so what!?!"
I take out my phone and jab at it, trying to find the picture. Simmi's cheeks are inflamed. "Jess, I'm... um, kind-a busy right now!"

Finally, I find it. I shove the phone to her eye level and say, "This is the Iceman Richard wanted!"

There, in all of its glory, is the picture of the giant penis ice luge.

She looks at it in complete shock. Her mouth gapes open and her eyes bulge. She covers her mouth with her hand in astonishment. She looks at me and then the picture again. Then she looks at her superhero Iceman miniature. Then she smiles. She looks back at the picture again.

"We are so getting this for my bachelorette party!" she announces!

We both snort loudly and uncontrollably! I am arched over laughing so hard I can barely breathe. I think I might pee my pants. We start babbling at each other between snorting and spitting and laughing so hard. We both are holding our sides which start to split with actual pain. Nobody else around us can understand what's going on.

Through laughter I say "You said it had a ramp ... you said its power is shooting out the—" I can't even finish the sentence.

We are bent over dying with laughter.

"—the ice ... liquid ...," I try to continue, but it's no use. Oh my, I haven't laughed like this with Simmi in a long time. It feels like we are back in college.

"Jessica, there you are!" comes a shrill voice.

"Yes, sorry," I'm still laughing, "Coming, Polly!"

I leave Simmi, who tries to gain her composure. But I can hear her break out into fits of giggles again by herself. At the sound of her, I can't control the giggles! And Polly looks at me several times with uncertainty.

Finally, Polly ushers me into Simmi's bedroom, which looks as if it has been turned into a makeshift command headquarters. She is all business and ignores my laughing.

"Wow," I say as I look around at all the equipment. I quickly regain composure! All around are TV crew equipment and enormous looking cameras.

Polly hands me some paperwork. "These are releases people will have to sign for photography and video use. We have to make sure everyone signs it for when we do the press release because things could happen in rapid fashion from there – you know twitter feed, blogs, etc. I will go over this at the beginning. Here is an itinerary of how the night will go. She hands me more paper." She is talking a mile a minute, and I am trying to keep up.

She begins again, "Our clients, Apogee Botox, are up with our operations team, which is setting up on the roof terrace in a make-shift spa setting under a heated tent. We will have a sectioned off area for the counseling in this room so you and Simmi can be incognito. There are two massage therapists up there as well. In case there is a line we wanted to have other options for people. The CEO of Apogee Botox is up there. She is thrilled about this. This is just the kind of underground marketing event we wanted to have in all the major cities across the country. We are very excited to pilot it here. But of course we are all counting on Richard! I hope your plan works. It's got too!"

"It will. This is exactly up his alley!"

Everything gets put into final places. We have a huge crowd of luxurious looking ladies who have arrived. Everyone is dressed to the nines. High heels, tanned bodies, glorious dresses, and hair that shines. People are merrily enjoying cocktails and hors d'oeuvres. Ladies are ogling the penis

216

cake and taking pictures of it, while giggling, on their phones. There are a lot of ladies I don't recognize. Some are folks invited from Apogee, some are from Polly's side of things and I have even invited Blanche, who has brought some girls too. Blanche tells me she loves this, and we must have a party just like this in the old neighborhood. She would invite tons of people. It would be *off the hook*, she says! Justin Timberlake's *"Sexy Back"* comes on. The beat is booming, and you can see people getting their grove on. This is turning into quite the event.

I grab a drink of water, and I decide to go upstairs to the roof-top to check things out. I stop dead when I take the final step to the top terrace. There is a giant whimsical white tent, hung with soft white lighting, and inside are sectioned off medical treatment areas with physicians and Botox specialists. I feel like I am in a spa, not on Simmi's roof. There is an area to sit down with beautiful potted greenery and pictures of before and after shots of beautiful ladies with Botox treatments. Women are huddled by the pictures examining them.

Someone in a long white medical coat is saying, "This is taken at maximum frown before and then after …" There are delighted gasps from those admiring the transformation of the photographed evidence.

I am standing there scanning everything. I twirl in a circle to take it all in. I don't believe what I see. My phone goes beep-beep.

> Nolan: Hi Doll, he's walking up to the building.
>
> Me: Thanks honey for being look-out! I love you!
>
> Nolan: Hurry home! I miss the mother of my baby!
>
> ME: XOXO

I run down the steps to the apartment and find Polly and Simmi. "Ok, Nolan says he's approaching the door."

Simmi and I go to our positions. Simmi has a cocktail.

"Simmi, you can't counsel people after drinking."

"Says who, this is a party! I call it party counseling!"

I roll my eyes at her. I take a deep breath. I'm nervous but excited. The place is alive with energy. Richard will flip.

There is a knock at the door. I can hear muffled voices. I hear Polly's voice.

"Please come this way," she is saying.

I can hear her ushering him into the room. Simmi and I are behind a curtain that has been set-up for private counseling. He has no idea we are behind here. I'm sweating bullets!

Polly begins, "Let me introduce myself. My name is Polly Huxley and I am the president of Huxley Communications and Publishing. Joy, whom you scheduled this party with, is a scout of mine. She saw you at a party she attended and highly recommend you for this event. We are combining this with a Botox party featuring our client Apogee Botox. We are initiating a new underground marketing initiative to make spa services for busy professional women more convenient, social and enjoyable. The sex-toy party is a new angle we would like to develop in conjunction with the Apogee suite of services.

"What the...?" Richard says in surprise. He must be stunned. I know I would be.

Polly laughs, "Richard, this could be your big night. If you are interested we want to audition you to be the next Dr. Ruth?"

"Am I on candid camera? I am, aren't I? Ok, give it up. Where are the cameras?"

"I assure you," Polly begins again. "This is not a joke. We are serious! And of course you will be compensated! We didn't want to tip you off too early because we want you to be as natural as possible. We also understand that you are a psychologist who minored in human sexuality and that's why we selected you. Is that true?" *That's a little known fact about Richard that hit me like a ton of bricks when I was standing outside of the Naked Chocolate Café the other day.*

218

"How do you know all this?"

"Like, I said, my scout Joy! She's very good!"

"Now, picture this, we want to break out an entire marketing campaign around a new sex therapist, sort of like the next Dr. Ruth … that's where you come in! We want this person to be an advocate for woman who struggle with the pressures of today's fast passed life and pressures of being a career-woman. But you know it doesn't stop there. These women are also expected to be super-moms, soccer-moms, fit and spry going to the gym 5 times a week, plus taking care of their parents and reading all the new amazon best sellers. And one of the things ladies are stressed over now-a-days more than anything else is looking their best, looking younger, and in many cases this means cosmetic enhancements. And we don't think there should be a stigma. It's a crazy world for us ladies!"

"Tell me about it, Polly, you didn't even mention the waxing!" Richard echoes. I can tell he's getting comfortable.

"Yes, of course, waxing too. Our market research shows that the area that becomes lacking for women most of all is sexual fulfillment. Women today are just so busy that they are having less sex! We believe that the next sexual revolution will involve the confident sexual woman, who's interested in having cosmetic enhancements to look and feel younger and at the same time perhaps attend a sex toy party to purchase items for self-pleasure or for use with her partner. This marketing will target women who want to look younger, feel younger and have better sex. We want to create a forum where women can come to an Apogee Botox party that offers sex therapy, psychologist services, Botox treatments, sex-toys and more. The sky is the limit. We think you might just be the face of this new revolution. The next Dr. Ruth, but in your case, Dr. Rich! What do you have to say?"

"Um, well, it sounds interesting," Richard says sheepishly. He is completely shocked, I can tell. I have never witnessed something that had the power to silence Richard before.

I am listening so intently that I notice my hands are gripped together in a prayer fold and I am sweating a little. Next, it sounds like Polly is taking him through an Apogee marketing presentation and I can hear her

219

explaining where he comes in to it all. She is getting to the part about providing counseling first to women considering cosmetic enhancements. You see, at this event, the Apogee folks will refer interested ladies to therapists, which is where Simmi and I come in. This was part of my idea too, which was greatly fueled by all my research on body dismorphic disorder. I wanted women to make educated decisions and also be counseled on BDD before leaving the party. Polly loved it. She calls it the Botox suite, a dynamic soiree that provides a suite of services. Each service will be a fee for service program, and ladies can choose to participate. I am beaming at Simmi as we hear the party continue to go on. Polly has Richard sign some paper work, and they leave.

"That went well, don't you think?"

"I don't know. I was busy drinking this cocktail down so I can go sneak another!" Simmi cracks!

"Simmi!" I say disapprovingly.

Simmi and I can hear muffled sounds, and I look over the itinerary Polly provided me. They will introduce Botox services first because you can't be intoxicated to sign the waivers to receive treatment, then they will introduce Richard for a sixty minute sex-toy forum. Then Richard will do a second showing for anyone who went to get Botox. My head is spinning just looking at all that is taking place. Then after that they can choose counseling, follow-up Botox for another day, ordering their sex-toys or just mingle and enjoy the party. I mean it's an entire orchestrated event. Polly's crew will be interviewing people and photographing the event, and if they like what they see with Richard, they will have him be the figure-head for the marketing campaign. It's amazing!

Simmi and I begin wedding talk while we are waiting. All the while we can hear Richard's muffled voice, and then fits of giggles break out and sometimes loud screeches. Lord only knows what's going on out there. After a few minutes Polly comes in behind the counseling curtain.

"He's incredible Jessica! You were right. He is simply amazing. You should see what's going on out there. He is gyrating about and passing around huge pink vibrators. The ladies are so, so loving him. He has all

220

these creative games, and he's just perfect. He is getting the ladies to really open up. They can't wait to order their items and then move on to the Botox suite. I really think we have something here! You have to see it!"

"I wish we could," Simmi says sulkily. Simmi is still upset that she has to be a psychologist at her own party.

"Simmi, if Richard saw us it would ruin everything; plus if this all goes to plan you can go to endless parties like this." I say to her empathetically.

Polly continues, "Jessica you really are brilliant. After this I am going to talk to you about some other ideas. The Apogee team loves this underground party marketing idea and the *suite of services*. They are thrilled!"

"Oh, no, Polly, this was only to redeem Richard. I'm not getting involved in anything else."

"You are a card, Jessica!" Polly pats my shoulder and exits.

Within a few minutes Polly's staff is ushering in ladies for counseling. One after the other they come in, and it's incredible. I go over BDD in detail, and the ladies really get into it. It's amazing how they open up. I don't know if it's because they are on the heels of Richard's performance and so they feel a little more uninhibited than normal. Or, maybe it's from having a drink or just being in a party atmosphere. But I receive all kinds of fantastic questions about sex, psychology, cosmetic enhancements and life in general: "... *Should I quit my job and stay home with the kids?*" this woman is asking me now.

I love it. When it's all said and done, I have counseled 26 people at rapid fire and Simmi has counseled just as much. I can hear the party dying down and things clearing out. Polly comes into the room just as I finish up my last counseling session. I can hear her shrill voice from behind the curtain.

"Dr. Rich," Polly is saying using his new moniker, "You are it. You are the new psychologist who will lead the women's next sexual revolution. We are going to make you a household name."

"I always thought I was meant to be famous," he responds.

"But first I want you to meet my scout in person, the person who made this all possible."

"Oh yes, absolutely, I have to thank her for all of this!"

I can't believe Polly is doing this. I wanted to remain anonymous. I'm looking around for another way out, but there is none. I'm trapped. Suddenly, Polly pulls back the curtain. There I am.

"Dr. Rich, I think you know my scout Joy. Joy is just her alias, but then you know that."

I look up at Richard modestly. He stares back at me in shock. His eyes, like huge Frisbees.

"I'm sorry Richard. I had to do something. And well, it's a long story but I told Polly you would be perfect for what she needed in her communications plan and … and I was just trying to help you and your mom, and I understand if you still hate me!"

Richard hesitates and cocks his head to one side. He takes a big breath and then he begins. "Jess-er you did all this? This is some mea culpa! And … hate you, girlfriend? I couldn't hate you after all this. Plus, if this works out I might just turn straight for you!"

Everyone stops talking and turns to Richard.

"Joke, people … a joke!" Richard calms everyone down. Laughter erupts in the room.

"You're not mad?"

"Jessica, I sold more toys tonight than all other parties combined. I got a free Botox treatment, and I'm going to be the next Dr. Ruth according to Polly. Of course I'm not mad. In fact I am grateful and touched. Nobody has gone to such lengths for me. You are a great friend!"

222

Friend? Richard just called me a friend. I'm completely gobsmacked. To my surprise he walks closer to me, grabs my hands and gives me a hug. I am stunned and just stand there. After a moment, a smile begins on my face.

As Richard turns around to exit the room he says, "Oh, Jessica think quick!"

Suddenly, I see a giant *"pink pumper"* flying at me. I scream in alarm as it hits my right shoulder and ricochets off. By the impact the power is activated, and it lands in my lap swirling and whirling and shaking. I yelp out loud and jump up. It falls to the floor and is vibrating on the hardwood floor, causing a reverberating sound around the room. I stand on my tippy-toes as if I've seen a spider and then run out sickened by the entire thing. Everyone is howling laughing, but I fail to see the amusement. I can hear all kinds of remarks behind me as I breathe deeply trying to get my heart rate down.

"Did you see her face?"

"Did anyone get that on video?"

"A picture … Please tell me someone at least got a picture!"

I screech from the hallway, "You guys are harassing a pregnant woman, you know! I could sue!"

TWENTY-TWO

It's full fledge winter. The days are shorter and the nights longer. It's cold outside, and Christmas is just a little more than a week away! I am going on week 16 of my pregnancy. I am totally showing, and I found super comfy and cute maternity clothes. The trick is to shop on-line. I was never really much of an on-line shopper. I always wanted to see my clothes up close, feel the material and try them on. But those days are over! It's so easy. You make a cup of tea. You browse in your PJ's and click away. I have ordered maternity clothes from the Gap, Old Navy and Loft. I am quite enjoying my growing belly! And I have to say this is the fun part of being pregnant. I don't have morning sickness anymore. I don't feel as tired, and shopping for new clothes is so much fun! And that looming anxiety, my entire first trimester, with Richard and that mess has been lifted. "Dr. Rich" has made a big splash! And I mean BIG! Polly has had him featured on several networks already. They gave him this incredible makeover before his TV appearances. He looks … well … I have to say … gorgeous! Even though he is totally out of the closet gay, they gave him that manly sexy look that makes you think as a woman that there is a chance he's not gay. And maybe one could have a chance with him. And even if you thought he was gay, there are some women out there who truly believe they can change that. Don't get me started on the psychology of that! These ladies are swooning over him. He is coming out with a book called, *"YOUthful Looks, YOUthful sex, YOU deserve it!"* He is already being compared to the next Dr. Ruth, just like Polly and I planned. It's amazing. His Mom is thrilled. He is able to pay all the bills and has hired several people to help take care of her, which she likes. She enjoys seeing Richard happy and likes the new company of the nursing staff. Captain Crunch has even noticed *"Dr. Rich's"* new fame! She apparently contacted Richard for his position back. Of course, he politely turned her down, but said he would be willing to come in twice a month to see his long-time patients. People like Ambrosia—who is doing much better now. It's a "win-win" situation. Captain Crunch gets access to Richard's new found cache', and Richard can administer to his beloved patients.

Tonight is Nolan's poker party. I told Simmi that I really need to catch up on some research and so—no girl's night—this time. She didn't seem to mind. All this on-line maternity clothes shopping has taken away from my normal research. I have organized my research needs in a "Ghant chart" that nicely depicts what is work related, what is pregnancy related, and what is baby related. I haven't been overloaded with this much research since my dissertation. I'm lying on the bed with the door shut in my PJ's. Nolan keeps coming in and asking if I need anything.

"Doll, the boys will all be here soon. Last chance for snacks?"

"I'm all good. You have fun Babe!" I smile back at him. He is so amazing. He already has brought me water, another fiber filled smoothie, a bowl of sliced kiwi and strawberries, and a tray of celery and carrot sticks. You would think that I had five people in here with me with all this food. It's set up on a table like a buffet. And on our bed, spread far and wide, are journal articles on breastfeeding, Rh- sensitivity, cord-blood banking, and proven relaxation techniques for Tourette's syndrome — for a new patient I have. I know I should get right to the research, but I can't help myself. I desperately want to watch my DVRd episode of "Birth Day" on the discovery channel. I'm obsessed! I found it one day over a weekend, and now I DVR every episode and watch it religiously when I get home from work. It's riveting! Just the thought of watching it conjures up a feeling of wanting a bag of popcorn and a large soda. Of course, being pregnant I have opted for the Nolan inspired menu this evening. So far I've watched tons of episodes. In one episode a baby is born with the umbilical cord wrapped around his little neck, and chaos ensues as the medical staff try to make sure he is safe. I start sweating every time it's on. Sometimes it is so scary that I practically pee my pants, but also it is so joyous when the baby is actually born. In yet another spellbinding episode chronicling the birth of twins', I journey through the agonizing moments with this new mother. I thought about writing to the show's producers to ask if I could send gifts to that heroic mother. This makes me ponder a bit. How come we don't hear more about this, you know, the actual amazing feat of birthing another human? I think we need like a cartoon character. Seriously, what women do to birth the children of the world is pure heroism. I close my eyes and picture a pregnant superhero. She would be able to grow things. Yes, that's it. Think about it, a woman grows an actual person over nine months. A freaking person! That is amazing! In order to do so, she has to double her blood supply, grow a placenta, expand her uterus by like 200 times, so of course her super power would be to grow stuff. She could grow organs for those poor patients who are waiting for a heart transplant, or a liver or a kidney. Gosh they could build a whole platform around it. She would be fully pregnant and glowingly beautiful, and she would point with her finger and – BAM - grow something. I would call her *Birth Woman*! She would wear a flowing green cape and a big B symbol emblazoned on it. I am smiling at the thought of this.

Then, I'm distracted by the doorbell. Ok, that's enough Jess, clam down!

Anyway, I'm learning so much. I'm learning about birth planning and birth positions, and I mean they should require you to watch this in my opinion as soon as you find out you are pregnant! It always ends the same way—A family cuddling their newborn and me in tears. Full-fledged sobbing tears! Then immediately I turn it off and put on my relaxation CD. When I get to the part of the baby's heartbeat, I always close my mind and imagine the first time I will hold my baby. By that point I am in such a Zen moment that I can move on from there.

I convince myself one quick episode will not deter my research too much! I fluff up my pillows. Relax and turn it on. Immediately, you sense there is a problem with the way the show is starting out. As I continue to watch I learn that the mother develops preeclampsia and has to be put on bed rest. *Note to self: research preeclampsia!* Now to me, bed rest sounds pretty awesome. I almost hope I get bed rest at the end. You just lay in bed, and people have to bring you all you need. It looks totally amazing. I mean think about the amount of research I could get done! However, in this case I am utterly abashed as the woman in this episode looks so miserable. As I'm watching, I hear the doorbell ring again. I can hear the volume from the next room pique a bit. It also sounds like Nolan has put some music on. The poker game must be starting soon. I am curious about this poker game. I've never been home when one has gone on. I wonder what it entails? I start to hear the door again and now the volume of the voices is quite high, edging on vociferous. I have to turn the volume up on the TV in order to actually hear it! Normally I would feel comfortable venturing out to say hello, but I am already in my PJ's and slippers. I also applied a rejuvenating cucumber mask that needs 30 minutes to set in. Maybe I'll just get Nolan to come in to tell me what to expect. But I can't go out there looking like this.

I think a bit about what to do and then … Brilliant! I have just come up with a great idea. I pause the show and I grab my purse and take out my phone. I jab into it:

> Me: So sorry to bother you. But could you make me a cup of tea when you get a chance?

Ok, that will do it. He should be in any minute.

2 minutes – nothing.

5 minutes – nothing. Right, he's busy of course. OK I'll just text him again.

> Me: Honey, I have a kiss waiting for you too!

That should do it! Problem is another 10 minutes goes by and nothing. He must not have his phone nearby. It's quite loud out there. He must not be able to hear it. And now I'm not really able to enjoy the show because I'm so distracted by all the noise. I start to imagine what is going on out there. First thing that comes to my mind is that iconic painting of dogs smoking and playing poker. You know the ones painted by C.M. Coolidge that were used to advertise cigars. I remember a grade school friend of mine had it hanging in her house. Her Dad would boast, "C.M. Coolidge, best painter ever was!" I remember from a very young age being very interested as to why he would think or say that. Not Picasso, not Monet, not Van Gogh, not Renoir, he picks the painting of dogs personified in a smoked filled room playing poker with pipes and half empty high-ball glasses strewn about? OK, this is the wrong thing to imagine. I shake it from my head and try hard to imagine something else. OK, now I picture a Tony Soprano type of scene with Tony holding a cigar in his hand and a gun on the table in front of him. I shake my head again. Ok, probably better to not imagine what's going on out there. But, my curiosity is killing me. I crack open the door. From the angle of our bedroom I can only see someone's feet sitting at the far end of the dining table. I'm listening. I hear banter about poker...

Raise you 10

... I fold

... Oh, Jack has his bluffing face on

... I call the clock

... Cassandra's win

... Grab me a beer

Well, I know I am eavesdropping, but this is kind of fun. And I am very proud of myself. I know most of these terms, except Cassandra's win. Wonder what that means? I Google it real quick. Hmm? Nothing comes up relating to poker. It must be a local Philadelphia poker dialect or something.

I decide I'm too distracted to watch the end of *Birth Day*, so I just turn it off altogether. Maybe if I read the research on breastfeeding or Tourette's I can engross myself in something else. So I sit by the crack at the door and grab an article. It's quite interesting, you know, breastfeeding. Like this bit I just read now about how breastfeeding takes care of all the baby weight for you. Your body uses the fat stores to make the milk. Fascinating! Just then I'm distracted again.

I hear Nolan's voice. "Dude, she's amazing! She always gets everything right!"

I begin to totally beam. He's talking about me to all his friends. I mean of course I know he must talk about me, but it is so nice to hear it with my own ears. It seems so unabated, just bursting out of him!

I hear another voice chime in, "Yeah and she's pretty hot too!"

I hear Nolan confirm with a grunt.

Wow, that's a little weird for a friend to call your wife hot.

Another voice interrupts. "Did you guys hear Joey had a date with her?"

I never dated a Joey?

Voices in unison give loud hoots and hollers. Suddenly I realize they are not talking about me. My brain feels like it's in slow motion. I am slowly processing all of this. Nolan said some girl, not me, is amazing and grunted in agreement to her hotness?

I am frozen with disbelief. Then out of nowhere I realize the door has tipped open more. I'm half way leaning out of it, and someone has turned into the hall to make their way to the bathroom. Shit! He sees me. I look up. He looks back at me startled. It's Mike from hockey and he looks crapulous, holding a beer.

"Jess is that you?"

"Yes, hi there Mike!" I say looking up at him in my *hello kitty* slippers and night-shirt that has little pictures of cupcakes on it. I totally look like I was snooping. I'm mortified.

"I...um ... I lost my earing. I'm just trying to find it."

He is staring at me with a smirk. "I never saw anyone who actually did that. Only in movies!" he says.

"Oh, it's nothing. You just kind of get down and feel around for the earring that's all. Don't want to wait and have it get vacuumed up or something!"

"No, I meant that stuff on your face!"

"Oh My God!" I turn around and jump up and face the mirror. Staring back at me is a green-faced monster with cracked looking membranous disfigurement. I look hideous. I look like Yoda, the grand master of the Jedi counsel!

"Oh, um it's great for the skin you know!" I try to sound confident as I quickly shut the door. Once it's shut, I lean up against it and fall to the ground in complete embarrassment. After a few minutes, I go to our private bathroom and rinse my face several times. I can't seem to shake Nolan's words … "She is so amazing and gets everything right." Who the hell is he talking about? The rest of the night I try to read through my research. Nolan never answers my text or brings me tea. On several occasions I consider getting out of my pajamas and getting dressed just so I can march out there and make my presence known, but I decide not to. I fall asleep at some point to the sound of what I can only imagine is a mix of dogs and tony soprano, carousing it up over some hot girl, not me, while drinking and smoking cigars. OK, I know Nolan would never let anyone smoke in here, but without going out there I can't imagine anything else.

TWENTY-THREE

"**S**exting, that's your answer!" Simmi says with determination and a look of ancient Indian wisdom.

"Absolutely, that and some boudoir toys, which I can hook you up with!" Richard adds with a double raise in his eyebrows to accentuate his intentions. "Jess-er, there is a new one that has your name all over it." I shiver at the thought of Richard receiving a new merch order and thinking "Ah, now Jessica would squeal over this little ditty!"

Simmi laughs!

"Shut-up both of you! I'm being serious here!"

"So are we," they say in perfect unison. Who are these two? A few weeks ago they practically loathed each other, and now they are bullying me into sexting and sex toys together as a unified front? Have they been having secret Yalta style conferences and excluding me? My eyes dart from Simmi to Richard and back to Simmi again in suspicion.

I can't believe the two of them. I texted them both the night before and called an urgent morning meeting at Naked Chocolate Café. Richard and I now meet here regularly. He is becoming, well, I guess he is becoming one of my closest friends. Normally when we meet, we catch up on how things are going, and then we go up and visit with his Mom. Afterwards, I always immediately call my mom to check on her health status and Dad's. She is getting quite used to it. Last week when she answered the phone she didn't even pause for a greeting and just said, "Hi honey, 2 good bowel movements, next check-up still not for 2 months, walking 25 minutes a day and eating fish for dinner tonight! Gotta run, I'm meeting your father in 10 minutes at the shop." Anyway, of course I need Simmi's input too to discuss what I overheard Nolan say. So here we all are in the café, each of us sipping on a decadent hot chocolate covered with fresh whipped cream followed by a topping of nutmeg and cinnamon sprinkled on top. This place is heaven if you ask me. The café is effervescent with the smell of warmth, coziness and calm … basically the smell of chocolaty goodness. I will drink this until I am chockablock, and I need to be rolled out of here. It's been about 12 weeks since I've had my precious s'mores martini, but this comes very close to the same level of enjoyment!

I take a sip of my hot chocolate and realize I probably should have kept this to myself. Simmi insists Nolan would never cheat on me but that he might find other women sexy or attractive and what wife wants that happening. And Richard has laid his cards on the table. He is adamant that I must step-up my game in the sex department to which Simmi has latched onto as well.

"First of all," I begin as I straighten my back up and sit tall in my chair, "Nolan and I are in so much love. In fact, I think we have a rare, soul-mate kind of love. You know we are still enjoying our honeymoon year? We are like Rose DeWitt Bukater and Jack Dawson. And have you forgotten we were only married a few months ago! I trust him completely, and I probably misunderstood the entire thing. And I do want to point out that contrary to your belief we have a magnificent sex life!"

Simmi and Richard exchange dubious glances, and they both start smirking. To which I look back at them totally agape!

"Hello, I can see you. I'm sitting right here!"

Richard speaks first and says "Who the fuck are Rose DeWitt Bukater and Jack Dawson?"

Simmi interrupts me before I can speak and in a muted tone says dismissively, "Titanic – the movie, Jess was obsessed." Again, I look at Simmi afflicted. Is she my best friend or what?

"Tell us the most exciting thing you've ever done in bed?" Richard says.

"No way, that's private!"

"I'll tell you mine." Richard looks proud as a peacock. I quickly cover my ears.

"No, I don't want to know!"

"Look Jess, all we are saying is don't give him a reason to wonder what it would be like to be with a more adventurous mate! Start a little sexting. Let Richard stock you up on some toys." Simmi looks at me encouragingly.

"And go buy some lingerie." She adds flippantly.

"Simmi, how dare you? I have plenty of lingerie!"

"I'm not talking about your angelic white wedding night thing. I'm talking naughty lingerie! And, Jess, don't get all upset. We are trying to help you!"

"Well, you're not!" I retort.

The next day I decide to end work a little early and go to Children's Hospital of Philadelphia (most locals just call it CHOP) to the Sports Medicine and Performance Center to surprise Nolan and grab some dinner out at a romantic restaurant. When I arrive and enter, I am always so impressed by CHOP's magnificent and welcoming entrance. As you walk in you immediately are drawn to look up to the expansive several story high atrium with beautiful staircases and artwork. Hanging from the ceiling are magnificent sculptures in bright colors. They remind me of a child's dreamlike version of the cosmos. You are so overwhelmed by all the popping colors that your eyes dart around not sure what to settle on first. I imagine that families who travel here from far and wide to get the best care for their children must feel a slight warmness as they enter these doors. Not that the aesthetics can calm the nerves of parents facing the worst with a sick child, but it must give a little solace. Although it's such an incredible place, I put my hand on my belly for a moment and hope I never have to endure what some of these parents are dealing with. As I walk through the equally stunning and colorful corridors towards the Sports Medicine and Performance Center, I recall the first time I came here to meet Nolan years ago. I remember being so impressed by his love of sports nutrition and helping children! I approach the familiar door where a kiosk beside the entrance lists the team members of the unit. I reach my finger up and scroll down to Nolan Reed, MS, RD, CSSD, LDN and run my fingertips over the

233

letters adoringly. I also remember the half hour conversation whereby Nolan explained to me what all those letters stood for. As I enter the door, there are young families and children waiting to be seen. Everything looks busy. It's been so long since I've come to Nolan's office. When we first started dating, I would come here often. But now that we are married, we don't need to find ways to see each other. I, Jessica Reed, wife to Nolan Reed, now wake up in his arms every morning and go to sleep by his side every night. I smile at the thought of that. I walk up to the counter, and a young man, must be a student, approaches me. "Hi, my name is Chris, may I help you?"

"Yes, Hi Chris, my name is Jessica Reed. I'm Nolan's wife. Could you let him know I'm here?"

"Sure thing, Mrs. Reed!" He looks at me with that young eagerness of a student wanting to please everyone. It's so refreshing.

"Oh, just call me Jessica!" I smile at him.

I start looking at the pamphlets. There is one on Fluid Management. This is actually interesting from the pregnancy standpoint. I'll have to ask Nolan about this. I take one and put it into my purse. Do I drink 8 glasses of water a day? I really need to consider this. I take out my phone and enter myself a reminder with an alarm. I've been using the alarm feature of my phone a lot these days. The alarm makes this horrible *eeeeeehhhhh-eeeeeehhhh* noise until you turn it off. I have an alarm for my prenatal vitamin, for pre-natal yoga morning and night, for kegel reminders, and for doctor's appointments. Now I just added one for water consumption. I'm feeling quite proud of myself. I mean how many expectant mothers take their prenatal care so seriously? Then suddenly, my thoughts are interrupted by someone calling my name. It's a woman's voice.

"Jessica Reed?"

I walk over to an attractive blond woman with teeth as bright as snow. Her hair is partly up with soft twirling tendrils dangling around her face. She has a white lab coat on, and her eyes sparkle at me.

"Are you Jessica?"

"Yes" I respond hesitantly.

She smiles broadly, "Hi, I'm Cassandra. I work with Nolan." She thrusts her hand out to shake mine. "He's such a great guy I wanted to come out and meet you. I've been bugging him to bring you round. He's with a patient introducing a new high caloric diet. He should just be a few minutes. Would you like something to drink?"

Still clutching the fluid management brochure that is partly in my purse I look up at her and begin, "Um, actually water would be great. Could you make it 8 ounces?"

I point to my belly and smile, "trying to keep good fluid management for the baby!" I try to say knowingly.

"Yes, that's very wise of you! And congratulations by the way. Nolan is very excited!"

"So Cassandra, how long have you been working here?" I ask.

"Oh, a little over a year."

...A little over a year? What? Nolan never mentioned a beautiful blonde named Cassandra –

Suddenly I stop mid-thought. Something is coming back to me. It's slow at first and then like a freight train it hits me. The poker night... "*Cassandra's win!*" I thought it was a poker thing. Oh my God! Is this who Nolan meant? Is this the amazing girl? The one that's always right? The one that dated Joey and garnered hoots and hollers? Is this the one who he grunted in agreement as being hot? I feel an abrupt sense of betrayal, and I can feel my face flush red. I can feel myself starting to breathe hard. For a moment I am frozen stiff. I just stare at her, and the room seems to slowly start to close in around her. I meekly raise my hand to my mouth in shock!

"Are you ok, Jessica?"

I quickly realize my eyes are wildly looking around, almost in a fight or flight response. I take a deep breath and summon all of my psychology training.

"Yes, of course, Cassandra. It's just that water would be great."

"Oh right, yes, I'm sorry. 8 ounces coming up!" She says jovially. She is very nice, but I don't care. I feel an instantaneous hatred towards her!

As she turns around, I can't take my eyes off of her. I notice everything about her. The shoes she is wearing – black and pink nursing clogs. The way in which she walks – a sultry saunter. Her hair gently swishing back and forth as she navigates through the maze of people. The fact that she is taller and more busty then me – probably 5'9 and a C cup. Before I even realize what I am doing, I have my phone out and am jabbing into it.

> Me: OK, change of plans. I need you to teach me sexting and stock me up on sex toys pronto!
>
> Simmi: Yippe, let's meet at Velvet Lilly on 2nd tomorrow at noon!
>
> Richard: I'm coming too. Will bring my best supplies! I love a good sex kitten make-over.

Cassandra arrives back with a glass of water. "So tell me how you've been feeling?"

"Oh, you know, pregnancy has its ups and downs." I begin then suddenly I regret saying that. Why would I want her to think my pregnancy with Nolan is anything less than perfect?

"Um … for most people that is… but not for me. It's been totally blissful. I have felt magnificent the entire time. Nolan is such a doting father already." I lean in for good measure and say, "you know sex during pregnancy is pretty awesome too!"

Suddenly, I can see her expression changing from a smile to an uncomfortable stare. I can read her body language as she shifts slightly to the left pointing her hips away from me, and then she even takes a step backward. My psychologist alarms are working overdrive – you've closed her up, and she wants to exit the conversation. Ok, maybe I shouldn't have added that sex comment.

"Let me just check on Nolan for you!" she says!

As she walks away again, I take her in again. This time I notice she has a tattoo sticking out from the bottom of her pant leg. I can't make out what it is, but it's green. Ha! I think to myself. Nolan hates tattoos. I crane my neck farther to see if I can see any more of it when I hear someone clear their throat behind me. I quickly turn around to see a young man and his family. He has his arm rapped up in a splint, and judging by the looks they are giving me, I must have been blocking them for some time.

"Oh, I'm terribly sorry. Please let me get out of your way."

I take a seat. About 10 minutes pass by, and finally Nolan comes out.

"Hey doll, what a surprise. Come with me." I light up at seeing him. A flood of memories come back from all the times I would come in to meet him here. But then I can feel my expression change when I see Cassandra pass by behind him and brush him on the shoulder in a friendly teasing good-bye gesture. She waves to me, but I'm too stunned to respond. How dare she brush his shoulder?

Nolan takes my hand and brings me to his office and shuts the door. Suddenly, his hands are all over me, but I am too distracted to reciprocate.

"You know I always wanted to have sex here!"

"With me?"

He stops mid-kiss on my neck and laughs. "Of course with you!" He gives me a look of confusion.

"Nolan?" I push him away. "Who was that girl? Cassandra?"

"Oh, Cassie?" … My eyes are like saucers … Now he calls her Cassie?

"She's a physical therapist here."

"Well, I don't like her!"

He laughs, "Cassie, why? She's great!"

I sneer at him and think — *Yeah, and she's amazing and she's always right and she's hot too, right Nolan?*

"She was kind of rude to me." I know… I know that's a lie. But I don't want him to like her either.

"Doll, I doubt she was rude. She was just probably busy. She's been dying to meet you."

I bet she has!

"Why haven't you told me about her?"

"I have. Remember when I told you the entire department was so happy to get this new great physical therapist who was transferring from California? I told you all about it. I told you how we were excited because she was certified in sports but also specializes specifically in knee injuries.

OK, this is sounding familiar. But he never used the appropriate pronoun. He never said "she." He said "this person" and "great physical therapist."

"You never said she was a beautiful blonde from California." I give into my feelings.

"Well, doll, I didn't interview her. I just knew we were getting somebody great. I didn't know if it was a man or a woman." "And besides," he is looking now at me with concern, "why does that matter?"

"It doesn't matter … I mean … well, um, it kind of does … I mean I just wish you had told me about her."

"Dollface, I did." He puts a hand on my cheek and then pulls me close to him. "You can't be jealous about her… are you? You are my hot wife! I'm your husband. Did you forget about that? You are carrying my baby! I am head over heels in love with you. She can't hold a tiny match to the raging fire of feelings I have for you!" He is pressing me up against his

238

office door now. And he has resumed kissing my neck. I take a deep breath in and can smell his scent, which makes me a little weak in the knees. I feel the heat from his chest leaning up against me. But I'm still so distracted. I don't give in. I mean why did he say all those things? I can't admit I was eavesdropping can I? What is the psychology take on this? I quickly muddle this over. So many thoughts are rushing into my brain at once.

If you tell him you were eavesdropping, it compromises your trust.

If you tell him the truth, it will create a strange dynamic with him at work and you don't want that, especially if you have read this all wrong.

If there is something going on, well then—

I shake my head. Of course there is nothing going on! This is ridiculous!

"Doll, what is it? I'm doing my best work here!"

"I'm sorry Nolan, I just am distracted. You know work and the baby. Listen, can we stay home next week, you know on Christmas Eve?" That was genius; at least I have used this moment to try to get out of the nightmare matching PJ family night at his parents with psycho-Rosanne. I can't believe that just popped into my head out of nowhere. I am quite proud of myself.

"Sure, doll, whatever you want!"

TWENTY-FOUR

I am standing across the street from *The Velvet Lilly* trying to look totally incognito. OK, so who has heard of *The Velvet Lilly*? Is this a place the in-crowd is supposed to know about? Do they have them in New York and LA? I mean I haven't seen this in my US Weekly. I had no idea this place even existed. I went on-line last night to look it up. I was half embarrassed to even enter the words onto my computer. For some reason I kept thinking what if some program in cyberspace logs my activity, you know, that I am looking up sex shops? I mean I'm a professional psychologist. Could that information get out to my patients somehow? And even worse, what if one of my patients sees me entering this um, this establishment? That's why I am standing clear across the other side of the street. I am standing there with my hair pulled back into a bun and a scarf all around my head with sunglasses on. I glance at my watch; it's 10 minutes after 12. Where are those two? I see a group of women approaching me. I hurriedly take my phone out to occupy myself. I turn to the side as if I'm reading a rather important email. They pass me, and I feel a wave of relief. I'm going to have a heart attack standing out here. Across the street I can make out a man and a women walking along holding lattes. Wait a minute, that's no man and woman – that's Simmi and Richard. Together! They are having Yalta conferences! I feel a fury rise inside of me, a bit of a sting of betrayal. I jab at my phone.

Me: What are you two doing? I've been waiting 10 minutes.

Simmi and Richard are still walking, sipping their lattes. Then I see Simmi react to receiving the text, and she pulls out her phone. She reads it and puts her phone away. Is she ignoring me? She doesn't bother to respond. To my utter astonishment, they arrive at the Velvet Lilly, and completely unabashed just stroll on in. They don't even notice me across the street. They don't look around to see if people are watching before entering. They just walk in like it's a supermarket, or a dry cleaners or a pharmacy.

I'm too stunned to move. If that were me I would wait for a diversion, like a big truck to rumble by before I would actually go in the door. Just then my phone beeps.

Simmi: We are in here. We don't see you.

Me: That's because you completely ignored me. I'm across the street.

The next thing I know Simmi and Richard exit and, once again, without an ounce of embarrassment, stand on the front steps of the store entrance. They are looking all up and down the street. They both look at me several times but don't acknowledge me.

My phone beeps again.

Simmi: Are you playing some kind of trick. You are not on the street.

Me: Yes, I am!!! I'm right across from you!!

Simmi: Look... all I see is some weird Hare Krishna lady.

Me: That's me you idiot!

Simmi shows Richard the phone. They both look at me and start doubling over in laughter.

Richard yells, "Jess-er, where is your tambourine?" between bits of laughter.

Simmi chimes in, "Jessica, get over here!"

In a hurried rush, I pull my scarf tighter around my face and scurry across the street. "Shh! Stop yelling my name."

"What the fuck are you doing?" Richard snaps at me.

"I don't know. I'm embarrassed to go in here. I'm not exactly the usual rabble that goes in here."

Richard roars with laughter and comes over and places his hands on my shoulders. He pushes me slightly to face the store front. He is behind me now. He says into my ear. "Close your eyes, take a deep breath. Stand up tall. You are Jessica Reed, a woman not afraid of her sexuality. Thousands of strong, confident sexual women have come before you and have entered this store. Now it's your turn. Follow in their footsteps. You owe it to your sexual being inside to explore what you've been missing. You owe it to the man you love to satisfy him in all possible ways in all possible forms of lovemaking. Do not be afraid. Let down your hair!" He has pulled off my scarf and untwined my bun and my locks of hair fall down around my face. "You have every right to enter this shop! When you come out, you will be a changed woman!"

God he is good at this stuff!

Simmi is beaming at me and shaking her head in agreement. I enter in first. I take it all in, scanning the room. All around are things I've never seen before with signs naming them. The words enter my brain and bounce back out again as if they can't enter my vocabulary. There is no space in my brain for this stuff. There are vibrators of every shape and color. I glance to my right and see an entire section of what looks like exercise wedges for gymnastics. I look above it and, it's labeled, "Sex furniture." All at once it registers. The movie "The Fockers," that's the thing the character played by Barbara Streisand used for her sex classes. Oh My God, they're real? They are real!!! I swivel to my left and see a section of lingerie.

Richard comes behind me and says, "Take a look up. You would knock Nolan's socks off with that!" I look up and above my head suspended from the ceiling is some contraption called a fantasy swing.

"What in the world is that?"

Simmi and Richard start giggling and I can't help it, I start giggling too.

Then we abruptly are interrupted by a sudden screech! "Dr. Rich, Oh My God, Dr. Rich, is that you?"

This woman with the most unruly bob of curly blonde hair I have ever seen comes running up to us. She is very short, about 5'2, and very curvy. Her boobs are popping out of her blouse and her arms are adorned with at least 10 bracelets on each arm. Her skirt is very translucent, and you can make out her undergarments if you look too long. She smells of some kind of herbal scent.

"My name is Rosalie! Welcome to The Velvet Lilly!! This is my shop! I can't believe it's you! This is my lucky day, Dr. Rich!"

Richard is beaming at her. I can't believe this. He has been recognized in a sex shop. Richard gives her a hug and says, "Rosalie, how nice to meet you. What a wonderful service you are performing for the women of this century." Gosh, he has really rooted himself in this "Dr. Rich" stuff.

Rosalie looks as if she's won a Nobel prize. She is standing erect, and her cheeks are coloring pink. "Oh, well Dr. Rich, it's you who has turned it around. My business has gone through the roof since you were featured on prime time! I mean there is an entire following of your blog, and people come in all the time requesting items you've mentioned! I have a huge wait list for your book!" She is batting her eyelashes at him. Can she not tell he is flaming gay?

And wait a minute … Richard has a blog? Since when does he have a blog? He hasn't mentioned that! Rosalie is completely ignoring me and Simmi. In fact, I get the sense she wishes we would leave the two of them alone.

Simmi comes beside me and whispers, "I smell an exhibitionist!" And I want to giggle but stop myself by squeezing my lips together hard, which makes my nostrils flair out.

"That's fantastic!" Richard says.

"Could I trouble you with a picture?"

"Of course, of course," Richard beams!

Rosalie asks if I will snap them with her phone. She doesn't even make eye contact with me, just holds it out as if it wasn't a request but rather a demand. She adjusts her boobs before looking up for the photo.

I take a picture of the two of them. She reviews it but is not happy with it. "Actually can you take it again and try to get the store sign in the background." After about 7 shots, I finally get it right.

"Do you mind if I post this on my twitter account for the store."

"Go for it," Richard says with a raised arm and flip in his wrist.

She is still standing there staring at him.

"Ok, well if you don't mind Rosalie, we are going to take a look around."

"Yes, yes of course and a 20% discount for you, Dr. Rich!"

"So generous of you!" he hugs her again.

She walks away, and I can see her rapidly jabbing into her phone. I imagine her posting the picture on twitter and then texting all her fellow exhibitionist friends that Dr. Rich has entered her building. *"This is now sacred ground. Our Messiah, Dr. Rich!"* There will be a walking tour of where he has walked, and people will touch the same door handle as he has and refuse to wash their hands.

"Guess who's famous, bitches?!?" Richard interrupts my thoughts and smirks, and we both high five him.

We start to browse through the store, and Simmi is picking up all kinds of things and yelling, "Oh My God, Jess look at this!" I am quite enjoying myself now. This is kind of fun! Then, I catch sight of something that draws me closer.

"Oh, that's right!" Richard says noticing that something has caught my eye. "Go with your instincts."

I walk over and can't believe it. I am staring at a shelf of "Kegel beads!" I pick them up and read the package "...*Designed to strengthen your kegel muscles. Hold on to the beautifully decorated Kegel bead to strengthen…";* I read on in utter amazement.

I have to get this. I need this for pregnancy. Everything I've researched advises you to work on your kegels during pregnancy for the birthing process. This is perfect!

"Oh, good choice," Richard is saying. "That will enhance your orgasms for sure. Now you're getting into it. That's an advanced purchase. Now I would start you off with a standard vibrator, but of course I have a little gift set for you in the car of the basics."

Simmi adds, "Here, let's go to lingerie." I am clutching onto the kegel balls. At least I got something useful here. Then suddenly I stop short.

"What, have you seen something else?" Simmi is saying.

"No, it's um …"

Suddenly I have this intense feeling that has come over me. I feel something in my stomach; it's like a butterfly feeling. Come to think of it, it's the same feeling I was noticing as I was waiting across the street. It's that same nervous butterfly feeling. But I have relaxed. I don't feel nervous now?

I take a deep breath. There it is again. It's like a wiggling, a little swooshing. I can't describe it. I close my eyes and try to visualize it. It's like a fish swimming through water. Then I pop my eyes open, and it occurs to me. Oh My God. It's not butterflies. It's the baby. Oh My God. It's the baby. I feel my mouth go dry. I don't have any words. Simmi and Richard have rushed to my side. My hand is over my abdomen, and I am aware of the shock that must be written all over my face.

"Is it the baby?" Simmi says with concern.

The tears start to come down my cheeks, and I nod yes, unable to speak.

Richard exclaims, "Quick, Rosalie, call 911!"

"Get her some water!" Simmi adds. "And a chair! Oh My God... it must be the shock of it all. It's too much for her. She just can't handle this type of stuff!" Richard is nodding in agreement. Rosalie arrives with a chair and then a moment later with water.

"Is she ok?" She looks at Richard while observing me as if I'm a freak show.

"We overwhelmed the poor girl. She's pregnant you know!" Richard answers.

Finally the ability to speak comes back to me. "No, No, it's the baby! I felt the baby!"

They are all staring at me not comprehending. "You know... I felt the baby move! Inside!" I point to my belly.

Simmi and Richard sigh in relief. Simmi hugs me. "You scared the life out of me. I thought we prompted pre-term labor or something!"

A moment later we see red, white and blue lights swirling out front. The medics rush in. I feel such horrible embarrassment. I am still clutching the Kegel Beads in my hands. What these poor medics must think of me — pregnant woman in a sex shop. I can just imagine them on their radios. *"False alarm, call off the back-up. It was just another freak in a sex shop. Pregnant this time... Over and out!"* They thought it was humorous, thank God, when we explained it was all a misunderstanding, but they still checked my heart rate and blood pressure to be on the safe side. By this time the store has drawn a crowd, and more people have started to recognize Richard. In order to get the hell out of there, I purchased my kegel beads, which were the only item I really wanted, and then somehow I was convinced by both Simmi and Richard to purchase several other items.

As we exit the store, the need comes back to hurriedly remove myself from the scene. Simmi and Richard obviously do not possess the same paranoia. They are lingering in front of the store. They even have the nerve to ask me to show them the contents of my bag again. Are they serious? Right there on the street they want me to pull out the *basics bondage* set Richard insisted on. No Fucking way!

I hastily grab my scarf and wrap it around my head again and pull out my sunglasses. The two of them survey me with a look of confusion. Both of them have furrowed brows, and their heads are jutting back as if they have seen a car accident. I grab the bag and shove them towards the end of the street.

"Let's get out of here!" I say.

"Some changed woman?" Simmi says to Richard.

They both giggle at my expense.

"I'm glad you both think this is funny!"

We part ways after Richard insists I also take the gift box he prepared for me. Simmi gives me a great big hug goodbye and tells me she is so proud of me. You would think I saved an orphanage from a fire the way she looks at me. And then I walk Richard to his car. He is actually quite sweet.

"Jess-er, you know, Simmi adores you!"

I smile.

He must have picked up on my jealousy. Being friends with all psychologists can be a drag sometimes. We all constantly psychoanalyze each other.

Then he adds in jest, "And I think you're all right!" I smile at his attempt to soften me up.

"Why do you guys seem so chummy, as if I'm not included?"

"We aren't. I'm only friends with her because of you! And I guess we bonded a little over your sex make-over. That's all!"

"But I saw you walking along with lattes. If I didn't know you were gay, I would have thought you were a couple!" He bursts out in laughter.

"Jess-er, don't get all paranoid. We just ran in to each other at the same coffee shop. Coincidence!"

"Oh, OK!"

"Now take this stuff all home. Review it. Call me with any questions. And just do what feels right. Light candles! Take a long rose petal bath!"

People actually take rose petal baths?

"And just awaken your inner sex goddess! She's in there!" He looks deeply in my eyes. "I can almost see her in there!"

We hug goodbye.

As I leave Richard, the first thing that I do is take out my phone and text Nolan.

> Me: The most amazing thing happened. I can't wait to tell you!
>
> Nolan: I have a surprise for you too!
>
> Me: I miss you.
>
> Nolan: Hurry home! I miss you too!

I rush home. When I approach the warm and familiar door to our condo, I feel a rush of embarrassment. How could I have bought this ridiculous stuff? I want to throw it all out. I put my key in the door. As I try to conceal the bag behind me, I quietly begin to open the door hoping I can sneak it into the closet before Nolan will notice. Except something is not right. I can't open the door all the way. It's blocked by something.

"Nolan!" I yell in.

"Hey doll, Surprise!" I hear Nolan's voice getting closer.

He comes to the crack in the door and is all smiles.

I smile back, "What's the surprise?"

"Well, it will cost you a kiss."

"OK, let me in!"

248

"Nope! Kiss first." I feel a little zing of excitement inside as he teases me.

I lean in through the crack of the door. He is still in a tee-shirt and boxers. His face has a morning scruff on it, which I have always found completely irresistible. The door is cracked only enough for me to just graze his lips slightly with the softest of kisses. He pulls away, but I want more.

"OK, this will just take a minute."

He shuts the door, and I can hear him moving things around and scuffling on the other side of the door. I giggle in delight. What could it be?

He then opens the door and blocks my entrance with a longer more intimate kiss this time. I'm holding both hands behind my back to conceal the bag from Velvet Lilly. He wraps his arms around my waist and thrusts me forward.

"What's in the bag?" he says softly.

"Oh, don't peek, it's a … It's a Christmas present for you!"

He laughs, and then he pulls me in and points to several large boxes. "Surprise!" I quickly usher the Velvet Lilly bag into the corner and survey the boxes.

I can't make anything out. The boxes are totally non-descript!

Nolan looks at me bemused. "It's the crib and feeding chair from the safety class!"

"Oh my God!" I gasp in delight. And jump up and hug Nolan. He lifts me up, and I am suspended in air being held by him. It's all getting so real.

As he is holding me above him, I look down into his eyes. I feel my eyes fill with tears. "Nolan, I felt the baby!"

Nolan pulls away, his eyes wide with surprise. "My baby? You felt my baby? Let me feel? Let me feel!"

I giggle at how adorable he is. "I know… I wish you were there."

Nolan makes me tell him the story over and over again of how I felt the baby. Of course, I couldn't say I was in the Velvet Lilly, so I just explained that we were in a boutique store where they sell pajamas (close enough). I explain the feeling over and over again. He lays his hand on my stomach. Even though we both know he can't feel it yet, we pretend he does. It's such a beautiful moment. He lifts up my shirt and kisses my belly. Then he talks to the baby and says, "I love your Mommy so much!" He kisses my belly softly then looks up at me. We make eye contact. Then I don't know what happens next. I'm grabbing at him, and he is grabbing at me. We roll off of the couch and on to the floor. The feeling of him … the scent of him … it provides me with pure pleasure. He lifts up my skirt with urgency and he makes passionate love to me on the floor. I have the most intense orgasm! Afterwards I lay silently wrapped in his arms. I feel pure joy! I replay what happened in my mind while smiling. Then I try to imagine what it would have been like if I had taken out those sex toys. I can't help feeling it would have ruined the entire moment. More and more I am convinced those things are for couples in stale relationships. Couples that need some fetish to get them going. All I need is Nolan, and all he needs is me.

Later that evening we put together the crib and the feeding table. We take turns getting in the crib and taking pictures of each other. We set it up in the spare room where I have begun to pick out color swatches for the nursery. I can't quite choose yet because I really would prefer to know if it's a girl or a boy before I decorate. Nolan and I haven't really discussed that yet. We keep saying to each other, "it's up to you!" Regardless if we find out, we have the most important piece, the crib, where our baby will rest it's head at night. And we know it's the safest possible one, so if all that exists in this room is the crib, then I will be at ease.

TWENTY-FIVE

OK, I am wearing a pheromone spray!

Before I sprayed it, I looked up every single ingredient to see if it was contraindicated for pregnancy. Then I lit 8 massage candles and placed them strategically around the bedroom. I am actually excited about these. You drip the hot wax on each other and massage it in to your bodies. Any form of massage is supposed to benefit the pregnant woman. In fact, the research I read on this indicates it can have a direct effect on fetal health while also reducing anxiety and stress in the mother, which I could really use. And of course it will also decrease joint pain. I couldn't help myself. I also checked the wax ingredients and everything checked out ok for pregnancy. I re-made the bed with fresh sheets, and on top I put rose petals, oral pleasure gloss and the vibrator Richard included in his special "Jess-er kit!" The oral pleasure gloss was highly recommended by Richard, and according to Richard I am supposed to just leave the vibrator out for Nolan to initiate activity with. I think I will die of embarrassment at that, but I'm going all out. This is my gift to Nolan. Simmi made me buy the chocolate edible thong but with my hemorrhoid situation I just can't bring myself to wear it. So the only other thing I purchased was this panty-less green lace slip, so I maneuver myself into it, which feels a bit like wrestling a bear. Finally, I get it over my belly, and I add the leather wrist cuffs, ankle cuffs and blindfold from the bondage for beginners kit. I wrapped the leather rope from the bondage kit around my neck like in the picture. I venture a sight of myself in the mirror. I look ridiculous! First of all, I am so ridiculously pregnant now. My stomach is sticking so far out that I really have to strain to see what's under it. A pregnant belly is actually quite strange looking. My belly button has spread quite far and wide, and it no longer resembles my belly button. It looks like an alien belly button. I stare at my belly. I look so big. According to my books, I shouldn't be so big. That reminds me, I am just a few days before 19 weeks. I run to my pregnancy journal while the leather strap flaps behind me.

Week 19:

Your growing fetus is about 6 inches in length. Your baby is growing by leaps and bounds. If you palpate your abdomen you should be able to notice your uterus in your lower abdomen; it will feel like a playground ball. It's beginning to push upwards on your other organs. You may have gained about 15 lbs by now. Continue to track your weight. Also, soon you will have your sonogram. You can learn the sex of the baby if you want or keep it a surprise. During the sonogram the technician will evaluate all of the baby's developing organs – heart, kidneys, etc. And the most exciting part aside from seeing your little bundle up on the screen is the picture you will get to take home with you. Make sure your spouse can be with you for this special moment.

Gosh, I really haven't been tracking my weight. But that's nurse Marge's job anyway, isn't it? Hurriedly I rush to the scale. I haven't weighed myself since, well, since Marge did it last and that's been nearly 4 weeks. As I am about to step on the scale I think I better remove all these leather straps and bands. Now, I just have the slip on which should provide an accurate reading. I feel my heart start fluttering a bit, feeling the nerves that the scale can bring on. I remind myself of how healthy I've been. I imagine a little angelic image of myself on my right shoulder. She sits there calm as a cucumber and says, *"Jess, don't forget you have a vitamin packed fruit smoothie every day. And you eat ridiculously healthy the rest of the day. Right? Lunch and dinner is either grilled chicken and vegetables or a salad or fish (but only the kind with low mercury) and always vegetables with a side of quinoa. You have nothing to worry about!"*

I feel more confident and am about to step up on the scale, but just then I imagine a devilish me dressed in red with blazing horns growing out of the top of my head gripping a pitch fork on my left shoulder. *"But don't forget dearie, you've been having those gazillion calorie hot chocolates and sometimes you splurge on those fattening cakes too! Say, why don't we head over there right now for a yummy hot chocolate? After all you're eating for two!"*

My face sours as I think of those cakes. Dammit, those cakes! My right shoulder me, dressed in a white dress pipes up, *"Don't listen to that heifer, you keep yourself on a strict prenatal diet. And those hot chocolates are like a little reward that you have only once a week."*

That's true. I shake my head and the images of them are gone.

I look down at the scale. It's dusty. I brush it off a little with a towel. Then, I gently step on as to not startle the scale. If I'm gentle with it perhaps it will give me back a nice number. I close my eyes and place both feet on the scale. I take a deep breath in and summon the weight gods above. Then I look down. 137! But it can't be. I take a deep breath. I step off and step up again. This time I take a huge gulp of air in and hold it. Again it says 137. WTF! I step off, and this time I don't care about being gentle. I stomp both feet on top of the scale with all my might, thinking it could be a little off and needs a good stomp. You know, sort of like what Fonzie would do to the juke box. I wait as it calculates, and this time it reads back 138. "How dare you?!" I yell out loud at it. That means I've gained 22 pounds, and I am supposed to have only gained 15. How could this have happened? This is not right. I grab my list of questions for Dr. Lange. My appointment is next week. I add question 22: Why am I seven pounds over my target weight? No wonder I look so big in this panty-less lace get-up. Oh, it's no use.

I text Simmi:

> Me: I can't do this!
>
> Simmi: Yes u can Jess. Just have fun with it!! Go out for a mani-pedi and relax a bit!
>
> Me: Simmi! I'm pregnant; I can't get a mani-pedi – the fumes! Honestly as a child psychologist shouldn't u know these things?

It's Christmas Eve. Nolan left early today. After he made me a refreshing mint, strawberry, lemon zing smoothie (it was really zingy), he reviewed his itinerary for the day, something about last minute gift shopping and food he needed to pick up and something about train station and stopping at the rink and … be gone for hours. I don't know. I was so nervous about all this sex stuff that I hardly listened.

I look at my phone again and text again.

> Me: Nolan is going to laugh at me. I look like the state puff marshmallow!

Simmi: You do not.

I take a picture of myself and send it to her

Me: buy me a sticker for my ass that says *"please tell this lady if her shoes are untied… She is too fat to notice."*

Simmi: Haha, sexy mama! You look like Buddha. Go with it!

Yesterday Simmi and I had a full day. In the morning we met for coffee – she, a large mocha-double-shot-latte and me a decaf green tea infused with cinnamon. Over our coffee and tea Simmi coached me on the art of sexting and seducing. Then we went Christmas shopping, and then we stopped at the Franklin Institute. That's where she has decided to have her wedding. It's going to be incredible. I mean this will probably be the grandest event I will ever attend in my lifetime. I didn't even know they had weddings there. The reception will be in the breathtaking George Washington Memorial foyer. If you haven't been there before, it's a must see. It's an enormous open space with a huge 82 foot domed ceiling. Beneath the dome is a 20 foot national monument of George Washington positioned in the center of the room. Abby Green, the head of events, showed us the wedding event picture book. Simmi already saw it, but she insisted that her maid of honor see it too for planning purposes. Being the maid of honor sure has its perks!

Abby provided us with her vision of the wedding: "After you delight in your brand new marital status, posting a relationship change to facebook first of course, you will nosh on decadent appetizers and share champagne with your elegantly dressed guests. Then you will enter the magnificent Mendel Center for a sit-down dinner, joining the ranks of diplomats, past presidents and other lucky brides before you who have dined here."

Simmi and I beamed in delight! Because of the extended family from India, they are expecting 450 people. How can that be possible? I mean, I don't think I even know 450 people.

I close my eyes and recall the moment in hopes this will relax me. There we were standing in some secret offices above the exhibits. Abby continued, "After dancing the night away, you will enter the infamous Giant Heart Room where you will cut the cake and enjoy butler passed dessert trays, a chocolate fondue and fruit station complete with hands on barristers to conjure up made-to-order espressos, lattes, cappuccinos and specialty coffees." At that I was practically salivating. Being in the Giant Heart Room has to be the most exciting part. I can remember as a child coming to the Franklin Institute on school trips, and even with Mom and Dad. I was mesmerized with that heart. You see, this heart is an actual enormous anatomical replica of a human heart, with the four chambers and all, and you can walk through it! It's a child's playtime dream! I would run all through the right side and the left side and then back in again, over and over until I thought I would vomit. I can't believe I'm going to be noshing on dessert with a married Simmi and Vishal right there in the heart room. I will have to go through the heart, bridesmaid dress and all. Of course, morosely I have to admit to myself at 38 weeks pregnant how could I even fit in the heart? My thoughts are interrupted by my phone beeping.

Simmi: Did you try the sexting yet?

Me: Nope

Simmi: Why not?

Me: It's too … It's too revolting. I feel like a hooker.

Simmi: I bet Cassandra does sexting

Every time I tried to brush away the sexting over coffee and tea yesterday Simmi kept making Cassandra comments to remind me why I started all this is the first place! That blonde-hair busty Cassandra! Ooh! She just angers me!

Me: How dare you, Simmi?

Ok, maybe she's right. If I'm going to do this right, I guess I should try. I look at the clock. It's almost six PM. I think Nolan said he should be back around seven. OK, this calls for a little self-talk, an old psychology trick. "Jess – you can do this. Jess – be confident. Nolan will be so excited by the new sexting it will make the rest of the night go even smoother! This will get your mind off those extra pounds! Ugh! Did I have to bring up the pounds with myself? Ok, Jess, stop it! Think sexy, think sexy, let the words flow. You can do it! You can do it!"

255

I pull out my phone, take a great big huge breath and start a new text. The cursor is blinking back at me, egging me on. Oh for the love of Pete here goes:

Me: You're going to be in big trouble when you get home mister!

I'm sweating and laughing at the same time. This is nerve-racking. I feel like I'm doing something that I will get in trouble for.

Nolan: Why? What did I do now?

Me: You've been a naughty boy!

Ha, ok, so this isn't so hard. I think I have the hang of it.

Nolan: Are you talking about the blender in the sink? Leave it. I'll clean it later.

OK, never mind, this is not going so well. He has no idea that I'm trying to sext him. Maybe I'm being too subtle. Maybe I need to pull out the big guns.

Me: I want to take a ride on your carousel!

Nolan: Are you feeling all right doll? You are not making any sense!

Me: My body longs for your touch! Let's make some Monkey Love Talk!

Nolan: haha nice try. I see what's going on here. Simmi give Jess her phone back!

Are you kidding me? Am I so un-sexy that he thinks I'm incapable of sexting? And why does everyone think Simmi is such the sex goddess?

Suddenly my phone beeps again. I grab it ready to respond to Nolan, but it's Mom.

Mom: Hi sweetheart. How are you feeling? We can't wait to see you tomorrow. Merry CHRISTmas! I have a birthday cake for Jesus that I'll bring to your house.

Me: Tx Mom! Love you! Merry Christmas!

Then I fire off another text to Nolan.

> Me: It's not Simmi. Don't you know what ride your carousel means? You're not making this very easy for me.

> Nolan: Doll, I will be there soon. Just try to get some rest. Maybe your dehydrated. Get a glass of H2O.

> Mom: love you too sweetheart!

> Me: I'm not dehydrated for Christ Sake! I want to fuck your brains out! There I said it.

> Mom: Oh dear me, honey, What does that mean?

Oh God! What have I done? Shit! That went to mom? Shit! Shit! I check my phone for verification. Oh my God! It did go to her. There should be some emergency prompt when you are texting someone. If a new text comes in, you should not be able to respond to a new one. There should be some policing, like a message window that says, "you just received this text. are you sure you want to respond to this person? Are you sure you want to use the word "fuck" when texting the contact, Mom? I mean these are supposed to be super smart phones. It should say – WARNING – WARNING – you are about to sext your Mom.

I am totally unsure how to address this. I think for a moment and come up with something. I don't think it will work, but I am completely desperate so, I try it anyway.

> ME: Not sure what you mean mom? My phone has been on the fritz. People have been telling me they are getting strange texts from me but I'm not writing them. The phone service said my phone could be crossed with someone else's. I'm getting it checked out after Christmas.

OK, I know that's not the truth but I can't let Mom think I'm sexting my husband. She'll be in therapy over it! And besides I don't look at it as lying. In psychology sometimes it is important to create a scenario that will protect the interested parties from psychological damage. And besides

257

when I did it, I made an immediate sign of the cross and asked for forgiveness. So hopefully it cancels itself out.

My phone beeps again.

> Mom: Well you could have it crossed with a jail inmate, dear. Horrible language coming from that phone. I have to get my rosary now and say a prayer for whoever wrote that.

She bought it! Yes!

Now that I'm mortified, I decide I can't sext anymore. It's too dangerous. Instead I decide to give a real touch of Jess to this evening. I decide to make a love-making CD. I choose some great songs, but I can't also help to feel it is completely cheesy. This isn't my normal CD creation. Well for starters I go with *"Let's Get it on"* by Marvin Gaye–that one's a must, right? I also throw in *"After We Make Love"* by Whitney Houston (RIP), *"I Will"* by the Beatles, and *"Nice and Slow"* by Usher. I check myself in the mirror one more time and re-attach the leather cuffs and rope. I cringe at the site of myself. I prime the CD and grab the remote so I can push play when Nolan walks in. I position myself seductively on the bed. As seductively as a pregnant woman can that is. And I wait. And wait. And wait. It's a little after seven. He should be getting here any minute. Just as I hear some commotion out in the hallway I have to pee. Crap! I jump up and pee quickly, wash up and then dart back to the bed. I hear the door opening. I quickly push start on the CD. Marvin Gaye is whaling away. I cross my legs one way, then the other. I try to find a good position for my arm and decide I should drape it over my forehead like you see on those romantic book covers.

"Jess?" I can hear Nolan's muted voice. He's saying something else, but I can't make it out. The music is too loud.

I try to turn the volume down, while I say, "I'm in here!" with my best sexy voice.

He must not hear me because I can here, "Jess, come out!"

"No, you come in," I'm saying now, again lustily.

"Jess, what in the world?"

Oh, forget the sexy talk. "Nolan, get in here!" I scream.

Finally he rushes in. "Jess, what's wrong—"

He pauses. He stares at me for a good 30 seconds with his eyes completely round like frisbees. I can hear other voices.

"Who the hell is that?" Quickly, I roll off the bed to the right to hide behind it.

"Who the hell is out there?" I whisper in shock!

"Jess, what on earth is going on?" He picks up the oral pleasure gloss and reads it. He smirks and starts to laugh!

He has ignored my question. I peak up from the bed. "Nolan," I grit through my teeth, "Who is in the living room?"

Then I hear it. That voice. It's unmistakable. "Oh, Jessica dear we have your pajamas out here."

Oh my God, it's his Mother!

"There awesome pajamas!" Rosanne adds! "Of course, I think mine are the best, but yours are ok too!" Rosanne is here too?

I screw my face up into half shock and half wince with a touch of fury!

Nolan is giggling. He calls out to the living room, "Uh, guys, Jess just needs a minute. She's not feeling well. Remember I thought she was dehydrated." Nolan closes the door behind him. He surveys the bed, the rose petals, and the vibrator. He looks at me and looks back at the vibrator.

"Doll, is that a—"

"Just stop Nolan." I lurch up and pull everything on the floor with me. I feel tears pricking behind my eyes. What a nightmare.

"Why didn't you tell me your family was coming?"

259

Nolan looks at me surprised. "Doll, you said you didn't want to go to mom and dad's this year. For them to come here! This was your idea!"

"No it wasn't!" I scowl back at him. "I meant a different day. Like after Christmas!"

"OK, well. You weren't specific. I just thought you didn't want to travel."

He comes over to the other side of the bed. He's looking at me intently, his eyes twinkling and his mouth turned up in half a smile. I can tell he is trying not to laugh.

"Jess, what is all this? And do you mind if I turn Marvin off?"

I stand up and stomp over to the CD player while the leather strap around my neck flaps behind me. I reach the CD player and hit stop. I turn around and cross my arms tightly in front of my chest. I can see Nolan looking at me up and down.

"I didn't notice at first … is that a … what is … Jess what's around your neck?"

"It's a …," I look down at myself and survey that part of me that I can see. I must look like the un-sexiest creature alive!

I begin again, "This was all just a mistake! Just leave me alone."

I turn to go into the bathroom to cry alone, but he stops me. He is standing behind me, and he places his hands around me hips. I'm still pulling away, and it's as if we are playing tug of war. He pulls me towards him, and I try to take a step away. I start to cry, as I step harder away, and he pulls back again saying, "I'm not letting you go. We can do this all night!" My tears quickly turn into laughter. Nolan gives one final hard pull, and we both fall to the floor in a thump. He is laughing, and I am laughing. Then he hugs me tight.

"Jessica Reed. What are you up too with all this stuff?"

I turn to him. I'm so embarrassed now I can't look him in the eye. I gaze at his chest and quietly say, "Merry Christmas. This was my gift to you!"

He laughs loudly again and says, "Wow, some gift! I can't wait to try it out. But Jess, this stuff–he picks up the vibrator and looks at it with a smirk–this stuff isn't you. What's going on here?"

I feel so many emotions welling up inside, then before I realize it the words just burst out before I can stop them. "I heard you talking at your poker night. You said someone was amazing and always right, and I thought you were talking about me, so I started to listen. Then I realized from the conversation that you weren't talking about me at all. You were talking about another woman, Cassandra." A new hurt seems to rise inside me, and I need to catch my breath. "Nolan, do you … Do you have a thing for that girl you work with?"

Nolan laughs out loud again. "Oh, Jess, you can get yourself so worked up. Of course not!! We just work together. And when I was talking, it was about the football pool. She is 9-0. We don't know how she does it. She's going to win the entire pot. Here we are a bunch of sports crazy professionals in the sports world, mostly guys, and she comes in from California and is going to scoop up the big win. There is $2,000 dollars at stake."

"You were talking about a football pool? That's it?"

"Yes, doll, that's it! I love you! Always have and always will."

But I heard someone say, "She's hot." And you grunted in agreement.

He roars with laughter again. "Jess, now your judging my grunts? I'm not the one that said that!"

"No, but you grunted in the affirmative."

"Jess, that's just the way guys are. They were talking about someone who likes her. I wasn't going to be rude. If you really want to know, I think she's a bit tawdry."

261

"Tawdry?"

"Yeah, she's great and all. Really smart and great with the patients, but she's got tattoos everywhere and that California look – bleach blonde hair. Doll, that's not my kind of taste. You should know that!" He pulls me closer. I feel such a sense of relief. If I had only asked him about it at first, I could have avoided this entire nightmare. I lean in and put my head on his chest, feeling his warmth and hearing his heartbeat. He pulls my chin up to his, and I feel his mouth on mine.

There's a knock on the door. "Is everything ok in there? We are getting worried out here!"

I pull away and smile lovingly at Nolan. We gaze around at all the paraphernalia and have a fit of hysterics. "Well, I'll put this stuff away for later. How about you get me these matching pajamas I'm supposed to put on."

Nolan helps me up and walks over to the door. He turns back and whispers. "I like my present though. Don't put it away where we can't find it!"

Next thing I know I'm trying to squeeze into a footy pajama that says "Santa's little helper inside!" But no matter how hard I try. How hard I wiggle, I can't get it over my belly. I try until I'm sweating and my belly is bright red from irritation, trying to get it to fit.

I exit into the living room in sweatpants and a tee-shirt. "Sorry guys, I rub my belly fondly. Santa's little helper is too big to fit into these."

"Come over here doll!" Nolan is lovingly waving me over to the loveseat.

"How can it not fit? It's a large!" Rosanne is saying to their mother.

Nolan's Mom whispers, "She must be really eating for two, if you know what I mean."

I can't believe the two of them. I can hear everything they are saying. I really think they pretend to live in an alternate universe where they can speak in code and no one else will understand them.

Nolan's Dad comes in from the kitchen. "Jess, dear, you are looking just radiant. Merry Christmas!" He hands me a gift. We sit there for hours, Rosanne in her, "Best Aunt in the world" pajamas and Nolan's Mom in her "Best Grandmom in the world" pajamas. They squeal in delight over all their gifts. When we get around to me I have to put on fake smiles complete with "oohs" and "aahs" to indicate I like a pie maker and a cupcake carrier. And Nolan's mom is overly excited when I open her bucket of kitchen cleaning items. As I open them she says, "Now that you are a mother you will see how much cleaning there is!"

I can't believe this. I'm pregnant, and suddenly they see me as Betty Crocker and Mr. Clean rolled up into one. Last year they gave me leather knee high boots and a beautiful purple scarf. In one year I've gone from trendy evening wear to domestic staples. What a load of crap! Finally the night comes to an end when Rosanne announces that she must get back to meet her girls out for Christmas Eve cocktails. She is going to change into her sassy elf costume she is saying, but I'm too tired even to diagnose her obvious affectedness.

After they leave and it's just Nolan and me, he dims the lights and says, "I have one more present for you, doll!"

I smile at him with warm affection.

"It's up to you. I thought we would do more presents tomorrow, but this one is really special. What do you think?"

"Well, I'm not sure you could top the cleaning supplies but, why not, hand it over."

To my surprise it's not a wrapped gift. It's a simple envelope. I look at him wondering, what on the world could this be. I open it slowly and pull out a gift certificate of some kind. I stare at it. It has a picture of a baby on it and it reads:

Ten Fingers, Ten toes,

But, what you are nobody knows!

Here is your gift certificate for your

263

Gender reveal ultrasound party.

You pick the date and our team at *Pink or Blue Reveal* will do the rest.

I'm staring at it, reading it over and over again. It takes me several minutes to take this all in. A gender reveal party? Does it include an ultrasound? How cool is that?

"Jess, say something! I know we didn't talk about this, but this really cool sonogram seminar was going on at CHOP. I attended, and anyway they mentioned these. I went up after and … we don't have to use it, but I just thought—"

He is babbling so I just lean over and kiss him gently. Then I meet his eyes. "Nolan, it's the most perfect gift! The most thoughtful, the most unique, the most … It's just … I love it! Thank you!"

"You really like it?"

"Is the new pope Argentinian?" I reply!

We hug for a long time, while he explains that we can invite all our close friends and family and the team. *Pink or Blue Reveal* will set up two big monitors, and everyone can watch the baby on the screens. Then they will reveal the gender, per our instructions to everyone, however we want. It just sounds so fun and exciting. I didn't even know you could do something like that.

We are silent, and I just hold onto the certificate. I stare at it, amazed at Nolan.

"Hey," Nolan begins, "I have to disagree with you on something. My gift is not the best gift." He gives a devilish grin. "Yours is pretty awesome. Can I open it again?"

I smirk back at him. He pulls me up from my lounging position and leads me into the bedroom.

Then we both are startled by the sound of "eeeeeehhhhh-eeeeeehhhh."
My phone alarm goes off for prenatal yoga, but I hit ignore!

TWENTY-SIX

If it's a girl, I'm going to rush right out and buy tons of those
adorable little dresses I've been seeing everywhere. My favorite colors are
green and purple, so of course those will be her favorite colors too. We'll
be best friends like Lorilei and Rory from the Gilmore Girls! And if it's a
boy, then I have to go buy a bunch of sports sets in honor of Nolan,
especially hockey, because our boy will love hockey like his Dad. I can't
believe tonight I will find out if I'm the new Mom to a daughter or a son.
This is such an incredible feeling. I am just buzzing through the day at
work. It seems like all my patients are exactly where I want them to be. I
mean, not a single patient hasn't made a milestone somehow! I just feel
light on my feet, as light as you can be when you are seven pounds over
your target weight, ok well make that ten. Anyhow, I'm not going to let
that get me down. My appointment with Dr. Lange is in two days. I
decided I couldn't wait for the reveal party. When I called "Pink and Blue
Reveal," they said this was a perfect time as I would just be turning 20
weeks, and I could have it any day that there was an opening. They said I
didn't need to wait until my next OB/GYN appointment. So, I picked the
next available date, which happens to be tonight, just two days before my
next OB/GYN appointment. Which I actually think is better anyway. I
mean surely the ultrasound will evoke more questions. This way I go into
Dr. Lange as an informed patient. And, personally, I feel an informed
patient is better than an un-informed one.

It was totally last minute, but everyone can make it to the big reveal …
Mom, Dad, Nolan's family, Simmi, Vishal, and some of Nolan's friends
from Hockey. Naturally, Richard will be there too, and he is even bringing
his Mom. I invited Polly Huxley too. I know she loves unique events.
She's a maybe. We are setting it up with all pink and blue colors, which is
surprisingly easy to do. We are going to have fancy hors d'oeuvres with
pink raspberry drinks and blue blueberry slushies'. I even found pink and
blue M&M's. Simmi is coming over early to help me make the "reveal"
cakes. What's a reveal cake, you ask? That's exactly what I was wondering,

but once I heard about it, well, it's simply genius. So we are making two cakes. One will be pink inside with white icing and the other will be blue inside with white icing. So, you get the picture. Outside the cakes will look exactly the same, but on the inside the color of the cake will reveal the sex of the baby! Don't you love it? Then tonight the ultrasound technician will take Nolan and I aside and tell us the news. After we have our private moment of bliss, we will bring out the appropriate cake to our family and friends. We will tell them it's a reveal cake, and we will hand a cake knife to my Mom and one to Nolan's Mom. They will both cut into the cake on the count of three and reveal to the entire party if it's a boy or girl. I mean is that super fun or what? I am actually quite fascinated by it all. I mean the psychology behind it is extraordinary. Think about it. The couple still is allowed their private moment. Then the jubilance is elevated by making it a happy party event. The sonogram is done safely in your home for all to see. There are no pregnant cranky women waiting in a waiting room to get in there next. You can take your time. Relax. Enjoy it! Spend some quality time with your baby up close. Then the revealing allows you to tell all those you care about the big news all at once. You don't have to deal with hurt feelings of who found out second or third or even last. Your friend isn't going to read it on facebook before you have a chance to tell her. You have the opportunity to see the excitement on their faces, too. It will bring the best out in everyone, and everyone will really feel a part of the baby's life. I mean from a psychology standpoint, I would call this a positive milestone trigger point. This single event could initiate many wonderful interpersonal affects. This is our rock in a pond. We will create the most wonderful ripple effect.

I can hear my phone in my purse, "eeeeeehhhhh-eeeeeehhhh." That has to be my kegel reminder. Quickly I do 10 elevator kegels. I don't mean to brag, but I'm getting quite good at these. I bet I have an easy birth because of all these kegels. Just in time I finish as my assistant calls out.

"Dr. Reed, Your 4 o'clock is here."

"Send him in, please!" I reply.

In comes Simon Dirk. "Mr. Dirk, Lovely to see you. How were the holidays?"

Mr. Dirk regards me with a smile. Then his nose begins to twitch uncontrollably. The first time he did this I said, "Gesundheit!" thinking a sneeze was eminent, but then he quickly informed me it was just one of his ticks. This is my Tourette's patient. He is a lovely man and enjoys talking about his grandchildren. He said he never realized he had Tourette's before, until his wife forced him to the doctor. Apparently, as their 34 years of marriage has gone on, his ticks have became worse until finally he agreed to go to a neurologist where he received his diagnosis. On his first visit with me, his wife Ethel attended our session. I can remember her account of his issues.

"Dr. Reed," she said, "It's God-awful. The nose thing I don't even notice and the grunts and noises he makes is no big deal either. But when we are driving his nerves are so bad, he starts rubbing his head and rocking forward and clearing his throat. It's gotten so bad the entire car shakes when he drives. I feel like he's doing the funky chicken behind the wheel."

As a professional, I know Tourette's is a neurological condition, so I can rationalize this. His anxieties are obviously increased in the car while driving. They were able to confirm that the symptoms worsen in heavy traffic. But Ethel seems to think he can correct this willingly. I explained to her that due to the underlying condition being neurological in nature, the best we can do is work on some relaxation techniques that may calm the anxieties that increase his Tourette's symptoms. Ethel cold not grasp that her husband suffers from a legitimate anatomical issue, something that can't be fixed with increased will power. This is very common. Many loved ones of an affected patient can't accept anatomical issues with the brain. But if I told Ethel it was his heart, his liver, his bones, his kidneys, anything other than the brain she would accept it at face value. But if you diagnose the issue as brain related, people automatically think you can just fix it on your own. Last time we met, I gave Mr. Dirk several calming and self-talk exercises to try. I also instructed him to allow other people to drive him places to see if that changed his threshold for symptoms. I made him a relaxation CD that I will give him today. I really hope this helps Mr. Dirk because I can tell he wants to get better for Ethel. I know he feels badly that this upsets her so much. So, I insisted we have private sessions to also work out the anxiety or guilt he harbors for upsetting Ethel, whom he loves very much. Ethel wasn't too keen on it, but I told her if she really wanted us to make progress I felt this was necessary.

"So, Mr. Dirk, tell me how your week has gone? Did you let others drive you?"

"Yes, Doc, yes I did!" He is bright-eyed, so I begin to assume the outcome must have been positive.

Then before I have a chance to comment he bursts out in laughter. He makes some audible lurching noises with several inward breaths; it comes from deep in his throat and he says, "Doc, it was an absolute nightmare!"

"Oh no, why?"

"Well, first I let Ethel drive. Well, what a crisis that was! We've been married 34 years, and I never realized what a bad driver she was. I mean she is awful. My nerves were even worse. We only lasted about eight minutes before I had to switch to the driver's seat to get us home."

"OK, well what about one of your sons—"

Before I can finish, he begins with the audible ticks again and says, "Tried that doc. It's no use. I'm the worst back-seat driver. My sons drove me crazy with the one arm over the wheel and the underhand technique on the turns. My other son keeps his hands on the lowest part of the wheel. In my day you never took your hands off of 10-and-2. For Christ's sake, it's 10-and-2. I taught them that. How can they not remember? And they have THAT music on." He starts shaking his head, and his face wrenches up into fits of muscle spasms. "That music they listen to. It's lunacy! I have to have the news on when I drive. I just have to."

"OK, well no harm done." I break him off as he's breathing hard. "That was one path to explore, and now we know that's not an option. But let me ask you a few questions."

"Shoot," he says.

"OK, I presume that Ethel and your sons must drive themselves places safely. Is that correct?"

"Well, I suppose, so," He answers dutifully.

"OK, and we know we need to get you in a calm state, right?"

"If that's what you say Doc."

"Well, what if you tried something else? I've made you a relaxation CD. It has some very selected songs from your era that you will recognize. It also blends in some classical music which should be soothing to you. I want you to listen to it each morning and night. As soon as you wake up and before you go to bed and practice the relaxation breathing we went over last week. Can you do that?"

"Sure, Doc!"

"Ok, then once you are familiar with it, I would like you to let your wife drive again—"

He interrupts, "Not gonna happen Doc. I mean she's awful."

"Mr. Dirk, please let me finish."

He lurches with an audible noise and adds, "I'm so sorry Doc."

"Not at all, don't be sorry. I just want you to hear me out." I smile at him and continue, "Sit in the back of the car this time. Get a portable CD player with earphones and listen to this CD. You could even put it on an ipod if you have one of those. Then try your best to block out who is driving and just close your eyes. Listen to the music and do the breathing techniques. Be present in the moment and don't allow thoughts of who is driving to enter your head. If they do, just try to ignore them. Do you think you can try that?"

"I guess we can try it. But I dunno, Doc."

"Ok, well give it your best shot."

We continue to try to figure out what other stress points could increase his symptoms. We come up with a few, like when his printer doesn't print or when his son doesn't hang up his coat when he enters the house or when his wife's friends come to the house to visit. That one made me laugh a bit.

The thing with these, albeit normal stress points, is that for him it becomes one building block in that day, growing and growing until the blocks tumble and the ticks emerge in full force. So we have to divert his attention from these stress points with relaxation techniques.

Mr. Dirk heads out, and I wish him luck. He notices my growing belly and says, "You too, doc. Is it any day now?"

His question takes me by surprise. "No, Mr. Dirk, actually I'm only half way there."

"Oh, my. There I go putting my foot in my mouth again." His nose starts to twitch and then there is an audible lurching, "I just meant, I mean you look wonderful of course. It's just that when Ethel was big like that it was towards the end, but you know she had small babies." He smiles and draws in several breaths making more audible noises.

I place my hand on his shoulder to reassure him. "Please, Mr. Dirk. it's quite all right." I whisper, "I am a little bigger than normal." We both give a little chuckle and I continue, "And thanks for the compliment. Do give my best to Ethel!"

After I return to my office, I wrap up my final paper work and practically run home. Nolan has beaten me home and is already busy with the hors d'oeuvres.

"There she is! My beautiful bride!"

We rush to hug each other. "I'm so excited, Nolan. I can't believe it!"

We spend several minutes guessing boy or girl, and then we both change our minds about three times each. This is so exciting!

Nolan warms my heart as he talks with fondness how a boy will be his little buddy at the rink and if a daughter is in store, how she will be his little princess.

I change into a more comfortable hostess outfit, black tights and my beautiful, yet comfy green and black maternity dress that makes my belly look smaller than it actually is (an on-line purchase of course). I throw on an apron and start making cakes. At the thought of baking, I eye that 4 miniature pie maker from Nolan's parents sitting above the cabinet, half wanting to wheel it into the trash can. But just then my spirits are lifted as Simmi arrives.

"Ok, Big Mama, here is your food coloring."

Simmi has taken to calling me "Big Mama." For some reason when she says it, I find it cute. But God forbid if anyone else should venture to say that to me! Even Richard asked me how Simmi gets away with that. And I tell him—at least she has stopped calling me psycho-mommy.

"Oh Simmi, you are too kitschy! Just wait until you're pregnant!"

"Won't be happening for some time girlfriend. I don't want to be anybody's baby mama just yet!"

Simmi enters the kitchen and opens a brown bag. I stick my hand out to receive the food coloring, but Simmi pulls out a bottle of red wine instead.

"Simmi?" I say incredulously.

"What, this is a party, isn't it?"

"It's a reveal party, not a booze-fest."

"Trust me, Big Mama, people will want a drink!"

"I got beer in the fridge," yells in Nolan.

"Beer? I thought we were having pink raspberry juice drinks and blue blueberry slushies?"

"We are doll, but you can't expect me to offer that to Mike and Chuck!" he laughs as if it's absurd.

I grumble under my breath.

"What's that Big Mama?" Simmi nudges me.

"I'm just ... Nothing ... nevermind."

So about 1 hour later, 2 glasses of wine for Simmi and at least 2 times mopping the kitchen floor, we have our cakes ready to go. I have to resist the urge to eat them as the freshly baked smell wafts before me. *"Pink and Blue Reveal"* have just arrived, and they are setting up the monitors. I feel almost like it's my wedding day. I'm the guest of honor again, how fun! And we are waiting for the guests to arrive. The anticipation for that "it" moment is looming above me wherever I go like a bright rainbow. And I can hardly believe this pregnancy journey is half way over. I went from completely thinking there was no way I could be pregnant to accepting the wonderful surprise that this family would now grow from 2 to 3. Nolan and I have grown so close throughout this time. I love him more now than that day on the beaches of Nevis when we first married.

Feeling slightly woozy, I take a seat by the front door and reflect. I suffered through morning sickness and came out the other side healthy and happy. I turned the fiasco with Richard into a win-win, and now he's one of my very closest friends. I've got down pat my pre-natal care —with my state-of-the-art alarm system— well ok it's just my phone, but it makes me feel high tech. I always know what I need to do. Prenatal vitamin, check! Prenatal yoga, check! 10,000 steps logged weekly on my prenatal pedometer, check! Daily fruit and protein shake, check! Healthy diet, check! Hold breath near smokers, check! No hair dying and no mani-pedis, check! No fish with mercury, check! No peanuts, check! No alcohol, check (well just that one s'mores martini early on)! Research on pregnancy, breastfeeding and the birthing process, check! Safest Crib and feeding chair known to man, check! Daily kegels, check! Cleaning supplies and all other death trap devices moved safely to storage, check! As I think of it all, I really am impressed. I finally feel calm, confident and relaxed. Now I can just enjoy the night and the rest of my pregnancy. There is nothing I'm not prepared for. I am a pregnancy goddess. I am psycho-mommy no more. I am such an expert on what to eat and drink that sometimes I don't even enter it into my pregnancy app anymore. That's right! Look at me ... I've grown!

Just then my thoughts are interrupted by Simmi!

"Shit, shit, Jess?"

Uh oh, she's not calling me Big Mama. This must be serious.

"What, what is it Simmi?"
"The cakes!"

I rush into the kitchen and look at the counter. The cakes look perfectly fine.

Well, remember you asked me to put a blue M&M on the blue cake and a pink M&M on the pink cake just so you would know which one to bring out for the reveal?"

"Yes!"

"Well, I went to open another bottle of wine. Nolan was making room on the counter and shifted the cakes around. Now I'm not sure which one is which!"

"SIMMI!" I exclaim and then I make a noise in my throat quite like Mr. Dirk, which surprises me. "I'm going to kill you! How hard is it to put a damn M&M on the cake?"

"I know, I know, I'm sorry," she's saying while she provides a lugubrious face complete with a frown.

And of course I can't stay mad. "Well, we'll just have to poke at it or something. And then slap some more icing on it. We'll worry about it later," I say resolute.

I check with the technicians, and they are nearly ready to go.

"Would you like a sneak peak before everyone gets here?"

I'm pleasantly surprised, "Can we do that?"

"Sure we can!" I can't hold back the excitement. "Nolan, Nolan, get in here!"

Nolan rushes in, "What's wrong?"

"We can do a sneak peek ultrasound now before everyone gets here."

Nolan looks as excited as I am. "Well, just give me five minutes. I have to get the asparagus wraps out of the oven and brush them with egg white."

"Ok, well, we will get Jessica all ready."

I hop up on their portable table and they turn on the buzzing machine. We are waiting for Nolan when the bell rings. Shit! "Simmi, can you get that?"
There is no answer from Simmi.

"Simmi?"

Where the hell is she now?

"Oh, I guess we'll have to wait. I have to get that, excuse me."

I go to the door, and to my surprise it's Polly.

"Polly, you made it?"
"Of course, love, you don't think I would miss a big reveal party. I'm loving these reveal things. They are all the rage." She's peering around our condo. "So this is where the famous Jessica Reed comes up with all her ideas."

I smirk at her. "Come in and let me get you a drink." In the background my reveal party CD is playing. All the songs have baby in it, of course. I made copies for each guest, and they are sitting by the doorway. Polly picks one up and studies it. "You clever, girl! I love this. Can I have one?"
"Of course," I say brightly. "Everyone gets to take one home."

Simmi finally appears. "Yeah, watch out though because those CD's are probably Big Mama's secret therapy CD's with subliminal messages in them."

"And over here in this vase you can enter your guess for the baby's sex." I completely ignore Simmi's little ping of humor.

"What does Simmi mean, therapy CD's?"

"Oh, you know, I incorporate music therapy into my patient's therapy."

275

"Really? That's genius stuff." I can see Polly's wheels turning, so I try to break away.

"Um, excuse me Polly … I'm going to check on that drink of yours."

The doorbell rings again, and it's Mom and Dad. "Darling!" Mom exclaims! "Hi Honey!" Dad pecks my cheek. "What a great little idea," Mom says. "We were telling everyone at the shop, and they thought it was really amazing!"

Nolan greets them from the kitchen, "There's the VP, and look at you Emilia, as beautiful as ever!"

Things are really getting cozy. More of our family and friends arrive and the big moment is approaching.

Richard's Mom is absolutely glowing. She is so happy to be at a party. She comes right over to me and holds my hand. It's frail and slightly cold. "I'm so excited for you dear!" she beams at me. Whenever I am near her, I feel calm and a true sense of what life is all about.

"Geez, Mom, you'd think I never take you out." Richard is joking.

Rosanne busts in and demands to have the seat right in front of the larger monitor. She puts her stuff all down on the chair and the chair next to it to save it for Barb. I hope the technician accidently squirts her with gel. When Nolan's mom arrives, I hear her say to Rosanne, "So will we have a baby Noelle or a baby Nolan?"

She better drop this Noelle crap. I'm not naming my baby Noelle just because it's Nolan's Godmother's name!

Just then, Anna from *Pink and Blue Reveal* approaches me, "Are we ready to get started Jessica?"

I look around and see that everyone is here, and they are all mingling. "I think we are. Let me find Nolan."

"Ok, then." Anna says, "We will boot up the machine."

This is it. This is when we will finally know how to decorate the nursery. I find Nolan who is in the kitchen with Mike and Chuck. "Nolan," I beam at him, "It's time," I say. He looks like a little boy on Christmas. He doesn't hide his excitement or try to be cool in front of his friends, which I have always loved about him. He grabs my hand. "All right, doll, let's do this!"

Nolan gets to the middle of the living room by the ultrasound machine. He holds up a glass and dings it several times. "Ladies and Gentleman. The moment you all have been waiting for. If you gather around the monitors, we are about to have a peak at what's been cooking in the oven."

There are hushed gasps of excitement all around the room. Rosanne rushes over, "That's my seat in the front."

Everyone gathers around. I can't think of a better way to share this news. I look from face to face, smiling at each person. They each smile or nod back to me as if they are with me in this journey. I step up onto the portable table once more. Before I lie back I tell the group how this will work, that Nolan and I will have a private reveal after the ultrasound and then we will bring out the cake. Everyone whispers to each other in excitement. I hear Rosanne say, "Is the cake gluten free?"

And then before I know it Anna is putting the gel on my belly and then within seconds there on the screen is what looks like a head. There are gasps around the room again. "Is that a penis?" I hear Richard say. Everyone erupts in laughter. Nolan is squeezing my hand, and everyone is craning their necks to get a better view. Anna plays the heartbeat for us. It's such a beautiful sound. Then abruptly she turns it off. I look at her and see a look of alarm.

"What is it?" I immediately know something's not right. Nobody else seems to notice. They are all busy joking about the images.

Anna leans in and says "Oh, um just a little something ... well ... it's um unexpected here. Mr. and Mrs. Reed can I see you alone?" I look at Nolan and feel I'm about to cry. Oh my Lord above, I silently say about ten prayers as I hobble off of the table, and we walk back to our bedroom.

As we shut the door, I look at Anna. "Tell me, what is it, what?"

"Well, um the heartbeat and the scanning appear to …"

She stops. "Appear to what? What?" I demand.

I feel like my legs are going to give out.

"I think you should both have a seat."

I start to cry. Nolan helps me sit on the bed, and he hugs me tight. "Just tell us Anna!" Nolan says.

"Mr. and Mrs. Reed, it appears there are two babies."

"What—?" Nolan and I respond in unison.

"Did your doctor ever indicate that you had multiples?"

"No, no she didn't. Oh my God! Are you saying we are having twins?"

"Yes, congratulations!"

"Doll, two at once. You're an overachiever at growing babies, too!" Nolan looks pleased as punch. His reaction is quite different from mine.

I open my mouth a few times, but no words come out. Two babies? Twins? I don't know anything about twins? I didn't do any research about twins! We only bought one super safe crib! We only bought one super-safe feeding table! We don't have enough room in this condo for two babies. We don't have enough car seats. No wonder I'm over my target weight. Oh My God! Oh My God! I start hyperventilating.

Nolan looks at me with alarm.

"Mrs. Reed … are you all right?" Anna is saying. Nolan rushes out and brings me a glass of water. As the door remains ajar I hear our guests talking to Nolan …

"What's going on in there?"

"Don't keep us waiting………………"

"We are dying out here………………"

278

He comes back in. I sip some water. I take deep breaths.

"Doll, say something!" Nolan kneels down in front of me.

Finally at last I blurt out, "We are going to have to get a minivan!"

Nolan roars with laughter. "OK! Is that all?"

"Nolan, I don't know anything about multiples. I'm in shock. I mean how do you even breastfeed two babies at once? That seems physically impossible."

"Ok doll, but 4 months ago we didn't know anything about babies—period—and now look at us. We can do this together. I know it will be tough, but you are amazing. And with me by your side, I know I'm mediocre at best," he says with a smirk and I giggle, "but we can do this!"

I have tiny tears dripping down my face. But I do feel happy. I do, it's just. TWINS? But, Nolan is right. Now that the shock is wearing off, I am getting excited and we can do anything together.

"Well, Anna should we go back out so you can figure out the sex of the babies."

"Actually, I did that already. Would you like to know?"

Several minutes later, Nolan, Anna and I all emerge from the bedroom and enter the living room. All our guests are staring at us with the greatest anticipation. Nolan and I are holding hands and grinning ear to ear. Wait until we let this cat out of the bag. We both go into the kitchen and pick up the cakes and bring them to the dining room table. I remind everyone by saying, "Now these are our reveal cakes. We would like our Moms to step up." I look over at my Mom, "Mom, here is your cake knife."

Nolan looks at his mom, "Mom, here is your cake knife," he follows. They both come to the table with the knives. Everyone is silent. I whisper in their ears what to do. Then I say, "Everyone count to three!"

"Hold on, Big Mama, remember about that crazy girl who forgot the M&Ms?" Simmi is shouting.

"It's ok, Simmi we figured it out! Ok everyone count to three!"

Everyone chimes in, "1, 2, 3!" On 3 they each cut into a cake. Simmi yells from the back, "No what are you doing. You are only supposed to cut one." Everyone looks confused.

Richard says, "Big Mama has lost her mind!"

Rosanne says, "What the hell, one cake is blue and one cake is pink?"

Nolan and I just lean on each other as mass confusion ensues. People are peering at us, and we are just enjoying it. Finally, Mrs. Amado, Richard's mom speaks. "Everyone, everyone. I understand what this is." Everyone shuts-up and turns toward her. It even seems like there is a luminescent glow around her as if she is the all-knowing-high priestess. Then with confidence she simply says, "Jessica and Nolan are having twins: A boy AND a girl. That's why they had their dear mother's cut both cakes!"

People gasp. They look from Mrs. Amado to me and Nolan and back again. I hear Barb mutter to Rosanne, "Oh, she will have to quit her job now!"

Richard exclaims, "Mom, you are like Yoda!"

My Mom holds my hand. "Honey is it true? Twins?"

I nod in agreement and Nolan picks me up and twirls me around. Everyone is screaming and laughing!

We are having twins! One boy and one girl! I get to have my tea parties every June and my super hero parties too! We have the most joyous evening.

When everyone leaves, I let the news really sink in. I stay up late and make a list. My list of questions for Dr. Lange now is 57 questions long. I plan to have a full weekend back at PENN library for research, and I have to really increase my calorie intake. I am worried about so much. Just when I thought I could relax. There are so many unknowns. Could they be at increased risk for any complications? How does the birthing process go with twins? What if I can't carry them full-term? OMG! – Will I get to be on bed rest? How is fetal development impacted? How much weight will I gain? Can we order another super safe crib and feeding table in time? Not only that, should we move to a bigger place? How much are minivan's anyway? Will my boobs triple in size? And, really, how do you breastfeed twins, anyway? What is the psychology of raising twins? I need to research. I need to consult with Simmi. Holy Cow! Psycho-Mommy is back, but back twice as much!

ACKNOWLEDGMENTS

I am eternally grateful to my first critic and Editor, Vince, who encouraged me, yet also provided the most critical comments to shape the book. Thank you to Barbara, without whom many a comma would have gone misplaced. Big thanks to my third reader and dear friend, Danielle, for pointing out my punctuation obsessions, and for being so supportive. Great gratitude goes to my talented friend, Shirl, for her creative design of the book cover and website (I may be biased but I think it's INCREDIBLE). To my gorgeous children who inspire me every day, not only as a creative writer, but as a mother, a woman, and a human being. To my family and especially my mother, who provided me much creative exploration as a child; I believe this allowed my creative writing to continue to blossom. Finally to every single person who is a fan of this book – THANK YOU! I hope you enjoyed it as much as I enjoyed writing it! To all mothers: Motherhood is a blessing and a challenge. You can do it … embrace your inner psycho-mommy!

ABOUT THE AUTHOR

MIRA HARLON has worked for over 15 years in the healthcare industry, specializing in the neurosciences. Her career has focused on diseases of the brain and on related treatments and drug discovery. She holds an undergraduate and doctorate degree in pharmacy sciences. Mira's career has taken her on a journey about the human psyche and affective disorders. Mira draws on her professional career and from her life experiences as a mother to bring you "Psycho-Mommy!"

If you enjoyed this book, please go to Amazon, now to write a review. It only takes a few minutes.

Please visit www.psycho-mommy.com

… write to Mira on her website with suggestions on what you would like to see in the next book.

Follow Mira Harlon on twitter at https://twitter.com/MiraHarlon

Visit Mira Harlon's website and sign up for her newsletter at www.miraharlon.com

Learn more about the next installment of Psycho-Mommy at

www.miraharlon.com or www.psycho-mommy.com

ᴊruce County Public Library
1243 Mackenzie Rd.
Port Elgin ON N0H 2C6

CPSIA information can be obtained at www.ICGtesting.com
Printed in the USA
LVOW07s1620300415

436757LV00016B/970/P